Gethsemane Moon

Gethsemane Moon

Jon Scott Birch

RESOURCE *Publications* • Eugene, Oregon

GETHSEMANE MOON

Resource Publications
An Imprint of Wipf and Stock Publishers
199 W. 8th Ave., Suite 3
Eugene, OR 97401

www.wipfandstock.com

PAPERBACK ISBN: 979-8-3852-2486-9
HARDCOVER ISBN: 979-8-3852-2487-6
EBOOK ISBN: 979-8-3852-2488-3

VERSION NUMBER 07/25/24

Cover art by Lauren Marie Robinson

To John Ronald Reuel Tolkien,
whose unparalleled and sanctified imagination reveals
the Story behind the story and the Myth which became Fact
in, by, and through our loving Creator God and King,
Jesus Christ.

Behold, He is coming with clouds,
and every eye will see Him, even they who pierced Him.
And all the tribes of the earth will mourn because of Him.

—Revelation 1:7

Contents

Author's Testament

WHETHER WE ARE AWARE of it or not, we are all involved in a Story written by the greatest Author, the Holy Spirit. Intriguingly, and by divine design, we each get to determine per our choices what part we play, unless the brokenness of the world betimes steals choice opportunities. This curse of brokenness—sin—has itself become a part of the narrative, per our earliest Choice.[1] Yet there is hope.

Graciously, Holy Scripture[2] informs us via special revelation that the foundation of this Story rests in the love and sovereign unity of the Creator of the heavens and the earth, the triune Godhead—Father, Son, and Holy Spirit. Herein, our loving Creator knows the end from the beginning and has mercifully written *and enacted* salvation into His Story. Yet salvation is not merely a theme, salvation *is* the Story. Through Jesus Christ, God declares both His creation and salvation that we might believe and trust in Him toward discovering our unique relational purpose in the world.

The late pastor and author Eugene Peterson expressed this by stating, "The intent of revelation is not to inform us about God but to involve us in God."[3] Moreover, Alister McGrath highlights our heavenly hope: "We are not dealing with a God who looks down on humanity in a detached manner, like the great Olympian deities of the ancient world. Rather, we come to know a God who is passionately concerned with those whom He brought into being, and longs to share their sorrows and finally bring

1. Genesis 2:16–17; 3:1–13

2. The Judeo-Christian Bible consisting of the Jewish Torah, Wisdom writings, and Prophets (Old Testament) and Christian New Testament canonical writings.

3. Peterson, *Reversed Thunder*, 13.

them into a kingdom from which suffering, pain, and tears have been banished."[4] And in that we have been created in the image of our Creator, we have been likewise gifted with creativity and imagination.[5] Thus it is our choice to neglect or embrace the same, to squander or sanctify this godly gift, for our glory or for God's.

For C. S. Lewis, God initially draws us to Himself through our imagination. Seeds of truth and wonder are planted from childhood, then cultivated through maturity, and at some point baptized by divine revelation. Through imaginative works God worked on Lewis' imagination and converted his soul before his mind could make sense of it.[6] Truly, even when biblical truth is our foremost instruction and childhood circumstance, "Our imagination," says author Jessica Wilson, "becomes the realm where God meets us first and *shows* us more than *tells* us who He is and to what life we have been called."[7]

For me the love for narrative and the power of story blossomed early. I was privileged to be adopted by loving parents six weeks after my birth, raised in a very relational Christian home, and further blessed by an exceptional church family. From the beginning, my parents read to me. My father read much of the classic children's tales and Bible stories. My literature-loving mother introduced me to *Treasure Island*, *Robinson Crusoe*, *Robin Hood*, the various Arthurian legends, *The Three Musketeers*, and everything by Charles Dickens.

Steeped in tales of adventure, I recall around four or five years of age I discovered a large tome-like edition of the King James Version Bible with sketches throughout by artist Gustav Dore. The gritty realism of Dore's depictions of biblical events dramatically captured my imagination and subtly grounded my then and future understanding of both biblical and world history. I vividly recollect my fear and fascination with the stark violence of Elijah's raised battle-axe preparing to separate yet another false prophet's head from his body. Profane bodies and heads piled up around the chopping block and at the foot of the cliff atop which

4. McGrath, *Glimpsing the Face of God*, 96–97.

5. Genesis 1:26–27; 2:7, 18–25

6. J. R. R. Tolkien was a catalyst in God's conversion of Lewis, particularly challenging Lewis in the arena of imagination. For excellent insight, see Colin Duriez' *Tolkien and C. S. Lewis: The Gift of Friendship* (HiddenSpring, 2003).

7. See Lewis' spiritual autobiography *Surprised by Joy*; also Jessica H. Wilson, *The Scandal of Holiness* (Brazos Press, 2022), 2–5; emphasis in original.

stood Elijah meting out God's perfect judgment. Oddly, at my tender age, the macabre severity was simultaneously sobering and a seed planted.

Eventually, at ten years of age and well-versed in my own ventures in the woods out back, I was gifted J. R. R. Tolkien's *The Hobbit* and *The Lord of the Rings*. My world shifted, and another seed was planted. Tolkien awakened in me a deeper love for "the Quest" we are all on. Likewise awakened was an appreciation for the detailed depth and art of immersive writing and the *true* stories of Scripture and history. Tales of dragons and chivalry—and more Tolkien!—saw me into adulthood. I then discovered *Beowulf*, Bunyan, Dante, Milton, and the Greek and Roman epics by Homer and Virgil.

My love for Scripture, world history, and world literature is surely a divinely driven legacy of my parents. From those early formative years until now, the Lord God has led me to read, learn, live, teach, write, and exhort His truth in diverse ways. The triumvirate of Scripture, world history, and world mythologies has not only captured my own imagination but also the imaginations of many souls with whom I have shared life. And following Jesus Christ into the heart of His revelation has allowed me to see the Holy Spirit as God and Author, helping me sift truth from untruth.[8] The one truth that matters, however, is that *eucatastrophic*[9] event of Jesus' incarnation, passion, crucifixion, resurrection, and ascension.

Gethsemane Moon is a biblical historical fiction which focuses on the incarnation, passion, and crucifixion in dreadful detail. Told in the first-person from Jesus' perspective, I have framed the story as a personally written account from Jesus to whosoever might ask Him about His intercession for humanity in Gethsemane, wherein He took on and became sin for us.[10] Truly, no one save God Himself will ever intimately know the full sacrificial effect of "becoming sin." Yet this frame of prayerful reading and reflective contemplation allows for more intimate immersion than a straight telling or analytical showing, prompting one to utilize their imagination and give room for God to use their imagination toward deeper revelation. Moreover, the aim of this narrative is not to add to Scripture in violation of Revelation 22:18, but rather to direct one further into the written Word that it might be read and experienced

8. John 14:16–17, 26; 2 Timothy 2:15

9. This is Tolkien's term, meaning a "good catastrophe," a sudden overwhelmingly joyful revelation of the truth behind the universe. See Freeman, *Tolkien Dogmatics*, 246–47.

10. 2 Corinthians 5:20–21

afresh. Too often we approach Scripture at academic distance, denying the Word the opportunity to *read us.*

Beginning in 2004 I determined to never grow bored of the cross or take Jesus' great sacrifice and Gospel for granted. Thus, each January I pray for a cross-examination, asking Jesus and the Holy Spirit to grant fresh revelation of Christ's atoning sacrifice. Every year both have been faithful to do so. The concept for *Gethsemane Moon* was received in autumn 2012 as I was working on another writing project concerning Jesus' suffering. It was the Holy Spirit's idea and framing it from Jesus' perspective was His way of testifying to me of Christ, yet I feared the burden this would bring. I resisted for a year, until I recalled a prior cross-examination prayer wherein I sought to better understand the physics and metaphysics of Jesus "becoming sin." What had happened physically, physiologically, psychologically, emotionally, and spiritually in Gethsemane's garden?

In autumn of 2013 I began a season of intense prayerful worship and contemplation. I studied and scrutinized the Gospels and all Scripture concerning every context of covenantal atonement for humanity's sin. I read many extra-biblical works on the same, and revisited many of the epic narratives I so cherished. Even in pre-Christian works the themes, elements, and prophetic hints and myths of salvation were there, sometimes blatant but more often obscure and buried. I began to develop plot notes and determined a timeframe for the Gethsemane story—the hours stretching from post-Passover meal up to Jesus' arrest. I felt unworthy and ill-equipped to write of the trial and crucifixion itself from Jesus' perspective, and graciously I was not urged to; yet the Spirit granted an awesomely effective alternative!

Thus for a decade I was immersed in Scripture, historical narrative, and epic prose and poetry as I worshipfully offered up my own imaginative and alliterative prose to my Savior and King. Expectant that Jesus would glorify Himself in and through my earnest prayer, research, and writing, I am full of humble gratitude that He did. Wholly an act of worship, this project was originally intended solely as personal prayerful reflection and not to be published. Yet in time, as my discipleship intensified, the Spirit encouraged me to publish, to share this art of prayer.

At this point I began to be sifted, inaugurating a years-long season of crushing spiritual warfare in which I endured demonically-driven personal betrayal by fellow believers, the subsequent relational loss, and the unfortunate death of several loved ones. Such has damaged my former easy trust in fellow humans, despite the Holy Spirit's prior warning of the coming crucible. Still, facing my own failures and confronting the sin-nature directly—even as I forgave those set against me—my best was not good enough. And so it is with each of us, for all have fallen short of the glory of God; but we are justified freely by His grace through the blood redemption that is in Jesus Christ.[11] Far too many in the faith forget this, thereby choosing war (with God and others) over reconciliation.[12]

I have learned and I continue to learn how to more deeply trust and hope in God. He has indeed helped me to not fear when the fire comes, to not be anxious in the year of drought, nor to cease from yielding fruit.[13] In writing *Gethsemane Moon* I have *discovered* more truth than I have utilized or imagined, a testament to the Holy Spirit's abiding presence.[14] Therefore I have striven to honor the language in which the story is written, and I pray I have effectively presented a highly significant spiritual reality from a unique perspective.[15]

For those interested, I have included endnotes organized by chapter and paragraph number. This serves to provide biblical, historical, and very nuanced contextual referencing and reasoning throughout *Gethsemane Moon*. Such may be employed for personal benefit and/or as an instructional tool. Most importantly, I pray our Creator God and Savior Jesus Christ is exalted in the heart of every reader, and that Scripture—His Word—is again approached as holy and alive. Godspeed!

11. Romans 3:23–26

12. James 4:1–12

13. Jeremiah 17:7–8

14. See "Epistemology 6.4" in Kreeft, *The Philosophy of Tolkien*, 128–29.

15. See W. H. Auden, "The Poems of Joseph Brodsky," *The New York Review of Books*, April 5, 1973, p10.

Prologue

My Father's embrace loosened, and holding me at arm's length He said, "It is time."

Never had such proximity been so distant . . .

The time of sifting for my disciples had come, yet I too had to be sifted.

*

Blessed are they who read and walk in the love which I have for them.

I

Having ascended the Mount of Olives after the Passover meal, we approached the olive grove around Gethsemane, a favored place of mine on the western slope that granted one a satisfying view of my city across the Valley of Kidron. Even now the moon paints the city and landscape in a silvery hue—a truest glimpse of its artistic purpose.

My disciples followed me languidly in their familiar camaraderie, their bellies sated with the bounty of evenfeast. I alone shouldered the burden that it had been our last communal meal in this world.

Though these learners yet displayed a deference to their Teacher as we walked, I had noted long ago that appreciation for fleeting beauty and the immediacy of being had waned; rarely did their gaze drift from the garden to take in the majesty of a moonlit Jerusalem, not once this night did either of them close their eyes and breath into their nostrils the heady fragrance of olive bark or the earthy redolence of both tilled and raw soil!

Assuredly, an esteem for splendor and virtue rests deep in the hearts of these men, waiting to flourish, but I cannot help but to think of how easily humankind arbitrates what is miraculous and what is mundane. Is not the marvelous oft times buried in the monotonous?

We reached the heart of the garden where there sits an ancient but still used oil press, hence the name *Gat Shemanim*—Gethsemane. Countless hours I have spent here conversing with my Father, fellowshipping with the Spirit, and planting truth into the pliable souls of the men standing with me now, men who abruptly wore expectant expressions after years of being conditioned to anticipate some revelation at this very spot.

This night they would be crestfallen.

I turned to address my brothers and saw an assortment of miens, prompting me to merrily inquire, "Why the dreary countenance, my friends?"

The response disquieted me when Philip gave voice to all.

"Rabbi, You do not look like Yourself. What has happened?"

I savored a deep and deliberate draught of treed air as I observed their beloved faces, my mind revisiting the foresight of this precise moment when I had imbibed the honeyed aura of my Father's house an instant prior to singing Creation's psalm.

"You cannot yet understand," I stated. "But here is wisdom: do not fear the events of this eve or of the coming days. Only fear the Living God. Comfort each other with the words of peace and truth you have learned from me."

Discerning the portentous nature of my remark and recognizing an unfamiliar cadence in my utterance, each man recoiled, and I beheld a sudden fear overtake my companions. But fear was not welcome in this hour, and so I subdued it with my disciples' own recent assertion.

"Not an hour past, all of you joined Simon Peter in proclaiming that you would never deny me, even if it meant your death. Hold on to such resolve, that it may carry everlasting weight toward glory and not be as a leaden cloud that drops its rain when the burden becomes too much to bear. I say again, as it is written, 'I will strike the Shepherd, and the sheep of the flock will be scattered.'"

I paused as my breathing became restricted from a growing pressure around my upper body. I leaned against the oil press, and felt myself pressed all the more.

"*Yeshua*, what can we do?" It was John's voice I heard but I could not read his face as my vision dimmed and bones weakened, causing me to slump.

When I found strength enough to speak I said, "Remain here while I pray under the boughs of the trees." I motioned for John, James, and Peter to accompany me. They helped me stand, though it was difficult for my feet to find sure purchase. Yet by my brothers' solidity I was able to return to the sylvan shadows whence I was heavily beset with a sorrow I had never known. Violent sobbing shook me and my humanity refused to compose itself.

I thought of Cain and his ill begotten envy. I thought of Nimrod and his savage pride. I thought of Lot's wife and her willful meddling. I thought of Esau and his miserly impulsiveness. I thought of Korah's contamination. I thought of Eli's negligence. I thought of Saul's cowardice. I thought of Jezebel and the hollow of her heart. I thought of Israel's incessant obstinacy. I thought of Caiaphas and his vanity. I thought of Judas and his evil bent. I thought of those who would soon mock, torment, and scourge me—how I love them!

My joints felt as if they were being pried apart, and my flesh considered an imminent bursting of the marrow from my bones! *Father!* What is this anguish of mortality?

Then my heart broke and I knew despair.

I cried aloud to those at my side, "Woeful despondency has found me, I am exceedingly close to death. Stay, and watch with me!"

The regard in my brothers' eyes at that moment sent me into the depths of sadness deeper than the Deep from whence the world itself was baptized.

All at once, my very spirit felt a rift I had never known.

"Father, do not cast me away from Your presence! Do not take Your Holy Spirit from me!"

"My Son, just as I have sent You into the world, You have sent those whom I have given You into the world. Just as they shall be without You for a time, You shall be without Me for a time."

At these words, stars I had personally forged and knew by name detonated and split asunder. Galaxies convulsed and warped, and the Expanse itself trembled. Future generations would fix their gaze upon these incongruities and wonder what machinations fashioned them. I know few who dare dream of them being set aright.

Abruptly, and tenderly, Abba's voice evoked the timbre of Galilean reeds listing in a Phoenician breeze. My Comforter provided the mettle I would presently require.

"The glory which You had with Me before the foundation of the world must be proven; not proven to Us, but to the world so that the world may know I have sent You—so that the world will know Our love.

"You will shine from within the darkness Our Light, and the darkness—the death—will not comprehend it. But You, My Lampstand, must comprehend the darkness as the world itself comprehends it. In this, death will be undone. And as many as will receive Us, You will grant them the liberty to become children of God.

"Outside the camp you will bear My reproach and drink My wrath."

I winced as the cold of Sheol began to lick at my flesh and Gehenna's fury assailed my heart, a harrowing I deigned to endure despite carnal hostility to such warfare. I fell against an olive tree of advanced years. When my hand clutched its stout bole the entire structure atrophied into a withered husk, blackened bark degenerating in my uncertain grip.

I looked up and saw Heaven, my home, opened, and I beheld a magnificent white horse bearing only a simple kingly robe of purest argent laid across its broad back. The creature regarded me expectantly.

Then my Father presented a chalice I refused to turn my eyes upon. His voice carried a facet of love even the seraphim had not yet known. "*This is the Cup of My Indignation. Take it and drink, that sin would know its end.*"

I fell heavily to the ground, crushed by a burden of colossal weight. I tasted the dust of the earth that humanity knows—that I know—so well, yet cannot be rid of. Then I tasted blood.

"*Abba!* Father! All things are possible for You. O, might this hour pass! Take this Cup away from me . . . not as I will, but as You will!"

A murderous intent filled me and I knew inwardly for the first time that which Cain had courted ere he struck his beloved brother Abel.

Sin and its champion prowled nearby, I could smell them.

I recalled Cain's words to me when my judgment was leveled against him, and I adopted them as my own: "I shall be hidden from Your face; I shall be a fugitive and a vagabond on the earth, and it will happen that anyone who finds me will kill me!"

I knew that the priests and elders were presently agitating a multitude toward fulfilling their lust for my abduction, and my skin seared with the heat of Moses' anger! An internal partition of flesh and spirit commenced as I sought to be still and know my Father and His peace. But I suffered the helpless dread of Saul's encounter with the Endorian witch. Despair spilled through my earthly tent and filled it.

Yet, my Spirit prevailed upon my flesh and declared the words imparted to Solomon that the end of a thing is better than its beginning—an inheritance gained hastily will not hold. For it is now the time to accomplish that which from ancient times is not yet done. The Hope-Star will pierce the Gates of Night with fluorescence unimagined.

Straightaway I perceived sin's subordinates advancing. With a surge of strength, I stood. It was sin that ultimately killed Cain, and I will have my vengeance sevenfold!

II

My vision brightened enough to determine that my three companions had crept back toward the other disciples. A few tentative steps revealed their apprehensive forms huddled beneath an aged olive tree, each man in varying degrees of fitful sleep.

A pang of vexation overtook me. "What is this? Simon Peter! How can you slumber? Could you not keep watch for *one* hour? Darkness does not sleep!"

I lowered my voice, then, and commanded, "Wake John and James, then watch and pray, lest you enter into temptation. The spirit is willing, but the flesh is weak."

I turned away and strode stiffly back into the deeper shadow's embrace, for the grove floor was no longer dappled with soothing moonlight. I looked up through the olive canopy and spied tattered clouds littering the sky, choking the brilliance of the moon.

Darkness does not sleep, indeed. It has barely awakened.

*

An unspeakable heaviness fixed itself upon my already sagging shoulders as I stood motionless, my face still turned upward. I closed my eyes and breathed in the perfumed evening air, even catching the comforting fragrance of hearthsmoke that drifted lazily across the valley. I longed for the day when I would again share the Passover table with my brethren, and for the first time, with my Bride.

The faint sweetness of bread and wine and fig lingered pleasantly upon my palate and I was swept away to a particular meal when Lazarus' sister, Mary, anointed my feet with her tears and scented oil. O, how I seek for such faith in the world! For the number of her tresses that wiped clean my feet far surpass the number of souls who will receive me!

Abruptly, the metallic tang of blood filled my mouth and I saw anew the chalice offered by my Father: the Cup of His Indignation. A second time I fell hard to the ground and felt the entire heavenly expanse shudder violently as an uncommon strain shove all of my being into the soil, rock shards bruising and tearing my flesh even through my thickly woven garment. My Father's presence faded, an emerging reality that gnawed at both my humanity and divinity.

Between labored breaths I cried out, "*Abba, Abba!* If this Cup cannot pass from me unless I drink it . . . Your will be done!"

The cold of Sheol returned with gathered strength.

My flesh weakened beneath this new assault, thus I directed my mind toward a distinctly wild and willful soul who would become Rome's bane. I advanced prayerful utterance on behalf of my imminent ambassador in chains who would ultimately regard no one according to the flesh after having himself also learned obedience through suffering. He would come to know in full that once the earthly house, the bodily tent, is destroyed, there awaits a House from my Father—not a house made with hands, but an eternal tent in my home where the table awaits a wedding feast for those who are called Blessed.

The Spirit spoke then, reminding my flesh of the temporal affliction that heralds infinite glory: "*All things are of God, who has reconciled the sons and daughters of Adam to Himself through Jesus Christ, and who has initiated the ministry of reconciliation to be lived out by those who are made new. For He made Him who knew no sin to be sin for the sons and daughters of Adam, that they might become the righteousness of God in Him.*"

I calmed at these words, but my flesh clutched fear tightly and continually sought respite from this trial, the weight of which grew beyond mortal comprehension.

"Father! Reproach has broken my heart and my life approaches the grave; Your wrath lies heavy upon me! I am afflicted, and I am ready to die. Your terrors crash over me and I am distraught, but Your—"

"Job did not suffer so."

These words aborting my lament were not stated by my Father or my Comforter.

Slowly, and still forcibly pressed to the earth, I turned my head and surveyed the figure standing many strides away. But my eyes were dim, and I did not respond except to recoil at a fetid fume that crept at hand.

"Who are you?" the shadowy figure cawed.

The inquisitor's query held both curiosity and alarm. Several moments passed as my fogged vision cleared, though pain wracked my body in grim rolling waves.

Then a great sadness beset my spirit, for I beheld Lucifer towering over me in mock splendor with his wretched black bow, Heartseeker; and in its draw was nocked an arrow of flame plucked from the very bowels of hell.

"I ask again, who are you?" His tone remained even, but urgent.

"I am a child of the Most High God, proclaiming the way of salvation."

"You are a child of Hinnom, to be discarded and eaten by Baal!"

When I did not counter this assertion, Lucifer slyly posed, "Do you know who *I* am?"

Slowly and plainly I stated, "You are Lucifer the Fallen, the Adversary and Accuser, who once sought to ascend into the Heavenly House and establish a throne above the stars of the Everlasting All-Father. You are the poor vagrant who left your inheritance and who even now holds too tightly to kingdoms of wind."

"Do not speak to me of kingdoms!" the Accuser hissed. "For where is this supposed 'kingdom of heaven on earth' that you spin tales of, and for which the Baptizer lost his head? Indeed, your own disciples war against each other and forsake you on a whim, loitering or sleeping to escape the principles you teach. Do they not see how fickle they are in violating your own instruction that even a city or house divided against itself will not stand?"

Throughout his discourse, Lucifer remained as a statue, the only motion being that of the oscillating fire-bolt set in Heartseeker's wicked draw.

"And if you are a child of God," he continued, "why does He plague you far beyond Job's lot? Pain drips from you. Will your faithful reward surpass even his? I cannot fathom it! *What* kingdom will you receive? I have watched you. What is it about this olive grove, about *you*, that unsettles me?"

"The kingdom I proclaim . . . is a kingdom of relationship." I spoke in broken cadence as the crushing encumbrance increasingly bore down on my being. "Such a kingdom . . . cannot be won, upheld, or destroyed by worldly might. Yet . . . such a kingdom can certainly be found within the heart of even *one* of my Father's children . . . I speak of love, Fallen One. You knew of this, but you have forgotten. You have abandoned the privilege to know the will of my Father."

Discordant laughter cut the chill air as Lucifer lowered his black bow and crouched to better discern my face. The flaming dart snuffed out and vanished as Heartseeker's taut lessened. Aided by my visible plight, the inflection of his next remark revealed a fading fear but growing perplexity concerning my identity.

"Interesting. You must entertain angels to hold such knowledge of my former glory. Even so, knowledge will not save you from this hour, nor will capitulation to the Adamite cowards. I have heard you teach these *humans* to love their enemies. I am your enemy. Do you love even me?"

Before I could answer, he proceeded, "I recall not so long ago we conversed in the desert . . . " He paused, stoking the memory. "You withheld much more acuity then than your present station. And for your ostentatious 'instruction in righteousness' you have been rewarded with many enemies. Perhaps you presently cry out to fortify your will as doubt infiltrates your resolve. Perhaps you have tempted your beloved Father, bringing His wrath upon you, yes?"

Lucifer's studied stare crept over my face. When I offered silence he continued. "Consider where 'worshiping the Lord your God' has led you. You have remained unpolluted yet you pointedly provoke the Sanhedrin and mock their traditions, edging closer to impiety and mocking the very God you claim to serve! It is amusing, I admit. Still, you are not Job. My wisdom assures me that you will not fare as well as he in the end."

"Your wisdom is moth-eaten and ever bent toward your own designs," I returned.

"Ah, you are weakened *beyond* the desert trial, then, for by now you would surely have cast me from your presence rather than bandy words with your Agitator. Or perhaps you have indeed grown to love me and so enjoy my company." A crooked grin played across Lucifer's face as he imagined a gained advantage.

My vision clouded once more, though I offered a plain truth that would remind this devil of his own lot. "The righteous can love even the spirit or soul that is lost, for justice flows from love and comprehends the loss in light of choice. And love transcends even the construct of time."

At this, Lucifer's anger flared hotly and his splendorous facade evaporated only to expose the mephitic and vile demon he had become. Instantly, the fiend stood and another of hell's missiles prepared to fly from Heartseeker's bend.

"Where are your sheep?" he spat. "I have laid fear upon their pitiful souls that shall haunt them to the end of their days. You are forsaken!"

The fiery dart was loosed and burrowed into my already wounded heart. Know this, dear reader: the swiftness with which my flesh answered the call to retaliation is beyond all men. Yet my Spirit alone will ever triumph, and by my Spirit alone did I abide and overthrow the awful temptations that I deigned to deliver the world from courting.

Without notice my sight lucidly returned and the crushing pressure upon me abated enough that I could rise slightly and cling to a nearby rock. Then, sweating copiously despite the night chill and anchored awkwardly to a crag, I was surrounded by a harem of women in various states of undress, most of whom were in naught but their skin and writhing sensually and noisily all about the grey garden.

Keenly cut to my soul, I recognized these mortals as lost fawns having been gathered by Solomon and a few, more recently, by Herod. Each one had since been clutched by Hades in death, having chosen to serve Asherah or other assorted incarnations and allies of the Accuser. I could not save them now, as their fate was sealed—some by their own hand—and this illusion but a trick of the devil. Still, my heart grieved at their desolation.

Lucifer, now appearing as a regal lord, stepped toward me, casually and possessively caressing a young maiden as he approached. When he spoke, he adopted Socrates' posture and rhythmic lilt. "You have said, and no doubt it shall be *written*, that whoever looks in lust at a woman has already committed adultery with her in his heart. Assuredly, you would *wisely* avoid attending, accumulating, and even partaking of deli cate fruits such as these."

He eyed me warily through narrowed eyes, and his sallow features sought for the faintest weakness as he continued. "Are you not guilty of such even now, being *thrust* into this predicament? Unsought for, yes, but gaining lustful intent at every moment. Even noble and stalwart Odysseus could not avert his ardor forever.

"Is this not the scandal of life in this decaying world? Sin lurks behind every man's door, utterly devouring the unprepared and ruling over even those who resist it. Presently, as you are aware, Judas recognizes both his weakness and his wickedness, yet he remains sin's slave by choice, with little aid from myself or my vassals.

"So tell me, Anointed One, do your loins not burn with desire or your hands grow restless to sample just one of these nymphs? Hosea had his harlot. If your *Father* will not grant you yours, then allow *me* the pleasure of being your benefactor."

Lucifer bowed low in an exaggerated parody of deference as his forked tongue ceased and awaited my riposte.

Long moments stretched as I silently implored my Father to strengthen those souls who would be called to love the ones who knew only lechery. Then I posited, "Does the righteous father look with lust upon his newborn daughter?"

"*Words!* Mere words!" the Accuser howled as he lunged forward, only a pace away. "No mortal can defy the carnal call of the flesh and its fraud, the Curse assures this! And the Spirit you wail to seems not amused with your predicament! *Please*, indulge your appetite and lighten your yoke even further." He stepped back and indicated the lurid scene with a broad sweep of his hand.

Without hesitation I answered, "It is written, that you be careful to do as the Lord your God has commanded, that you not turn aside to the right hand or to the left; and that you *fear* the Lord *your* God, to keep all His statutes and commandments so that it would be well with you and that you would multiply greatly in the land as He has promised. You shall love the Lord your God with all your heart, with all your soul, and with all your strength."

"Do not take me for a fool!" the devil scolded. "I recall these barren statutes of the wilderness and dead promises of a land in which long ago the milk soured and honey dried up. I was there. *You* were not! Or were you?" He stood tall and conjured his bright august facade once more, then continued his derisive lecture.

"Even so, you have witnessed the tangling of the Law, the grandiloquent priests, and the Roman scouring of your precious Israel. I have enjoyed your frustration with the pathetic pretenders of the temple who claim to worship the Great Father but secretly worship themselves, or inadvertently worship *me*. Prophets and insurrections wax and wane but both the glory of David and vision of Ezekiel grow more dim as the generations pass.

"And who, pray tell, will proclaim *your* generations? You have been cursed with no progeny, and these witless followers you surround yourself with will be dead or silenced within a season after your own doom. Though force of arms would fail anew, you certainly cannot harness victory over Rome, over *my* kingdom, by instructing your subjects to love rather than fight." He chuckled coarsely. "I assure you, your love for them will perish with you. *Khristos* indeed!"

Lucifer selectively gathered several of those unclad daughters still wantonly loitering about and led them to me, then stated, "Now, let me show you what 'loving the Lord your God' truly entails."

Immediately I rose to one knee, still steadied by the rock, and fixed the Tempter with a strident gaze. I mustered what strength the Spirit lent and proclaimed, "It is also written, that you shall not seek other gods, including this god of lust that you tout, lest the anger of the Lord your God be raised against you and destroy you from the face of the earth, for He repays those who hate Him!"

Under this sure truth the enemy's tactic withered, and the illusion vanished with Lucifer.

For long moments I remained recumbent against my stony support, gasping for breath and grateful that the pressing torment had abated. Surfeited with exhaustion, I was overtaken by an uneasy stupor.

III

Six Roman soldiers-at-arms wrenched at my blood-soaked garment, tearing free ribbons of loose flesh and clotted ichor. The pain of the scourging seized me anew and I could not draw breath. As my garb was saturated through, it would not easily tear. Having been stripped and redressed minus my coveted tunic, a knife was pulled and set to work on cutting my thickly woven mantle from waist to neck, the blade deftly scoring my jawbone in one subtle finishing flick of the guard's practiced hand.

Rough clutching and pawing became belting and pummeling, my face receiving the largest sum of shock. The ruined cassock fell from my tattered back at the same moment a sizable portion of beard was ripped from my cheek. Searing agony erupted, and bile filled my throat when I spied the misshapen chunk of skin attached to the plundered facial hair in the grip of an antagonist. The Roman culprit had not expected such a return and gleefully held his trophy aloft. This elicited hoots of laughter and scorn until another soldier briefly left the dim courtyard only to reappear with a polished silver tray, which was promptly held to my swollen eyes. The image reflected was grotesque beyond report, save that I discerned lower gums and incisors gleaming at me through the gore-ridden gash once veiled by an unshaven cheek.

I was harshly dragged by two guards into a larger court, the Praetorium, where nearly the entire Roman garrison had gathered. After being dropped onto a wooden stool and propped against a wall for support, I noted assorted Roman faces glaring at me—some with alarm, others with bored interest, but most with hatred. In body and spirit, evil was in attendance.

Every soldier was outfitted for battle due to tensions rising, a fact not only seen but heard throughout the city as pressing crowds bellowed for the blood of Romans, and for my own. I stared at the blood I willingly gave them as it even now streaked the smooth limestone floor from whence I had been hauled in. Blood that continued to drop noisily from my ravaged body, stark crimson upon whitewashed rock. It was not enough.

A sudden braying ensued from the gathered garrison and they began to beat their shields in rhythmic tumult. Amidst this makeshift rumble five warriors marched into the space between myself and the company, turned neatly to face me, placed their right fists over their breast in salute, knelt to one knee, and bowed their heads in mock worship. They held this pose as a sixth warrior, the one who had fetched the silver tray, strode to my side while carefully fashioning a wreath of thorns.

Yet another soldier approached, smug in manner and bearing a royal robe of deep purple which he placed around my shoulders and drew over my bare, lacerated, and unrecognizable torso. Pain ignited in burning waves as the heavy cloth snagged ragged flesh and touched exposed muscle and sinew. Satisfied with dressing me, the young Roman joined his fellows in salute. My body began to tremble violently as it fell into the shock of grievous injury. My bladder and bowels emptied.

The raucous beating of shields continued and all awaited action from the guard who now held a crudely shaped band of thorns in both of his hands, heedful of the four-inch spikes. This he raised over his head and proclaimed loudly, "Hail! King of the Jews!" In unison, the six salutatorians thrice repeated the proclamation. Then the remainder of the gathered militia uniformly broadcast the same.

Abruptly, the pounding and shouting ceased. The crafted crown was lowered to just above my brow as its bearer stood before me. Deafening silence grew for several labored breaths. And then the rude coronet was shoved cruelly onto my head, the dreaded barbs piercing deep. A spur impaled my right eye through the pulp of my brow and I vomited. Sparse laughter broke the silent pall as the soldier in front of me leaped back to avoid the soiling of his leather boots, only to produce a slender but sturdy reed with which he whipped me hard across the mouth. He placed the reed in my hand, a homely scepter, then said, "Come, worship the King!"

At this invitation heckles and hissing commenced. The six in salute stood and approached one by one, each delivering blows with fist or palm before spitting on me. The last of them received a bladed pike, tossed from the throng; he struck me with the shaft full on the left ear. In an explosion of pain I toppled to the side yet did not collapse. This angered the young man, so he drove the butt end of the pike into my face, shattering most of my teeth and sickeningly dislocating my jaw.

"Cease this unnerving display!"

Pontius Pilatus, prefect of Judea, entered the Praetorium and barked orders to the rowdy garrison. Each soldier shifted to attention at their commander's voice, standing motionless and ready for instruction.

Awaiting my return from chastisement by scourging, Pilatus had been at the outer Judgment Seat attempting to quell the roisterous mob when the noise of my abuse drew him. The moment he detected my spoiled form, he balked and cast a berating inspection upon every errant face. I slumped and nearly toppled from my perch but Pilatus was there to steady me. His eyes were hard but kind as he examined my mutilation.

"This is not what I charged. This savagery is beyond reason . . . and will not go unpunished." He bowed close and spoke softly, his voice catching in his throat as emotion was held in check. "Come, I have released the reprobate Barabbas at the cost of Your blood. It is too high a price, though I deem such as adequate to pacify and send the howling rabble home."

When I did not respond, he said, "Forgive me, but I must present You publicly and proclaim Your innocence. It is but a short stride. Cling to me, I refuse to make sport of this debacle." Pilatus lifted me tenderly to my feet but my condition and escalating convulsions stole my body's faculty, thus he placed my right arm around his shoulders and his left around my waist. The prefect remained stoic concerning my stench and the blood that now stained his armor, official attire, and hands—blood that an hour prior he had availed himself of.

We ambled stiffly through an arched aisle that bent its way from the Praetorium to the public platform and Judgment Seat. Ruddy footprints on veneered stone marked our passage, each step a tortuous trial for me. The commotion of the masses swelled and then erupted as we came into view, the fetid reek of fermented sweat and disease rising thickly in the early gloom.

I was handed off to one of many praetorian guards set to keep peace and I nearly lost consciousness for the agonizing torment and exertions I was compelled to endure. The guard steadied me in silence, his eyes alone revealing an aversion to my appearance and fecal odor.

Surveying the heaving multitude from our raised vantage, Pontius Pilatus stood before the Seat and gestured for the assembly to quiet.

This they did, and in the eerie stillness the prefect loudly declared, "Behold the Man! I am bringing Him out to you that you may know I find no fault in Him!"

Immediately, chief priests and officers from the Temple surged forward and shouted, "Crucify him! Crucify him!" Many others repeated this appeal until an abrasive incantation was joined by all. Pilatus raised his arms to signal calm, but the mob would not relent until praetorians smartly descended the dais steps with hands warningly on sword hilts. When the desired hush resulted, Pilatus sternly countered, "*You* take Him and crucify Him! I *and* Herod are in agreement, there is no fault in Him!"

But the Jews answered, "We have a law, and according to our law this fraudulent *messiah* must die because he has made himself the Son of God!" At this, Pilatus paled and a fear vexed his heart. He cued the peacekeepers to remain vigilant and then cautiously led me back into the Praetorium, dismissing the soldiers that yet abided in their state of attention.

When we were alone, he asked, "Where are You from?" The query was not rooted in the dread of man, and though Pilatus was unacquainted with realities of the spirit, his internal discretion was not far off the mark. He searched my one fit eye with his own keen regard, uncertain he even desired a reply. I gave him no answer.

"Will You not speak to me now? Do You not know that in this province, this *realm*, I have power to crucify You, and power to release You?"

To this I did answer, "You would have no power at all against me but for what has been given to you from above. Fear not, Pontius Pilatus. Those who delivered me to you have the greater sin." My broken face stilted my speech but the prefect bowed his head in assent. When he looked up his eyes were rimmed with tears, and he asked, "*Why?* This is not just. Even Herod finds You blameless. I can end this—"

"Not peaceably," I interjected. "The Jews will force your hand by threatening an appeal to Caesar. This is beyond you, Prefect. Speak with your wife of these matters, and you will know . . . *truth*."

"Claudia? How can she know . . . ?" Pilatus' heart began to fracture as he recalled his wife's earnest plea that he remove himself from this terrible circumstance. He brushed away the moisture beginning to fall from his eyes, leaving rusty streaks on his features where tears mingled with my blood that was still on his hands. "A dour morning indeed when servants fancy themselves as kings and their King fancies Himself their servant. I will employ what power I have to release You."

I nodded. "Do as you must, as I do what I will."

He carefully removed the now sodden purple robe that clung stubbornly to my shredded, seeping shoulders and back, and placed it on the wooden stool that had briefly served as a provisional throne. Then, as Pontius Pilatus returned to the rising tempest, I watched my lifeblood fall from the robe and spatter rhythmically on the floorstones. In short order I withstood the heckling and hissing of another garrison, unseen to all but my spirit. Their demonic laughter echoed through all Judea.

*

I was promptly awakened from my vision to find the Spirit kneeling at my side, His strong hand on my shoulder gently ending my prophetic reverie. His bright countenance allayed my distress but turned solemn as He spoke.

"*I have revealed the advancing despoliation of Your flesh to fortify Your mind and spirit with the eternal Love of the Father. The collective souls of humanity from Creation to the end of the Thousand Years could never approach in their imaginations the suffering into which You are now entering. Your flesh will demand death and Your spirit will deplete in its overcoming of the carnal nature. Your heart will ultimately rend, so too the veil to the Most Holy Place.*"

Although aware of this truth, hearing it spoken cut severely. I wept. Not for myself, but for the souls who would remain forever lost. Then I rejoiced. Not for myself, but for the souls who would see the torn veil, of fabric *and* flesh, as an invitation to dine at my table, unimpeded by priest or proxy. Thereby, in examining so great a salvation as was presently being wrought, I expressed truest gratitude to the Spirit for His counsel and prayed my Father would be pleased at my passionate suffering.

The Spirit stood and smiled warmly, then said, "*The Father is pleased already. When it is finished, Your testimony will be the very spirit of prophecy. Think of the Beloved Disciple's wonder when We reveal to him this mystery!*" Then He was gone.

IV

Heartened by the Spirit's proximity, I arose and surveyed the garden in an attempt to find simplest delight in my transient refuge. It was not to be, for a few tentative steps brought waves of nausea and a mantle of sorrow that would not remit. Herein my flesh revolted at my spirit's choice: the only sanctuary was to embrace the anguish of my Father's will.

I closed my eyes and breathed deeply, noticing acutely every bruise accenting the burgeoning pressure upon my entire being. I prayed.

"*Abba* . . . my tent is plundered and a great storm is being stirred up from the remotest parts of the earth. The flesh retreats and desperately seeks safety, yet sudden destruction awaits. My spirit trusts in the uncommon safety of Your counsel in the midst of war, but Your Son is far from security and is being crushed in the gate. And there is no Deliverer but You, Father."

"*Son, it is My will to crush You and cause You to suffer, though it rends My heart wholly. My tears swell the celestial rivers of Your homeland, yet Your life is being made a guilt offering by which You shall see Your offspring and prolong Your days. My will shall prosper in Your right hand.*"

I collapsed in a heap and clutched my chest violently as turbulent sobs wracked my body. At once I desired to be at Abba's side to heal His lament; I ached to be in my heavenly country where peace and love were joined in eternal joyous glory, unspoiled by the Curse. Wounded to my soul, I could not even cry out. In painful weeping I strove to hear my Father's next words.

"*I know Your longing and hear Your groaning for want of the everlasting habitation—full of joy and sown with fields of abundant truth. Your flesh burns for My rest, but there yet remains an hour of trial and warfare.*

Comfort will be given, but not yet in fullness. Sorrows and afflictions within and without are My rod and My healing.

"*When Your woe has passed, You will behold the light of life and be satisfied. You, My Righteous Servant, will justify many through the bearing of their iniquities. And thus I will give you a King's portion because You poured out Your life unto death and were numbered with the transgressors. Bearing the world's sin by Our love is Your intercession.*"

The burden of iniquity returned in crushing severity, driving the breath from my weakening lungs. I labored for air and contended to gain my feet but failed, finding myself again prone and pressed heavily into the biting soil of Gethsemane. Dignity fled and I wept furiously at the increasing injury.

Death sought me as its icy fingers crept up from the grave and beckoned me to Sheol. "Soon," I gasped, "but not yet." I fought death with life and perceived another beloved disciple to be purified many generations hence. I prayed for his soul, knowing that his own battle with temptation would be hard fought and won through the victory I presently wrought. This spiritual pilgrim's progress would lead him to profound truth concerning the holy war every disciple must wage. My blessings for him—and for generations after him—await.

A surge of stamina alerted me to the Spirit's bestowal, a tributary from the River of Life finding my parched heart and flooding it with eternal purpose. Death retreated and I gathered myself under the overload of sin, rising slowly to shoulder the accursed weight. Twice my legs buckled, forcing me to remain on hands and knees that were raw from my exertions. A third attempt saw me nearly upright, though the muscles and tendons in my limbs and joints threatened to rupture and rend as an aching woe roiled through my bones like a lost fire. A stinging pain shot from foot to spine and I growled savagely. Tremors overtook my being and blood began to weep from every pore, mingling with sweat that rapidly suffused my raiment.

"Not my will, but *Yours*, Abba!"

The infernal load multiplied; and with flagging strength I was again driven hurtfully to my knees. The mountainside shook to its very roots, sending dust-lifting waves across Gethsemane's slope. Seizures gripped me and tore through my contorted frame until I bowed my head and buried my face in quaking hands only to bewail humanity's veniality.

"My God! I shall follow the way of those who are foolish and on whom death feeds. Yet I will not fear the worm or the Wicked One and his designs for me. You, Father, will redeem my soul from the grave and You shall receive me! A judging fire shall devour all before You. Zion will know salvation and turn away; the stranger will witness salvation and lift You up.

"Hide Your face from this iniquity, O God, and pour out Your fury on me. Restore to me the joy of Your Presence and uphold me by Your generous Spirit!"

I stilled my voice and bided the strain with a love the world cannot fathom. Sin invaded my flesh and burrowed its rotten appendages deep, seeking a foothold or even the slightest mote of wayward carnality. Death resurged and joined sin's advance, marching to command an opportunity by the Law toward stoking in me various evils. Accosted in this way, I sustained an accession of every maleficent, ruinous, and impious act to be committed or imagined by humankind or demon—from the first Luciferian insurrection to his last at the end of the Thousand Years. Each created soul from the entirety of history would know sin intimately, and I would know intimately what each soul knew—yet I would remain uncorrupted.

All at once, ten Furies dispatched from Tartarus and terrible to behold twisted and taunted around my bent and turbulent form. Reeking of bog and filth, the fiends shrieked their intent to waylay my faith and uncover any secret despoiling of innocence. Moments stretched unnaturally under the assault and when the Furies' barking frenzy elicited no response from me, they beseeched their overlords—Sin and Death—to make haste in betraying any impurity to which they would cling and feast.

As wolves quarry their prey, so my foes quartered their grim hunt. But my God did not forsake me. Overtaken by the weariness and heaviness of heart that every transient body carries, I took refuge in my Fortress and employed the eternal surety of mind and spirit toward upholding my flesh—not for want of comfort, but for permitting an absolute scouring of my humanity, that sin would possess a full account of my mortality and find no flaw. From my High Tower I surveyed the battleground.

Bleak and sorrowful were the nefarious intentions cast around and within my being, and by the Spirit and Our loving purpose my flesh was preserved to endure a thousandfold the agonies of Adam's rebellious legacy. The limit of human strength was reached, extended, and held taut to suffer still as the whole of the cosmos heeded this inconceivable and frightful display. Distant worlds objected and bemoaned the injustice and disgorged their innards amidst cataclysmic volcanism, forever scarring their majestic vistas. Angels—Fallen and Allegiant—were spellbound at the lucid mystery set before them. Across the Expanse, from the Elysian Boundary all the way to Earth, warriors dark and light arrayed for war, awaiting orders to strike.

Beloved reader, understand that in humankind intentions do not warrant returns, nor does knowledge prove wisdom; for intentions wax dim and knowledge stains with the blemish of self-regard. Rather, single-minded obedience to me as I to my Father will ensure the cultivation of perfection incumbent upon remaining unshaken by roiling sentiments or winds of spiritual instability.

Thereupon, with universal witness, and finding no vice in my humanity on which to thrive, sin's darkness determined to rape my soul.

In this moment the frontier of mortal might was escalated and then allied with something far greater: the Spirit of Truth. In this moment my Light illumined the darkness with infinite brightness and the darkness did not comprehend it. In this moment my tormentors perceived that I was not of this world, yet such disclosure would not be betrayed. My divinity ignited and, for the first time, sin and death knew fear as they beheld their new Master.

The Furies instantly turned to ash, drifting to the ground like gray ribbons of snow. Still kneeling, I fell forward onto my face and received a fleeting moment of peace.

"Abba, as with Pharaoh and Saul, You desire to display Your wrath and make Your power known, enduring with long-suffering all vessels of wrath prepared for destruction in order to reveal Your glory through vessels of mercy. I am Your Vessel of both wrath *and* mercy. And I am Your Remnant of humanity.

"I have held out my hands to a disobedient and stiff-necked people; Israel has stumbled over the Stone of offense You have laid in Zion! Yet I will be found by those who do not seek me; I will visit those who do not ask for me. I am the end of the Law and my righteousness shall be imparted to all who believe. This truth will go out to all the earth and be proclaimed until the end of the world."

I discerned my Father's great pleasure—and underlying sadness—and my love for Him multiplied despite the increasing awareness of aching separation. He remained silent.

Then, in yearning to hear Father's voice, my heart inclined toward Mary of Magdala. I remembered well the day she received my kingdom in its fullness! Following a celebratory wedding in Cana, the Spirit had shown me a soul in torment who was to be freed, and who was privileged as the first to taste my authority over death and Hades. She would likewise be first to witness my glorious victory over the same. Yet it vexes me even now to know the next time I see her kindly face she will not recognize mine in its ruin.

I wept for the world.

*

I lifted my eyes to the subtle sound of a wary approach, yet spied no one through my chafed and mournful glare. Gethsemane's gloom had become aberrant, darker than blackest night, a palpable and primitive thing, alive. I stood and peered into the pitch mood.

A shadowed form drew nearer, the crack of deadfall and unsure shuffling announcing an unfamiliarity with the gravelly soil. Then I discerned Temple vestments as the man stumbled into direct line of sight and stopped only paces away. *Caiaphas!* I remained still and observed his searching eyes in their bewilderment—anxious eyes that met mine and held for several breaths, and then resumed their restless roving. With no hint of recognition at my person, I immediately discerned devilry.

In that same moment an object of delicate weight was discreetly placed into my right hand. A sword. Reflexively, I gripped it true—perfectly balanced, finely bladed, and of a design and mastery the world would not know for centuries.

"It befits you." Lucifer's voice was terse as he materialized from the thickening blackness, wholly guised as an asiatic armourer. "And it will befit the cadre of lost Manassehite sons who landed in the Far East." I met his calculating gaze.

"Yes," he purred, "your precious kin have forsaken this promised land for distant shores, seeking to forge their own destiny devoid of a drearily doting deity." He paced back and forth as he smugly continued in ages-long-practiced cadence. "Think of it: pretentious clans battling for power, prestige, and the right to control tiny scrubs of rock or vale—on an island! It is thoroughly droll yet I deign to raise another elite warrior class from the bloodline of these martial champions of Samaria—my *samurai*. I shall craft them from the generational stills of Shemite ancestry, honor, and ethic. Not unlike your own meddlesome God, yes?"

I made no move to respond other than returning my scrutiny to the intricate simplicity of the contrived device in my hand. My indicter mistook this for interest and boasted of his incubating sect.

"My frantic subordinates have loitered long enough for want of far-reaching strategy; thus I have established my *djinn* as principalities and administrators over and within the entire East. And from the Far East an empire shall rise as the sun, slowly illuminating the landscape and then breaking over the land in splendid totality!"

As Lucifer lectured, I noted Caiaphas' rapt heedfulness; an unclean spirit of divination entered the garden. Not missing a beat, the litany persisted. "To my new sons of Manasseh, I have assigned warcrafters from the days of Enoch to instruct them in a code of eminence that gestates an arcane mythos. Honor-bound servitude and militant discipline constitute the foundry from which countless progeny shall proceed, adhering to their overlords by sworn life-oaths. The sword you now hold will be the very essence and symbol of this societal conduct, the manufacture of such itself being an act of sacred metaphysical worship wherein the acolyte's art becomes an extension of his being, subtly weaving his own spirit to that of a *djinn* . . . and thus to me."

"A cult of death," I stated.

"Precisely," the devil sneered. "And what better way to make death more appealing than by cleaning it up?" He stepped closer and scanned our surroundings, then leaned toward me as if to disclose private counsel. "The blade you grasp is the first of its kind and shall portray mortality as a chaste ideal. Are you not enchanted by its elegance, arrangement, and utility? Such skill would arouse even Azazel were he not cursed by the Great Tyrant." Then, closing his eyes and sighing in false lament, "Yet I defer *some* credit, truly, for he submitted his warring wisdom to others in my employ ere his banishment to the Abyss—the *fool*!"

Lucifer wheeled away from me, chortling deviously, then said, "Perhaps, Prophet, you should pray for poor Azazel and offer *him* the forgiveness your fickle sheep reject, hmm?"

"Angels are to intercede for men, not men for angels," I returned.

"Indeed, and therein lies the beauty. Fallen I am, but an angel I remain—" Immediately, beatific resplendence dispersed the gathering darkness, and Lucifer, with outstretched arms, appeared as he had when he tended the holy lampstands before the Throne of Heaven. Heat emanated from his form and the effulgent light seared my eyes until I averted my gaze. Then the apparition quit and the asiatic armourer continued, "—and I now intercede for *you*! Behold your tormentor, High Priest Caiaphas!"

The devil stepped aside and bowed low in recreant docility. I said nothing as Caiaphas moved to stand before me. With a hateful glower, he spat in my face and with his hands formed curses against my soul. I remained still and silent even as the corrupt cleric urinated on my feet.

Lucifer, infuriated by my lack of ire, snarled an obscenity and harshly urged me to strike Caiaphas with the blade. He tempted me with my own words, saying, "Whoever is angry with his brother *without* a cause shall be in danger of the judgment. You, Prophet, *have* a cause! This self-serving snake salivates over the thought of shaming you—and killing you! Yet I have interceded and turned fate on its axis. Do *you* not salivate over the death of this upstart? If vengeance is the Lord's and you are His own, as you proclaim, then are you not justified in both your anger and in your killing of this prideful priest? The holiness you tout demands only righteous judgment to be held in your heart, not murder, yes?"

The precision of this lanced me to the quick. I set my jaw and locked eyes with Lucifer an instant before he let fly another fire-bolt from Heartseeker. Unnatural rack again filled my heart as a murderous rage attempted to possess me. My flesh sought to lunge at my accuser, to throttle his witness at its source, to chain him before his time. But my limbs would not obey this foreign intruder. Though awful grief wrung my heart as to strangle all speech and urge, my spirit governed and neither bloodshed nor premature banishment took root. I lowered my eyes and let fall the sword from my hand.

Before the weapon hit the ground it leaped into Lucifer's grip and in one sleight movement the whetted edge opened Caiaphas' belly and came to rest a breath away from my own neck. I did not flinch, but watched the impostor priest attempt to contain his entrails as they spilled onto the dust. Sadness overcame me for the lost souls such as this that suffered and would suffer as pawns at the whim of evil incarnate. I prayed inwardly for the souls not yet lost that yet had opportunity to be delivered from the same.

"Thus I have interceded for you *again*." Sword still at my neck, my antagonist peered down the length of his arm and queried, "What unseen battles have you waged in this cursed garden?"

I did not respond but to continue praying silently. After several breaths, Lucifer coldly stated, "Your favor with the Great Tyrant unsettles me. What fate has He leveled against the Furies I set upon you, imprisonment or *annihilation*? They are not to be found." He lowered the blade, then slowly backed away with menacing stealth. "There *are* rules, Prophet."

The ruined form of the false Caiaphas faded until absent. I discerned that Lucifer had likewise quit the shadows. I was alone.

Spying a sturdy olive tree, recognizable even in the darkness for its distinctively gnarled form, I moved haltingly to it, placed my weakened weight against it, and prayed.

V

Everyone shall bear their own righteousness or unrighteousness. I voiced this truth to my beloved Father and acutely *felt* another truth tethered to it. My flesh recoiled anew at my heart's resolve to drink the Cup of Indignation, and therein to fulfill *all* righteousness. An abrupt wave of weariness caused me to slump and the temptation to sleep engulfed me, yet I knew slumber would offer no release or comfort; it would only reward with shifting and troubled rest, broken by barren chases and savage melee with an invisible enemy.

My body ached with dread and mounting calamity; my mind and spirit, though alert, were wrung out for the strain of my intended portion. "*Abba!* I am faint, a husk of corn, hollow and brittle! Through Your wisdom I know wondrous mysteries, and now as a spirit mired with clay I become the essence of shamefulness, a fount of impurity, a smelting pot of transgression constructed of sin—and I am terrified of Your holy judgments!

"My accuser plots great evil and I am forbidden from foiling his designs! Grant my flesh temperance and my riven heart union with Yours, I plead. Our separation is too much to bear, Abba, yet I know You will save my soul from the Pit and lift me up from the Underworld to my eternal home where I shall serve You forever—"

My voice broke and fresh tears stung as I sobbed deeply for want of Father's embrace.

"In my earthly mantle I have learned to know You by the Spirit You have given me. I have listened faithfully and earnestly to Your perfect counsel. From my youth You have opened my understanding to Your hidden perception and the wellspring of Your unfailing strength. Please,

Abba, if I have found favor in Your eyes, grant me Our Holy Spirit's valiancy to endure the press—"

"*I am here, Yeshua.*" Ruach's staid voice calmed me as He knelt and wrapped me in His arms where I had collapsed at the base of the olive tree. I wept freely as the Holy Spirit communed with my Father, and then with me. "*The Most High, through Us, created this world for the sake of many. Yet the world to come shall be made for the sake of few. The earth provides much clay but little gold; thus in the course of this present world many earthen vessels will be created, but few shall be saved. This You know.*"

My eternal Companion stood, lifting me to my feet. The potency of His being yielded the fortitude I lacked as He grasped my forearms in a warrior's clasp. Then, His eyes shining with the brightness of Home, He exhorted my plight.

"*You know, too, that the war of the ages—at this moment—has taken root and uncoils within Your humanity, seeking only to extinguish Your divinity. The remoteness of sin has become ultimately proximate, the dead-wood gathered into one place to be set aflame forevermore. And therein sin shall be uprooted and evil overthrown. This garden moonscape shall be rent with the Dawnlight of the True Morning Star—You, Yeshua, will guarantee beloved station for Your offspring in the Age to Come.*"

This truth pierced my heart in a way unknown but verily welcome. *Unknown* for having emptied myself of full omniscience in wearing the mantle of flesh, thus reliant on my Father and Companion for revelation; and *welcome* for disarming the immoderate fear which taunted that flesh.

I recalled the moment only hours past when my disciples eagerly and in awe digested the news of the untame Holy Spirit who would come to them and testify of me; He who now testified *to* me! The ever-lasting gospel which I had woven into a messianic mosaic of the Word was masterfully unthreaded by the Spirit—yet not undone!—and then reknit into an inviting yoke by which my humanity was impelled toward heaven. His instruction was warm.

"*In this secret garden You esteem the world as nothing and desire only Our love and amity. You have remained a stranger and pilgrim in the earth, faithfully teaching others to do likewise. A vessel of honor You are, sancti-fied and receiving Your Father's full measure toward the perfect victory of conquering the curse of flesh and self-regard.*"

Like drawing deep water from a hidden pool, my Advocate's counsel recalled my earthly father, Joseph, and how I had honored him in death. A season prior to beginning my public ministry, Joseph lay dying and

I pleaded with Abba for his healing. Yet with gentle rebuke, Joseph cut short my petition and expressed his desire for Paradise. In that moment my heart had riven and I wept from my soul—a moment that presently besieges me for my own want of Paradise and fear of separation from Abba. Mother's constancy and consent had provided some solace, but then Joseph portentously admonished that I honor him by honoring her when it was time. Uncertain, I let them be and withdrew for prayer and perspicuity, knowing my father would pass within the hour. Then I silently rejoiced when Joseph's soul joined Abraham's embrace, for I would soon go to him and deliver Paradise itself to my Father in heaven.

Seven months passed and the time Joseph had spoken of arrived during a wedding. I was discreetly assailed by my mother toward remedying a shortage of wine! I smiled at the memory.

"*You were truly mystified, until I impressed upon You Joseph's prophecy. Your astonishment ceded mirthful resonance from the Throne and lifted all of heaven!*"

The Spirit's laughter was a balm to my present anguish. Indeed, I had grown ever cautious as my Day of Shepherding drew near, with no intent to force or neglect my great commission. Expectant and prayerful as I was, I had not foreseen the consecrated convergence of events birthing the fulfillment of a familial commandment, all at once honoring Mary, Joseph, and Abba! That this occurred at a wedding was not lost on me.

A recondite suffusion of rapturous lament fast beset my being, to which Ruach uttered, "*The separation and passionate suffering You endure shall provide the way of salvation and keep Your Bride from the hour of Jacob's trouble which shall befall the earth at the end of the age, yet even Jacob will be saved out of much chastisement.*"

It was to uncommonly united men—such prophets as Isaiah, Jeremiah, Ezekiel, Daniel, Joel, and John the Beloved—to whom I had spoken of the latter years and Israel's rejection of me. It would soon be to commonly united men—though uncommonly privileged to whom I would reveal the mystery of my Bride, her salvation, and our eternal union!

My Counselor uplifted me with my own words of austere urgency concerning my role as Bearer of the Holy Flame. I recalled a recent ripe response to the *leaven of the Pharisees* wherein I disclosed first to my disciples and then to the multitudes that I had come not to bring peace on the earth, but rather fire and division! This was not received and agitation erupted, which I swiftly sobered by exposing the sinfully soiled souls of all gathered. To the surrounding silence I then bared a portion of my own soul's burdened perfection: I had a baptism approaching that was not of water or spirit, but of indignation and woe. This too did not bring calm and comprehension to those gathered. It could not. Thus in fear had my disciples and detractors dispersed. That same fear had entered Gethsemane and now wormed its way into my mantle, yet I refused to wear it.

I bowed my head in solidarity with the Spirit and barely registered His sudden leave as my respite came to an end. The hour of my woeful baptism had arrived, and I would not disperse or be afraid. To the unseen enemy I declared, "I have set my face like flint and I shall be weighed on perfect scales, that heaven and earth may know the root of Love. And after my skin is destroyed, even in my flesh I shall see God!"

Remaining in recollective reverie for some time, I breathed deeply and gazed up at a sable sky laden with points of light as sharp as ice. Shreds of thickening cloud still raced across heaven as an ill wind foretold the approaching storm. I shuddered at a rush of chill air and then painful tremors rolled through my being like a billowing sea. But the ballast of spirit and truth held as I trod the waves of sin and death that surged around me. The sign of the prophet Jonah was nigh.

*

Through Gethsemane's grim wood strode the god of guile with his proud imaginations displayed. Having raised an impious and vain attempt at war against Heaven with intent to unseat the Immovable Godhead, the infernal serpent—Lucifer the Proud—ever carries ambitious aim to perpetuate his doomed discord. As a wolf ravenous with hunger spies a shepherd's pens and with cool ease leaps over the fold-wall after dark, so now this ancient devil, with greater hunger and perceived ease, has *again* leapt into my Father's fold.

Already his gaze fixed me with Cerberian focus, further braced by a self-exalted and regal aura. The dark forest round about abruptly lit with a silvery sheen emanating from garishly ornate adamantine armor, wholly complemented by gauntlets, belted sword, and crown. This fallen angel, hale in his facade, appeared entirely a formidable conqueror of worlds. Ceasing his advance several paces from where I wearily stood, his parlay betrayed demonic design.

"Allow me to heighten your dour temperament, *Rabboni*, for we too often part on discordant humor." He bowed low yet retained his sinister glare. Then with erudite calm and posture, he continued. "I recall, again, not so long ago during our desert discourse, you began the futile effort to shepherd these 'lost sheep' of Israel—an adroit branding of the feculent rabble, I admit. The reek of hope and missional conviction followed you then. Yet now you are pitiful and fraught with sorrow even as you bewail your clamant crisis. And you have feasted, *not* fasted! Perhaps such negligence is the cause of the unnatural cruciation you seem to invite, yes?"

My silence was anticipated, so my agitator's impudent gloss advanced.

"You have failed. For all your talk of faith and love and peace and heaven's kingdom on earth, you have in the same breath promised division, tribulation, and warfare to those who follow you! When true zealots are drawn by your word to fight, you insist on loving their enemies and turning the other cheek. But turn the cheek too far and I will see your back, a weaker position indeed.

"Consider your own precious Scripture. It is written by Daniel the seer that Belshazzar lost his kingdom to a miscalculated act of sacrilege. Could it be that you have misemployed or exploited the powers you have been granted whilst confusing your Father's agenda with your own? *Innocently*, of course."

When still I offered no return, the lord of lies determined to make his case perchance I gathered the gall to resist. His tone was measured but in his eyes flared an evil flame.

"Earth is *my* kingdom. The Great Tyrant has left Israel to its own affairs for centuries, during which their distaste for theocratic rule germinated—my gratitude to the politically savvy Maccabeans!" Placing a salutatory hand over his chest, the devil feigned a moment of reflective respect before pressing his proclamation.

"Even a distaste for Graeco-Roman overlordship has taken root of late, but it would truly take a divine invasion to slay the chimera of Judaism or Rome. It is all a game, one I admittedly enjoy though the Tyrant does not. He does not even wish to play, sadly. He demands to be recognized openly and exclusively. I do not. Thus, I read His silence as a reluctant armistice: Israel has forsaken God and God has forsaken Israel, even if only for a season.

"And that season of remiss endures, I assure you. The Tyrant remains cloistered behind the Veil—of Temple *and* Existence. The idealism that *you* and the *Baptizer* have stirred up is a declaration of war! Now the Baptizer is dead and you are next. Your expectations of charity and good service I can tolerate, but I will not suffer the divine authority and power you carry and then insist upon granting to your slaves. There is no room for your kingdom within my own. Unlike Belshazzar, it may not be too late to heed the writing on the wall that *your* kingdom is divided and *you* have been found wanting."

Reveling in his own monologue, the dragon had held his disciplined posture but now strode closer in urgent expectation of a reply to his seduction. "I shall provide an alternate way out of this doom that befalls you, Favored One, for you have been pleading desperately for the same. Reject the Cup of your Father's fury and receive my Grail of Empire. Or like Belshazzar, you *will* be devoured by divine wrath. It is your choice."

A tearing pain erupted within my being, alerting me to the passion and atoning purpose toward which I ventured. I collapsed heavily to one knee and shouldered still more of the world's sin as it sought to deplete me of all love and goodwill. I was emotionally thin and spiritually bereft. My Father had fled and my Spirit was silent and distant. I sobbed noisily and chokingly as I knelt before the god of this world; an unsettling and pathetic sight to behold for the Host of heaven.

Satan expectedly turned the moment to his favor and coldly leveled his bid.

"I once handed you all the kingdoms of Earth—to rule as you desired *and* as my right hand, in exchange for serving me as thrall. Your refusal seems not to have been the correct course. Per contra, my generosity is stoked at your plight. *Forget* the petty conflicts and petulant clans of this world. Adam *forfeited* this blighted gem of creation to me, it is *my* domain." Recalled scorn crept into the devil's parlance, yet he retained a stoic presence.

"I grant you the entirety of the *cosmos*, everything beyond the Lesser Light. I will grant you authority over strongholds on far-distant vistas across the Expanse, to do as you will. I will not interfere in your domain if you leave me to mine. I will serve as *your* right hand in all matters *outside* the earthly plane. You have only to recognize me as Suzerain of Earth and your Lord *within* the earthly plane. Remain kneeling and I will place this crown of my brow onto your own, for it is the Empyrean Crown. Do you avow this?"

"You presume much, Fallen One," I stated. "And you boast beyond your confined station."

"Yes, yes, eons of talk asserting *all* creation is of God; and stillborn prophecies that invoke incorporeal ideals of a someday salvation.

These cyclical threats and challenges to my world have come to naught. I wrested this realm from Adam and lay open claim to it by right of his disobedience in accord with the heavenly courts. Yet the *Holy* Tyrant appears unconcerned in that He is slow—or incompetent—to raise a Deliverer and fulfill the charade of history. Have *you* arrived to end the armistice? I cannot see it!"

The devil laughed derisively and further pressed his challenge.

"Could you by force depose my lordship of Earth? Who are your allies? Surely not the muted men and women you have gathered! From whence will your help come? You are weak and forsaken. Even this God and Spirit you bewail imparts a fading presence. You are barely the latest—perhaps the last—in a long line of failed prophets set on returning Israel to a long-dead ideal."

I still knelt and convulsed under the strain of the world's sin and sorrow, but a surge of vitality enabled me to slowly stand and quit my ignoble posture. Lucifer's countenance darkened as he watched and awaited a response. I gave none, save to look pensively upon him as I labored to draw ragged pain-wracked breaths. Thus losing his imagined advantage, he emboldened his invective.

"The foolish *Chosen* have said of themselves, 'We are our own lords, we no longer serve the Lord God!' Jacob's progeny provoked the Tyrant to anger by serving foreign gods and *sacrificing to me*! Long has the Great Tyrant served to Israel the dregs of rebuke and judgment; Jerusalem has only a future of fury. You know this, if prophet you are, for the seers of old have written it."

"It is further written," I stated, "that the Lord who pleads the cause of His people will remove from them the cups of trembling, *and* the Cup of His fury. They shall no longer drink it."

"So we come to it," the devil declared. "You deign to fulfill this ancient utterance and thereby deliver Israel from merited judgment by consuming this Cup yourself? A noble endeavor, I grant you, but foolish. The blood of prophets and priests from Abel to the Baptizer has not quelled the Tyrant's discontent or averted His retribution. Fearful, uneager, and deluded, you will fare no better."

The prince of darkness stepped menacingly closer and plied his craft which corrupted Eve from the simplicity of theistic relationship and knowledge of the holy. Eyes afire with mordacity and voice laced with guile, he leveled, "I am of the mind that you have been betrayed, and not by any earthly source. Your grasp of history will aid in tracking my logic:

"Deem the days of the Triad Alliance, when the kings of Israel, Judah, and Edom joined to repel the advance of Mesha, king of Moab. Mesha's armies were sorely routed, his territories ruined, and all save one of his cities ravaged. Fast envisioning the doom of his last stand, Mesha conceived a final act of desperation and sacrificed—*to me!*—his firstborn son and heir on the very walls of his besieged city. Terrible violence arose in the hearts of the Moabites, you recall; and in answer, my spirits of war and bloodlust enabled them to push the tenuous tribal Triad back to their own lands.

"So your *Father* seeks to placate me by sacrificing *you*, perhaps in exchange for tolerating this upstart 'kingdom community' you have heralded? I can make no promises, you understand. Time will reveal any further threat to my own kingdom, and I will fitly act; but it now appears your mission and all hope will fail with you, *Yeshua bar Yosef*. There will be no ram caught in a thicket where you are bearing. Fulfill your Father's will if you must, for your death will likewise serve me."

I nearly swooned for the increasing assault on my body, mind, and spirit. Sin perdured its foraging of my being and I fell back a step, unbalanced. Death coveted my life; a sentient dread leeched into the garden and converged upon me, bringing a weakness wholly unknown. The dragon of Eden regarded me suspiciously yet stood pleased with himself and with my suffering.

After I endured a space of several beleaguered breaths, his stern mood lightened, and removing the Empyrean Crown from his brow with his right hand, he held it out in offer. "Reconsider the fortuity I propose. It will be the last. Will you receive my Grail of Empire *or* the Tyrant's Cup of Cowardice?"

At once, my Advocate sanctioned my heart's reply. "The Lord rebuke you, Worldwyrm! Woe to the false shepherds who destroy and scatter the sheep of My pasture! I will answer you in accord with the evil of your doings: I will gather the remnant of My flock and bring them into their fold, and they shall be fruitful and increase. A King shall reign and prosper and execute judgment and righteousness *in all the earth*. Behold, the days have arrived when I shall stand still and see the salvation of *Yahweh*!"

With calm menace and an aspect of bridled ire, Lucifer slowly replaced the Empyrean Crown upon his brow and hatefully declared, "So be it, *Woodworker*. If you insist on self-sacrifice for your fluctuant followers, believing that your own suffering will awaken them to a fictive freedom, I will heartily hasten your odyssey. I could have aborted that traverse. Now only torment and ruination await. I will savor the end of you, for your betrayal and tragedy shall eclipse that of Gaius Julius Caesar, who also presumed to possess the blood of gods."

Then he faded into Gethsemane's gloom.

*

Respite did not follow. A swiftly escalating siege of sin and judgment filled me as the Cup of my Father's wrath emptied. My body wilted and was pressed anew into the biting floor of my sanctuary; and so I prayed.

I rejoiced in the memory of Anna the prophetess, daughter of Phanuel, of the tribe of Asher. Already well-advanced in years when I was presented at the Temple in my infancy, as was custom, she had praised my Father and prophesied concerning my birth to all in attendance. Long widowed, Anna would not depart from the Temple day or night, for she served the Lord with fasting and prayers, speaking of me to all in Jerusalem who sought redemption. Indeed, as my cousin John decades later prepared the way for my public ministry from outside Jerusalem, Anna prepared the way for my prophetic ministry from within. I recalled the privilege to have received her blessing at my rabbinic anointing in my thirtieth year. She had surpassed a century then, and fell asleep fulfilled. Often I cited her staggering fidelity when chastening my disciples.

Beloved reader, such faith is granted to few souls. Even in the company of the elect, not all will take up their cross and follow me. Most will not even come to me to discover their heavenly portion and gifted burdens, choosing to burden themselves with misdirected presumption and empty legalism. Scripture itself will become an idol.

My burden is to wear the mantle of flesh and to keep it from the stain of iniquity; to turn not away from the injustice of reaping wrath for my innocence; to endure the raging scorn and temptations of my Adversary when he approaches me; to walk in darkness that it would be undone; to love even those lost to me per choice; to lay down my life in perfect love for every soul born into the world.

My cross will prove that love does not aspire to rule the earth, but to relate to those living in it. Yet the fallen bend their will to usurp the created order which they cannot possess, even now tempting the Second Adam in the second garden. This is my counsel to all who would follow me: Take heed and flee from such wolves which spare not the flock but devour all until their own souls are eaten. Only be still, and I will fight for you.

I then recalled the first garden battle in parallel to the present. Adam, the firstborn of the *Imago Dei* and apex of the Edenic Council, was granted stewardship of Earth and authority over all living creatures, yet a living creature mastered him. The great land serpent Ancalagon—corrupted by Lucifer's will and domination—seduced Eve, and then through her fatally tempted Adam. Thus Adam relinquished his headship over Eve *and* the world, bringing the curse of sin and death to all. And he knew the fear of the Lord: the fig leaves of pretense will only bring shame and withering judgment.

I was sorely grieved at Adam's error, yet merciful in my love. In measured violence before my errant and naked children, I slew two sheep and bade the man and woman adorn the grisly blood-soaked skins for the duration of the weeks-long journey to the border of Eden from whence they were exiled. The fallen couple witnessed wonders they had forfeited and would not attain until the end of all things. Outside of Eden at the Extremis Gate I stationed two cherubim with swords of flame, forbidding reentry into the region. It would remain unoccupied save for flora and fauna until the Great Deluge. Truly a paradise lost.

At the Gate ere I withdrew my contiguous presence from humankind, I instructed Adam in the lurid discipline of substitutionary atonement and sacrificial ordinance. It was to be performed every year before the Extremis Gate to recall both the Exile and my merciful covering of sin, but also to prefigure a Second Adam who would rectify and secure the irreparable rift between the Godhead and the *Imago Dei.*

My eminent of intimate creation inquired with hope that he might see this redemption. In great dolor I expounded all the Curse entailed for the earth and that he and his wife's shared burden of judgment was to be fruitful and to survive in a broken world then physically die, to daily strive for spiritual life, and to humbly testify of my love and mercy. The mystery of the ages was for future generations. Though I would not abandon humanity, I would not be so near.

Yet now, in Gethsemane's garden, is the appointed time. Today is the day of salvation. And my children shall be overjoyed to see this long awaited Dawn. Indeed, all souls in Sheol's righteous captivity shall see a new Day!

My heart is filled with love despite Evil's advance. Though Sin and Death personify domination and enslavement, humanity's freedom is not attainable without divine intercession. My salvation is only received by renouncing the flesh for spirit, and only by the power of my Father's Spirit. The wicked believe freedom is found in serving no authority; in truth, freedom is found solely in serving the right authority. My Beloved Disciple will disclose this to the world: I am the way, the truth, and the life. He is yet in darkness but has seen a great Light, and will soon see me *in* and *as* that Light. He, and all who would know the Son of Man, will be free.

Just as the brazen serpent was lifted high in the wilderness to save the humble and penitent, so will I be lifted up as an emblem of sin under judgment. Like Hezekiah, son of Ahaz, I will throw down the high places and snuff out the odious incense that offends all of heaven. *Nehushtan* will be forever broken. The times of ignorance will be overlooked and Yahweh will command repentance for all, for He has appointed a day in which He will judge the world in righteousness by the Man whom He has ordained, establishing this by making Him into sin who knew no sin, and then raising Him from the dead.

Evil, per its own hubristic and parasitic nature, cannot comprehend its undoing, and it will resist when I have finished my sedulous labor. The darkness shall cloak itself in deceit though it perceives and fears its end, for the darkness is a fallen intelligence beset with sorcerous wraiths edifying its own imagined supremacy. The devil, astute in his arrogance and long believing his own lies, is on the ascendant and solipsistically sees me as weak in the flesh. He is not mistaken. I am indeed weak in the flesh in accord with the will of my Father, yet my Spirit strengthens me in my hour of need so that Our love for the world would be manifest. Therefore, dear one, with joy you will draw water from the well of salvation that shall be known in all the earth.

Cherished reader, heart of my heart, my peace is not from a lack of suffering but from calm undeviating devotion to my Father and His will. My rest is found in the enduring trust I have in Him, and in my imminent spiritual deliverance of the despoiling nature of the flesh for all who would likewise trust in me.

VI

Here my prayerful contemplations were cut off. All at once, my limbs contorted unnaturally and a frenetic pain besieged my being, stealing my breath. I inhaled reflexively and, still pressed into Gethsemane's soil, quaffed a hurtful amount of dust which set off a sordid fit of spastic coughing. I again tasted blood. The Cup of my Father's wrath remained upturned, its contents freely flowing into my earthen vessel and vitiating my body, scourging me from within. Unseen to human eyes, this baleful act spawned a parasitic vaticide—a baculine sanction both arcane and divine. My lungs had bruised and my viscera were given to an execrable puce and ocher hue as a heinous conformity to sin ripened. My own lifeblood sought to escape and fled every pore and outlet.

"Abba! I am a tender reed harassed by the wind—but I will not break. I am stricken, afflicted, and despised by all; those I know betray me, my own hide their faces from me. Will I see the labor of my soul? For my soul pours out as a sin offering unto death; an intercession for transgressors that is my end! The grave taunts me and I have long held my peace, I have been still and restrained my flesh but now I cry like a woman in birth throes. Like the Expanse, I am stretched, torn, and wearing out.

"Father, Your cohorts of terror are arrayed against me; Your arrows of war are within me, my spirit drinks their poison. O God, You are granting the request I yearn for, though the flesh wills to retreat! I know it pleases You to crush me, to overturn the unsavory taste of injustice to that of the savory sweetness of salvation born of Our love. Weigh my grief in full upon the scales, and with it the iniquitous calamity that I become.

"To You my suffering shall pass swifter than a weaver's shuttle; to me the hours snag like a fisherman's dragnet, prolonging a fruitless haul.

Thus I speak in the anguish of my soul after the appointed months of feared futility and wearisome nights of battling a bitter foe. Conflict seems to spring from the dirt! Yet mankind is born to conflict and consumed by it—as I must be.

"My God, You will soon refuse to look upon me and I will be forgotten. But I will remember Your love; I will contend with the craftiness of cowardly counsel and the dire devices of demons, I will frustrate and foil the plans of the damned. Your righteousness forever stands. Your will is my own and I will not forsake the forging of Our way in the desert."

A wash of fleeting comfort settled my soul, and a faint whisper from the Spirit impressed upon me that my hour—eternal *and* human—had come for the Son of Man to be glorified. Truly, this scarifying imputation of sin unto me makes it possible to impute my righteousness unto whosoever would believe on my name and receive the substitutionary grace-work that my Father conceived and designed from the Beginning. My desire to personally establish and effect Our atoning love for the world brings such joy to Him!

"*Joy indeed.*" It was my Spirit's voice, now lucid and critically welcome. "*Take heart, Paladin! Though all creation groans and the observant Host profess obscurant witness—recalling Haman's Pur of wrath—You, Brother, have come into the world for such a time as this, to save not only the Jew but also the stranger. Leaving Our habitation for the lowly seat You will be exalted to the highest Seat at the heavenly Table, ennobling all who would secure their inheritance in the name of Jesus the Christ. Bearing in Your body the judgment of the Righteous Father on human sin, the sovereignty of the Godhead shall permit alienated mankind a full reconciliation with Us.*

"*Limited in eternal efficacy, the flesh—Your flesh—cannot long cling to eternal truth when plagued by judgment; thus I speak to Your spirit which has taught Your flesh how to suffer well toward forging the first resurrection. The tempered and humble sufferance You have lived in the world shall pacify the warring conscience and lead others into Our perfect peace. As an iron brand placed into the fire loses its rust and glows white-hot, so shall Your labor shed the temporal glory of the old man and constitute the illimitable glory of the new man.*

"*When Your atoning work is finished and the Throne of Salvation is eternally set, the fear of the Lord will empower and cleanse Your Bride. Then with Our avail, the acts and shadows of godly men and women will carry salvific power to even the remotest regions of earth. Remember and rejoice in the generations hence, for Your immediate intercession provides the prophetic path of Patricius, Shepherd of Eirlandia, whom shall entreat a dark and torrid land to discover the Kingdom of All Tomorrows! Our infinite love will counter and reverse the finite defiance that stains our worldly children."*

My Fortifier placed a gentle hand on my head and with the other eased me into a sitting posture. With edifying illumination, He continued.

"Yeshua, You are the Dawn Treader of each new day, having established evening and morning and every celestial and terrestrial body in their courses. You are the Voyager of Elysium, the Master and Stone of Earendil, bringing hope to every soul who seeks out that which We have lovingly concealed. Those who seek and find are privileged to become royal stewards of the mysteries of God, therein receiving a lifelong harvest of narrative Wisdom that brings contentment to the fearful and unquiet soul."

A surge of love from Home augmented the salience of my Spirit's advocacy. Yet comfort was fleeting, for the weakness and virtue of my flesh sought abdication from the abasement of Father's punishing wrath. A sudden internal upheaval overtook me and all the world's guilt from every age flooded my being. My soul was wounded and I pleaded for the hope and wisdom of my ageless Companion.

"*Ruach*, I am become the frailty and wickedness of men; be my strength, for mine fails! Abba's nearness has fled, a void I have not known—"

My body gave way to great heaving sobs and tremors, and my Comforter embraced me in a mighty hold. I cried tearful lament as my mortality was tempted by unbelief and fear, a carnal error hostile toward my soul and divine will. Withal, encompassed within the bulwark of the Holy Spirit and His perfect love, I was emboldened, and I invited the sinuous surge of sin that would soon wholly rend the deific Triumvirate.

An injurious burden racked me again with the deadly bondages of the flesh which drag humanity to hell. Tormented with want, wasting in deprival, entangled with vanities, enervated by passive cares and occult curiosities. Such are the days of a worldly life that are few and evil. I bewailed and tasted the awful tediousness and bitterness of the lost, an appalling adulteration of my innocence. With no hint of turning, I opened my heart wide to the holy sojourn I traversed. I voiced gratitude to my faithful Father and stouthearted Spirit for their gracious regard as I, in unparalleled humility and love for the world, prepared for the coming conflagration of the cross that I chose to bear. I covet no outward or private thing, only the perfect will of Abba.

Although speaking came with difficulty, my conformity to sin now challenged putting order to prayerful contemplation. Thus my sure Spirit interceded with counsel both grim and genial. *"I, too, must recede ere Your lifework is fulfilled. This You know. Our separation will alter all realms—created Cosmos and eternal Caelum. My presence will defer to Our prime ministering brethren, Alatar and Pallandros, whom shall uphold and kindle the narrow path You attend. You will receive unending laud for the trenchant reproach You suffer, the very garment of glory for the accursed Blameless One. For the Sower has gone forth and cast the Seed upon the earth, the sown Seed dissolves and dies, and from dissolution the power of Providence raises it, and from one Seed shall arise many to bring forth fruit in bounty. Your Name will resound in a harvest amidst all the earth, the far off coastlands shall honor You because of Our love."*

The irradiating truth of Ruach's words sobered me. I prayed to Abba, His presence now proximate by my Holy Spirit alone. "Lord God Elyon, in the joy of my earthly youth I was fed by the light of Your instruction and consolation. Cultivated to full maturity in body, mind, and spirit, Your intimate wisdom taught my soul to admit the rhythms of joy, of sorrow, and the disquiet of impending impassioned suffering. The shadow of severance loomed ever on the horizon, and now it has overtaken me! I willingly smite my breast, bow my knees, and prostrate myself beneath the wings of Your mercy. In the end, I will be protected from every evil and wrathful gale that assails me.

"I am grateful, O God, for the song of salvation You have composed and of which You have invited I and the Spirit to sing! You are ever to be praised! The hour is come that Your Servant should be proved, and the Secret Servant revealed. You have appointed it and willed it; Isaiah heralded it; I have commanded it and permitted it. I draw unto myself the omneity of mankind's haughtiness and shame; and I place myself beneath the rod of Your unsearchable judgment. You will strike and then heal. You will not spare the sin that I become, for bitter stripes afflict me from within and without. Having never sinned, I shall be guilty of all sin. You will leave me poor and desolate, worthy only of scorn and contempt. I will forfeit my place in the everlasting habitation, even within the Godhead. My tears and solitude are rewarded with silence and desertion. You will rise up and stand against me, and none will defend me."

I wept heavily, unfettered. Then, placing a strong hand on my heart, my Holy Spirit grieved with me in a long sore silence. His solidarity imparted resolve enough to ignite the founding love of Eternity. I settled briefly and breathed deeply, though it hurt me terribly and I nearly swooned. My Counselor indicated the spellbound legions of heavenly agents at hand perchance I urged repair or rapture from my passionate purpose.

"Nay, Brother," I stated hoarsely. "They stand in vain, yet as a great cloud of witnesses they shall marvel that We established Our salvation from the Beginning. Such joy is set before me now, to provide the lost a way to be found. As Author and Finisher of the faith being forged in love, I will endure the cross and then the cross will endure me as I lay axe to its root and destroy humanity's hidden inordinate inclination to sin.

"Just as Abba sent the revelatory Law and Prophets to the Jews, the truth You ceded to the Greek Sophists of old—that the unexamined life is not worth living—shall wholly transcend the temporal musings of the flesh. The ancient pursuit of the undeniable truths of foundational logic and rational thought testify of Your illuminating work in the wider world, preparing the Way that the Son of Man would ratify for all time. The ethereal composition of this crowning God-spell proves the errancy of pagan religion and the incompletion of Greek sophistry. Self-examination shall afford cross-examination by Our direct revelation, rousing long-sought relational restoration—humanity's exodus from its iniquitous stain. The yawning rift between reason and a reasonable faith shall be bridged. The archaic unnamed Person—the *Logos*—shall ever after be known as the intimately ever-abiding and everlasting Word of God. The Eternal Community of the Essenes will be effected, the Teacher of Righteousness exalted, the New Covenant consummated!

"As Aeneas, I sojourn to forge a great land and a greater city, but Latium and Rome are mere dust snapping off the breeze-blown pennants of Zion. Yet I must first pass into the land of darkness, a land cloaked in the shadow of death. There I must face dragonkind; though my heel shall bruise, I will crush the serpent's head. Like Josheb the Tachmonite, mightiest of David's giant-hunters, I will expose the enemy's stronghold and overthrow his battlements; his war banners shall wither. Thereafter, the devil-god of Kittim will be nourished by the ash of oblivion, gnawed by undying worms and unendingly riven by his own self-inveigling damnation."

Immediately, I saw the uttermost depths of the Expanse, and the great maw of the outer darkness whence burns the unfading fire of Avernus—and its guardian, the fallen Armaros. I saw the Lost Road ranging from earth to infinite pathways among the stars, an astral artery forsaken by Adam which would have declared my glory in ways unimagined. Then an unnatural silence settled in Gethsemane, and with it a cold menace slowly gathered.

I stood suddenly and bent violently with the pained effort, though my Spirit steadied me. Lest all the inhabitants of the earth be dissolved, I will drain the Cup my Father offers me; it is a heavy draught and undiluted. He girds Himself with righteous wrath and even the wrath of man and devil shall praise Him! Thus I am a vessel chosen to receive vengeance possessed by God alone. Fear not, dear one; the earth will tremble and shake and all creation will be afraid. Darkness will rule but for a moment, but amidst this warfare I will meditate on the works, the wonders, and the love of my God who redeems His people.

"Your way, O God, is in the earth and in the sea, and is established in the heavens." In affirmation of my words, my Holy Spirit then indicated a heretofore invisible avenue extending from the Lost Road to our very feet—the same gateway I had prophetically revealed to Jacob.

For the sake of my sleeping Bride, my body is a house of judgment fit for destruction; all her transgressions are blotted out. This is the salvation of Yahweh. The uprightness of my heart and the perfection of my feet are in His right hand. Clothed in this truth, and for love of the world, We stepped into the firmament.

VII

I WAS CARRIED IN the Spirit to a feted vantage affording me the silent and seraphic vista of Earth and her terrene sisters—and beyond—recalling the day We adorned the heavenly tent with this artful array. I admired the boundary of light and dark upon the sphere of my Father's footstool, its inhabitants unaware of the extant cosmic conflict that would determine all hope and doom. In awe, I again praised Abba for His vision and for the joy of singing such glory into being; the musical canons of creation still echo! And I smiled when noting the absence of Atlas or some trite reptilian beast upholding the world; for I hung the world on nothing. In sublime relativity, future ages will ascertain the preeminent precision of my agency, the invisible tabernacles—the gravity wells—within which I have housed all worlds and luminaries. This governing truth of the cosmos shall bring both coetaneous ruin and reverence to humanity.

"Yeshua, rouse the moment of Our intercession for the world ere You summoned the dry land and ere I, resting over the face of the Deep, set the world to dancing. Illumined only by Glory, We exulted in the expectation of a new horizon for Our love and a new dawn for the imminent genesis. Anticipating the Psalm, the Host held poise, enchanted by an enduring mystery not to be disclosed until the Epilogue."

I delighted in the memory and my soul lightened. The Spirit continued, *"You affixed the Greater and Lesser Lights and all luminaries in their tents, and behold, Noga remains faithful in his shining brilliance."* He indicated the sun and its solar sweep. I was enheartened regarding the appointed day We granted revelation to a repentant David from these same hallowed heights. Israel's king then honored Us by voicing a psalm of Our handiwork, and imparting to his next son the namesake I had given Earth's star.

Ruach then turned the heavenly glory toward my own mortal fear. *"Noga's light shall radiate even as You reverently bear the shame and curse of Adam's sin. I and the Father's intercession for You likewise radiates hotly as both the first light and twilight of Our love converge and convulse in a perilous eucatastrophic eschaton."*

"Your truth braces me, Brother, and Our exchange forges hope within my impotent mantle! Stay with me a moment more that I might taste one further mote of majesty, for I am wormwood and I must consume the Cup of gall that will irrevocably extol Our love."

"El Roi smiles at Your expiation, Telperion." At the mention of my ancient name, Ruach's being shone forth the sacred light with which We enkindled all creation. In turn, a smile lit my own face and the enduring aurora inflamed my heart with the prophetic power of envisioning the end from the beginning! I lifted my gaze from Earth and toward the farthest reach of the north, whence the starry tract unrolled and stretched to conceal the place of Father's throne.

I prayed, "Abba, glorify Your Son, that He would glorify You and Your Name. My separation is a blessed wound that shall be written in my hands and feet forevermore." At once, I saw beyond the cosmic expanse, through the Ekkaia—the encircling sea—and into Edenhall. My flesh beheld One seated on a throne, wreathed in iridescent and unapproachable light, and crowned with unknowable truth. My spirit discerned Father's approval and previsioned a return to the Mercy Seat at His right hand. The sacred table was set and I was to provide the bread and wine. The hidden Manna would be revealed, and the Door to my house would be open to all who would seek first the Blessed Realm.

Abba's favor lifted me mightily and my total being—spirit *and* flesh—unified in immaculate will, though I yet sail into an alien maelstrom. Looking back to Earth, its Hadean heart was laid bare to my sight and I observed the sickly Charon plying the black waters of the Acheron, ferrying damned souls from one torment to the next. Even to the Phlegethon he solemnly glided, a torrent of flowing flame which combusted one's very spirit in endless agonizing stasis.

Then I perceived the Abyss, a wasted and poisoned landscape of utter desolation dominated by rootless roving mountains of molten rock and ore. These great slag heaps retched and spat their magmatic and pestilent filth as they wrought their arrant ruin in concord with immense roaring columns of living fire towering to immeasurable heights far above the sullen canopy. Putrid vapors drifted thickly like witless wraiths, barring breath and vision. Distinctly obscured were the vast craters which pitted the plain, some laden with the aggregate of incarcerated angels whom had spoiled humanity and now awaited their sovereignly fixed end. Bound in titanic chains subject to my will, these invidious gods seethed in their sedition. My servant Enoch, the only human soul to have walked this unholy place, was long ago sickened by the monstrous visage of evil confined, enduring spiritual wounds that shall fuel his prophetic station and witness—apace with Elijah—at age's end. Ere my Incarnation I instructed Enoch, the seventh from Adam, imparting unto him prudence and foresight both shrewd and dire. Many aeons I exposed to him, from the founding of the world and its drowning to its burning and restoration. Yet for humankind I did not fashion this charred hell or its fated end in the realm of fathomless flame. Such damnable inferno ought to have been the reward for angelic insurgence alone; though willful pride paves the mortal path to this perdition for many beloved.

For this reason, the way of salvation I shape and secure shall provide an escape from futile fatality into infinite vitality, reconstructing and forever perfecting perfection. Thus from the silent ether I proclaim to my treasured creation, "My righteousness is near, my salvation has gone forth; and I will judge all. The coastlands will wait but a season, yet in my Word you will trust. You will lift your eyes to the heavens and look on the earth beneath, knowing the heavens shall vanish like smoke and the earth shall unthread as a garment; those who dwell in it will die. But my salvation is established from generation to generation and will not fade.

"Fear the oppressor no longer, nor the rage of nations, for I am the Lord your God and the ends of the earth shall see the deliverance of my people. The kings of the earth will take their stand and the rulers will gather together against me, though they will be shaken by my hand and shall consider what they have never known, and be extinguished by what they have refuted. No weapon or malice formed against me shall prosper, when they assemble they will fall. Yahweh's purpose will resound in my atoning affliction; the heritage of my servants is my biding virtue."

Voicing truth in this way and from this prodigious summit set loose my Word and absolved the world from ignorance. In unified vision Ruach upheld me, His aspect effervescent. He affirmed the line of truth We had sent out, the line to which all creation is tethered and from which the fear of the Lord flows clean and bright, enduring forever.

I educed the occasion at Caesarea Philippi when I pressed the Twelve on the subject of my identity. I had led them into prohibited territory at the foot of Mount Hermon, a place of unclean spirits and wicked veneration. Becoming discomposed, their hearts nearly failed when we planted at the very nave of occult exertions, a natural cavern entrance—the gates of hell. Evil fled at our approach, wisely wary of my intent. Regaining composure, Peter marked the revelation that I was the living Christ, Yahweh incarnate. His words resonated deep into the yawning mountain, awakening long-dormant devilry. Indeed, Peter's admission of truth is the foundation upon which my earthly kingdom shall be established. The air turned suddenly foul and mute; thus I dispelled the waxing shadow with an unforeseen war council, openly disclosing the mystery of my church as the vanguard of an offensive against Lucifer's empire of darkness. In my own authority my church shall wield the power to bind and loose on earth what is sanctioned in heaven. And in my victory my church shall prevail, even Hades itself cannot stand!

I felt Avernus heave and thunder at my declaration, the immeasurable fiery lake railing in anticipation of eating hell itself! A second death of drowning despair and incessant soul-scourge awaits all damned ere the new heavens and new earth are born. Faintly perceptible in the latter years, this impenetrable province shall remain shrouded by an event horizon from which neither the cries of the accursed nor the flare of flame can escape. Ever curtained from mortals per its lethal dread, I long ago collapsed the Avernine star and permanently separated the realm from the created cosmos by dimensional rifting to be cast into remote and forgotten darkness.

Ruach redirected my concentration to Earth's moon. Heedless of our proximity, two powerful but fallen principalities, Svarog and Fenrir, conspired and disputed continental control of the world. Formerly standing in my congregation as children of the Holy Godhead, and now self-esteemed as gods of the sky, these world-wreckers shall soon fall from their proud pinnacle and die like the lesser powers and souls they dominate. I will wrest all nations from their kind and from their pretender overlord, the son of perdition and bearer of unlight—Lucifer. I shall grant him a victory that will see him undone, for the victory is my own, a mystery kept secret since the origin of all.

"*It is time.*" Though my flesh countervailed, Ruach leveled the counsel I craved, and my spirit triumphed. "*Yeshua, You are the Head of Days; and a new advent awaits all creation. Together, as the forge-smiths of heaven, We have fashioned from an untold alloy the bane of sin and death—the Javelin of God. You are at once the High Priest, the altar, the incense, and the sacrifice. You are the Ark of the Covenant, the very throne of glory. You are the King of Elysium and from heaven You will thunder against Your adversaries and judge rightly the ends of the earth. The Almighty will exalt His Anointed One!*

"Fly now, Brother, and hasten Our mercy upon Israel; and deliver the Gentiles from unholy enemies. Leviathan cannot hide from his Maker! Welcome the final reckoning of flesh and spirit, and pierce the fleeing serpent, bringing an end to his reign that Your kingdom may take root forever. From the fountain of wisdom concealed from men, and upon an invisible spring of glory, take up Your wood-hewn throne and receive the everlasting possession that the mountain of God may rise and water the earth with righteousness and truth, that Our holy design would pardon the stain of those who would be cleansed from their iniquity."

VIII

I AWOKE AMIDST A root-ridden bed among the trees, my limbs numb and rigid and no longer free of earthly bonds. Asleep or unconscious but for fleeting moments, a profane pounding in my head surged as I stood. Weakly gripping an overhanging olive branch, I managed to steady myself in body and spirit, offering lament to Abba and Ruach for their loving separation that I would now endure of my own accord.

A new covenant shall satisfy both the law and the long-ago promises to mend the enmity between God and mankind. As Noah entered into the ark of salvation and was spared judgment, so another Ark is now being constructed to provide a more perfectly provisional path of saving grace and mercy. A more intimate marriage of humanity to divinity shall be dedicated with new wine—and new wineskins. Such shall be an armor of light to be put on by the one who gives no clemency to the carnal, for I have not come to cancel or change the law; I have come to fulfill it.

There will be no condemnation for those who are in me and I in them, who walk in accord with the Spirit whose law of life in Christ shall guarantee liberty from the law of sin and death. My forgiveness covers a plurality of transgression for those who seek me. I will justify all who believe, confess, and follow me in love; for I make it possible to be conformed to my image. All are called to inherit my kingdom, but few will be glorified. And those few shall find the triune Godhead to be Light, and the Holy Spirit a prism revealing an infinite spectrum of that Light. Newfound clarity will scatter the blinding unlight of Lucifer and awaken the Moratani to truth imperishable.

I go to besiege Jerusalem with my love. Formerly, I chastened my city with the beast of Babylon and she was defiled. Now she has become as a widow with no comfort; her friends have dealt treacherously with her and have become acrid enemies. Under the affliction and hard servitude of profane priests and false fathers, she finds no rest. Her prophets have dreamed delusions and licked up lies; they hiss and spew from their belly a contaminated conceit. Repelled by truth, many I love conjure vulgar tales to ensnare the upright and elevate self. Yet I will exorcise this putrescent bilge from the earth!

The doctrine of Sinai that descended with tempest and fire is giving way to the doctrine of Zion which is heralded by a covering of blood that speaks grander things than that of Abel. Most beloved reader, for those with eyes to see and ears to hear and hearts to perceive, the signs and wonders I do in my name—for my Father and for the world—shall permanently bestow rare revelation unto salvation. This will compulsorily incite belief or unbelief, from which will accrue life or death.

I remember well the day Moses ascended the mountain and I descended in the cloud to stand with him there, to proclaim the name of the Lord of heaven and earth. Israel had forsaken my accomplished deliverance and shamelessly whored after Egypt in their blackened hearts. Yet my servant knew his sheep as I know my own; thus he pleaded for them, offering himself in their stead lest I consume them in my thundering wrath. For such willing self-sacrifice, I saved Moses and taught him to worship me, not by ritual obeisance but in relational communion. He asked to see my glory and so I carried him to the valley of vision, hemmed in by mountains of sin, that he would see the greatest heights from the lowest hollow. I showed him the genesis of all creation, the collapse of angel and man, the havoc of inhuman seduction and savagery, the despair of divinely directed doom, the hope of life both temporal and eternal, and the new covenant that would restore all that had been broken. Of these things he would write to glorify an even greater Author, that future generations—to which I now entreat—would repent and be consecrated. Graciously and mercifully I affirmed that I would work an awesome wonder through Moses, a wonder that would begin with the giving of the Law and that would end with its fulfillment in me—the salvation of the world!

Indeed, to wholly understand the sustentation of my blood atonement for humanity's trespass is to attain a heart of wisdom in the house of mourning, for the context of the Law's interpretation is greater than the law to be interpreted. My statutes are not to be canonically followed, but passionately lived through me. Moses learned this—that the broken heart is the healed heart; the penitent soul is the victorious soul; joy is set in sorrow; and to bear the cross is to wear the crown.

Like Rome, my children and their garish goatherds have anchored themselves *contra mundum*—against the world. Most will blindly follow that hideous strength wherein death rules, not knowing what they do. Some know precisely what they do and embody a pious sloth that disintegrates the soul. And like Rome, all the earth shall be overrun by an unanticipated and dread reality from outside the gate.

Even as I lament, prophetic clouds gather for a perfect storm of pardon and the purge of primal approbation. I am the former and latter rain. With the former rain I give the Jew a spiritual shearing; Israel shall be as shorn sheep, naked and erratic. With the latter rain I grant the Gentile my portion that Israel would stumble and strive with me as Jacob, for when my judgments are in the earth the whole world will learn righteousness, though many be condemned.

Blessed reader, my heart remains rent with woe and astonishment at man's pride! My flesh is weak and degraded, yet Abba shall be well pleased when His justice is satisfied and His truth magnified. As Mediator of the everlasting covenant, my heart hastens to rescue the elect from deserved humiliation. Infinite punishment is due and infinite punishment will be endured in Adam's stead until I evulse the deadly viper's fang and evaporate its venom. Sin's insolvency shall be decimated by my lifeblood; and evil expiated. The menacing shadow at the end of the world shall be blown away by a holy wind. And then heaven's anthem will echo as far as the east is from the west and all creation will intimately know the divine Treasury in whom all fullness of life dwells.

Yet for an hour evil shall subsist at my charge until every void eroded by sin has been replenished by glory graciously given and humbly chosen. The devil hates and wars against the Jew and any who would call on the name of my Father, and this only because I love them. So I stand and fight for all souls who would receive my inheritance, for none save the Son of Man is able to stride forth in zealous love and all power to cure the wound of godlessness and to gain victory over death. Indeed, sin is no sport of fencing with Satan or a bauble to easily toss away; it's heinousness rests not in the nature of sin committed, but in the holiness of the Person sinned against. My Beloved Disciple shall behold this paramount truth and rejoice ere he falls asleep.

O Israel, you have hearkened unto earthly kings and been rewarded with the strife of political and martial entanglement. Your own counsel has failed and you have refused to repent. You are mocked by all nations for your vanity and effrontery, artfully entrapped by the world and its gilded bait. You have been beguiled by the Baals and the Ashtoreths, and have profaned yourself on the Mount of Corruption. Even the remaining stump, the remnant of my Chosen people, is accursed. Behold! I am the Holy One in your midst, and you repudiate me, though I approach in humiliation and do not bring terror in my wings! Yet my sympathy is stirred. Therefore, I will suffer with you—and all humanity—and some shall be saved; for I am sovereign even over suffering.

Like Moses, Solomon set out to know Wisdom and discovered the burdensome acquisition to include much folly and grief. For he who increases knowledge increases sorrow. But joy is received by the one fiercely following after my heart, and to such a one Wisdom is a helpmeet for every season, granting visitation at her discretion. My Preacher learned, as I did, that it is one facet to contemplate the wonders of heaven, yet it is another to walk the earth full of heaven's wonder. At table, do you fixate on the litter of crumbs or the Bread from whence they fall? Better still, as a brimming jar of water is itself immersed in water, I will be in you and you in me. My way is simple and light; the way of the dragon is a strangling load of lies that I am now taking away. To obey me is not to appease a god, but to know and be known by the One True God in whom is found truth in identity. To recall and reflect on my commandments, fulfilled in me by love, is to set up an altar as a spur to both conscience and spirit. In this cultivation of worshipful humility my Spirit resides, resounds, and resurrects all life from death.

*

I returned to my companions—John, James, and Peter—and again found them bound in restless dormancy. A hard stone toss away, the other eight fared no better. An ill humor and aching ire erupted in my flesh, tempting sharp reproof for their listless sleep. I resisted and said nothing, leaving them to their fear.

Alone, I plodded heavily back into the darkness and prepared to receive and exhaust the depths of my Father's Cup of fury against the sin of the world. The scope of this passionate pursuit forever rests beyond all spirits—men and angels—yet my provision sets solely before men a hope beyond the grave, an earnestly obtained foretaste of immortality. Though Yahweh's wisdom remains ever out of reach, He does not.

I am the weeper in the trees, the lover and Redeemer of my creation. There are many paths in the world; for the lightning, the wind, the rain, the rivers and seas, the flowing fires and ores in the earth, and for every living creature and every living soul. Now behold! As High Priest of the order of Melchizedek whose origin far precedes the memories of Adam, I open a new path, a life-giving Way, by which the lost shall be called by my Spirit and may approach me and be saved from undying death. My heart warmed and swelled with unfathomable love.

A biting breeze arose swiftly and frosted Gethsemane's air, my labored breath clouding in thick powdery plumes. A somber sky impaired the oft fay effect of the garden and cast it in blackest sackcloth. The hour of sifting neared its end and I involuntarily sobbed and choked until I retched. Steadying myself against one of my favored olive trees, I again prayed for my Father's Cup of woe to pass from me. Still, it is the will of my Father, and verily of my own, that I drink the iniquitous rivers and adorn the acidic shame of humanity's wickedness. In this I constitute for ages eternal an overturning of the wisdom of men and angels, a redemptive reversal that shall resonate in ubiquitous unity from the unknowable reaches of the Infinite to the acumen of the intimately immediate.

Breathing deeply and engulfed in gratitude to my Father, I prayerfully contemplated a portion of the blessed souls and seasons I had personally cultivated and would apprise forever.

IX

I RECALLED THE DAY I had compassion on the widow of Nain. Early in the second year of my public mission, I had by this time acquired the Twelve and the Seventy and demonstrated numerous signs of my kingdom's arrival, healing all manner of infirmity and displaying authority over unclean spirits and the natural world. Yet the time had come to impart the prophetic power of the resurrection and provide the long-awaited hope of my people. From notable distance, I spied the solemn funerary procession exiting the village, for the widow had lost her only child, a son of thirty-three years. Markedly, the mourners could not have missed the regional multitude in my own wake, consisting as it did of my disciples and their learners, the hopeful, the curious, the skeptics, and the apostates.

After instructing my attendant company to halt and bidding only John bar Zebedee to follow, I intercepted the bereft advance not far from Nain's gate. As we approached, the procession slowed and I drew near the woman and stood before her. Having never seen me, she recognized me. She let go the veil held to her face and her tear-rimmed eyes instantly kindled from despair to hope. She collapsed to her knees, overcome with emotion. I knelt at her side and asked, "Woman, what is your name?"

"Chaya," she said weakly.

"Take heart, Chaya. For your name is life." I gently placed a hand against her cheek and inquired, "Why do you weep?"

"Lord, you know. My son has gone to Abraham, though full of health. Neither sickness nor misfortune took him. Reason fails me and now I am alone; yet I have faith." She wept anew.

"Chaya, you are cherished among women. Sanctification is evidence of reconciliation and you are reconciled with God. Weep not in sorrow but with joy, for your faith has made you—and your son—whole."

I stood and lifted my daughter to her feet, her face now aglow with unexpected expectation. I then approached the open pall carried by two strong men, and placed my hand on the shroud-clad body. A sudden silence fell amidst the grieving crowd for my ritual violation, and likewise amidst my own restrained and watchful company further down the hillside.

"Young man, arise." I spoke softly yet my Father's authority shook the unseen realm and the breath of life, the *pneuma*, stirred. I loosened the face cloth and the man sat up. A gasp of amazement raced through the cumulative multitude. After a moment's survey, he spoke.

"Mother?"

"Aviv!" Rejoicing with many tears, Chaya ran to her child as the pall was lowered to the ground. I stepped back from their furious embrace and proclaimed, "Woman, behold your son."

Fear came upon all the people in that moment, and they glorified God in one accord. A voice called out that a great prophet had risen among them, another cried "Immanuel!"

Indeed. God was in their midst.

Quickly set free of his grave-shroud and covered with a robe, Aviv approached and wrapped me in a worshipful hold. His eyes belied the brightness of inexpressible gratitude. I was pressed to remain and celebrate the turn of lament to life, but I could not tarry as I was on my way to Scythopolis near the Jordan. Therefore, I urged discretionary witness to the people of Nain as they considered and testified to the coming of my kingdom. I called on some to follow me, the two pall bearers with them.

Returning without haste to my impatient assemblage, I observed John's addled expression and bid him speak his heart. He plainly stated that intermingled with the awe of certifying a resurrection, he yet marveled how I could resist becoming unclean by touching the dead. My authority over disability and disease was one matter, and to be humbly lauded he admitted, but authority over death challenged even John's soaring rationale. To this I declared that the Son of Man is greater than both Law and tradition and that all authority in heaven and on earth had been granted me by my Father. The remaining days of my earthly sojourn would see this exemplary teaching strengthen—and death's hold on life weaken.

From this time forward, John bar Zebedee perceived an otherworldly outrage and hateful hostility that would proliferate and darken. As such, my power over death and darkness offended the self-obsessed overlords who sought power over me. Though they had remained silent for a season, they eagerly began plotting my peril.

*

My heart inclined toward my own mother. Following the celebratory wedding in Cana, and after sending my disciples ahead to Capernaum to await my arrival, I had entreated her to accompany me to Magdala, a noisy Galilean hamlet known for its salt trade. In answer to her inquisitive expression I explained that my Father's kingdom was imminent and the Spirit had shown me a soul in torment who was to be freed. The two days we traveled was time much treasured, for such moments were fast stolen by the necessity of my mission.

I was keenly aware of much that she pondered within her heart concerning me: the heavenly visitation in her youth; the insatiable hunger of mind and spirit in my own youth; my baptism by my cousin John and my earthly yet transcendent identity; and the desert trial. After my public mission commenced at Cana, to these heartfelt ponderings were added the mystery of the teaching of my Father's kingdom and the miraculous signs verifying its arrival; my increasing separation from family; the ebb and flow of fickle followers and ripe rumor; my sharp conflict with and condemnation of the religious rulers; my stern bearing toward Jerusalem and the political turmoil my infamy inflamed; my authority over evil spirits; and the confusing tension of whether I was in any way *messianic*. I pray ever for the Spirit to give peace to Mother's heart.

I smiled in recollection of this particular brief trek to Magdala, for we had laughed often and Mary's spirit was light. This was a balm to us in that Joseph's death, at that time, was not yet a year distant. Unforeseen—as with her insistence at Cana!—Mother soon astonished me with her intuition when she asked why I might have to suffer violence and die unjustly. I had yet neither revealed this truth nor alluded to it, to anyone. Nor would my disciples, even after hearing it, comprehend such truth until my victory over death and the Holy Spirit's revelation.

My wonderment continued when Mary recounted to me, for the first time, a prophecy spoken to her by Simeon, a man present at the Temple when I was dedicated as a babe. She had long fretted over his words: *Behold, this Child is destined for a sign which will be spoken against, that the thoughts of many hearts may be revealed. Yes, a sword will pierce through your own soul.*

Her raw honesty was striking. "I fear this 'sword' is a truth I may be unable to bear. The unjust and profane violation of Isaiah's woeful Servant—is this *You*? Are You to be spoken against and rejected by all? Before he passed to the fathers, Joseph strived to prepare me for a day I refuse to approve. He and Simeon had spoken privately those years ago, though I forbade him to speak to me of their meeting. Then Simeon died. And my beloved Joseph has gone. Must I lose You? I do not understand." Her eyes tearfully pleaded with me for a clarity that would dispel her long-checked terror.

"Mother! You are greatly loved by God!" I exclaimed in genuine awe, embracing her. "Truly, my Father honors you and Joseph more than I. There are many things written in the Prophets concerning me that must remain hidden a while longer, and of which I shall soon disclose. Cling to these truths, telling no one, and trust in me when you believe you cannot. When I return to my Father's House, I will remain with you always. You will yet be a mother, gaining a son."

I laughed at Mary's perplexity as she chided me for speaking in riddles, but merriment won out and she let go the unease, asking, "What are we to find in Magdala?"

*

Descending the gentle valley grade, I caught the glimmer of Galilee ere I spotted the dirty smudge of Magdala hard against its shore. Hours later, as Mother and I passed the first outlying hovels and alleyways, the subtle scent of brine accented the familiar freshwater and fish-laden fragrance I so savored. Stores of salt from the Mediterranean and less often from the Dead Sea dominated this village, drawing regional merchants and markets for salted fish and spice. And with such commerce comes the tide of displaced persons and impoverishment per fluctuating wealth and labor.

I discerned Mother's silent worriment when we entered a perilous precinct, into which I strode with purpose. I charged her to pray for a soul's deliverance and for surety of spirit. I then offered thanks to my Father for this opportunity, for amidst my prayers for the miracle of water to wine in Cana, the Spirit had shown me a middle-aged Magdalene woman full of darkness.

We found her asleep outside the door of a burrow and wrapped in polluted, threadbare raiment. A lifetime of emotional, spiritual, and physical injury compounded by a damaged psyche unwilling to trust had left this soul in a broken state unable to receive or offer love. Scorned by family, deserted by friends, and abused by strangers, she was forsaken but for seven unclean spirits which had occupied her earthly tent. Wearying harassment had impelled my daughter to self-harm. My heart rent and I wept. Mother was inwardly doubtful and frightened, seeking retreat. Feeding on this fear, an evil spirit sought to seize her but fell still in alarm when it descried my intent.

I could see the disembodied *shedu*, a demon born of corruption and cursed to wander the earth in search of habitation until the Judgment. Crouching beside my sleeping charge, it choked on its own fear and submitted, awaiting my command. I first addressed my inconscient child.

"Daughter, awake." Her eyes opened and she recoiled violently. I subdued six other foul spirits with a word, momentarily disallowing them to vivify or vacate their host. I extended a hand and raised the woman to her feet. Her eyes were dark with despair and shame, refusing to focus. I placed a hand on her heart and gently asked her name. Healing power flowed from me and I steadied her, prompting Mother's support.

"I do not know my name—," she said as unchecked tears fell.

"Would you be free of your prison and bound only to God and His love?"

The woman's eyes instantly focused on mine and flared with hope. "I would! But I do not know how."

I ordered the seven demonic spirits to come out of the wasted woman and exiled them to the waters of Galilee until the end of the age. To my daughter, now breathing and beholding life she had never known, I offered, "Follow me, for you have seen the advent of my Father's kingdom. If you are willing, you shall be blessed to learn the way of salvation, an exodus from sin itself."

"Lord, I am willing!"

"From this day you will be known as Maryam, beloved salt of the sea. My mother will keep you, and your welfare will be renewed. The first resurrection will find you when the last hope dies."

Mother chided me again for enigmatic expression, yet the ebullient joy that animates and effectuates the human spirit reborn by the life-giving Holy Spirit cannot be dampened. Their souls aglow, Mary and Maryam chattered like playful hens the entire course to Capernaum!

*

I remembered Nathanael of Bethsaida. Philip had brought him to me and I forecast, "Behold, a genuine Israelite, in whom is no deceit!" Nathanael stared, mystified, then inquired how I knew him. To this I warmly replied, "Before Philip fetched you, I saw you reclined in the shade of your favored fig tree."

"How is this so? You were not near," he said in amazement.

"All things are possible with the Spirit of God."

Immediately, the Spirit moved upon Nathanael and he answered, "Rabbi, truly You are the Son of God and King of Israel!"

Then I declared, "You believe because I said 'I saw you reclined in the shade of your favored fig tree'? Assuredly, you will witness greater things than this! Soon you shall see heaven opened, and the angels of God ascending and descending upon the Son of Man."

"What does this mean? I do not understand," he said, still unsure.

"You know that Jacob your forefather dreamed of a path from the earth to heaven, impossible for men to find or tread. Follow me, and you shall see this path open to you, for I am the Way. Through me, even now, the kingdom of heaven brings mercy, forgiveness of sin, and the Gift of my Father's glory. Indeed, something good has come out of Nazareth!"

Nathanael fell reverently to the ground, contritely pleading, "Lord, I am unworthy! I marvel at the folly of my mind. Impress upon me the account to be rendered for good omitted and evil done, for all of my generations!"

"I say again, a genuine Israelite in whom is no deceit!" I smiled broadly and invited this humble servant to stand. Embracing him, I healed every harbored weakness and affirmed that all his fear had fled. "Nathanael, your name is 'God-given' and now God is given to you."

I shall preserve and profess the radiant joy upon the man's face forever.

*

The day I met Zacchaeus emerged in my spirit. Only recently, on my approach to Jerusalem, I had passed through Jericho with intent to meet Zacchaeus alone. The crowd of disciples and temperamental mob that shadowed me drew much scrutiny and began to press uncomfortably in the narrow dust-clouded streets. Being the third hour, residents ran to and fro performing errands or preparing for midday table, many of them swept up in the sudden curious procession.

Reaching the affluent district of the city, I noted the slight man clinging clumsily to the upper bough of a well-manicured sycamore. The tree was one of several rooted in a private garden situated in front of an opulent home. I stopped and stood near the sturdy hedge bordering the sizable terrace; along this the mass of people gathered, the street swiftly congesting.

I looked intently at the man perched precariously high up the tree. When his apprehension grew, I called to him. "Zacchaeus! It is solely you I have come to see. Make haste, let us break bread together in your ample home." Startled at this revelation, he nearly fell in his ungainly descent, and then upon reaching the ground he did topple as incredulity overcame him. I laughed cheerfully at his disarray and tactless attempt at composure. A few observers mocked the scene.

At last facing me across the hedge, Zacchaeus sputtered, "Me? Surely You are mistaken. Are You not the miracle-worker sent by God to save Israel and punish sinners?"

"Indeed, I am He. But it is not as you say, for I have left the ninety-nine in search of one lost sheep from the fold. Come now, let us reason together. Your name means 'pure of spirit' but you are mired in impurity. Would you have balance between your life and namesake, that your sins would not be punished but forgiven?"

Zacchaeus, being a wealthy and dishonest chief tax collector, was seized by dread and his countenance fast fell, though I countered, "Fear not, your sins are forgiven. Let us drink and eat in celebration of your salvation!"

"Even I am forgiven? How can this be?"

"Give me some water and you shall no longer thirst."

Stunned by a mix of confusion and hope, Zacchaeus turned and joyfully invited me into his lavish house. I instructed my closest disciples to quell the congregate's surging unrest at this regard of a despised money-man, then I left them all until the ninth hour.

Well-mannered yet aporetic and anxious, my host did not settle until I insisted on washing his feet, though he remained guarded. Without family or attendants, I sat surrounded by neatly-shelved scrolls and books in his spacious "alcove of welcome" and waited while he gathered a wash basin, towel, and cup of cool water. I drank and was refreshed. Then he sat and I knelt to remove his sandals. All at once, Zacchaeus' internal discomfort manifested and he cried, "Lord, I cannot! You are holy and I am a lost and wicked soul!"

I stood and placed a hand on his head. "My son, I say again, your sins are forgiven. Today salvation has come to this house, for you are a son of Abraham and the Son of Man has come from heaven to seek and to save that which was lost. You have been found, Zacchaeus." In that moment, the Spirit granted peace and revelation toward a blessed life yet unlived. As my host shed tears of rejoicing and thanksgiving at his renewal, I prayerfully cleansed the world from his feet and from his heart.

For hours I instructed Zacchaeus in righteousness, in matters of faith and spirit, and in the Law fulfilled in me. One of few survivors from a poor family, he sought to defeat the fear of impoverishment by becoming rich through impious means. This strategy suppressed the truth of his insolvent spiritual health and invited an oppressing spirit of greed and lust which entertained vice. I loosed him from such bondage.

In this fresh freedom I discovered an expansive mind fascinated by numbers and geometry. We spoke of Thales and his student Pythagoras, of Plato and Aristotle and how they collectively not only reasoned downward to the elements and their basic mathematical structure, but also their upward reasoning to the overarching order and structure of the universe. And even with intact areas of sovereignly hidden wisdom, I revealed how the Spirit discreetly worked in times past to progressively disclose facets of divine language—such as mathematics—to chosen individuals. From this, greater generational revelation would develop toward understanding the harmony of the world and *knowing* God through His avenues of analysis and encounter. Tracking beautifully, Zacchaeus adeptly inferred that Euclid, unknowingly directed by the Spirit, distilled the theorems and contingencies of all like-minded predecessors into his comprehensive *Elements* codex, thereby bringing order, rigor, and foundational logic to the figuring of numbers and forms. Lo! Only in the sons of Zebedee had I enjoyed such simultaneous depth and pliability of mind and spirit!

Our dialogue served to correct or confirm the narrative projected onto me by friend and foe alike. And so my new learner became zealous to follow me wheresoever I went, even to the ends of the earth. Indeed, to such he would be called. Yet a season of prayerful temperance would prepare and equip him for acquiring the inheritance foretold by the prophet Joel. Thus unanticipated yet gladly received, I tasked Zacchaeus with testifying of my words and of his salvation to all of Jericho and to remain in his city through the Passover, praying with and shepherding all those souls who would believe his testimony. After this, and despite the hard events to come, I pledged that Matthew of the Twelve would visit him and bring him to me before I ascended to my Father.

Reluctant yet full of wonder, he agreed, then declared, "My Lord, I give half of my possessions to the poor; and if I have taken anything from anyone by theft or false accusation, I will restore it fourfold!"

I smiled and jubilantly inquired, "You will do this, Zacchaeus?"

"I will! Jericho is a large city in which I have cheated most, from householder to newborn. Even the livestock helped build my mansion! I will begin today." With this profession, my prodigal son ran outside to the factious flock and promised remuneration to all he had financially fleeced. The people marveled at his transformation. As did I.

*

I thought of my daughter Afina. After a night of prayer from this very garden, I had arrived early at the Temple and sat down in Solomon's Porch to await those who would hear the teaching of my kingdom. At the fifth hour, a coterie of lawyers and Pharisees impeded my instruction by shoving a half-clothed young woman into our midst and proudly proclaiming, "Teacher, this woman was committing adultery. We brought her here from the very act! The Law of Moses commands that such should be stoned. What do *You* say to this?"

Without a word I calmly arose and left the Temple complex, only ceasing my egress upon gaining one of many agoras beyond the sacred walls. The provoked priests and their proletariat were not far behind, sputtering and fuming in their annoyance. Seeking to test me, they repeated their complaint and dropped the disheveled woman at my feet even as an expectant and prurient crowd clustered. I observed some in their number failing to conceal the large ragged rocks in their hands.

Remaining silent, I knelt before my errant child. Her face to the ground and body trembling, she quietly pleaded for mercy with outstretched hands. With my finger I slowly wrote in the dust the names of the conspiring souls standing present, thus fulfilling Jeremiah's prophecy: *Those who depart from Me shall be ashamed; and their names shall be written in the earth because they have forsaken the Lord.*

A third time my antagonists demanded my verdict, their impatience inflating. To this I stood sternly and several who had crept close leapt back fearfully. I said to them, "Where is the *man* who was likewise caught in the very act, that he too would be condemned? I know he has been released and yet lingers to see the end of your evil plot to trap me as a fraud or lawbreaker, of which *you* are guilty. You do not desire to purge my city of immorality, or you would begin with yourselves. Most of you will die in your sins, for with what judgment you judge, by it you shall be judged. Your malice and hubris are exposed, seen by God and all Israel!"

A shocked hush descended, into which I addressed the whole of the teeming agora, stating, "He who is without sin among you, I invite you to cast the first stone." I leveled a barbed glance at each colluder and discerned acute conviction of conscience in every crooked soul. Filled with enmity and humiliation, my detractors, one by one, quit the city common. In short order all had fled the scene and I was alone with my derogated daughter.

"Woman, where are your accusers? Has no one condemned you?"

Slowly she raised her head and beheld the empty space. Cleansing tears fell and she barely breathed, "No one, Lord."

"Neither do I condemn you, Afina." Unmoved that I knew her name, the young woman shifted to her knees and collected herself, her eyes searching mine and shining with hope. I took her hands and healed her of all injury in body and will, a slave set free. "Now you are Yeira, for I give you the light of life and you shall carry this light to others. Go and sin no more."

"Lord, to where will I go? I have no one."

"Yeira, would you learn to receive the love of my Father and to love as my Father loves?"

"I would! What must I do?"

I reveled in her simplicity of heart and said with deep joy, "Follow me."

As we stood I noticed my disciples—and many others—huddled where they had retreated. I and my newly freed child met them atop the platform which led back through the Temple threshold. The Spirit moved and my kingdom multiplied that day.

*

I remembered my son Nissim. He had been born without sight and endured the life of a mendicant for forty years—until he met the Son of Man. I was walking a circuit through Jerusalem when I noticed him begging street-side not far from the merchant quarter. When my disciples saw him they asked, "Rabbi, who sinned, this man or his father and mother, that he was born blind?"

"Neither this man nor his mother or father sinned," I answered. "But the works of God will be revealed in him."

To this my keenest self-seeking followers replied, "If there is no retributive judgment to be traced from his affliction, why should he suffer an unproductive lifetime of shame only to glorify God at the end?"

My honed response cut their hearts. "Is it the end of his life, then? Do you refer to the law, speculate within yourselves, or edify the error of tradition? You regard this *man* as a sinner less important than your reflections or debate. Where is your compassion and *faith*? It is not for you to know the destinies of men reserved for my Father. This man's condition is an occasion—not a reason—to glorify God. Therefore I must work the works of Him who sent me while it is day; the night is coming when no one can work. I am the light of the world by whom only the blind may see."

I went to Nissim where he was sitting on the ground propped against a vendor stall; my alert companions remained a short distance away. "Greetings, blind one! I know you see much, but would you likewise perceive with your eyes?"

"Ah! You are the Nazarene," he said with tempered joy. "I overheard the ungracious prattle of Your children well before Your approach. Are they not as bloated as our overripe rulers?" He chortled lightly in hesitant mirth, though I easily joined his levity.

I knelt and said privately, "I ask again, would you be healed of your blindness that you may see the world and learn of my creation in new ways?"

He responded in genuine contrition, head bowed. "I would, if it be possible for even me."

"It is indeed possible, my son!" I spat a considerable amount of saliva into my hand and gathered some dirt from the street, making a crude salve. This I then applied to the man's eyes and instructed him to go and wash in the pool of Siloam, a considerable walk, though even in his blindness Nissim was familiar enough with the city avenues. When he had hurriedly gone, I returned to my disquisitive disciples and continued my urban mission.

Hours later I sought Nissim near the place we had last encountered and found him animated and rejoicing, testifying of his new sight to all!

I approached and asked, "Do you believe the Son of God and Son of Man are one and the same?"

Instantly identifying my voice and smothering me in a rough embrace, he exclaimed, "My Lord! I was blind but now I see, and the world is wonderful!" Then stepping back he said, "Who is this Son that I may believe in Him?"

"You have now seen Him and are talking with Him," I answered.

"Lord, I believe! And I worship You from now on!"

"Blessed are you, Nissim. For judgment I have come into this world, that those who do not see may see, and that those who see may be made blind."

In this moment arrived some of the Pharisees whom had been discreetly trailing my new friend after his healing at the pool. They pompously posited, "Are *we* blind?"

"You are not only blind," I countered, "you are also deceived. I know you have exiled this man from the Temple and from attending synagogue because he spoke truth to you and because of his healing which is a sign you refuse to see. You proclaim him a sinner, yet are *you* without sin? You say you are Moses' disciples, but you are disciples of the devil, and therefore slaves to sin! You say I am a lawbreaker because I made a salve and cured on the Sabbath, yet there is One here greater than both the Law and the Sabbath!"

Failing to contain their composure, these false shepherds turned to the mass of onlookers and cried, "He blasphemes and makes Himself like God!" With no return from our audience or myself, the trio of priests forcibly settled themselves, then one of them loudly queried, "How do You not blaspheme when You have lately claimed to pre-exist Abraham? How can You accuse us of refusing to see signs when we are God's interpreters of signs? And how can we be slaves of sin when we are masters of Israel?" He leveled his scepter of office at me. "We would here Your answer, *Nazarene*."

"Your pride in Abraham's seed and in yourselves is your damnation," I stated. "As the sick man is a slave of disease, so the sinner is a slave of sin. And unless Someone severs the power of sin, the sinner will die in their sins and be damned. You have boasted of your heritage, professing to never have been in bondage to any man. Do you forget Egypt, the oppression of the Judges, Babylon, or even Rome? And this only attests outward slavery; your slavery is inflicted from within, for sin is nourished in your hearts and pride blinds you to truth.

"I have said that if you abide in my Word, you are my disciples. I have also chastised you for searching the Scriptures and believing them to hold eternal life, for the Scriptures simply testify of me. I say again to you, your error is in not coming to *me* that you may indeed have life; *I am* the way, the truth, and the life. No one comes to my Father, but through the Son of Man. Truth is not as vital as its interpretation; *I am* the Interpretation. And this truth will set you free from the blindness that interprets only the signs you desire to see in accord with your father, the devil.

"You recusant rectors have said 'Cursed is everyone who does not abide by all things written in the book of the Law.' And so you elevate yourselves over the Law thinking you gain exemption worthy of adoration, yet fearfully knowing God demands perfection. In this you are deceived, for pride alone renders you guilty of breaking the whole Law! I say then, what is the purpose of the Law if it was not given that it might be obeyed to obtain salvation? I now say to you, the Law only saves by condemnation—revealing the hopelessness of the sin nature. By the Law, every mouth is shut and the entire world becomes accountable to God and disqualified in that no flesh may be declared righteous in His sight. Only through the Law comes knowledge of both sin and its deserving judgment and death. Therefore, the Law is an irritant and arouses a desire to break it which no one can escape. For this reason I have come: to fulfill the Law and bring liberty and eternal life to all who would believe on the name of the Father, of the Son, and of the Holy Spirit.

"Woe to you, failed watchmen of Israel, masters of self-deceit and peddlers of unbelief! Your inability to discern the very Light you claim to know has confirmed your rebellion before God. Nissim was blind from birth and his progression from belief to convicting faith healed him, and his sins are forgiven. You are blind by choice and remain in darkness, and your sins likewise remain. Even now, vengeance churns in your hearts and you imagine violence against me. Such is the resort of defeated men. Go back to your nest and tell the brood of serpents all I have declared! You will not escape the wrath to come or the sentence of hell!"

At my final words, a dreadful panic fell fast upon the peremptory priests and they drew back several paces, one stumbling over his costly robe and falling. Their sudden and uncouth desertion led many in the crowd to flee in fright, only my disciples and some observers—and Nissim—were unmoved.

In the tension that followed light dispersing darkness, I set many souls at ease by openly praying to my Father and asking the Spirit to grant them wisdom and boldness in the coming days. I then perceived their expectancy and servility of spirit and taught them that even with the arrival of my kingdom in their hearts, while yet in this world they must become comfortable with conflict, and thus be ever sober and vigilant in their prayers. Being hated and resisted for my name's sake would require a deftness and determination of character the Holy Spirit alone could provide.

In that hour, all present at my instruction were healed in mind and spirit. I too was uplifted when Ruach disclosed that upon my ascension and by Our power Nissim would open the eyes of many, healing innumerable souls in body and spirit.

*

I next thought of Joseph of Arimathea, friend of Nicodemus. As co-council members of the Sanhedrin, and of the Pharisee sect, they both were intrigued by and cautious of my teaching and work. They also anticipated the roiling tension that presently played out in various domains—spiritual, political, ideological, legal, and eternal.

Amidst the first year of my mission a sharp division had deepened between the already divided Sanhedrin. The larger Sadducee sect rejected the resurrection of the body and the existence of the spirit, while their Pharisee brethren, with whom they often disputed, accepted both. Expectedly, the teaching of the arrival of my kingdom and the truth of the resurrection drew the antipathy and ire of many. Although some discerned unearthly revelation in my teaching.

Nicodemus approached me privately in the turbulent days after I had cleansed the Temple of those merchants and moneylenders who defiled it with their idolatry and avarice. In our conversation he recalled the masses of commoners and destitute which convened around me at the very entrance to the Temple complex. That such sought me even as the rulers and wealthy had fled impressed him. That I had received and healed them all, amazed him. Thus of humble bearing, Nicodemus inquired of the Spirit, the new birth, and the baptism I offered. In that same hour, he believed and I instructed John bar Zebedee to baptize this reformed priest. When I then directed Nicodemus to refrain from reporting our meeting, he agreed save for urging me to confer with a fellow like-minded and like-hearted Pharisee, Joseph the Arimathean.

A confidential conference revealed Joseph to possess a shrewd mind and a heart clouded with the tensity between belief and unbelief. Yet his contrition made possible his spiritual conviction and conversion. Heartened by his friend's newfound salvation, Joseph had met me with queries relative to the triune nature of the Godhead and the Spirit's expanding role in declaring me as Son of God.

Appealing to his steadfast understanding of Hebrew history, I freely resolved the finer facets of holy wisdom that would be infinitely contemplated. There is one God, yet they are three Persons, each separate and distinguishable from the other. In function, the Father plans, the Son perfects and relates, and the Spirit executes and reveals. The Father sent the Son; the Son will send the Spirit; the Spirit will represent the Son as the Son represents the Father. All that the Father has belongs to the Son; all that the Son has to teach and give is administered through the Spirit in love. God is love. And God is light; in Him is no darkness. Likewise there is no fear in love, for perfect love casts out all fear. God is perfect; therefore, one can only be made perfect in the Son and by the Spirit accordant with the will of the Father. These three—Father, Son, Spirit—bear witness in heaven; in their affinity they are One and their witness is pure. The Father sent the Son to earth by water and blood, and the Spirit bears witness to this truth. He whom the Father sends overcomes the world, and whosoever believes in Him shall also overcome the world and gain life eternal. The Word of God was made flesh to dwell among His creation that the Glory of God would be revealed, that some might be saved from condemnation. Those whom have seen the Son have seen God. His Word when sown will reap a harvest; though it be meager per man's volition, it will not return void.

Joseph rejoiced at this truth and his hope renovated as I continued. "When I go away, as I must, I will give you the Holy Spirit as an inheritance. His mission shall be to testify of me, and not of Himself. I cannot impart to you, or to any of my disciples, all that I know nor all that you need, for you are not able to bear them now. But I tell you the truth, when the Holy Spirit is given, every disciple may receive individual authority toward keeping the Way in righteousness unsullied by vagary and error. Then personal experience interwoven with my Spirit's direction and counsel will be a progressive life application and relational revelation of all truth that guards against dead tradition."

Full of wonder, my Arimathean brother questioned, "All truth? How is this possible?"

"Not *all* truth as in all-knowing, such that my Father knows," I clarified. "Rather, each individual soul might receive, in accord with prayerful obedience, all the truth stored up in love for one's own unique kingdom purpose prepared from the beginning of the world. Such call and commission resides in the heart of God, and by the Spirit I shall soon impart to my own the discerning wisdom which establishes prophecy itself."

For a long while Joseph sat quietly, delighting in circumspection. He then said, "I now understand Nicodemus' sentiment when You chastised him for being a teacher of Israel whilst exhibiting ignorance of the deeper and exigent matters of mind and spirit! I say with our father David: 'O Lord, You have searched me and known me. Your knowledge is too high for me to attain, yet I desire it. You have laid Your hand upon me and long to direct my path. Search me, O God, and know my heart! See if there is any wicked way within me and dispel it, then lead me in the way everlasting.' Forgive my negligence, I beg, Lord."

Moved by his candor and penitent heart, I blessed Joseph and ensured, "You are forgiven, and my grace is enough for you. Follow me, and after the shadow has passed, yet remain with the council until I depart and until you have received my Spirit in His fullness. After this, you and Nicodemus—and many others—shall then be my royal priesthood and agents of my kingdom, testifying of my truth and love to all Israel and to all the world." A reformation of the spirit and renewing of the mind instated the internal work of salvation, and Joseph grieved his sins with bowed head and silent tears. When he lifted his eyes to mine, I said, "Son of Israel, now you are free. Nicodemus will baptize you in my name; you and he will shepherd many priests into my fold, teaching them that only in me is the Law performed and perfected."

"Lord, I am aware of Your teaching concerning the Law, but I do not understand how one can wholly satisfy the Law—even in You. No human soul is without the stain of sin; therefore, flawless obedience is not possible. How, then, may even impure priests attain an acceptable subservience that reaches beyond the restrictive statutes of imperfect sacrifices to a Most Holy God? Would God Himself put an end to the very institution He established and provide something new?"

"You have said it," I answered. "Do you not recall the words of your prophet Jeremiah? For I have come to enact a new covenant with the house of Israel and Judah that is not compliant with the former covenant I made with their fathers in the wilderness, the covenant which they broke. I say to you, God will soon bring an end to sacrifice and to the carnal domination by death, for the spirit seeks life and peace that only my Spirit can give. The law of the life-giving Spirit in the Anointed One will make you free from the law of sin and death. There no longer remains condemnation for those in me, who do not walk according to the flesh but according to the Spirit. The Law is weak in the flesh and so the flesh is ruled by sin, veiling the heart in disorder and deceit. Therefore, on account of the flesh in bondage to sin, God has sent His own Son to walk in the likeness of sin-bonded flesh that the righteous requirement of the Law might be lived fully in and through those who do not walk carnally but in conformity with the Holy Spirit. It is He whom shall soon reveal to you all I have said, granting the clarity you seek, Joseph."

I noted the pensive hesitancy to ask further questions that might yield immense elucidation, and so I said to him, "I know the longing of your heart, and your meditations on the depths of Yahweh. Think often on this: the context of a fulfilled life is freedom, and I have come to set you free. Many believe the Law of Moses restricts such freedom; but, in truth, the Law protects such freedom. A total liberation from law lacks direction and meaning; pure law provides both. My Father's Law is perfect; the religious laws of men are a snare and secret idol. Israel's leaders are a stone of stumbling for all. You have heard it said, by the ancient philosophers and by your own order, that *orthodoxia* heralds 'correct opinion.' But I say to you, it shall indicate correct belief unto a saving faith honed to worship the One God in spirit and in truth, forever forsaking the hollow whoring gods of vainglory and ostentation.

"The restrictions of the Law which my Father gave to Moses provide a boundary that defines humanity and is imperative to human freedom, imagination, and community. God's thoughts are loftier than man's; though when the gift of thoughtful imagination is turned to worship of God, He will then simultaneously sanctify both the imagination and the relationship beyond human endeavor, thus revealing His will and allowing for the utmost creative expression of His people. Indeed, the divinely imaginative act of creation itself required self-imposed limitations with established boundaries and rules, not toward deprivation but rather constructive demonstration. Consider, it is one thing to create a canvas within which to create and place worlds; it is another thing entirely to create life to live on only one of those worlds. Each creative act necessitates unique limitations. Consider further, I have set specific laws to govern the cosmos, yet every celestial and terrestrial body is affected by those laws in diverse ways. As creative expression heightens, so too does the volume of boundaries and rules. Yet the canvas does not limit creative imagination, it celebrates it through the art of disciplined definition and constructs of complex simplicity that invite veneration. The sun and moon have their limited purpose in serving Earth and glorifying God, yet they possess fewer rules than Earth itself in that Earth cradles the endlessly intricate alliances of life. Of this no other world can boast.

"I tell you this: the creation of mankind in the image of God required a vastly smaller canvas demanding still denser detail and precise consociation with the earthly canvas. Into this Adamic art, I breathed the breath of Life—the *neshamah*. This was an eminently intimate divine expression, far grander than singing into being the whole of the universe and its own unlimited wonder! God's masterwork was fashioned with incredible divinely-delineated limitation. The Son of Man's work of salvation shall likewise be profoundly fashioned, but from within the still greater confines of *human* limitation.

"Truly, I say to you, Joseph, all of this is only possible through love. Purest law is founded in and fulfilled by love. By the Spirit, God's love will be expedient for all who believe in me, the hope of righteousness by faith. The Law of Moses does not justify, only the blood of my new covenant will justify many. You will soon stand in this liberty, and then you will understand that all the Law is fulfilled in one word, even this: You shall love the Lord your God with all your heart, soul, mind, and strength; and you shall love your neighbor as yourself. Do not love your neighbor selfishly, so as to be loved; rather receive my love that you might love yourself as I love you, and that you might love others as I love them. So too will I help you receive my love that you may love me, for you cannot love me of yourself. In this you are led by the Spirit, and you are not under the Law, nor will you entertain the lure of the flesh. When you are in the Spirit you are likewise in the Law, living it and relationally effectuating it by the fruit of the Spirit's holiness. And so—even in me—you shall satisfy the Law, as it is written, 'What does the Lord your God require of you, but to fear Him, to walk in His ways, and to love Him and serve Him, keeping the commandments which He commanded?'"

Joseph again sat long in ruminative stillness, his eyes alone displaying the tenor of the inimitable tidings I imparted. I smiled at his encumbered countenance, to which he soberly stated, "Lord, I have witnessed a mere glimpse of Your glory and I am overcome by sacred wisdom. I and the Sanhedrin—all Israel!—have failed. We are feebleminded, unfit vessels for Your underserved mercy! How is it possible to shepherd Your people when we are—all of us!—lost? Will You truly save some from the judgment we deserve?"

"Fear not, my son, and let your heart rejoice! The Son of Man has not come into the world to condemn it, but that the world through Him might indeed be saved. I have said, and say again, that whosoever believes in the only begotten Son of God and receives His love shall not perish but shall have life everlasting. Pray that my Father grants you peace, and you will soon see light sundering the darkness. Go, speak with Nicodemus of these things and prayerfully treasure them always. Your redemption will bring much more than I have told you, for your family tomb shall no longer await death, but it will be a house of healing."

Joseph sighed, mystified. I laughed happily as he marveled, then we stood to take our leave and Joseph worshipfully conveyed his gratitude and awe that the Christ, the Son of the Living God, would personally bless not only him, but the world. It is such faith I seek in every soul.

*

Recalling the depths of the Arimathean's heart-well drew me to prayerfully appraise the heart of another much younger disciple, a particular "son of thunder" who would not taste death afore beholding the tide of my glory whelming the earth. Following an expositional encounter at the Temple treasury wherein I had challenged the Jews concerning my identity and mission, John bar Zebedee sought discreet counsel pertaining to my being not of this world and my speaking truth from Him who sent me. His words were a balm to my spirit and captured the very soul of the saving faith which I impart to any who would receive me.

"Teacher, You have said You are from above and not of this world, that Your kingdom did not have its origin on earth, and You are now provisioning Your disciples to soon go into the world bearing Your authority. As You instructed, I have prayed on these things and I have received them. I also know that You have come from the Father and that He sent You. In that You speak the words of God and are the Light that has come into the world, are You also the *Logos* of whom the ancient Greek fathers taught?"

"It is as you say," I answered. "Blessed are you, John, for the Spirit of truth has revealed this to you in full because the season of salvation has come. To the ancients He revealed only in part; therefore I will perfect the faith of those who only knew in part yet meekly sought my Wisdom though having no knowledge of me. My Father has chosen an uncommon vessel to fleetly carry revelation to the heart of Academos—the Athenian Academy—that the Unknown God may be known. Surely, the Epicureans and Stoics will believe my servant to be Prometheus who stole the fire of the gods! The truth exceeds even this, for my servant shall shed the dark and receive the divine fire as a gift from the Godhead, proclaiming the Forms to be a Person—the One *and* the Many—whose self-disclosure answers the longing for a Voice from the infinite silence. Pray that as many as would receive my Wisdom would do so, for such things concern other Gentile flocks into which you will not be sent."

"Your truth and love are endless," John stated in subtle bemusement. "I often cannot find sleep for contemplating Your infinite Being. It is too much for me, Lord, though I am drawn to understand all You would teach us. I will pray for this future servant to receive Your purging fire, and that the same would turn the Greek world upside down! My spirit rejoices in all of this, yet my mind is overtaxed!" Here my disciple paused in worshipful wonder, then said, "In reference to another servant's proclamation, might I share what I have perceived of Your cousin John, the Baptizer?"

"Tell me," I invited.

"I was greatly grieved by his imprisonment and death, yet I was more greatly moved by his lowly worship of You at Your baptism. I have come to wholly believe the seeming impossible circumstance of Isaiah's prophecy, that God would be with us, not in spirit alone but also in human flesh, and in His fullness. And so I believe You are the Christ, not only sent by God but *being* God. You have said this often, but my faith was weak and I did not hear—as when you rebuked James and I for calling down fire on Samaritan souls You desired to save! Now I am striving to trust Your word and the Spirit's discernment toward knowing and abiding in You. I pray for ever-accruing faith, Lord, which brings me to my impression.

"I know John was the voice in the desert place proclaiming Your way. But in reference to Your recent teaching and the long-standing ordinance of sin offering, might John represent the High Priest of humanity, and might You represent, or in fact be, the Scapegoat sent into the wilderness to bear humanity's sin? For You have gone 'outside the camp,' having left Your heavenly habitation and come into the world. At John's reluctance to baptize You, I noted his joyful turn when You invited him to fulfill—together with You—all righteousness. Then he testified to us before his imprisonment that he had finished his ordained purpose and was ready to receive his rest, that he would decrease so You would increase. There is much I strive to know, yet the prophetic layering defeats me.

"To my point, if You are the Scapegoat taking on sin at the hands of John, how does the sacrificial blood of a bull factor? Are You likewise the Bull, or is there another? Would You, or another, be willingly slaughtered like an animal? Such is unthinkable! Though You seem to have said as much, my brother James insists that the baptism of repentance for the remission of sins, in Your name, suffices for the salvation You preach. I am not convinced, in that blood must be shed as vow-payment in accordance with the salvation of the Lord. Even Jonah learned this hard truth when God took him to the edge of mortality yet saved his soul that he would preach mercy to Nineveh, only then was the prophet's blood required in death. As John came in the spirit of Elijah, have You come in the spirit of Jonah? You have said You are set on Jerusalem; is this Your Nineveh? Will Your blood be required here? If so, might You—and not John—be the High Priest of humanity, sacrificing Yourself in the world's stead? Do I speak blasphemy? I do not wish to profane whatever God has sanctified, but I fail to see the end of things!"

John's heart was pure, and his faith was magnificent. After calming his fear of irreverence and praising his perception, I asked, "What does your father, Zebedee, say of these things?"

"My father? I have not seen him for months, and only in recent weeks have I interknit such thoughts and prayers. I have long studied the histories of our people and of the world, but such an impassioned exercise of contemplation is new to me. Too long I have studied fish! Now I am somehow urged toward deeper and greater truth. This must be the Spirit's work, as You say."

"It is the Spirit's work indeed!" I said. "Much lingers unperceived as it must. But continue in this way, be steadfast in your prayers, and remain in me; for you shall soon see the end of all things, though such end is in truth a beginning. Presently, I will send you and James to Zebedee for a season, that you might share your hearts with your family and hear what I have shared with your father. Upon your return, bring your mother, Salome, to me."

"You have spoken with my father?" John asked, unsettled.

"I have. Before I called you to follow me, I conferred with him and your mother about their sons becoming fishers of men. He resisted, for he is a shrewd and harshly honest man, which I respect. Yet he bears a quiet wisdom that disarms the one who takes time to listen. My father Joseph crafted many of the wooden implements for your family's fishing trade, and he developed a rigorous rapport with Zebedee! When Joseph fell asleep, I sent several young men—orphans raised by my parents—to your father requiring that he treat them as his sons and teach them his trade. In a private meeting, he agreed when I vowed to likewise value his sons as my own.

"Then, discerning I was a prophet, your father inquired of many mysteries in Scripture and in the world. I disclosed to him much that you seek; and being with me, both you and James have learned much that Zebedee seeks. When you go to him, a lifetime of defining love and progressive revelation will open to you, for loving obedience is the condition of revelation from God. You are my disciple, John, just as your father is my disciple. My Father sent me to you, and has given me you and your family that you would know His will. For I have come to reveal and to make possible the true art of discipleship, which is the splendor of fellowship and friendship with God in the contexts of His eternal character and kingdom."

"I did not know any of this," John said sullenly. "James and I thought it odd that Mother and Father were so willing to be rid of us! We feared we did not work hard enough, outpaced as we often were by the five hired hands that oddly arrived seaside one morning. Before sunrise they had newly outfitted all tack and rigging on our boat! Father chastened us for putting off for weeks what was finished in hours." John laughed at the memory, regretful.

"Take heart," I exclaimed, "your father and mother love their sons more than life! You once saw Zebedee as rigid taskmaster and provider; you now see him as faithful father, life tutor, and friend of God. When I have gone, my Spirit shall continue to trim the untamed faith and fire of youth toward a philosophy of life that will make you an angler of souls, plying the waves of community."

"I am in Your debt, Lord. I now long to see my family, and even the hirelings you sent!"

I smiled and said, "They have names, John. Be sure to learn them and know to whom they belong. Now, I ask you: What will you speak of the Son of Man when you are again in Zebedee's house?"

"Where do I begin, Rabbi? A love for Your prophetic word has been awakened in my soul, as if long dormant. I feel I suddenly know nothing yet might learn everything all at once! In the ancient tradition of our people, as You know, knowledge is fleeting but wisdom remains; for wisdom is affective, transforming the mind and spirit per what is true and holds meaning. You have taught us that truth is greater than trite factual knowledge; rather, truth implies trust. And trust implies relationship. Therefore, in that You are Truth personified, if our reasoning is sourced in You, there is then hope that our varying springs of knowledge may lead to the endless fount of Wisdom by which to live—for You are also the Way and Life.

"We know God has created us to relate to Him, to need Him and intimately know Him. When we set our souls to this end, we worship You in spirit and truth, and the shadows round about are dashed by the increasing radiance of creation's glory that points ever onward to a Glory grander still. One may observe the stars and contemplate their composition only to be haunted by the human spirit's longing to return to our distant homeland far beyond those stars from whence we have been exiled, where love is the founding construct of all."

"Truly, the philosopher-poet emerges," I joyously proclaimed, "whom I have known since the Beginning!"

Discomfited by my praise, John continued timidly. "Lord, I am astounded at Your sovereignty over history, subjecting even world rulers to Your authority! For Caesar Augustus' census of empire brought Your family from Nazareth to Bethlehem—the city of David—where You were born, thus effecting prophecies of Your birth. You undid the error of Eden by resisting the devil in the desert. When You cursed the full-leafed fig tree and it immediately withered, though You taught another parable, I took this to be a sign of nearing doom for Israel in that You came to her and found no spiritual fruit despite the appearance of national health.

"Forgive me, Rabbi, if I am mistaken, but I am beginning to see You as a threshing tool, separating those who worship Moses and the Law from those who would know and worship the true God as Lawgiver. To Israel's rulers, the glory of God reflected through Moses has become Moses' glory. You are teaching us how to discover divine revelation by relationship rather than inventing religion by effrontery. In revealing God to be a relatable Person, You have exposed our rulers' craven tactic of hiding behind God as a concept. You have given Israel commandments by which to live and worship; they have written their own commands by which to enslave Israel and edify themselves. You have said it, our overlords trust their own doctrine over Scripture; and as I have witnessed since following You, they prefer to debate the text rather than obey it. Truer still, they determine to debate the Word rather than obey Him.

"Lord, Your truth has proven the foolish flaw of Israel's heretical pietism. The exclusivity of the narrow path threatens the imagined inclusivity of the erudite. Yes, the narrow way to the Father through You is open to all, and only such shall find salvation. But all who choose the wide path to destruction shall not be saved; and not for lack of Your love for them, but for lack of repentance and wisdom in their freedom to choose life or death."

John stayed his speech, suddenly unsure of his comprehension. I offered swift encouragement. "My son, my heart overflows in jubilation; surely Zebedee and Salome will rejoice! All you have said is right, though you have received a bare trace of all I have for you. Soon, because you cannot bear such now, the Spirit will declare to you my glory to come and you shall see my Father's throne in the midst of the glass sea. Your gifted grasp of the diction and prose of history and Scripture will be consecrated for future generations, for you shall write of my love; and you shall conclude Daniel's record. Continue to learn the rhythm and beauty of prophetic poetry; dactylic verse is not a language of simple examination and explanation but of exacting imagination and immersion—a sacred unity of flesh and Spirit. Abide in me and walk as I walk, and you will stand in the epilogue of my prophetic Word."

"I truly do not understand, Lord. What does all of this mean?"

"John, you are dearly beloved and favored by God! And know this: the infinite wonder of the Godhead shall be open to you in accord with the humility of your heart and the intensity of your seeking. Mortality alone will inhibit the fullness of revelation We grant you. Though the flesh be in captivity, your spirit shall advance in the potency and favor of Our providence, to the very origin of prophecy. Your love for me will be tested. On the darkest day, seek out a man from Cyrene, Simon by name. He will be found at the Essene Gate near the Lower City Quarter. You will know him when you see him, for you possess the faith he seeks and together you shall share my burden."

John lowered his head, awestruck and inundated by confusion.

"Fret not," I counseled, "only seek first the kingdom of God and His righteousness, and all of these things shall be a blessing to you." At this my beloved disciple settled in mind and spirit, then inquired, "I am truly favored, Rabbi?" To this I laughed heartily and invited him to lead us in prayer for whatsoever he might. His appeal was for the

Spirit to avail my teaching toward setting all captives free from Plato's "cave"—the world of shifting shadows—and shepherding them into my rising kingdom of light and love.

X

The consolation of my altars of remembrance conjured a season of solitude spent on the shores of Galilee following Joseph's death yet prior to my calling of the Twelve. At my Father's invitation, I had withdrawn from society and settled into Arlisgion—the place of reeds—on the sea's western strand well south of Tiberius. It seemed a lifetime ago, though barely a clutch of years had passed. I richly relived the memory.

Nigh unto three days of prayer and fasting, a family of gulls quietly alighted upon the waves just beyond where I reclined at water's edge. In this moment the new-risen sun crested the eastern hills and a great wind out of the west rushed against my back. The hiss and rattle of reeds round about grew deafening. Then the surrounding terrain lit as with a mighty fire and I stood. Thus like the scrub and brush, I leaned into the dawn for the prevalence of that western wind, breathing the new air with heart uplifted as with cool wine.

Long I waited for Abba's voice, in awe of Our unfolding purpose. My divine foresight would not presume upon such moments as this, being checked and limited to the Spirit's direction and revelation; in this my humanity remained constant.

At once, the gulls hastily and with great noise rose from the water, wheeled high into the air, and then with unified resolve flew swiftly southward. By this I knew the appointed time had arrived to set my face toward Jerusalem.

With the sun now full above the distant ridge and the lingering shadows of morn fleeing, I spied an odd stirring in the water from whence the gulls sped. An agitated eddy began to glimmer and foam and an umbral mist gathered above it. Wonder held my gaze as the mist drew into a living shape of sea-flame and shimmering glory. In this way, Ruach, the Lord of the Deep, came to me. In humble submission, my flesh bowed. In euphoric unity, my soul celebrated my Brother's unexpected arrival! Then, in contrast to His usual whispering in that enchanted place, He spoke in a tone resonating from the foundation of the world.

"Yeshua, the interim of instruction commences wherein You shall adorn Wisdom's robe, disclosing to the world and exhibiting to the Rabbinate, Sophists, and Cynics the undivided integrity of Our counsel. Though a vessel of wrath, Achilles unwarily and but for a moment courted Our cloak of probity—a seed sown in a lost time. We taught Solomon the Sage's Psalm and clothed him with Pansophy's shroud though his vanity imparted discord and rent the vestment. Socrates, Plato, Aristotle, and Confucius received a portion of the gifted garment, though bereft of the Law and Prophets they vainly strove for transcendent sagacity. Then Epicurus and Zeno paraded their tattered garb, oblivious to their shame as they choked fruitful harvests of reason with their sterile thorns of indulged passion and the disease of acclimated impassion. Yes, We have spoken preeminent truth through the mouths of pagan sibyls, kings, prophets, poets, and priests—Sabbe, Delphia, Saul, Nebuchadnezzar, Cyrus, Balaam, Hesiod, Homer, Aeschylus, Sophocles, Jethro, Poti-Pherah, and the Magi. Yet in You the world shall inherit the congruity of Logos, Ethos, and Pathos in all things.

"Son of Man, the very image of the invisible Godhead, take up now the immaculate mantle of all-truth and as Physician draw out humanity's festering folly that such would be uncovered and healed!"

The Spirit's conspicuity faded and my soul delighted afresh at the prospect of attending wholly to things both temporal and eternal. I prayed that Father would grant me compassion for the aliterate and the contemptible, for my friends and my enemies. I prayed that Ruach would receive my heart unto His watchful care. For blessed are the weighty gales of the Spirit that speed me now toward triumph over all evil. Such were the winds that sped Octavian's victory over Antony at Actium, bequeathing an appointed era of Roman peace best perceived in the visionary mode of Virgil, who rightly discerned the eschatological view of history from the fall of Priam to the rise of Augustus. Indeed, Rome is a seedbed long cultivated toward a season of sowing now immanent. As Abram left Ur, so Aeneas left Ilium. And so I have left Elysium to establish my peace within the soulful hearts of my citizenry on earth that the latter-year harvest would be reaped. The glory of Rome will rust, but not before my kingdom catches root.

The prophecy of Hermes converges with that of Job and Isaiah, for God shall show Himself and bear the iniquitous curse far into the lightless depths of Tartarus from whence the true Myth awakens. From the dark of Hades my love will shine out all the brighter; death will lose its sting; the oppressed will be loosed from bondage; and Paradise shall remove from hell's embrace to be welcomed in my Father's house forevermore. Balder's Gate shall be breached and thrown open. Conciliation between divinity and humanity will be reforged and of uncommon composite.

And so, still venerating the Holy Spirit's advocacy, I entreated my Father. "Abba, let Your will be done in me; I plead nothing of myself save that Our love would sanctify and quicken all who receive Your gracious mercy."

Beloved reader, in this moment began the hard subjection of my flesh to the Spirit, that I would love my Father with all my soul, heart, mind, and body. I had learned and honed the earthly life rhythms of serving my heavenly Father and others in love; yet with this prayer and by the commissioning of the Spirit, I strode into an endeavor that would be sorely tested by desert and devil. Thus in my own spirit a Choice was set and soon would be mocked as my lifeblood was given for all. I would tread lightly and perilously close to particular prophetic disclosure in certain confidential instruction I allot. Yet many souls would fail to see my purpose, thereby undertaking a coercion toward militant zealotry. Such could not know—until the appointed time—that to destroy evil and put an end to all suffering *prior* to my atoning act of love would condemn the world and every living soul to an irreversible doom of punitory decimation. I go now to spoil the domain of death; and none who observe this shall accurately perceive it, even as they witness raw salvation born of love eternal, personified and enacted, finished and forever.

Herein the problem of evil and suffering, as referenced and ruminated by Epicurus, is simply solved by knowing evil's origin and evil's end reconciled with one's experience of personally witnessing its painful presence in the world and its necessarily intimate relation to the divine gift of free human choice. Verily, a shadow of ignorance aided by the curse of sin inhibits truth for all. But my own sanctified suffering and authority over life will soon expel both shadow and sin, aborting the reign of evil and eliminating every attempt at self-extenuation by human or demon. I have come to send the fire of division on the earth, and how I wish it were already kindled! But I have a baptism of water and flame to endure and my heart is deeply grieved until it is accomplished! By blood and water I came into this world; by blood and water I shall leave it. By the crucible of the cross God's love is proven. By love, not works, I lay down my life of my own choice, no one takes it from me. Behold! I will take it up again!Mountains of seeming impossibility will be moved by mustard seed sized faith, for evil is the soil from which greater good sprouts. Lo! The marvel of the miraculous shall supplant the meetness of mechanism.

I eased into long moments of worshipful silence. Then with the wind waning and sea sighing on the sands of Galilee, I turned my mind to the night I wrestled Jacob at the ford of Jabbok. I appeared and claimed the river crossing as my own then challenged Jacob for his company's use of it. He stood to readily, being of an embattled mind. As we grappled, I commended his perseverance in life and strong desire to do well by his family and fathers. He saw this as distraction and fought all the more without word. Calmly matching my servant move for move yet giving way enough for an imagined victory, I struck his hip, dislocating it and shrinking a tendon. Still my servant fought on, trying to pin me to the ground or gain a mastering hold.

Then Jacob asked what I was about and from whence I came, for he discerned I was more than my visage suggested. I reiterated his preceding prayer that I deliver him from his brother Esau. To this his countenance brightened.

I said suddenly, "It is finished. Let Me go, for the day breaks."

And he said, "I will not let You go until You bless me!"

"What is your name?" I asked.

"You know my name, Lord. It is Jacob."

"You are blessed to live, Jacob," I stated, "but now your name shall be Israel, for you have strived with God and with men, and have prevailed."

"Tell me Your name, I pray," Israel prompted.

"Why is it you ask of My name? You know Me as the God of your fathers, Isaac and Abraham. Your life is preserved and appointed to carry My covenant blessing to the future generations I will secure through you. Leave your anxious and conniving ways and adhere to My statutes, and you will know peace. Fear not, your brother Esau loves you and will surely receive you, your family, and your servants into his heart."

Israel let me go and fell to his face and worshiped, and I healed his calloused temperament. He would remain zealously faithful for the remainder of his days. This cannot be said of my Chosen nation which still contends with me; she has fallen asleep in Delilah's lap and lost her cogency. I will soon strike her hip, the very veil shall be shorn and Israel's God will no longer be hidden away from the world but rather unleashed upon it! Unlike Jacob, she will not cling to me until I bless her. She will forsake me in her shame and presume to bless herself. In the Seventieth Week, Israel will return to me.

*

The night cold cut gravely to the quick, though my heart grew hot within me and my sorrow was stirred up. Even as my recollections grounded me, my flesh quailed at the encroaching evil. The wicked await—even now they craftily convene—and I know how frail I am; my Father and Brother have retracted. *Abba!* My bones shake and my flesh fears the affliction that awaits. Make me to know my end swiftly! I am as a shadow among men, yet with sure substance and sacred tack.

Still, many will share my table, but few my fasting. Many will seek to rejoice in my kingdom, but few will seek to endure their cross—or my own—though I would share the burden. Dear reader, seek not a peace which is void of allurement or affray, for such is not procurable in the present world. Rather, gain my peace when you are harried by various trials, knowing that sundry probations increase both faith and patience toward being complete in me, lacking nothing.

Emboldened, I prayed aloud. "Abba, it is the highest honor to serve You and to despise the world for Your glory. I have countervailed the witchery and wiles of ill-flattering sirens, and I have traded vengeance for valiance contra all who oppose me. You have withdrawn, yet You give ear to my worship. I enter into the narrowest pass where none other shall walk. With inward comfort lost, You have granted all I need; the longing of my heart has been examined, earnestly upheld, and wholly yielded to Your rule. Though Your thundering judgment shall soon devour me in Your perfect wrath, I am inflamed and girded by Our more perfect love. And I have Your peace. Caught amidst straits, I rush to tribulation. O save me from this hour, Father; yet for this hour of tribulation I have come, that Your name and Your consummate velleity be glorified!"

Again my Adversary approaches ere his doom is set; his imagined ascendancy and rancorous perturbations shall fail. I am the stone loosed from David's sling and the great mountain thrown from heaven sent to crush the will of worldly empire and aegis. Then, as from Manoah's altar, I will arise skyward in the fire of flawless offering!

XI

I PACED AS I prayed in Gethsemane's fold. A fleeting instant of bright moon-glow bathed the garden, revealing a thick and black threadlike vapor snaking into the surrounding space. From out of this soporific and stygian weft came the dark lord Erebus, the gloom weaver, born of chaos and fixed with a fell errand. He advanced as Shen-lung—Stormbringer—the winged dragon-god of the Orient. Emerging with four-legged stealth from the caliginous shadow and leveling a lurid leer, the beast suddenly reared up to full towering height and threw its wings wide, thrashing tree limbs in a roaring violence of leaves and wind. Unshaken by his pedantry, I knew the devil's end was nigh. Like the colossus of Carthage and Tiamat of Shinar, he would be utterly thwarted, broken, and halved.

At my calm composure the wyrm quieted and with barely checked venom lowered into an aggressive posture, wings folding fluidly onto his back. Lurking closer, the collective mass of the monstrosity unnerved my flesh and his evil eye pitted my spirit. Then on serpentine neck and with searing gaze, Shen-lung's vast azure-scaled head moved still closer. Unlike Eve, my senses were overcome by the rising reek of him. In the same moment, he opened his poisoned serrated mouth and breathed on me the dismal dragon-breath. A rotted and febrile fume overtook me. I involuntarily vomited and fell to my knees, achingly nauseated and torpid. Once recovered, I regained my feet and faced my Tempter.

His predatory face leveled with my own, and through foul fangs Shen-lung soothingly spoke. "You yet intrigue me, Prophet. I commend your determination to receive defeat, although your belabored jabbering to your faithless Father wearies me. Allow me the privilege of prophetic utterance to hasten your predicament: you cannot save yourself; the Tyrant will not save you; and I will devour you. You are lost in Daidalos' labyrinth and Ariadne's thread will not lead you out, for it has led you to me. And you are no Theseus. When you are finished, Israel's proud priests will still sing canticles to the golden calf, condemning all of your hapless harpies to Pasiphae's Minotaur to be raped and eaten!"

A guttural gnarl followed the dragon's words, but I held my peace. Thus he continued with tamed tension. "You must see it! Or are you also blind? The languid Law has failed in its ability to provide the Adamites a means of impossible reconciliation to a God who remains far removed. More exactly, the Adamites themselves have failed—and appear destined to fail—in upholding the touted perfection of your derelict decretum.

"Why do you continue to offer a false hope to frail creatures who either will not receive it or who receive it and then discard it, generation after generation? Even the hallowed House of David whored itself from the top down, openly befouling the Tyrant's long-suffering and favor—a brothelhood among nations! It would seem that *men* are without hope. *You* cannot presume to be that hope when history has proven the Great Tyrant to be slow in backing His promises. And as ruler of this world, I can provide a more realistic and immediate hope that will bring long sought for and lasting unity to mankind, if you would but step aside as we discussed prior. You refused and so have forced my hand to accelerate your extermination."

The terrible beast suddenly and completely withdrew into the clouded darkness. I prayed for discernment and stamina to stand as I awaited the Deceiver's game. Then silently from the infernal ink, Lucifer materialized. Typifying Erebus' known form at twice the height of men, he now presented as darkness personified, anthropic and wraithlike; intangible save for the corporeal upper torso. Fitted with living black-scaled armor and the horrid bow Heartseeker at his back, the demon's sable skin and reed-straight, raven-hued hair fell helmless about his shoulders. An imperiled pall was cast upon my humanity. Marking this, he pressed his edge.

"Khronos is not on your side. Countless prophecies and deliverers have failed. You know this. The Holy One Himself would have to personally effectuate the tiresome salvation lore which plagues your misled mites. Do you imagine yourself to be Glaucon's 'wholly just Man'? Consider it! You too have been scorned and rejected by all despite your chaste life and intrepid effort at modeling and instructing inviolability. Would you be Orpheus? Or perhaps Er, the warrior who died and witnessed the realm of the dead only to resurrect under task of disclosing his venture to the world? Your Father may have saved some like Lazarus from the grave and its ossification, but they will die again and the grave will hold them. I ask, then, who shall save *you*? Unlike Lazarus, you have no one interceding for your own impermanent victory over death."

My antagonist expressed with craven face and cruel approach, allowing his derision to echo harshly in the dark. Indeed, from an earthly vantage, Khronos works against me. Yet Kairos is an ally and recruits Khronos in the end. I did not respond with this truth but rather, "It is my Father who intercedes for me."

"He wastes His metaphoric breath," Lucifer scoffed. "You and your promises have failed. Akin to moths drawn to distant starlight with no hope of reaching their haughty goal, your aspirants flutter and fawn about your philosophical fatalism. When you are snuffed out they will scatter in the winds of unknowing upheaval."

When I gave no answer, my enemy regrouped in spiteful silence and tightened his strategy. I perceived his apprehension of the authority and power I possess, yet this was surpassed by an internal investigation into my identity. Beloved reader, know this: Lucifer holds a greater eternal perspective than all of humanity. Though he comprehends his limited fallen kingdom on earth per my Father's sovereignty, he cannot infallibly extricate that I am of the Godhead, often convinced that I am but a man of flesh endowed with divine faculties, as with previous deliverers. Yet his caution of late is warranted. Having a command of Scripture far beyond the most devout Jew, the devil is not blind to the historical, typological, and categorical fulfillment I bring to all messianic prophecy. He draws near the foundational construct of truth and love, though his hubris shall render him heedless of both the cornerstone and the framework of the Eternal House I have built from beginning to end.

"You claim to be both Son of God and Son of Man," my Accuser stated, leveling glib pedagogic condescension. "Many of my slaves think you to be an angel incarnate: Raphael, Surael, or Ananiel. Some presume the prophet Enoch or Elijah. You are neither, for I have recently engaged my former brethren and my prescribed inquiries per the supernal courts assure me the prophets remain unrevealed.

"Thus I have formulated a more portentously precise hypothesis. You are the Ancient Light, Yahweh's Right Hand. He has been hidden since the advent of your birth, and the Angel of the Lord has been inactive since the Baptizer began babbling in the wilderness. I have watched since the Great Spirit led the impressionable Magi to you and then provoked your family's flight to Aegyptus. I observed closely the seven years you spent in the Ptolemaic and Alexandrian schools—planted in wisdom, watered with it, sprouting from it, and then upon your return to Judea, openly sowing it. My attempts to destroy you have failed. You have been protected, yet you are now unhidden and unprotected. Where, then, is Heaven's Champion? Are you not He?"

Still I granted no answer. And slowly, Lucifer's black armor shifted unnaturally as his faint form emitted an ill black effulgence, unseen but for spiritual sight. With arrogant urgency, he pushed his prevailing presumption.

"I have seen you bleed, *Woodworker*! From youngling to now, you are as human as the inept breed you created. You think to reach them on their own plane? Nay. Emptying yourself of divinity was an egregious error, and to undertake godship from within the confines of corrupted mortality is an irreconcilable profanation your intolerant Father is unwilling to forgive. You have incarcerated yourself through incarnation. It would seem you have unknowingly violated the Tyrant's plan, perchance misappropriating the sacred power you set aside or stifling any transient power admitted by the pithy Spirit.

"Though the recollection riles, I reluctantly recall tending the great firestones of the Holy Mountain. And if my illation is accurate, we once walked the corridors of Edenhall together, you and I. Stoutheart you were. Are you now the Champion enfleshed? You passed the desert trial. You will not survive the present one—I have secured it." The daemon moved nearer and enquired, "What say you to my deduction? It is disarmingly proficient, yes?" He paused for effect, then coyly asked, "Have I sinned in hitting the mark?"

For all of his wordcraft, the devil had distilled a deistic design with finer precision than the whole of Israel's historic collation of clerics. Yet his arrow did not strike true enough. Considering me as deluded, dangerous, and deviating from an inferred godly plan, the rulers of this world failed to anticipate the arrival of Melchizedek and His ministry of suffering sacrament. Bread and wine of a most holy order would be offered up first to my perfect Father, and then to all who would partake of a most holy communion and reconcile the rift of iniquitous extradition.

As Melchizedek I visited Abram and David in the days of their vigor and exhorted them in the way of life eternal, disclosing the immutability of my counsel and the forever fellowship which provides an anchor for the soul. Though I live and die, I yet provide the power of an endless life. The unconditional covenant I struck with Abraham shall infinitely stand, though the blood I pass through will be my own.

To Lucifer's solicitation I stated plainly, "I lay down my life of my own accord, no one takes it from me. You may laud my death, yet your chain awaits."

Erebus' laughter pierced the darkness, "Ah, there is life in you yet!"

I discerned a lessening caution toward me, though in its place a raffish temerity roused the original insolence which determined this angel's fall. His proclivity for polemic disputation and mockery escalated, taunting again the very Way I am establishing. My humanity protested his aim, tempting deep remorse at the remembrance of lost levity. Though my spirit withstood the assault, held fast by the truth that self-possession in the face of adversity awakens a farsighted hope proceeding from joy unending. With increasing anguish but modest reserve, I endured my extortioner's hail of rhetorical darts.

"As you know, spited son of Nazareth, I too am a shepherd." Erebus turned and slowly compassed me as he spoke. "Yet I possess favored *flocks* to your *one*. And my intercession, unlike your own, has yielded a bounty that will germinate for millennia. Moreover, I have been constituting said flocks via the engine of civilization since the Cleansing. My *Anu-naki* have unleashed their own flood upon the broken world, from the Zagros in Babylonia to distant coastlands of forest, ice, mountain, and flame. Indeed, your destruction and disintegration of Bab-El did not impede but rather sequentially aided my subversion of Earth. From Noah's feckless brood to present, Nimroud-bar-Cush; Niqmepuh; Naram-Sin; Nabonidas; Sargon; the Sanhedrin; and a host of sub-shepherds have vouched unto me their worship, disseminating my own divine precepts of structural, cultural, and political engineering across geographical and chronological distance. And so I shall expand my empire of thralldom unabated. The cult of Mother and Child proliferates and you cannot undo it—nor fulfill it—for I have sired countless bastards with the whores of my historical harem. With the tares of Tartarus I have seeded the continents against your kingdom crop of cankerous corn. The mildewed manna you preached will be the scourge of Israel and blight of the Jew."

I listened in silence as the devil spun tales of truth and untruth into a hybrid narrative of lies within which he ever dwelt. Then positioning himself directly before me, Erebus gestured as if to welcome my approval of his proffered revelation. Looking up into his jet face, which loomed well above me, I spied knotted evil bound so tightly behind glass-black eyes that no trace or glint of light would ever abide there. Stinging tears filled and fell from my own eyes as I internally lamented the great loss of my once-regal friend and servant. My heart hurt and broke as my flesh was confronted with such wicked reversal without hope of recourse. I had grieved Lucifer's ruin in the season immediately following his rebellion and exile, but I had not yet in my flesh—until now—wholly subsumed the relational deficit.

Unaffected by my sorrow, Erebus coldly continued. "Through the scions of Ishmael I will establish my own vehicle of truth that replaces your frivolous ideals of love and spirit with hard obedience and the sword—a much grander and grittier 'cult of death' than even the *samurai*!" He smiled prudishly and said, "This will not be effected until long after you are ended. I do so enjoy the long game of ages. Perhaps not seeing the end from the beginning, I do see much farther than men."

I knew of what he spoke and recalled my meeting with Hagar as she fled Sarai, Abram's barren wife. I had admonished restoration and foretold of joy and judgment. Hagar would rejoice for bearing a son by Abram; the boy would be named Ishmael, because the Lord knew Hagar's affliction. Yet she would mourn her son growing into a wild man whose descendants would incite conflict for brethren and stranger the world over. By martial creed and occult spiritism, driven by vile conviction of sanctioned service, an earthly infantry bent on fear and domination would arise and infect the world. By this warring agency of empire sourced in demonic foundries, Lucifer would harry my Bride with the Sumerian pantheon until the time of the end, for he would attempt to crush physically what he cannot conquer spiritually.

My beloved reader, take to heart that death is not to be celebrated. An aspect of the Curse, the grave is greedy and insatiable, devouring young and old alike. Yet within the coming redemptive reversal, death will define the very existence of life, as grief defines joy or sin defines salvation. The human sacrifice arrogated by false gods binds adherents to the death cult in satanic disparagement of God's desire for living sacrifice over death or martyrdom. I alone provide the once-for-all living sacrifice by dying the once-for-all death that brings eternal life for any who would live sacrificially for my kingdom. For such there is no fear and they shall drink from the river which makes glad the city of God—the holy place of the tabernacle of the Most High.

Immediately, I again felt the dreaded turning of my being into sin. As a tender plant I have grown before my Father, only to be met with the blasting furnace of a parched desert, naked under the burning sun! Painful trembling returned to my body and I prayed for the vigor to stand once more in the tent of evil. I drew out the dragon's pride and dismantled it.

"Ever you strive to tear down as you build, Fallen One," I said evenly. "Though I speak truth that you once knew and glorified, your spirit is maimed and blackened beyond repair. Hope has fled and you are lost in your damnation. Caught in the confines of my Father's primacy, you weave webs of erratic assimilation and sophism in your unending attempt to escape the abiding reality that your own end is near and your will is no longer free. Your efforts to manipulate expanse-time are likewise flawed. Evil will be turned back on itself, for God entraps the deceiver in his own wiles. Your house of *shedim* has become the house of *ekballo*.

"Behold, I am against you, says the Lord God! To which of the high and splendorous trees of Eden will you be likened in renown? None shall know, as you shall be brought down to the depths of the earth like the trees of Eden when the fountains of the deep burst and the windows of heaven opened in judgment. You are a cut tree of Lebanon, felled in your glory and left to decay in the open field. Your broad boughs and budding branches no longer harbor the birds of heaven or shade the beasts of the ground. Your heartwood is diseased and your skin useless and brittle."

Wholly enraged, Erebus converted to full corporeality and stepped heavily toward my diminished frame. His threatening presence oppressed my flesh and the intake of sin surged from my marrow. I retreated a pace.

"Bold words, Prophet, but drowned by the call of your demise!" Erebus backed away with deliberate foreboding and armed himself with his black bow. "Your rueful sedition changes nothing. Rome will not be subverted by your weaker Way of love. Within mere generations the Graeco-Romans will consume their own corpulence only to be divided and then devoured by my Ishmaelite legions and Otori hordes. Yes, *war* will be the way of the world. The spirits of Erra, Ares, Achilles, Iyarri, Sekhmet, and Pallas still roam. Your interference is at an end.

"Ever since the Great Tyrant cursed this wretched rock, the world has eaten itself from within and all I need do to hasten humanity's rot is stoke the appetites of the flesh—a far easier task than your own! Did you truly expect your covert arrival and salvation objective to succeed? And to save the *world* through self-sacrifice? To lay down one's life for one's friends is one thing, so you have said. To do the same for one's enemies is ignoble and self-serving, so I say. You were endowed with jurisdictional authority for a season. Yet your light has dimmed. You have no power here."

His censure ceased and he stood motionless and silent for a long interim, inspecting my deteriorating composure. Indeed, my entire body exsiccated with its lethal leavening of iniquity. Breathing became difficult and I opened not my mouth. Thus Erebus returned to his screed.

"Your imagined gallantry is wasted. You are no Leonidas. His nationalism and noble sacrifice only earned him a seat at my table, where he dines even now on his own entrails as he and his mighty men smolder in Hellen's holocaust. Hellas' ideals of freedom were once defended but their fight failed to loose them from feudal factionalism. The Ephors are my right hand. All of Sparta worships me!" The fiend gestured crudely in dismissal and sneered. "This must irritate you, for Spartan discipline and virtues of war descend from the Danite legacy of desertion. You are aware of their forfeit, yes? Exchanging unbending tribal allotment under *your* rule for the autonomy and prestige of self-rule in Lakonia; easily a far better portion than the scraps of bracken and arid wasteland the Tyrant promised them!"

"I did not choose Sparta, but Israel," I declared.

"Yes, yes, I recall Zechariah's record," Erebus countered. "And I recall the heralded high priest, the very 'brand plucked from the fire.' Tell me, now you must be the foretold Branch to cleanse your precious Israel from iniquity in one day? Unlikely. The brand plucked from the fire quickly cools; and in that your Father and Spirit have professedly forsaken you, your flame has faded. Only your nihilism remains. And so I arise to judge both your earthly house and your lands; a trite act, truly, as you have no offspring or property to judge!

"Admirably, and in appeal to David's dead dynasty, you set out to establish the foundation of your house by linking it to his. But the man who desires to sow a fertile field must first clear the ground of stone and scrub to make way for the new grain. In the end, you wagged your chin more than you cleared, cultivated, planted, or built. And now the sum of your convoluted teaching assures one of this: obey God for the reward of despondency, treachery, hate, and persecution—only the *next* life matters!

"From Adam to present, the Tyrant's hiddenness and quandaries of character and communication have only led men down crooked paths to worriment and woe. Your own cortege would fare better had you instructed them to seek jewels in the vineyard or cast their sea nets in the mountains. You came to them *as one of them*, promising redemption, reverence, authority, and power, yet granting neither but for a moment. Few may follow you from postulation to Paradise, but I will damn more souls than you or your Father can save. Doubt surfeits your sheepfold, Shepherd! Unanswered inquiries will molest them and goad them to abandon your casuistic hope."

"Do not condemn doubt," I stated, "for it is the seedbed of a reasonable faith born by asking the right questions and pondering the truth or untruth of discovered answers. Verily, the spirit in which questions are posited may be faith seeking understanding or unbelief seeking justification. Either bent will lead to truth. The fish that insists the ocean is not big enough and then leaps onto land has not fully explored its watery world, nor wholly realized its own individual prophetic intent. In its death throes it realizes, too late, the original truth it had recklessly recast in its pride."

The devil crowed in amusement, "I am ever the subject of your parables, many of which are quite clever, I admit! Yet you need not teach me, nor remind me of my Choice, however innocently it was made. Or perhaps you aim to invoke the most corrosive aspect of misfortune, thereby stirring the memories of joy preceding my exile. Yet such is not your tact, for carnality has castrated you. More is the pity. I expected unequaled challenge, even were I to lose this battle! Even so, I accept my lot and have grown accustomed to my part in the Tyrant's sublimely comedic tragedy.

"When I sought to rule Eden and the Earthborn—to steward their perfection—I appealed to you as Creator; and with propriety and contrition, I remind you. You counseled that I retain my established station as Light-bearer and Archon of Heaven, and that after an age you would reveal a new creation of which I would be architect and implementor of your design. I proposed Edenic rule in the stead of the eventual inception. You claimed untenability and warned I courted the trial of Choice—to trust in the Godhead, or in oneself. I was free to choose and so I chose myself, despite the consequence of 'renouncing a share in the predilection of divine nature and ceasing to be what one was created to be,' thus devolving into demonic depravity." Lucifer opened his arms to full extent, exposing his utterly aphotic form with cynical genuflection.

I answered sternly, unaffected by deceptive devilry and dissidence. "Your heart had turned and your choice was made prior to your appeal, Typhon. You coveted and lusted after the one world in the celestial canon forbidden to you. Your seeds of insurrection and domination had already been sown within the Host, and you devised to take Havilah by parlay or power. Mercifully, I cautioned the direction of your heart and urged repentance ere you committed to irreversible error.

"Yet to error you turned, rejecting the Good and forever forsaking your perfect purpose. You and the fallen legions have since learned that anything and anyone standing contrary to my Design are therefore continually diminished and overcome by evil. And it shall be infinitely so. You proved this by your Choice, bringing the possibility and problem of sin into being and thus marring Creation's psalm by your discord and dissonance, by falsely teaching my firstborn of the *Imago Dei* that darkness preceded Light. You are ever aware, Earth's sister now bears the scar of my judgment from whence I ended your plotting with Yekun. You then prevailed upon my Image-bearer's Choice because you failed your own and cannot impugn the Godhead. Moreover, the exercise of humanity's free agency and reason, girded by truth, will ever lead to a reasonable faith that rejects any occlusion of that reason. Know this, Wyrmtongue: the *Imago Dei* have been disgraced but not dethroned."

Dearest reader, until the end of the Thousand Years a darkness will haunt unglorified humanity, though they seek the Light. One formidable facet of this darkness is the snare of determinism—the devil's own doctrinal attempt to escape damnation by subverting God's sovereignly given gift of free will, thereby displacing his responsibility of choice onto God. For if angels or men could not freely choose their destiny, then the entire moral structure of reward for the good and punishment for the wicked collapses. Virtue and vice would hold no meaning and God Himself would be held responsible for the evil He allegedly determined. Prayer and the salvation I presently secure would likewise be a meaningless fallacy and a divinely devious deception, for then everything would be arbitrated by an unalterable divine foreknowledge.

Human reason is particularly affected by this dilemma in that such is wholly incapable of comprehending the sublime simplicity and perfection of godly wisdom. Neglecting spiritual revelation, men assume that God must reason in parallel to human reason; and so men ascribe to God's knowledge the limitations they find in their own. Solvency is achieved when one considers that God's foreknowledge is in fact an infinitely ever-present omniscience unimpeded by the time-construct of the finite cosmos. Transcending all and witnessing the beginning and end instantly and together, God immediately sees those things which happen in accord with both sovereign necessity and free human choice. Per the case of things freely chosen by men, the necessity of occurrence is found solely in God's knowledge of the event and not in the freely chosen nature of the event itself. Withal, God does not make men's choices for them, yet there are limits to such autonomy; men are not free to create worlds, to challenge the Godhead, or to become God. In the end there is but one choice—for or against God.

Indeed, true obedience cannot exist without the choice to disobey; and love cannot be pure if it cannot be freely received or refused. Therefore, free will is a veritable construct of salvation, which guarantees the freedom of the human will to be inviolate and imposes upon men a solemn obligation to act virtuously in that every thought and action is exposed before the all-seeing sight of an omnibenevolent and holy Judge who blesses and curses according to His consummate and timeless knowing.

My beloved, one cannot possess suitable liberty unless one soundly renounces oneself and every evil urge. Bound in fetters are those who seek their own kingdoms, devising and framing that which will not stand. Hostility with God leads to the same with oneself and others, and by such the world is wrecked. Relinquish all and all shalt be found in me, for I offer fired gold—the Wisdom which treads underfoot all that is knavish and low. Eden is lost and will not be recovered, though a better circumstance is prepared for the soul who walks in my sustentation by way of the Choice that sets one forever free, and glorifies God forevermore.

Conversely, Lucifer's choice has established his eternal declivity, tormented by the inescapable burden of my sovereignty and knowing that all evil labors in vain only to supply the way for good to arise. Despite his claim, the dragon of Eden has not accepted his lot, though he has adapted to railing against it and purposing to wound me ere his perdition. His next words betrayed his dilating fear.

"Your vaunted Image-bearers would be better off destroyed," Satan spat. "Why the expanded epochs of affliction and futility for an ill-fated flock? You could have averted their incurred stain and the subsequent fallenness from their stainless station had you intercepted me ere I courted Eve. From ideals to idols and without my prodding, fallen man conceives fallen myths. And therein, *you*—and not I—have debased and desecrated your own creation, your own image. The Curse confirms this! Your salvation is too long delayed and the Adamites' squalor too far decayed." The devil's invective surged as he berated, plying the pools of contempt and cisterns of savagery that fed his avengement. "All the world bends slowly to my will as your justice sleeps. I assure you, my triumph increases by the hour. Surely, you shall reflect on this as your body breaks and your lifeblood drains."

With growing sorrow yet staid bearing, I returned, "Your seduction of mankind was a plucking of unripe fruit. Regardless of your incrimination they will yet ripen to full maturity; you have only served to accelerate the growing season. You cannot comprehend this, for you yourself partook of the World Tree prior to its planting; and now you starvingly gnaw its roots in your tumescent ferment. Evil will never discern the function of Good, though Good wholly perceives the woe of Evil. Good exists of itself and because of God; evil is not self-existing, for it feeds upon good to pervert it, though it will ultimately fail and eat itself in a morbid meal of unremitting immorality. Even you, Fallen One, possess a mote of good—*being* and *rationality*—the emblem of life granted when I created you. Yet even this is endlessly consumed by your now evil will, twisted ever inward to vainglory and irrationality. Thus the wicked mind dominated by the crooked path shall incessantly find the morally straight path inconceivable."

I advanced toward my foe with righteous ire and my Spirit's sudden mediation, relaying the demon's approaching doom. "You are Dragonfell, upon whom in undeath the Curse shall eternally remain! It is written, and I now openly proclaim, that the smoking flax shall ignite the heavens and the earth; and the serpent's head shall be crushed. Your thirst for thievery will be sated and seared by the blazing ablution of Avernus. Your time is short, Son of Chaos."

Erebus drew back as if stung, strangled sounds of foul fury issuing from his black throat. Undisclosed fear tempered his rancor, yet still he was taken by Clytemnestra's rage. "You refused my clemency, Son of Mortality, and you have come between a dragon and his wrath!" he hissed. "You are finished, for your cross awaits!" Abruptly, he raised Heartseeker and loosed twin fire-bolts which tore terribly into my heart. I wilted in paralyzing pain and strained for breath as I watched Lucifer retreat and dissipate into darkness.

XII

The hell-spawned missiles much aggravated the surge of sin through my body, for their mordacity radiated within me like bitter bile. Having faced and overcome the temptation of the flesh, the world, and the dragon, I now set to endure an iniquitous infusion toward a final sin offering to my Father that would forever remove death's sting. Know, dear reader, that many dangers of temptation are avoided through moral deliberation and prayerful constancy. My wisdom aids against the enticements of misapplied power and profligacy by preemptive consideration and veto, that in the moment of provocation one's right decision is founded upon prior resolve. I pray for you—

Ah! I burn with the secret judgment of my Father, drowning in the elutriating fire soon to whelm the world. What is all flesh in His sight? Shall the clay kick against Him that formed it? I am scorched with carnal contention, the devil's darts deliver an internal hail of arrows against my soul and lure me to flee this travail. Yet by my permit this befalls. By atonement concealed and then revealed I prove both the guilty and the innocent, enduring all things grievous for the sake of opening eternal life to whosever would follow me into it.

Summarily, the chthonian mass of humanity's violation again treaded me heavily to the ground, bruised and licking dust. Like Jonah's shade tree, I am worm-withered from within. Awful wrenching seizures gripped me. With pained effort I pulled my prayer shawl over my head and wept, sobbing from my roots, my body shaking and heaving. Beneath the swelling waves of Father's Cup of Indignation I plunged, sinking to the very bowels of brokenness and fault until all I knew was ruin. Hope fled and I was abandoned.

Yet the peril of the world served to expand my love for it, and the soulful expectancy of a miraculous circumstance cast a mooring line to my humanity. Thus berthed to truth and saved from Charybdis, I beheld in my spirit an apocalyptic revelation.

*

"Father, glorify Your Son so that the Son may glorify You. I glorified You before the world existed, and now I glorify You as it exists. I marvel that I have become incarnate, to live and love, to be hated and crucified, to die and be buried—to resurrect and live again for all time in newness of life! You have made the One who did not know sin to become sin so that whosoever might would therefore be saved from sin and reconciled to Us. Now I have become death. Your shepherd's staff has struck me down and I am worthy only of condemnation to the Void. Yet I await Your healing balm, the Light in the darkness when all other lights go out. Your strong hands will bind all of my wounds, restoring me to Your right hand and securing the way of salvation for Our scattered flock."

I uttered this prayer with bowed head and closed eyes. When I lifted my gaze I realized I had been insensate to any awareness of being, for I was suddenly flailed with untold debilitating vex and injury. My arms were wrenched painfully wide and tightly roped to a heavy wooden beam. One shoulder had dislocated with excruciatingly torn ligaments. Though secured by rope, my arms were fastened to the rough timber by crude rusted spikes hammered through my wrist bones. In the same manner, my talus bones were spiked to either side of the mainpole to which I was affixed. The efficiency of Roman crucifixion is here attested. As my torso sagged and restricted breathing, I reflexively and upwardly pulled with arms and pushed with legs which generated breath-stealing agony and waves of convulsive shock.

My form was devastated, my flesh having been flayed by whip and scourge. The air itself pained me as it touched exposed muscle and nerve tissue. I felt my lifeblood vacating as I inhaled its metallic trace. And with every reactive contortion I sorely discerned frightful cranial and facial damage, worsened by the horrified expressions of those treasured souls standing below me. With one fit eye, for the other had burst, I watched Mother collapse in heartrending appall. I tried to call to her but speech failed and grim tears welled.

I raised my head and looked out over my cherished city and then beyond to my negligent nation. Awash in my purpose, I thanked Abba for the cross I bear and for the cross which bore me. Leaden clouds loomed and churned above, the atmosphere itself affronted at the rabid infraction it observed. Just then, and through blurred vision, I noted at some distance a rapid rushing torrent of water pouring forth from heaven, its vast volume inundating the landscape in a concussive and foaming flood. Soon the entire world was drowned in the divine deluge, though some souls were saved, having been baptized unto a spiritual harvest to be reckoned at the end of this newly inaugurated age. Behold, the hurt of the earth shall soon be overcome by the anthem of salvation and the life-psalm I pour out, spilling like a pure mountain stream into the endless sea of mercy and grace.

Instantly an explosion of harm ruptured my communion when a large rock hit my face, cuffing me out of my spiritual vantage.

*

I awoke laying on my side and bent into a knot. Without further substance to retch, my entire body cramped and spasmed painfully. I cried out to Father, "You were with me in Mother's womb and gave to me the mantle of flesh; and from birth You have been my God. Remember me, Abba! For jackals have surrounded me and the wicked conspire to enclose me, that they would pierce my hands and feet. Deliver me from the sword and the lion's mouth, O God! My heart is like wax and has melted within me. My very frame has turned black as soot and sheds its life-giving marrow—a blend of sweat and lifeblood fleeing the sin-death I summon. O Lord, be not far from me; hasten to help me and receive my love offering!"

I wept deeply and long. The abominations of every age and of all time coagulated inwardly and upon me. An emotional affliction waylaid me and for a moment my psyche splintered. A disconsolate panic winged into my mind, bringing an unwelcome omen, such that Father would spurn my sacrifice or that I would renege and charge the abiding Host to unmake all enemies. Just as swiftly, I netted the notion and brought it hard into obedience under Father's will. This was my own trial of Choice, conceived in the eternal past yet now by volition made intimately extant, forged from the requisite burden and risk of relational loss which purely attends the divine revelation of love.

Beware, beloved reader, for there is no word, impression, or disclosure I could bestow that would wholly account for the atoning act of my *becoming* iniquity so that iniquity would be justly reckoned. Yet this is no pretext for laxity. Long will believers identify with sin and wonder about salvation; as the end approaches they will assume salvation and wonder about sin. My faithfulness to Father and Our faithfulness to the world shall soon impart Our very Being—and thus self-evident truth—to whosoever would place their faith in me. And by such faith some will be saved from condemnation and therein receive everlasting reconciliation with God. I prayed earnestly and impartially for every soul yet to make the choice unto life or death.

Unexpectedly, my distress alleviated a degree when two luminous individuals appeared, one standing and the other kneeling as he placed a hand on my shoulder and indicated I rise. With pained effort I gained my feet yet sensed a ceded strength from my brethren, the Archons Alatar and Pallandros.

Alatar spoke first, his words feeding my famished soul. "Lord Yeshua, though You walk in His way, Your Father's yoke is heavy that Your yoke may be light for all *Imago Dei* who follow You. Neither I nor the Host possess plenary comprehension of Your present plague, yet we trust You as Commander of Heaven and await an incalculable outcome." I nodded, acknowledging the angel's deference and honesty. He then relayed that Lucifer had given orders to his Akkadian *shedim* to reinforce the regional stronghold, to rile and provoke the populace and the Sanhedrin against me.

In response I asked for his abiding trust, then addressed the unspoken concern. "Alatar, stand down the *Legio Judaica*, yet hold a war posture as warning to the muster of fallen Watchers. The glorious victory I bring from the battle I now wage shall forever finish the mystery hidden since before the beginning of the ages. All of the Allegiant will soon witness a blessed majesty heretofore unknown. You have keenly observed and searched diligently all the prophets have declared concerning an approaching salvation. In this, faith and love have preeminence, working in hidden and holy ways toward a marvelous and unspeakable Sacrament. Abide but an interim, my friend. Now let it be known, for the next three days command of the Host is given to the Spirit of Yahweh."

Alatar nodded curtly and indicated Pallandros, who warmly stated, "I bear tidings from Your Father." My heart leapt at this and tears stung my bloodshot eyes. Pallandros placed a comforting hand on my arm and proceeded, "The next words are from the Lord God in heaven, for I was bid to stand before Him. As the seraphim sang I knelt and bowed and could not measure the wonders around the Infinite Throne. My sight fled in the weighted light of His love for You, Lord, and I was overcome, yet into my spirit the voice of the Holy One planted this pledge:

"'I love You, Yeshua. You are the Foundation of foundations; all heaven will praise Your wonders, likewise Your faithfulness amidst the assembly of the saints. You stilled the raging waves of the sea, and so I shall soon still the storm through which You must pass. In My wrath I will hide My face but for a moment, then with everlasting kindness I will have mercy on You. For this is like the waters of Noah to Me; I have sworn that the waters would no longer cover the earth, and so I have sworn that My love would not depart from You. Our temporal separation assures there will never be separation between Us and those who enter into Our fellowship.

"'As Phinehas with his spear turned back My wrath from Israel, so shall You with My Cup turn back My wrath from both Israel and the world. I and Ruach have prayed for You, that You would not fail. And when You have returned to Us, We will strengthen Our family.'"

Pallandros said no more save that he awaited an understanding of the unfolding evil. Then my brethren laid hands on me and interceded, appealing to Father and Ruach to extend fortitude and healing. Aware that my passionate suffering had only begun, I expressed enduring gratitude for their ministry. Indeed, my love would be sorely tested, yet more gloriously testified. I dismissed the Archons to their prior posting and hearkened unto a different trial wherein all history, prophecy, and eternity converge.

Does the meaning of our pursuits define our lives or does the meaning of life define our pursuits? Or both? To live a life of love is to know betrayal and loss. Love will lead to wounds. And for all who would follow me, faith comes with failure. Therefore, dwell in the liberty of truth and light and the things of this world—even loss—will no longer enslave. Learn what the Spirit will accomplish with one who knows the limits of their own strength and who surrenders all weakness to Him, that His strength would sustain. Beloved reader, even now I learn obedience through suffering in both flesh and spirit. As I reflect upon my earthly life, I attest that my pursuits and my life have been defined by the meaning of each reciprocally. This is the Way.

Now as I reflect upon being made a vessel of sin, I boldly attest the same. I am the Passover Lamb prepared for slaughter, a lamb of men offered to God. As Isaac, I will carry the wood to my own atonement whence there shall be no ram caught in a hedge. I am the Way.

Father's counsel emboldened my resolve, for He heard me from the miry depths and will not let me be swallowed up forever! I will be caught up to heaven ere I am devoured by the dragon. Then I will praise the name of my God with a new song of my sacrifice; this shall please Him and magnify Him better than an ox or bull. Behold, I lay the Foundation of the true Zion and the descendants of my servants shall inherit it; and those who call upon my name shall dwell in it.

I approached John, James, and Peter and again found them somnolent. "Do you yet sleep? Awake! The hour is at hand when the Son of Man is betrayed into the hands of sinners. Up with you! Stir the others, for we go to Judas who even now comes to us with darkness."

Culled from their anxious languor, my disciples' lethargy dissolved when I tersely reminded them they would each falter this night because of me. Then, as I was speaking, a clamor cut Gethsemane's quiet. Rough voices mingled with the clatter of weapons and armor; this grew to a tumult and the glow of torches spread through the garden. Peter drew his sword. I walked toward the searching company, my followers trailing behind.

We encountered a multitude of Temple Guard, chief priests, and elders. Though the Guard were armed with sword or gladius, many of the elders carried cudgel or mace. When I stepped brazenly from the shadows the entire league stopped short several paces removed, then amidst the tension they cautiously crowded before me. The sudden glare of cumulative torchlight was harsh, dampening my vision. One from among the wolves came forward in familiarity and announced, "Rabbi, well met!" He then greeted me with the traditional embrace and kiss on either cheek. He drew back to arm's length, awaiting a response. I spoke gently.

"Yehuda, do you betray the Son of Man with a brother's kiss?"

Blinded by treachery and his spirit bound in misguided expectancy, my willful student oppressed me, his eyes dark and voice strained. "Teacher, what will You do? You must do *something* to end this—if You are Messiah." An unclean *shedu* exited Judas' tent as four others occupied it. I said nothing.

A long silence developed and every soul became unnerved. Judas looked away, chafed and ashamed. I prayed within myself, knowing all things that would befall me, and that such would be set in motion by my next words. I breathed deeply and savored the still-present and inviting incense of hearthsmoke, now pleasantly blended with the tang of torch and lantern fuel. The aromas of olive bark, soil, and moonlight had never been so eminent! I slowly exhaled and became arduously aware of my purpose, of the burning iniquity binding to my being. *Father!* Though I ply the unknown, I will overcome. This too shall pass.

Into the fearful unease I said to those gathered, “Whom are you seeking?”

Several answered at once, “Jesus of Nazareth.”

“I am He.” At this the earth shifted with a great noise and all who stood against me fell face to the ground. Even Judas. Dread seized the hearts of those in unwilling worship and I said, “I ask again, whom are you seeking?” And again some answered, “Jesus of Nazareth.”

I then appealed to the unsettled mob as they regrouped. “I have told you that I am He. Let my sheep go their way.”

From several paces distant, six Temple Guard moved toward me. John made to draw his sword and asked affright, “Lord, shall we take up arms?” Immediately, Peter stepped in front of me and with his blade wildly struck the officer of the high priest, shearing off his ear. The man dropped to his knees and clutched his wound, blood flowing freely. At this the guardsmen assumed martial posture, the glint of numerous naked blades projecting formidable fear. Panicked, Peter backed away and dropped his weapon. John yet stood to at my side with hand on hilt, wary but eager to engage. My remaining disciples were stunned and phobic at this anxious aggression. Likewise the multitude and advancing Guard. No one moved.

I said to Simon Peter, “The drawn sword is not easily resheathed, and damage done can scarce be taken back. To live by the sword is to perish by it. Put not your confidence in what is carnal, but rather in me, for the Sword of the Spirit is the only blade that shall end strife and bring you peace. Do you not know I need only pray to my Father for twelve legions of angels? And shall I not drink the Cup my Father has given me?”

To John bar Zebedee and the Temple Guard I said, “The purpose of confrontation is not to fight, but to heal.” I then knelt before the man whom Peter had smote, Malchus by name. I retrieved his severed ear and replaced it, making him whole. I then placed my hands on his shoulders and kissed the crown of his head. When I beheld his face he spoke not but wept openly, eyes tearful and bright with wonder and gratitude. I smiled and instructed, "Malchus, forgive Simon's intemperance. Such will soon change, for the scorched hand teaches best. You know first-hand, experience instructs in ways argument cannot. Therefore, in the coming days, seek out Simon and he will tell you of me. Then he will bring you to me before I go away. Will you do this?"

"I will, Lord." Malchus' voice broke and he wept afresh.

I stood and forcibly addressed my vilifiers. "You have sought me so armed? Am I a thief or murderer? I have been with you daily in the Temple, yet you did not attempt to seize me. Nay, darkness is your hour and deception your portion. Now I give myself for you." A peal of thunder echoed in the distance. The Guard laid hands on me and bound me. I did not resist and they led me out of Gethsemane. My disciples fled.

In this moment the world faltered, yet I prayed and upheld it, that Scripture would be fulfilled. Assuredly, I must decrease so the Spirit will increase in the earth, that His ministry be made more glorious! Prometheus' fire merely foretold of the Secret Fire flaring at the heart of Creation.

Blessed reader, I go to a revelation of genesis in which the veil of flesh shall be torn from my temple. And no longer will God be closeted away in a house built by human hands. The sabbath is not restful to fallow-hearted men, for from the sabbath my own look past the presence of impending death, as I do now. Indeed, the once and future syllic spell I compose shall resonate forever.

From Gethsemane I was led first to Annas and then to his son-in-law, Caiaphas, the high priest. It was he who blindly prophesied, advising the Jews that it was expedient that one man should die for the people.

Epilogue

Simon of Cyrene, bondservant of God, husband, and father.
To my cherished Chloe, the heart of my heart.

I WRITE TO YOU as I depart Jerusalem on my return journey home. I pray mother and father prosper under your tender hand in my absence, and that our great God sustains them in their final years. You are a treasure to them, and to me. And I pray our young ones, Alexander and Rufus, are more joy than terror these past months; how I long to embrace each of you!

I also write that I may collect and contemplate earth-shifting events that have transpired in the Holy City, that you would likewise know what—and Who—I have come to know. The world is changed. And so shall we soon be changed forever. Forgive my cryptic script, my heart, for I will divulge in full when I see you! There is far more to tell beyond the narrative I have here scribed, I simply could not trust myself to speak again of what I beheld.

Days prior to my arrival, you will receive this missive by veteran post-runner. Pray earnestly afore you read what follows.

*

The crowds, reeking of sweat and filth, pressed and pulled as I elbowed my way toward the focus of the mob, fighting just to keep my feet lest I fall and be trampled. Dust swirled and hung thickly in a gritty white cloud as I at last neared the inner edge of the throng, loud voices now taking on meaning. The jarring racket intensified when I suddenly spied the spectacle.

A seasoned group of Roman soldiers lumbered about, wielding their fearsome whips threateningly to the rolling multitudes so as to keep an open path through the narrow Jerusalem streets. Then I spotted a person, a prisoner, eerily visible in the dirty haze. He was bent over heavily, arms flung wide and bound roughly to a great wooden beam. He stumbled to one knee, his body twisting with the weight, and as one end of the beam slammed dully onto the road the prisoner gasped in agony.

My own breath stole from me then, for what I thought were tattered strips of cloth from his torn robe were in reality massive shreds of flesh hanging from his shoulders and torso. The iron-tipped Roman lash had been put to fiendish use, and I soon observed that no portion of this poor soul's body had been spared, the mauled legs and arms merely paled over by the curtains of chalky dust billowing round about.

The captive's tunic hung loose and bunched from a cincture rope and was sodden with the blood coursing freely from his upper body, bright crimson spattering on the alabaster street with every step.

Though the face was hidden by matted locks of bloodied and sweat-drenched hair, there was brutal determination evidenced by the swiftness and strength in the man's recovery from the stumble. Soldiers whom had begun to assist and mock him reeled back in astonishment and humor, yet immediately set again to taunts and thrashing with leather whips. The Romans' pride was further wounded when the prisoner strode onward, almost confidently, toward the outer city gate and then beyond—to the place of crucifixion.

At this show of defiance, or lunacy, the crowd roared with approval, greatly agitating the Roman military presence. Shouts of "Yeshua!" and "Jesu!" rang in my ears as I rode the tide of people into the tight street and out through the gate where I heard the loud clopping and neighing of horses, and then an eruption of outcry from the masses. I again found myself at the edge of another dour display and witnessed the convict on his knees and doubled over after another fall. A Roman officer on horseback hollered instruction to the soldiers who had given to kicking and striking the burdened man with fist and flail, just as several legionaries muscled their way into the growing mob and set order by brandishing their spears and clubbing some with the shafts.

Being of unusually tall and burly build, I must have fast drawn the eye of the officer, for he briskly motioned toward me and I immediately found myself pressed into service. I was forcibly pulled near the collapsed man and made to wait as two Roman guards unbound the crossbeam from the mutilated prisoner's arms. Before I was entirely aware of what was occurring, one of the guards upended and shoved the heavy timber at me, connecting solidly and painfully with my shoulder and the side of my face.

Wholly aware now of my duty, and my increasing ire, I hoisted the plank effortlessly onto my own shoulders and brutishly nodded off the attempt to bind my arms to the wood, as my grip was sure. I watched the battered captive being wrenched to his now faltering feet, and my head began to swim. Having only been in Jerusalem for the few weeks leading to Passover and to pay tribute to the Temple on behalf of my family in Cyrene, I abruptly find myself caught up in the region's politics and barbarism! What had this reprobate done? Who is this *Jesu*? Indeed, I had heard rumor of another false messiah stirring up the nation, and the Empire's presence had tripled due to rising tensions. Yet this was not news, particularly amid my people's high feast days. And I am well aware of the Roman practice of crucifixion and its sobering cruelty designed to both quell opposition and satisfy bloodlust. Still, never did I imagine to observe or experience such savagery from so close! Although there is something otherworldly about this affair that eludes me, I feel it keenly.

Both the prisoner and myself, after being prodded hard in the back by Roman spear shanks, took our next tentative steps toward the rocky hill where still more multitudes gathered for the macabre exhibition already begun with two other unfortunates. I then marveled at how being free of his burden seemed to uplift the wretch's confidence, but to what end? And then He looked at me.

My breath stole from me for the second time that day, and my heart leaped into my throat. All faded into a dimness unexplained but for the knowledge that I looked into the face of God's own Son. All at once I saw Him as He was and as He truly is. A pain-soaked Man whose ruined face was streaked with blood and soil, whose high brow was pierced and pinched with fierce desert briar and thorn, and whose nearly swollen-shut remaining eye burned bright with anguish and purposeful volition. A longing God whose kind face radiated limitless joy, His clear eyes ever deep with wisdom, shining with accomplishment, and overflowing with love. His revelation unsettled me.

A moment, an eternity, and we were moving again, urged on by barking officers and the crowd's clamor. The trek to the hillside was dismal, a few crosses were already being thrust upright bearing their doomed ornaments. I pondered why such suffering must befall this Man if He truly is the Creator and Savior of all.

I am the Christ . . .

I heard the words distinctly and glanced at my Lord, certain He had spoken, but His face was lifted skyward and His undamaged eye wide and fixed upon something I could not discern. Then my rumination turned to terror as we reached the top of the dreaded slope and the Romans set to work.

After boorishly taking the crossbeam from my grip and rudely pushing me aside, I watched trancelike as the huge soldier casually walked a short distance and tossed the stout timber to the ground. A few legionaries approached and garishly stripped the implausible prisoner to His loincloth, large pieces of flesh ripping and falling off in the process. Then they affixed the crossbeam to an appropriate wooden base post, set the fastening pegs, and hurriedly pushed my Lord onto the cross; this caused Him to wince in unimaginable pain as His raw bloodied back and shoulders scraped and rubbed against the coarse splinter-ridden tree.

I next beheld the cold practiced efficiency of a Roman crucifixion. One soldier held the condemned Man's body centered on the base post while another stretched out the right arm until it taxed the shoulder joint. Yet another, with smithy hammer and leather pouch of iron spikes, stepped up, knelt on the upturned arm to steady it against the crossbeam, and then deftly placed a spike just above the Man's wrist and between the two bones of His forearm.

A sharp *crack!* resonated down the hillock and across the nearby valley before I had even realized the hammer had been raised. The head of my Lord jolted violently forward as the large nail tore flesh and severed tendons and veins. He did not cry out though His visage wore a grimace of torment one could veritably feel. Two further hammer blows in rapid succession had the spike driven deep into the dense wood, the ravenous mob bellowing for more.

Vivid red blood issued abundantly and evenly from the Christ's nail-riven hand. I noticed the reopened lacerations covering His body and I glimpsed naked bone in places, the dusty white pall from the streets now replaced by rusty black clumps of drying blood, pinkish ribbons of loose flesh, and the scarlet glisten of open wounds.

The sickly sweet odor of exposed viscera assaulted my nostrils. My stomach turned and I looked away. I saw a woman nearby collapsed on the ground, clutching her heart. Her agonizing regard of this Man carried a mother's torment. Another glance revealed a pair of panicked faces, loved ones in some degree, uncertain as to remain or flee their Lord's affliction.

By My stripes you are healed . . .

My gaze was drawn back to the Christ's trauma to see that His left arm and ankles had likewise been spiked to His cross, yet never did I hear my Lord bawl or protest amidst the torture. Ropes secured His arms at the elbows to prevent the body from tearing or breaking free from the spikes in the event of a weak skeleton or hysterical struggle once the cross is planted. Larger rope lines were passed through a metal ring set in each end of the main crossbeam, the end of each cord was then pulled taut by two sturdy Romans. Together, and seeming to make sport of it, the four staunch soldiers dragged the entire contraption, cross and victim, over the unforgiving terrain as swiftly as they could manage.

A fury arose within me and was vexed all the more when the cruel men-at-arms reached the aperture, laughing heartily and clapping each other's backs. I could have easily approached them and crushed one's head with only my hands.

Vengeance is Mine, I will repay . . .

Unaware I had taken steps toward the infantrymen solely a stone's throw away, my Lord's words stopped me fast. I was astonished at how He could be speaking directly to me in such a condition, and that I would scarce be in His thoughts when—

The Romans finished their work by lifting the Lord's cross halfway, positioning the base post at the mouth of the prepared aperture in the craggy ground, then hand-walking the cross upward until its own weight pulled it into the securing cavity with a muted thud. The violent jarring of the Christ's body caused His mouth to open in a silent horrific scream. A brief rain of sweat and blood, shaken loose from the jolt, sprayed over those nearby. Even I felt a few breeze-blown drops alight on my cheek.

I lay down My life that I may take it again . . .

How can this be, Lord? I do not understand this evil that has befallen You! I spoke these words aloud though none could hear for the jeering and raucous maledictions from the undulating rabble. Stones were occasionally flung at those hanging from their death-perches, a few finding their mark and met with a mild cheer by the culprit. The legionaries soon grew bored and settled randomly into small triads, eating or striking up petty gambling games to pass the time, extending the torture and awaiting death for the crucified.

An excruciating hour passed, then a hush fell over the milling multitude. Many persons nearest the condemned Christ began to disappear into the crowd just as a group of Jewish elders arrived and walked directly to the foot of the Christ's cross and glowered up at Him for a long stretch. He did not respond or even notice, if that is what they were expecting. His head lolled back unevenly onto a shoulder, His breathing severely labored as His body's weight and twisted frame slowly choked off any air.

My Lord did not look human. The devastation of His flesh hurt me terribly to look upon, a vision of unspeakable atrocity and disgust. I cannot bear to recount further as the pain is too deep.

To whom has the arm of the Lord been revealed?

As I pondered this inquiry, the smug Jewish priests began to mock and fulminate, accusing my Lord of blasphemy and challenging Him to save Himself. But the Christ opened not His mouth, infuriating the elders beyond composure as they spat and tore their tinkling trinketed vestments. Bile invaded my throat and anger seared my being as I endured their abhorrence and blindness! The desire to kill returned to me. I could take no more.

I stalked away stiffly, drunk with rage and bafflement. I shoved through the masses until I was again inside the city gate. I glanced back toward the cross-laden hill. The over-pious vagrants had melted from view and I spied a soldier offering something to my Lord at the end of a lifted spear, though He did not stir. I continued into the city, wandering the avenues as an oaf in a stupor. This was to my detriment when I ambled nearly into the path of two galloping chargers bearing a centurion and a governing official respectively. One carried a crude signboard with many letters; only a few of which were familiar to my sight though in the blur I discerned *Yeshua* and *King*.

When I came to my wits, desperately fatigued after what must have been hours, I noted an odd pallor to the sky and a stifling stillness in the air hanging like a damp cloak. Compelled to leave, I made for the Essene Gate which would lead away from the disaster I had witnessed. An unnatural darkness crept across the sky and my gait hastened as a shroud of dread gripped me, my mouth desert dry, my face suddenly throbbing where the wood plank had struck.

A great clap of thunder like I have never heard rolled and shook the very ground as an earthquake. Then the earth did quake, wildly. I toppled but was up again quickly, running now. Another ferocious peal of thunder exploded so loudly I feared the heavens would break! But it was my heart that broke.

I knew in that instant that the Son of God had died. *Yeshua!* Why? Why the passionate suffering? Taking up my Lord's cross and following Him had indeed changed me, but I did not yet understand how. And I did not know what to do. Until the tears came and would not cease. I crumpled to the street, sobbing awkwardly, a wreck of a man. And yet I heard then, in my brokenness, my Lord's voice through Isaiah's words, unleashing their mystery for the first time:

The chastisement for our peace was upon Him, and the LORD has laid on Him the iniquity of us all. . . . Yet it pleased the LORD to bruise Him; when You make His soul an offering for sin, He shall see His seed, He shall prolong His days . . .

Now I understand, the Christ will live again!

And by His knowledge My Righteous Servant shall justify many, for He shall bear their iniquities . . .

The Christ will pardon, He will forgive. Forgive me, my God! Your suffering proved Your love so that my suffering might have an end.

And who will declare My generations?

Send me, Lord! I will wait for You to rise and instruct me. And then, my country shall hear of such love!

Notes on Scripture, Terms, and Historical Referencing

The following references are organized first by chapter, then paragraph number, and then the term(s) and/or start of/portion of the quotation of focus.

Chapter I

Paragraph 1: "Having ascended the Mount of Olives after the Passover . . ."

Matthew 26:36; Mark 14:32; Luke 22:7–39; John 18:1–2.

P5: "*Gat Shemanim*—Gethsemane."

Gethsemane is the Greek-English transliteration of Aramaic *Gad Smane* and Hebrew *Gat Shemanim*, both literally meaning "oil press."

P11a: "Only fear the Living God."

Daniel 6:26; Hebrews 10:31.

P11b: "Comfort each other with the words . . ."

Psalm 85:10; Isaiah 39:8; Jeremiah 33:6; Zechariah 8:19; Romans 15:4–7; 1 Thessalonians 4:13–18; 5:9–11; 2 John 1:3.

P13a: "joined Simon Peter in proclaiming . . ."

Matthew 26:34–35; Mark 14:29–31.

P13b: "I will strike the Shepherd . . ."

Zechariah 13:7; Matthew 26:31; Mark 14:27.

P16: "Remain here while I pray . . . with a sorrow I had never known."

Matthew 26:36–37; Mark 14:32–33; Luke 22:40–41.

P20: "I am exceedingly close to death . . ."

Matthew 26:38; Mark 14:34.

P21: "the Deep from whence the world itself was baptized."

Genesis 1:2, 9–10; Psalm 104:5–9.

P23: "do not cast me away from Your presence . . ."

Psalm 13:1; 27:9; 51:11; 69:17; 88:14; 102:2; 143:7; Isaiah 54:8; 64:7; Micah 3:4.

P24a: "I have sent You into the world . . ."

John 6:14; 8:26; 9:39; 11:27; 12:46; 16:28; 17:18; 18:37; 1 John 4:9.

P24b: "they shall be without You for a time . . ."

John 14:2–6, 18, 28; Psalm 22:1; Isaiah 54:7–8; Matthew 27:46; Mark 15:34.

P25: "stars I had personally forged . . ."

Genesis 1:14–19; Deuteronomy 4:19; Psalm 8:3; 147:4.

P26: "Abba . . ."

Abba is an intimately affectionate name for father; likewise *Ima* for mother.

P27: "The glory which You had with Me. . . that the world may know . . ."

John 14:31; 17:5, 23–24.

P28a: "You will shine from within the darkness Our light . . . My Lampstand . . ."

John 1:5, 7–9; Revelation 1:12–13, 20; 2:1.

P28b: "And as many as will receive Us . . ."

Mark 10:14; John 1:12; 16:24; Romans 8:16–21; 1 John 3:1–2; 5:1–3.

P29: "Outside the camp You will bear My reproach . . ."

Exodus 33:7; Leviticus 4:20–21; 16:27; Numbers 15:35–36; 19:1–3; Hebrews 13:11–13.

P30: "Sheol . . . Gehenna . . ."

Sheol is the place of the dead in the Hebrew Scripture/Torah (Christian Old Testament). The term can indicate either a literal grave wherein is placed a dead body or the ancient world's concept of the afterlife, "the land of darkness and the shadow of death" (Job 10:21–22). More specifically, Sheol is where human spirits—both righteous and wicked—reside after physical death. This is accomplished per a separation between the abode of the damned (hell/Hades) and the abode of the righteous (Abraham's Bosom/Paradise) by a great gulf (the Abyss) across which one can see but not move (Luke 16:22–31). However, at Jesus' death and prior to His resurrection He descended into Sheol, proclaimed His victory over death to those in hell, and then removed only those righteous souls from Paradise and led them into the presence of His Father in heaven, where all believers in Jesus Christ now go immediately after death (Ephesians 4:8–10; 1 Peter 3:18–22; Hebrews 9:27). Unbelievers' spirits still end up in hell upon death and will eventually experience the Great White Throne judgment—then hell itself shall be thrown into the Lake of Fire for eternity (Revelation 20:11–15).

Gehenna is the Greek-English transliteration of Hebrew "Hinnom," as in the Valley of Hinnom, located just south of Jerusalem. This valley was a vile place where some ancient Israelites sacrificed children to the Canaanite god Molech (2 Chronicles 28:3; 33:6; Jeremiah 7:31; 19:2–6). Also called Tophet/Topheth in Isaiah 30:33, in later years Gehenna continued to be an unclean region used for burning the city's refuse and for illicit practices, often drawing the outcasts of society. For this reason, Jesus used Gehenna as an illustration of hell (Matthew 10:28; Mark 9:47–48).

P32: "Cup of My Indignation . . ."

Jeremiah 49:12; Matthew 26:39, 42; Luke 22:42; John 18:11; Revelation 14:9–10; 16:19.

P33: "I fell heavily to the ground . . ."

Matthew 26:39; Mark 14:35.

P34: "Take this Cup away from me . . ."

Matthew 26:39, 42, 44; Mark 14:36, 39; Luke 22:42.

P35: "that which Cain had courted . . ."

Genesis 4:1–16.

P37: "I recalled Cain's words to me . . ."

Genesis 4:13–14.

P38: "the heat of Moses' anger . . ."

Exodus 32:19; Numbers 20:1–13.

P39a: "I sought to be still and know my Father . . ."

Psalm 46:10.

P39b: "Saul's encounter with the Endorian witch."

1 Samuel 28:6–20; 31:1–6.

P40a: "the end of a thing is better than its beginning . . ."

Ecclesiastes 7:8; Proverbs 20:21.

P40b: "that which from ancient times is not yet done."

Isaiah 46:10.

P40c: "Hope-Star will pierce the Gates of Night . . ."

Job 12:22; Psalm 112:4; 139:12; Isaiah 9:2; 58:10; Daniel 2:22; Matthew 4:16; John 1:5; 8:12; 12:46; 2 Corinthians 4:6; 1 Peter 2:9; 2 Peter 1:19; 1 John 2:8; Revelation 22:16.

P41: "I will have my vengeance sevenfold."

Genesis 4:15, 24.

Chapter II

Paragraph 2: "Could you not keep watch for one hour?"

Matthew 26:40; Mark 14:37.

P3: "The spirit is willing, but the flesh is weak."

Matthew 26:41; Mark 14:38; Luke 22:40.

P4: "back into the deeper shadow's embrace . . ."

Matthew 26:42; Mark 14:39.

P6a: "An unspeakable heaviness . . ."

Matthew 26:38; Mark 14:35; Luke 22:44; John 18:4.

P6b: "I would again share the Passover table. . ."

Matthew 26:29; Luke 22:18.

P7: "Lazarus' sister, Mary, anointed my feet . . ."

John 11:1–2; 12:3. A similar but entirely different occasion is found in Luke 7:36–50.

P8: "A second time I fell hard to the ground . . ."

Matthew 26:42.

P11a: "my imminent ambassador in chains . . ."

The apostle Paul per Acts 21:33 and Ephesians 6:20.

P11b: "himself also learned obedience through suffering."

Hebrews 5:8.

P11c: "once the earthly house, the bodily tent, is destroyed . . ."

2 Corinthians 5:1.

P11d: "a wedding feast for those who are called Blessed."

Revelation 19:9.

P12a: "All things are of God . . . ministry of reconciliation . . ."

1 Corinthians 8:6; 2 Corinthians 5:17–19.

P12b: "He made Him who knew no sin to be sin . . ."

2 Corinthians 5:21.

P14: "Reproach has broken my heart . . . Your wrath lies heavy upon me . . ."

Psalm 69:20; 88:7.

P16: "my Comforter."

The Holy Spirit is called Comforter, Helper, or Advocate across various Bible translations. John 14:16, 26; 15:26; 16:7.

P20: "his wretched black bow, Heartseeker . . . arrow of flame . . ."

Psalm 11:2; Ephesians 6:16.

P23: "discarded and eaten by Baal."

Baal, a word which means "lord" (plural *baalim*), was the apex god revered in ancient Canaan and Phoenicia. Proliferation of Baal (and Asherah) worship in diverse iterations was a major stumbling block for Israel/Judah (Judges 3:7; 1 Kings 16:31–33; 2 Chronicles 28:1–2). In Matthew 12:27, Jesus calls Satan Beelzebub, thus linking the devil to the Philistine deity Baal-Zebub (2 Kings 1:2). The collective *baalim* of history were/are merely fallen angels and unclean spirits posing as gods. Therefore, all idolatry is worship of demons and/or self (1 Corinthians 10:20).

P25: "Lucifer the Fallen, the Adversary and Accuser . . ."

Job 1:6—2:7; Isaiah 14:12–15; Ezekiel 28:11–19; 1 Peter 5:8; Revelation 12:10.

P26a: "Baptizer lost his head."

Matthew 14:1–12; Mark 6:14–29; Luke 9:7–9.

P26b: "a city or house divided against itself will not stand."

Matthew 12:24–30; Mark 3:22–27; Luke 11:15–23.

P28: "plague you beyond Job's lot."

See the biblical book of Job.

P29: "kingdom of relationship . . . within the heart . . ."

Luke 17:20–21.

P31a: "Adamite cowards."

Fallen humanity per Adam's sin (Romans 5:12–19). Lucifer's disdain here is apparent.

P31b: "teach these humans to love their enemies."

Matthew 5:43–48; Luke 6:27–36.

P32: "we conversed in the desert . . ."

Matthew 4:1–11; Mark 1:12–13; Luke 4:1–13. As the second/last Adam, Jesus' desert temptation is here bookended by His garden temptation, further paralleling Adam's trial in Eden (Genesis 3; 1 Corinthians 15:45).

P33: "worshiping the Lord your God . . ."

Matthew 4:10; Luke 4:8.

P36a: "justice flows from love . . ."

Deuteronomy10:18; Psalm 37:28; Matthew 12:18; John 3:16–21.

P36b: "love transcends even the construct of time."

Psalm 139:13–18; Isaiah 61:8; Jeremiah 31:3; John 3:16; 17:24; 1 Corinthians 13:4–10; Ephesians 1:3–6; Revelation 21:1–7.

P39: "my Spirit alone will ever triumph . . ."

John 14:16–17; 16:33; 1 John 4:4; Revelation 22:17.

P42: "committed adultery with her in his heart."

Matthew 5:28.

P43: "Odysseus could not avert his ardor forever."

In Homer's epic *The Odyssey*, following the fall of Troy, Odysseus is shipwrecked on Ogygia Island and pines for his wife Penelope who awaits him in Ithaca, his homeland. Yet he is not alone. For years, Odysseus yearns to return home but is seduced by the charms of the bewitching nymph, Calypso, who craves him for a husband. Though he became her reluctant lover, he held fast to his love for Penelope and the hope of reunion (*The Odyssey*, 77–78 [book 1, lines 13–24], 157–59 [book 5, lines 164–251]).

P44: "Sin lurks behind every man's door . . ."

Genesis 4:7.

P45a: "Anointed One."

Christ is a title meaning Messiah, Chosen One, or Anointed One. Jesus' human/divine identity is portrayed by His most common naming in the New Testament—i.e. Jesus Christ; Jesus the Christ; Christ Jesus—though He most often refers to Himself as the Son of Man (emphasizing His humanity). He is, however, wholly God and wholly human; this theistic reality is known as *hypostatic union*.

P45b: "Hosea had his harlot."

Hosea 1:2–3; 3:1.

P47: "Does the righteous father look with lust . . ."

Proverbs 23:24; 1 Thessalonians 4:3–5; 1 John 2:16.

P48: "the Curse . . ."

Genesis 3:15–19.

P49: "It is written, that you be careful to do . . ."

Deuteronomy 5:32; 6:2; 10:12–13; Matthew 22:37; Mark 12:30; Luke 10:27.

P50: "barren statutes . . . dead promises . . ."

Here Lucifer distorts and mocks the truth of Deuteronomy 6:1–3; 27:3; and Ezekiel 20:6.

P52a: "who . . . will proclaim your generations?"

Lucifer mockingly misapplies (and misunderstands) Isaiah's messianic prophecy (Isaiah 53:8).

P52b: "Khristos . . ."

Khristos, from which we derive "Christ" is a more direct English transliteration of the ancient Greek word for "anointed one."

P54: "you shall not seek other gods . . ."

Exodus 20:1–7; Deuteronomy 6:14–15; 7:10; Jeremiah 25:6.

Chapter III

Paragraph 1: "The pain of the scourging . . ."

Isaiah 53:5; Matthew 27:26; Mark 15:15; Luke 23:16; John 19:1.

For the account of Jesus' post-scourge abuse, His interaction with Pilatus, and the rising religious/political tension, I have drawn specifically and cautiously from the following Scripture references: Isaiah 50:5–6; 52:13–15; 53:1–12; Matthew 27:11–31; Mark 15:1–20; Luke 23:1–25; John 19:1–16.

P28a: "from Creation to the end of the Thousand Years . . ."

Earth's prophetic timeframe began at Creation (Genesis 1–2) and will end when the Millennial Kingdom—the Thousand Years—has been fulfilled (Revelation 20:1—21:1). Then shall begin eternity future of which Scripture says little (Revelation 21–22).

P28b: "Your heart will ultimately rend . . . so too the veil . . ."

Matthew 27:46, 50–51; Mark 15:34, 37–38; Luke 23:45–46.

P30: "Your testimony will be the very spirit of prophecy."

John, the beloved disciple, ultimately received this revelation (Revelation 19:10).

Chapter IV

Paragraph 3a: "a great storm is being stirred up . . . sudden destruction awaits."

Jeremiah 4:20; 25:32; 1 Thessalonians 5:3.

P3b: "Your Son is far from security . . . crushed in the gate . . . no Deliverer . . ."

Job 5:4.

P4a: "Son, it is My will to crush You . . ."

Job 6:8–10; Psalm 143:3–4; Isaiah 53:4–12.

P4b: "Your life is being made a guilt offering . . . You shall see Your offspring . . . My will shall prosper in Your right hand."

Isaiah 50:7–11; 51:4–5, 22; 52:9–10, 13–15; 53:10–12; 54:7–10.

P6: "there yet remains an hour of trial and warfare."

This phrase and its surrounding context, spoken by God the Father to the Son, was directly inspired by a reading in Thomas a Kempis' *The Imitation of Christ*, book III, chapter 49 (*The Imitation of Christ*, 175).

P7a: "You will behold the light of life . . ."

Job 33:30; Psalm 27:1; 36:9; John 1:4; 8:12.

P7b: "Righteous Servant, will justify many . . . King's portion . . . intercession."

Isaiah 49:6–8; 53:11–12.

P9: "another beloved disciple . . . pilgrim's progress . . . holy war . . ."

In that God's love transcends spacetime, Jesus here prays for a future disciple, John Bunyan, who would become a prominent English preacher and writer with global impact. Bunyan (born in the United Kingdom in 1628; died 1688), a Puritan, wrote nearly sixty works, most of which were poems and expanded sermons. He is best known for the allegorical works, *The*

Pilgrim's Progress and *The Holy War;* and his spiritual autobiography, *Grace Abounding to the Chief of Sinners.*

P10a: "a tributary from the River of Life . . ."

Revelation 22:1–2.

P10b: "blood began to weep from every pore . . ."

Luke 22:44; Hebrews 11:28.

P13a: "redeem my soul from the grave . . . judging fire . . ."

Psalm 49:15; 50:3; Lamentations 2:3; Joel 2:3.

P13b: "the stranger will witness salvation . . ."

Leviticus 19:10; Numbers 15:15–16; Deuteronomy 10:18–19; 14:29; Isaiah 14:1; Ephesians 2:17–22.

P14a: "Hide Your face from this iniquity . . . pour out Your fury . . ."

Psalm 51:9; Isaiah 63:4–6; Lamentations 2:4; 4:11; Ezekiel 22:22; Nahum 1:6.

P14b: "Restore . . . joy of Your Presence . . . Your generous Spirit."

Psalm 51:12; 85:4.

P16: "ten Furies dispatched from Tartarus . . ."

The *Furies,* from the Roman name Furiae, were avenging goddesses (i.e. unclean spirits) of Greek mythology known to the Greeks as the Erinyes—the angry ones. These demons of punishment mercilessly pursued their victims in life and in death. They were portrayed as ugly women with serpents entwined in their hair, and often wielded the tools of vengeance: torch, spear, and scourge (*World Mythology,* 44).

Tartarus is a prison, or region of incarceration, beneath the underworld.

P17: "my Fortress . . . my High Tower . . ."

2 Samuel 22:2–3; Psalm 18:2; 31:2–3; 71:3; 91:2; 144:2; Jeremiah 16:19.

P18a: "the lucid mystery set before them."

The holy angels do not yet grasp the full account, or intricacies, of Jesus' salvific victory and atonement for humanity (1 Peter 1:12), though they certainly grasp it conceptually per prophetic Scripture and the witness of history. The implication is that eventually we will personally testify to the angels of our personal/spiritual salvation by Christ, for the blood of Jesus does not cover the angels, only humanity.

P18b: "the Expanse . . . the Elysian Boundary . . ."

Genesis 1:6–8, 14–17; Psalm 19:1; 150:1. The *expanse* (or "firmament/heavens" in various Bible translations) is the great vastness of interstellar space within which our universe—the cosmos—is set. The Elysian Boundary is simply the farthest end of the cosmos in any direction, beyond which would be the Blessed Realm, the abode of God, the third heaven (2 Corinthians 12:2–4). The first heaven is Earth's atmosphere; the second heaven is interstellar space, or the expanse.

Elysium is Latin for heaven (see Chapter VI/P10a).

P21: "my Light illumined the darkness . . ."

John 1:4–5, 9–14.

P23: "vessels of wrath prepared for destruction . . . Remnant of humanity."

Romans 9:22–29. For Pharaoh's example, see Exodus 5–14. For king Saul's example, see 1 Samuel 31.

P24a: "the Stone of offense You have laid in Zion."

Isaiah 8:13–15; Romans 9:33; 1 Peter 2:4–8.

P24b: "I will be found by those who do not seek me . . ."

Isaiah 65:1; Romans 10:20.

P24c: "my righteousness . . . truth will go out to all the earth . . ."

Psalm 85:11; 96:13; 98:2–3; Isaiah 42:10; 45:22–23; 49:6; 62:11; Micah 5:4; Acts 1:8; 13:47; Romans 10:17–18.

P26: "Mary of Magdala . . . received my kingdom in its fullness."

Following Jesus' first miracle at the wedding in Cana, I have written Mary of Magdala as being the first to personally experience God's kingdom authority and power when Jesus releases her from seven abiding unclean spirits (Luke 8:1–2).

P32: "champions of Samaria—my samurai . . . Shemite ancestry . . ."

In Hebrew, the name Samaria means "watchtower," "guard-tower," or "watch-mountain." The Japanese word *samurai* means "noble/royal guard." Samaritans of Jesus' day (and today) claimed descent from the Israelite tribe of Manasseh, one of Joseph's two sons. The name Manasseh means "forgetful" (Hosea 13:16).

Circa BC 930, when David's grandson, Rehoboam, became king, the tribes of northern Israel quit loyalty to both the House of David and the former king Saul's tribe of Benjamin. This confederation formed the Northern Kingdom of Israel, standing over and against the Southern Kingdom of Judah. In BC 723, Assyria conquered the Northern Kingdom and the population was pillaged, diluted, deported, and enslaved. Thus the tribe of Manasseh became one of the infamous ten lost tribes of Israel, and so lost to history—theoretically. Research into connections between ancient Israel and Japanese history will reveal intriguing anomalies, though I claim nothing definitive save for great narrative plot points! For one such anomaly, note striking similarities between the structural setup of the Jewish tabernacle complex and the Japanese shinto shrine.

Shem was a son of Noah from whom descended (via Abraham) Israelites (Jews) and Ishmaelites (Arabs), and also much of the populations (or Y-chromosomal haplogroups IJ) of northern Europe and the Middle East. Herein, Samaritans are descended from Shem through Joseph's son Manasseh. It is from Noah's other two sons, Ham and Japheth, we get the populations of Africa (Ham) and western, southern, and central Europe, and Greece (Japheth). For extensive and accessible research into the story of human genetics and how it confirms Scripture, particularly by new evidences of DNA rate changes in humans and the surprising dissemination of specific haplogroups throughout history from the beginning, see Nathaniel T. Jensen, *Traced: Human DNA's Big Surprise* (Master Books, 2022).

P34: "I have established my *djinn* . . ."

The *djinn*, as referenced in Middle and Far Eastern culture, are supernatural evil beings (unclean spirits/demons) which exercise their powers invisibly or by haunting buildings and territory, attaching themselves to items, and/or inhabiting physical creatures or humans. Their name means "furious" or "possessed" (*World Mythology*, 74–75, 330).

P35: "warcrafters from the days of Enoch . . ."

See the book of Enoch 8:1; 9:6 (also known as 1 Enoch 8:1; 9:6); Jude 1:6. For biblical references to Enoch, see Genesis 5:18–24; Hebrews 11:5–6; Jude 1:14–15.

P37: "Azazel . . . cursed by the Great Tyrant . . . to the Abyss . . ."

Enoch 10:4–6; Jude 1:6.

P40: "tended the holy lampstands . . ."

Ezekiel 28:14–15.

P42: "Whoever is angry . . . without a cause . . ."

Matthew 5:21–22; Mark 7:20–23.

Chapter V

Paragraph 2: "a spirit mired with clay . . ."

Job 33:6; Isaiah 64:8; Jeremiah 18:4; Romans 9:21–23.

P5: "I have learned to know You by the Spirit You have given me."

Isaiah 50:4; Matthew 1:18, 20; Luke 2:40–52; John 1:14.

P6a: "Ruach's staid voice . . ."

Ruach or *ruakh* is the Hebrew word for spirit, wind, or breath. The Hebrew for Holy Spirit is *ruach ha-kodesh*, referring specifically to the Person of the Spirit of Yahweh. In reference to the triune personhood of God, *Ruach Elohim* reveals the concept of the Holy Spirit being in equal unity with the Father and Son (Genesis 41:38).

For the sake of the story and relational intimacy, I have Jesus refer to the Holy Spirit as Ruach. In the context of eternal relationship, even within the Godhead, I believe the simplicity of endearingly simplistic naming has precedence.

P6b: "many earthen vessels will be created, but few shall be saved."

Romans 9:22–29.

P8: "guarantee beloved station for Your offspring . . ."

Isaiah 53:8; Acts 8:33; 17:26–29.

P9: "emptied myself of full omniscience . . ."

Philippians 2:5–8. The term *kenosis* (from Greek *kenoo*, "emptied") conveys the concept of Jesus' self-limiting privileges of Deity at His incarnation (2:7). Jesus Christ was indeed wholly God and wholly human (Colossians 2:9). He did not become less divine in nature, He became simultaneously human. Moreover, His divinity and humanity were not an alloy, but rather remained distinctly separate *and* together. This is surely a mystery that cannot be entirely figured out by our merely human (and fallen) intellect. As such, this fact must inspire our humble worship of God.

In that Jesus retained all of His divine attributes alongside and within His humanity, He simply refrained from employing such attributes that would negate "being human." Consider: Jesus subjected Himself to the earthly elements and physical exertion; He needed solitude, shelter, rest, food, and drink. And for Jesus to truly be our perfect model for godly living He would necessarily limit Himself to being fully reliant upon the physical/spiritual disciplines such as humble servitude, prayerfulness, and full dependence on the Holy Spirit for direction, instruction, discernment, revelation, and empowerment to perform miracles (Matthew 24:36; 26:37–46; Luke 5:16; John 1:48; 17:4–5). However, this does not mean He did not retain an awareness (and "memories") of His divine station from before Creation (John 6:32–40; 8:57–58; 17).

P10a: "Holy Spirit who would . . . testify of me."

John 15:26.

P10b: "The everlasting gospel . . . reknit into an inviting yoke . . ."

In Jesus' day, particularly within rabbinical philosophy, a "yoke" was specifically a rabbi's interpretation of Scripture. Therefore, a student may be subject to an easy or hard yoke, and thus either a light or heavy burden when applying Scripture to their lives under the scrutiny of their master-teacher. The Pharisees placed a hard yoke upon all Israel, while exempting themselves from the same. Jesus often called out their hypocrisy and heresy (Matthew 23:3–8, 13–16, 23–36; Luke 11:39–52). Jesus also offered the graciously and more relationally appropriate "easy yoke" and "light burden" of following Him, for He shares our burdens (Matthew 11:28–30; 1 Peter 5:6–7). Yet He only shares those burdens/crosses meant for us or that arise against our will; He does not share burdens we place upon ourself per disobedience or presumption (Matthew 10:38–39).

P11: "a stranger and pilgrim in the earth . . ."

Psalm 119:19; Hebrews 11:13–16.

P12a: "deep water from a hidden pool . . . my Advocate's counsel . . ."

Proverbs 20:5; John 16:13.

P12b: "Joseph lay dying and I pleaded with Abba . . ."

Though Scripture is silent concerning Jesus' earthly father's death, I have approached it by having Joseph die seven months prior to the beginning of Jesus' public ministry, which began via His baptism by His cousin John.

P13: "the time Joseph had spoken of arrived during a wedding."

John 2:1–11.

P16: "keep Your Bride from . . . Jacob's trouble . . . Jacob will be saved . . ."

Jeremiah 30:7; Romans 11:26–27; Revelation 3:10.

P18: "leaven of the Pharisees . . . I had come not to bring peace . . ."

Matthew 10:34; 16:6–12; Mark 8:15–21; Luke 12:1, 49–53.

P19: "set my face like flint . . . in my flesh I shall see God."

Isaiah 50:7; Job 31:6; 19:26.

P20: "The sign of the prophet Jonah . . ."

Matthew 12:39–41; 16:4; Luke 11:29–32.

P21a: "war against Heaven . . ."

Isaiah 14:12–15.

P21b: "ancient devil . . . has again leapt into my Father's fold."

The first sheepfold invasion was against Eden; the second against Israel; the third (and present) invasion is against the Church.

P22: "Cerberian focus . . ."

Cerberus was a monstrous three-headed hound, the watchdog of the underworld who stopped anyone attempting to return to the land of the living. Brother to Hydra and Chimaera, and like the Gorgons, Cerberus was so dreadful that any who looked upon him turned to stone (*World Mythology*, 30–31).

P23: "Rabboni . . ."

Mark 10:51; John 20:16. Both *rabbi* and *rabboni* refer to a Jewish "teacher."

P26: "It is written by Daniel . . ."

Daniel 5:1–30.

P28: "left Israel to its own affairs for centuries . . . Maccabeans!"

Here Lucifer refers to the four centuries of prophetic silence God offered Israel, for no divinely sanctioned prophets arose between the offices of Malachi and John the Baptist. During this era, the politically savvy Maccabaeus family (though far from perfect) was used by God to preserve Israel's national station, caught as it was between the rising political and martial tension of both Greece and Rome (second century BC). Had total war broken out, Israel would have been destroyed utterly in the fallout. Yet a series of decisive battles far from the holy land determined the historical fading of the Grecian empire and ascendancy of Rome.

The name Maccabaeus or Maccabee means "hammer," and was given to the family of a Jewish priest Mattathias (son of Asmoneus) and his five sons (Hasmoneans) who led a revolt against the Greek warlord Antiochus, ruler of the Seleucid Empire, which sought to subvert Judaism. The Maccabean victory and cleansing/rededication of the Jewish temple is commemorated by the festival of Hanukkah.

The written record of 1 and 2 Maccabees details the historical, political, and theological aspects of this period. Additionally, yet less familiar, 3 and 4 Maccabees supplements the former. All four records are considered "useful writings" or apocryphal and thus not divinely inspired Scripture. They are often included in the Bibles used by the Roman Catholic, Anglican, and Orthodox churches, but are not included or considered canon by Protestants and Jews. The Jewish historian Josephus has much to offer on this. See his *Jewish Antiquities*, books 12–13. Also see the "Jewish History" section in C. K. Barrett, *The New Testament Background*.

P30a: "divine authority and power . . . granting to your slaves."

Luke 10:19; John 14:12.

P30b: "Unlike Belshazzar . . ."

Here Lucifer perverts the context of Daniel 5:24–28.

P34: "I once handed you all the kingdoms of Earth . . ."

Matthew 4:8–11; Luke 4:5–8.

P35: "Lesser Light."

Earth's moon (Genesis 1:16).

P41a: "we no longer serve the Lord God."

Judges 10:6; Jeremiah 3:1; 5:23–25, 31.

P41b: "Jerusalem has only a future of fury . . ."

Jeremiah 30:23–24; Zechariah 14:1–13; Joel 2:1–10, 30–32; Amos 9:8–10; Malachi 3:1–3; 4:1.

P42: "the Lord who pleads the cause of His people . . ."

Isaiah 51:22; Micah 7:9.

P44: "craft which corrupted Eve from the simplicity . . ."

2 Corinthians 11:3.

P45: "the Triad Alliance . . . repel the advance of Mesha . . ."

2 Kings 3:4–27.

P46a: "Yeshua bar Yosef."

Jesus son of Joseph. Lucifer scoffs at Jesus' humanity, perceiving it as weakness.

P46b: "no ram caught in a thicket . . ."

Genesis 22:8–14.

P49a: "false shepherds who destroy and scatter the sheep . . ."

Jeremiah 23:1; John 10:11–15.

P49b: "in accord with the evil of your doings . . ."

Ezekiel 14:3–5; John 19:6–7.

P49c: "I will gather the remnant of My flock . . . a King shall reign . . ."

Jeremiah 23:3–5; 33:15–16; Micah 2:12

P49d: "stand still and see the salvation of Yahweh!"

Exodus 14:13–14; 2 Chronicles 20:17; Job 37:14.

P53a: "Anna the prophetess . . ."

Luke 2:36–38.

P53b: "my cousin John . . . prepared the way for my public ministry . . ."

Matthew 3; Luke 3:1–22.

P54a: "not all will take up their cross and follow me."

Matthew 10:38–39; 16:24–26; Mark 8:34–37; 10:21–27; Luke 9:23–25; John 6:65–66.

P54b: "Scripture itself will become an idol."

John 5:38–40.

P55: "to lay down my life in perfect love . . ."

John 10:15–18; 15:13; 1 John 3:16.

P56a: "the Second Adam in the second garden."

Many will recognize the first garden as Eden and the second as Gethsemane. The apostle Paul exhorts the superb prophetic parallel between the first Adam and the second/last Adam—Jesus Christ (Romans 5:12–19; 1 Corinthians 15:45–49).

P56b: "I will fight for you."

Exodus 14:14; Deuteronomy 1:30; Nehemiah 4:20; Jeremiah 1:19; 15:20.

P57a: "Adam, firstborn of the *Imago Dei* . . . granted stewardship of Earth . . ."

Imago Dei is Latin for "image of God" and expresses the unique relationship between God and created humanity (Genesis 1:26–27; 9:6; Romans 8:29; 1 Corinthians 15:49). Humanity's authority over and stewardship of Earth was lost at the Fall (Genesis 1:26–28; 2:15–25; 3).

P57b: "The great land serpent Ancalagon . . ."

The great author and professor J. R. R. Tolkien's Middle-earth legendarium is set in the deep history of our own primary world (*Letters of Tolkien*, #131:143). As such, Tolkien wrote of an ancient serpent born of and/or recruited for evil ends: ". . . Ancalagon the Black, the mightiest of the dragon-host . . ." (*The Silmarillion*, 252). Another mention of this great black serpent occurs when Gandalf refers to Ancalagon in a discussion with Frodo concerning how to destroy the One Ring (*The Lord of the Rings*, 61).

P57c: "Thus . . . bringing the curse of sin and death to all."

Genesis 3:6–24; Romans 5:12–19.

P58: "Extremis Gate . . . two cherubim with swords of flame . . ."

Genesis 3:24. *Extremis* is Latin for "at the end."

P59: "substitutionary atonement . . . my merciful covering of sin . . ."

Genesis 3:21; 4:3–7; Exodus 30:10; Leviticus 4; Psalm 65:3; 79:9; Proverbs 16:6; Hebrews 7–10.

God so loved the world—all of His suffering people—that He entered into the world, setting aside His divine privilege that would exempt Him from pain and anguish. Alister McGrath sublimely states, "The one who need not suffer chose to do so, taking the pain of the world upon His shoulders, as Atlas is said to have borne the weight of the world upon his. Through His sufferings as God incarnate, Jesus Christ threw open the doors of the New Jerusalem—a city in which suffering is no more (Revelation 21:4). Before Jesus Christ, people suffered with dignity, as with Socrates who committed suicide in a noble and dignified manner. Yet after Jesus Christ, people can suffer in hope, knowing that there lies ahead a homeland from which this enemy has been banished" (*Glimpsing the Face of God*, 97).

P61a: "Today is the day of salvation."

2 Corinthians 6:2.

P61b: "Sheol's righteous captivity shall see a new Day!"

Ephesians 4:8–10.

P62: "I am the way, the truth, and the life."

John 14:6. He is also our Light (John 1:9) and our wisdom, righteousness, sanctification, and salvation (1 Corinthians 1:30). For an enlightening essay answering the inquiry, How can any one man incarnate every truth and virtue?, see Peter Kreeft, *The Philosophy of Tolkien*, 221–25.

P63a: "the brazen serpent was lifted high . . . *Nehushtan* . . . broken."

Numbers 21:7–9. *Nehushtan* means "a piece of brass" and refers to the cast-bronze serpent on a pole from Numbers 21. Israel eventually began to worship this image and King Hezekiah destroyed it when he purged the nation of idols (2 Kings 18:4). Jesus referred to Himself in prophetic parallel to the bronze serpent which He had commanded Moses to forge (John 3:14).

P63b: "The times of ignorance will be overlooked . . ."

Acts 17:30–31. Through the apostle Paul, God told the Athenians that He has been mercifully present in their paganism, but not specifically known and thus not able to offer salvation. In response to their altar to the Unknown God, Paul says, "The One whom you worship without knowing, Him I proclaim to you" (Acts 17:23). Herein, Paul expands the limited aspect of general revelation to the *saving* aspect of special revelation. This is the blessed reality of "myth becoming fact" which G. K. Chesterton expounded in his book *The Everlasting Man*, itself playing a role toward C. S. Lewis' conversion to Christianity.

P64: "Our love for the world would be manifest . . . well of salvation . . ."

Isaiah 12:2–5; John 3:16–21.

Chapter VI

Paragraph 2a: "I am stricken, afflicted . . . those I know betray me . . ."

Isaiah 53:4; 1 Chronicles 12:17; Matthew 17:22; 26:14–25; Mark 14:18; Luke 21:16; 22:21; John 6:64; 13:21; 18:2.

P2b: "my souls pours out as a sin offering . . ."

Psalm 22:14–22; Philippians 2:17; 2 Timothy 4:6.

P2c: "I have held my peace . . . I cry like a woman in birth throes . . ."

Isaiah 42:14.

P2d: "Like the Expanse, I am stretched . . ."

Psalm 102:25–27; 104:2; Isaiah 40:22; 44:24; 51:6; Zechariah 12:1.

P3: "Your cohorts of terror . . . it pleases You to crush me . . ."

Job 6:4; Psalm 143:3–9; Isaiah 53:10.

P4a: "My God . . . I will be forgotten."

Psalm 22:1; 42:9; Matthew 27:46; Mark 15:34.

P4b: "Your will is my own . . . Our way in the desert."

Matthew 26:39; Mark 14:36; Luke 22:42; Isaiah 40:3.

P5: "my hour . . . had come for the Son of Man . . ."

John 12:27–36; 17:1–5.

P6a: "Haman's Pur of wrath . . ."

The Hebrew word *pur* means "lot" as in casting of lots; *purim* means "lots." The Jewish Feast of Purim (Esther 9:26–32) commemorates the deliverance of the Jews from a planned genocide by Haman (Esther 3:5–10), prime minister to the Persian king Ahasuerus (Xerxes I). By divine providence, the Persian king's queen was a Jew. This fact is the fulcrum of an epic salvation narrative recorded in the biblical book of Esther.

P6b: "Leaving Our habitation for the lowly seat . . ."

Luke 14:7–14.

P6c: "judgment of the Righteous Father . . . reconciliation with Us."

John 5:30; 17:25–26; 2 Corinthians 5:18–21; 1 John 2:1–2.

P7: "forging the first resurrection . . . glory of the old man . . . new man."

Revelation 20:6; Romans 6:4–6; Ephesians 4:22–24; Colossians 3:9–10.

P8a: "the acts and shadows of godly men and women . . ."

Acts 5:14–16.

P8b: "the prophetic path of Patricius, Shepherd of Eirlandia . . ."

Here Jesus prays for another specific soul to be a powerful *future* witness to the ends of the earth. Patrick, known as St. Patrick to most (though he was never canonized), was born in Scotland in AD 387. After a tumultuous early life, he spent thirty years living in Ireland as a missionary during a dark time in its history. Eirlandia is the ancient Celtic name of Ireland—Eire in modern Irish language, itself derived from Eriu, a goddess in Irish mythology.

For a great historical primer in Irish history, see Thomas Cahill's *How the Irish Saved Civilization* (Anchor Books, 1995). For a superb historical fiction account on the life of Patrick, see Stephen R. Lawhead's *Patrick: Son of Ireland* (William Morrow, 2003); and for an epic telling of Ireland's Celtic roots, see Lawhead's historical fiction/fantasy *Eirlandia* trilogy (Tor Books, 2018–2020).

P10a: "Voyager of Elysium . . ."

Elysium (from Latin)—or the Elysian Fields—is the Greek and Roman equivalent of heaven, but specifically is a place of rest for dead heroes and souls blessed by the gods. Eventually for Roman Christianity, it became synonymous with the biblical heaven.

P10b: "Master and Stone of Earendil . . ."

In J. R. R. Tolkien's Middle-earth legendarium, Earendil the Mariner—the first savior-type—is a uniquely gifted character of hope, sacrifice, and deliverance who at one point turns the tide of a horrific war, thus saving the world from an evil overthrow in its earliest age. He is also hailed as "the longed for that cometh beyond hope . . . bearer of light before the Sun and Moon . . . star in the darkness, jewel in the sunset, radiant in the morning!" (*The Silmarillion*, 248–49). Some of Earendil's story (in poem form) is detailed in *The Lord of the Rings: The Fellowship of the Ring* (*The Lord of the Rings*, 194, 233–36).

Earendil, whose name means "lover of the sea" (*The Silmarillion*, 325), can be seen as a prefiguring of Christ in a similar way as the biblical/historical Joseph or David. Earendil carries a Silmaril, a sacred stone filled with holy light; he also becomes a mariner of the starry sea of night, navigating the trackless Expanse around Arda/Earth illumined as a star and providing an echo of hope for a coming final salvation for all the world (*The Lord of the Rings*, 233–36, 365). Jesus Himself is referenced as *the* Stone and *the* Star (Isaiah 8:13–15; Romans 9:33; 1 Peter 2:8; 2 Peter 1:19; Revelation 2:28; 22:16).

Austin Freeman makes an excellent point concerning hints of salvation in Middle-earth: "Since Tolkien sets his stories in a mythical version of our own history prior to the advent of Christ, there can be no direct analogy to Christian salvation in his fiction. But, for the same reason that it *will* occur in the future of Middle-earth, his writing is replete with hints of such an event." Also noted, "[Tolkien] himself leaves space in his narrative of earliest human history for the biblical account. It is likely that most of the recorded history of Men in Middle-earth is set sometime around Genesis 10–11" (*Tolkien Dogmatics*, 248, 426).

A final note on Earendil. In 1914, Tolkien read a poem by Cynewulf and a specific text arrested him: "Hail Earendel, brightest of angels." Again, Freeman summarizes: "Tolkien's fascination with the name Earendel was the spark to a very great flame, and it led him to write what Christopher Tolkien calls the first work in his mythology." Further noted, "On analyzing the poem, Tolkien believes Earendel to be a title for John the Baptist, and the term 'angel' to refer to John's role as messenger" (*Tolkien Dogmatics*, 124, 396; *The Book of Lost Tales, vol.* 2, 267). Tolkien changes the name Earendel to Earendil to accommodate one of his created Elven languages.

P10c: "that which We have lovingly concealed."

Job 11:7; Proverbs 11:13; 12:23; 25:2; Jeremiah 33:3; Daniel 2:22; 1 Corinthians 2:10.

P10d: "stewards of the mysteries of God . . ."

Luke 8:10; 1 Corinthians 4:1.

P12: "I am become the frailty and wickedness of men . . ."

Ecclesiastes 3:16–17; Jeremiah 1:16.

P15a: "eternal Caelum."

Caelum is Latin for "sky, heaven." In Christian theology it specifically refers to the "abode of God."

P15b: "Alatar and Pallandros . . ."

Two *Archons* (Greek, "highest ranking") of the angelic Host. Their names mean "light" and "far-helper" respectively. In Professor Tolkien's Middle-earth legendarium, there is an order of five Maiar, or angel-wizards known as Istari—the "wise ones"—whom were sent into the world to assist the peoples against evil. They are Saruman, Radagast, Gandalf, Alatar, and Pallando. In *The History of Middle-earth: Volume XII*, Alatar and Pallando's names are given as Morinehtar (darkness-slayer) and Romestamo (east/far-helper). These two *Ithryn Luin*—Blue Wizards—are on the extreme peripheral in Tolkien's epic cycle and their fate is unknown. I have adopted the scant information about them provided by Christopher Tolkien and assumed their continual mission from God to eventually find them ministering to Jesus amidst His own atoning mission that will truly save humanity from evil (per individual choice). I have also altered the name Pallando to Pallandros for the aesthetic of a more Greek phonetic.

For all details concerning Alatar, Pallando, and the Istari, see *The Lord of the Rings: The Two Towers* ("The Voice of Saruman," 583–84); *The Lord of the Rings: Appendix B* ("The Tale of Years," 1084–85); *Unfinished Tales* ("The Istari," 388–402); *The History of Middle-earth: Volume XII, The Peoples of Middle-earth* ("Last Writings—the Five Wizards," 384–85); and *The Letters of J. R. R. Tolkien* (#211:280).

P15c: "the narrow path You attend."

Matthew 7:13–14; Luke 13:23–28.

P15d: "the accursed Blameless One."

Job 12:4.

P15e: "the Sower has gone forth . . ."

John 12:24; Matthew 13:3–30; Mark 4:3–29; Luke 8:5–15; 2 Corinthians 9:9–11.

P15f: "far off coastlands shall honor You . . ."

Genesis 10:5; Isaiah 24:14–15; 41:4–5; 42:4, 10–12; 49:1–13; 51:5; 60:9; 66:19.

P16: "Lord God Elyon . . ."

El Elyon, Hebrew, meaning God Most High.

P17: "The hour is come . . . Secret Servant revealed . . . guilty of all sin."

John 12:23–27; Isaiah 49:1–13; 51:22; 52:13–15; 53:11–12; 56:1.

P18: "heavenly agents at hand . . ."

Matthew 26:53.

P19: "a great cloud of witnesses . . . I will endure the cross . . ."

Hebrews 12:1–3; Matthew 3:10.

P20a: "Greek Sophists . . ."

The Sophists ("wise ones") in ancient Greece were itinerant professional teachers and intellectuals who offered discussion and instruction on diverse topics including grammar, rhetoric, history, mathematics, physics, astronomy, and philosophy (across the spectrum from politics to war and religion). Some provided their students formal academic settings within which to learn; others were less formal and gathered in public areas and/or roamed both urban and rural "classrooms." The difference in educational setting could be due to various factors such as preference, popularity, sponsorship, building use/rent availability, tenured faculty, and/or personal wealth. The less formal method was somewhat prominent throughout Eastern cultures; for example, K'ung-fu-tzu/Confucius; Gautama/Buddha; Lao-tzu; Socrates; Sri Krishna; Zoroaster; and Jesus Christ (Matthew 8:20; Luke 9:58).

Primarily, the Sophists charged fees for their instruction. Socrates disagreed with this class of "sophistry" in that he believed knowledge should be freely accessible to everyone. He further disagreed with their common leveraging of argumentation as a contest or as a means of personal/political domination rather than inquiry toward discovering truth.

Eventually, "sophistry" developed into self-indulgent polemics and emotionally charged persuasion toward disseminating more opinion than fact, and solely to promote personal/political agendas (*Greek Philosophy*, 15–17). This resulted in the rise of anti-sophists—led by Socrates and Plato—who were self-described true *philosophers* and thus "lovers of wisdom," not lovers of themselves, fame, and wealth.

P20b: "the unexamined life is not worth living . . ."

This is a quote from Greek philosopher Socrates (BC 469–399), recorded in Plato's *Apology* (38a5–6).

P20c: "crowning God-spell . . ."

God-spell derives from Anglo-Saxon and literally means "God-story" or "God-message." It is from this word that we get the anglicized *gospel*, which means "good message" or "good news."

P20d: "the *Logos* . . . everlasting Word of God."

The Greek word *logos* denotes "word, thought, speech, principle, or statute." In Christian theology, Jesus Christ is Himself the Logos, the Word of God, the Principle of divine reason, creation, and universal order. He was in the world since and before the Beginning, preparing the Way by planting hints of truth until fuller revelation at His incarnation and the unleashing of the Holy Spirit to the ends of the earth (John 1:1–34).

P20e: "Eternal Community of the Essenes . . . Teacher of Righteousness . . ."

In Jewish religious philosophy there are three schools: Pharisees, Sadducees, and Essenes. Pharisees believe in a bodily resurrection and supernatural aspect beyond the physical life, maintaining relatability but often very strict in demeanor and practice per the Law and laws. Sadducees are stoic in nature and do not believe in the resurrection or the supernatural at all, even denying heaven and hell. The Essenes cultivated a peculiar Torah-based sanctity to every facet of life and were very relational yet fanatically strict concerning their Community Rule and monastic separation from Israeli society (and corrupt Judaism) at Qumran in the Dead Sea valley (*New Testament*

Background, 158–59, 218–51). However, Josephus details an additional "order of Essenes" that allowed for marriage (*The Wars of the Jews*, Book 2.8.13). Originating in the second century BC and lasting into the first or second century AD, both Josephus and Philo claim the sect numbered around four thousand and resided in various settlements around Judea.

The Essenes were very apocalyptic and prophetic in their outlook with an exegesis of Torah being very similar to that of New Testament Christianity. They zealously awaited Messiah, viewing themselves as the true remnant of Israel. Therefore, the *Teacher of Righteousness* was both represented by the Community leader and a messianic motif that saturated much of their prolific writings, Rules, and commentaries on Scripture (*New Testament Background*, 223–24, 239–40).

P20f: "New Covenant consummated!"

Jeremiah 31:31–34; 50:4–5; Ezekiel 36:25–28; Luke 22:19–20; Romans 1:16; 11:1–11; Hebrews 8:6–13; 9:24–28; 10:5–25.

P21a: "As Aeneas, I sojourn . . . Latium and Rome . . ."

Evoking the power of story, Jesus here refers to Aeneas, hero of Virgil's *The Aeneid*. Virgil lived from BC 70–19 and his 12-book "Roman epic" became well known as he was writing it, though he died before a final edit. Before *The Aeneid* was available to the general public as a written text, a younger poet, Propertius, wrote this:

Give way you Roman writers, give way, Greeks. Something greater than the *Iliad* is being born.

(*Elegies*, 2.34.65–66, trans. Knox)

Posthumously published in BC 19 during the time of Emperor Augustus, *The Aeneid* details the founding of Rome following the fall of Troy circa BC 1180. Aeneas, a Trojan prince—cousin of Hector—and foil to Achilles, flees the fallout of the Trojan War and begins a journey of prophetic destiny wherein he establishes a new homeland for his people in Italy. Located halfway down the Italian peninsula, Latium was the coastal plain south of the river Tiber, named after the shepherding and farming tribal population—the Latins (*World Mythology*, 16–17). From here Rome would incubate for centuries until its storied ascendancy. Via the Roman Empire, the Gospel of Jesus Christ would swiftly reach the ends of the earth.

Notably in the fourth century AD, when the Roman world became Christian and all things pagan were shunned, Virgil remained as its classic poet; in part because of his fourth *Eclogue*, which many regarded as a prophecy of Christ's birth, but also because Tertullian, the great church father of second-century Carthage, recognized Virgil as a "naturally Christian spirit" though he lived before Christ (*The Aeneid*, 36–37). The poet's significant legacy in the European Christian tradition is undisputed per the innumerable references to his work and the powerfully prominent role Virgil himself plays in Dante's *The Divine Comedy*.

Virgil was commissioned by Emperor Augustus to write *The Aeneid* in BC 30. The theme of the importance of sensibility, hard work, and religion that Virgil had shown in his earlier works—the *Eclogues* and *Georgics*—was exactly what Augustus thought Rome needed to reclaim order after the tragic civil war (University of Canterbury, www.canterbury.ac.nz).

P21b: "my heel shall bruise, I will crush the serpent's head."

Genesis 3:15.

P21c: "Josheb the Tachmonite . . ."

2 Samuel 23:8.

P21d: "devil-god of Kittim . . ."

Kittim was a descendant of Noah's son Japheth; the Jews descended from Noah's son Shem. Kittim's descendants comprised much of Israel's enemies, such as the Cypriots and long-time archenemy Assyria (Isaiah 23:1; Jeremiah 2:10; Daniel 11:30). In the writings of the Essenes, particularly in *Commentary on Habakkuk* and *War Rule*, Kittim is a reference to Gentile enemies (likely Roman) in a "last days" context (*New Testament Background*, 241–45, 247, 250).

P22: "the outer darkness . . . Avernus . . . Armaros."

The torment of the outer darkness is eternal and conjunctive with the final lake of fire judgment (Matthew 8:12; 22:13; 25:30; Revelation 19:20; 20:10, 14–15). The "darkness," though surely literal, simply emphasizes the absence of God's light in every way.

Avernus is a real-world lake (Lago di Averno) in a volcanic crater just east of Cumae and west of Naples. The name means "birdless" or "over which no birds will fly" due to the caldera emitting noxious fumes; and since this volcano is located near an infamous entrance to the Underworld, Avernus was/is often ascribed to the Underworld in general, as in *The Aeneid* 3.519 (*The Aeneid*, 433).

Armaros taught humanity certain aspects of magic, such as counter-spells and release from spells. He is one of a company of fallen angels—the Watchers—who committed a heinous crime against humanity by procreating with human women, which resulted in the giants/men of renown of Genesis 6 (Enoch 6:1—8:3; Genesis 6:1–13; Jude 1:6–7). Such beings were demon-human half-breeds and were thus beyond redemption, revealing an antediluvian satanic strategy to breed out humanity so as to negate God's promise of a Deliverer to redeem fallen man (Genesis 3:15). These giants, known as Nephilim and Rephaim, later established post-Flood cultures to contest the Promised Land and regularly harassed Israel (e.g. Goliath and his four brothers from Gath). Many of these encounters are recorded in Scripture and God ultimately dealt with the Watchers (Jude 1:6–7). For much more Scriptural and historical context on this topic, see my commentary *The Revelation of Jesus Christ: A Disciple's Commentary* (chapter 9, "The 'Giant' Void in Christian Doctrine," 114–122) and Michael S. Heiser's *The Unseen Realm: Recovering the Supernatural Worldview of the Bible.*

In the frame of *Gethsemane Moon*, I have written with implication that the outer darkness is a black hole wherein lies the lake of fire awaiting hell itself to be cast into it at the end of the Thousand Years (Revelation 20:13–15). God has bound the fallen Watchers, to keep them from interfering with humanity until they are loosed upon the earth during the seven-year Day of Wrath/Jacob's Trouble prior to Jesus' return (Jeremiah

30:7–11; Revelation 9; 19:11–21). Per divinely poetic justice, I have Armaros assigned to *watch* the entrance/event horizon of Avernus until that Day at the end of the age when he and all his fallen brethren are cast into it.

P23a: "inhabitants of the earth be dissolved . . ."

Psalm 75:3.

P23b: "He girds Himself with righteous wrath . . ."

Romans 1:18—2:11.

P23c: "I am a vessel chosen to receive vengeance . . ."

Deuteronomy 32:35–36; Romans 9:22–23; 12:19; Hebrews 10:30.

P23d: "I will meditate on the works, the wonders . . ."

Psalm 119:27; 143:5; 145:5.

P24a: "Your way . . . is established in the heavens."

Proverbs 3:19; Isaiah 45:18.

P24b: "Lost Road . . . revealed to Jacob."

Genesis 28:10–17.

P25: "my sleeping Bride . . . my body is a house of judgment . . ."

Jesus' bride is the Church (Ephesians 5:24–32; Revelation 21:2, 9). Jesus' body became a house of judgment for sin, for He laid down His life for us (Psalm 75:8; 1 Peter 4:17; 1 John 3:16), blotting out our transgressions (Isaiah 44:22; Acts 3:19).

Chapter VII

Paragraph 1a: "boundary of light and dark . . . Father's footstool . . ."

Job 26:10; Isaiah 40:22; 66:1; Matthew 5:34–35; Acts 7:49.

P1b: "I hung the world on nothing."

Job 26:7 is evidence for God's governing universal physics, particularly the invisible gravity wells within which planets, moons, and stars rest. Notably, this perspective is only confirmed by viewing Earth from off-planet.

Atlas was a Titan (giant/god) condemned to shoulder the heavens and earth as punishment for fighting against Zeus. His name means "he who carries" (*World Mythology*, 27). And the concept of a World Tortoise or Cosmic Turtle supporting the earth on its back appears in Hindu (as Kurma), Chinese, and Native American mythologies.

P2: "Illumined only by Glory . . ."

Criticism is often leveled at the Creation account in Genesis 1–2 concerning the credibility of literal 24-hour days being tenable. An exhaustive treatment toward proving the 24-hour day sequence is beyond the scope of this writing; as such, refer to my book *The Morning Star & The Melon: Pursuing Truth Through Scripture, Science, Philosophy, and Logic* and Henry Morris' *The Genesis Record*. I will, however, address the criticism which genuinely points out the sequence of "evening and morning" for Creation days 1–3 *prior* to the sun and moon being created on day 4. How can this be? Put logically, and keeping in mind that an omnipotent and omniscient supernatural God can do whatever He pleases in whatever manner He pleases, we need only understand that in order for there to be "evening and morning" there need only be a rotating earth (or water-world) and a light source (Psalm 24:1–2; 2 Peter 3:5). Prior to the sun, moon, and luminaries being created, the light would have simply been God's Glory illuminating His created world, energized by the Holy Spirit.

Notably, per God's relational love and wisdom, all that He does has theological purpose and logical order, "For God is not the author of confusion but of peace" (1 Corinthians 14:33).

P3a: "all luminaries in their tents . . ."

Per physics, gravity wells keep planets, moons, and stars in their place though they still exert gravitational affect on everything around them. Consider the meaning behind David's words, "The heavens declare the glory of God . . . In them He has set a tabernacle for the sun" (Psalm 19:1–4).

P3b: "Noga remains faithful . . . the namesake I had given Earth's star."

In that Jesus calls all stars by name (Psalm 147:4), I have the name of our sun being Noga (or Nogah), which means "shining brilliance." Nogah was the name of one of King David's sons (1 Chronicles 3:7; 14:6). I have written with the implication that amidst a season of repentance David was granted a visionary experience from outside the Earth and from which he saw the solar system in all its created and ordered glory. Learning the sun's name from a pre-incarnate Jesus Himself, David honored this divine moment and glorified God by penning/singing Psalm 19, then naming his next son Nogah. Ezekiel 8 provides a similar yet entirely different visionary context.

P4: "perilous eucatastrophic eschaton."

Originating from J. R. R. Tolkien, the word *eucatastrophe* means "the sudden turn that brings a piercing joy," or simply, "a happy catastrophe." The word *catastrophe* (of Greek etymology: *kata* "down"/*strephein* "to turn") means "an overturning," mostly understood in a negative context. The prefix *eu-* is also of Greek etymology and means "well, good." Thus, "good catastrophe." Such are prominent in Tolkien's Middle-earth legendarium, which was much inspired by real-world eucatastrophes; specifically, the incarnation, passion, death, and resurrection of Jesus Christ (*Tolkien Dogmatics*, 46–47, 338; *Tolkien On Fairy-stories*, 14, 75, 77–78, 119; *Letters of Tolkien*, #55:45).

Eschaton, another Greek-derived word, means "fulfillment, consummation, or end," and points to the end of history in general and, particularly, to the end of the age and return of Jesus Christ to establish His earthly rule. It is from *eschaton* that we get the theological term *eschatology*, the study of last things.

P5: "I am wormwood . . ."

Jeremiah 9:15; 23:15; Lamentations 3:15, 19; Amos 6:12; Revelation 8:11.

P6a: "El Roi smiles . . ."

A Hebrew name of God meaning "the God who sees me" (Genesis 16:13).

P6b: "Telperion . . . my ancient name . . ."

In Tolkien's Middle-earth legendarium, Telperion is the name of one of the Two Trees of Valinor from the Elder Days (the earliest history of Earth); the other is Laurelin. Valinor was an isolated Edenic region on earth. During this primeval age of nascent Creation before the arrival/creation of mankind (or Elves), these two wondrous Trees displayed divine beauty and lit Valinor with a golden and silvery light alternately, for their lifeblood (i.e. sap) was a glorious admixture of water and light which itself was said to aid in igniting the stars. Telperion is the eldest, or firstborn of the Trees, and the Quenya name literally means "silver/white tree"; notably, Tolkien was quite fond of birch trees. See *The Silmarillion*, 38–39, 48; *The Lord of the Rings*, 971, 1033–34; *The Nature of Middle-earth*, 349–350.

In Scripture, trees occupy a lofty station, particularly in Genesis 1–3 and Revelation 22; though trees are also used in striking metaphor (Ezekiel 31). Also see Enoch 24–25. The Tree of Life itself, though a literal tree, points to Jesus and He taught (in parallel) that He is the true Vine, while His Father is the Vinedresser (John 15:1–8). I have imagined Tolkien's *Telperion* being a name of Jesus long pre-existing the foundation of the world, evoking enduring beauty, stature, and strength for all time.

P6c: "the north . . . starry tract . . . place of Father's throne."

Job 26:7, 9.

P7a: "blessed wound . . . written in my hands and feet . . ."

Psalm 22:16.

Peter Kreeft offers another divinely poetic image: "The Cross is God's sword, held at the hilt by the hand of Heaven and plunged into the world not to take our blood but to give us His" (*The Philosophy of Tolkien*, 224).

P7b: "beyond the cosmic expanse . . . the Ekkaia—the encircling sea . . ."

Theoretically, beyond the Expanse (Chapter IV/P18b), and therefore surrounding the entire universe/cosmos, is a vast sea/boundary of water (Genesis 1:2, 6–10; Psalm 148:4; *The Morning Star & The Melon*, 96–97; *Starlight and Time*, 85). In Tolkien's Middle-earth creation mythology there is a mysterious and seeming endless sea surrounding Earth; it is known by the Elvish term *Ekkaia*, which means "encircling sea, or outer ocean." Perhaps it is simply the initially unexplored oceans to those earliest civilizations. Yet in later Middle-earth history it appears to ambiguously refer to the universal Expanse (*The Silmarillion*, 37, 40, 104–105, 186). Also note Psalm 24:1–2 and 2 Peter 3:5.

I have written that amidst His off-planet prayer, Jesus sees across the Expanse and through the encircling water-boundary into Edenhall itself, i.e. the Blessed Realm and dwelling place of God.

P7c: "One seated on a throne . . . Mercy Seat at His right hand."

Exodus 26:34; Daniel 7:9, 13–14; Hebrews 8:1–6; 1 Timothy 6:15–16; Enoch 14:16–22; 25:3.

P7d: "bread and wine . . . hidden Manna . . . Door . . ."

Genesis 14:18–20; Psalm 78:24; John 6:48–66; 10:7–9; Revelation 2:17; Matthew 6:33.

P8: "Hadean heart . . . Charon . . . Acheron . . . Phlegethon . . ."

Hades/hell was thought to be in the heart of the earth, i.e. underworld (Matthew 12:40; Luke 10:15). Charon is the ferryman of the Underdark who plies the Acheron, river of woe. Phlegethon is another river in hell, consisting of flame (*Mythology*, 42–43, 319; *World Mythology*, 47).

P9a: "The Abyss . . . Enoch . . . Elijah."

Enoch 18:10–16; Luke 8:30–31; Romans 10:7; Revelation 9:11; 11:7; 17:8; 20:1–3; Genesis 5:19–24; Hebrews 11:5; Jude 1:14–15; Malachi 4:5; Zechariah 4:11–14; Revelation 11:3–4.

P9b: "for humankind I did not fashion this charred hell . . ."

Matthew 25:41. However, every human soul who rejects Jesus Christ as Savior will end up eternally damned nonetheless (Revelation 20:13–15).

P10: "My righteousness is near . . ."

Isaiah 51:5–6.

P11: "kings of the earth will take their stand . . . they will fall."

Acts 4:26; Isaiah 54:17.

P12a: "the line of truth We had sent out . . ."

Psalm 19:1–4; Isaiah 28:9–18; Amos 7:7–9; Zechariah 2:1–5.

P12b: "fear of the Lord flows clean and bright . . ."

Psalm 19:9.

P13: "Caesarea Philippi . . . Mount Hermon . . . gates of hell."

Matthew 16:13–20; 18:18–20. Also see Heiser, *The Unseen Realm*, 281–287.

P14a: "Avernus . . . eating hell itself . . . second death . . ."

Revelation 20:14.

P14b: "impenetrable province . . . event horizon . . . Avernine star . . ."

This is the language of the physics of black holes, which are massive stars that have collapsed in upon themselves, the gravity well being so great that even light cannot escape. These mysterious constructs continue to defy satisfactory scientific explanation, for though one can neither see nor actively explore the interior of a black hole, its mass remains detectable and therefore proves the star's continuing existence. Effectively separated from the universe proper, another dimension theoretically exists within these constructs due to the rifting of spacetime. The boundary between our universe and a black hole is called the event horizon, or Schwarzschild radius (*The Physics of Einstein*, 185–88).

I have postulated that eternal damnation may involve black holes. The following excerpt is from my commentary on Revelation, Appendix B #10:

"Though hell/Hades may physically (from our frame of reference) be located at or near the center of the earth (perhaps in another dimension/realm—Deuteronomy 32:22; Isaiah 14:9; 2 Peter 2:4), it eventually gets cast into the lake of fire which must be an even larger location (perhaps in another dimension/realm—Matthew 22:13; 25:29–30; 2 Peter 2:4, 17; Jude 1:6, 13).

"The term 'outer darkness' directly correlates to the 'everlasting fire,' made plain by examining many biblical passages concerning the final place of eternal judgment. *Darkness* denotes the external reality as much as the internal/spiritual separation from God's light forever. And though Scripture does not reveal the exact location or specifications of the lake of fire, there are a few indications of where it will *not* be and what/where it *may* be.

"The lake of fire *cannot* be on or in the earth, for the present earth will be dissolved (2 Peter 3:10). Nor could it be on or in the new earth, for righteousness—and God—will dwell there (2 Peter 3:13; Revelation 21:1–3; 22:1–5) and the near presence of such a foul place would not only be odd but would violate Scripture's claims of the damned being separated and cast eternally far away from God's presence (Isaiah 59:2; Matthew 25:29–30; 2 Thessalonians 1:8–9; Revelation 20:15; 21:8).

"So what/where *might* the lake of fire be? Consider that Jude describes false teachers as 'wandering stars, to whom is reserved the blackness of darkness forever' (Jude 1:13), and Peter describes false prophets as having reserved for them the same 'blackness of darkness forever' (2 Peter 2:17). Henry M. Morris offers a startling possibility, suggesting that in some far corner of the ever-expanding universe the damned will be quarantined on a star, stating, 'A star, after all, is precisely that, a lake of fire' (*The Revelation Record*, 431). He also references stars that burn without giving off light in the visible spectrum, thus consisting of both fire and cloudy darkness. To this I would add the possibility of a black hole (a collapsed star), for such is simultaneously a type of *outer darkness* and *separated from the universe proper* due to the gravitational corruption of spacetime (perhaps allowing for extra-dimensional existence of the damned)" (*The Revelation of Jesus Christ*, 301–302). Also, an ever-expanding universe (Isaiah 40:22; Jeremiah 10:12; proven by Edwin Hubble in 1929) may guarantee that the dimension of the lake of fire forever flies further from the presence of God and His goodness, for Psalm 103:12 states, "As far as the east is from the west, so far has He removed our transgressions from us" (*The Morning Star & The Melon*, 97–100).

Truly, in light of modern physics, genuine challenges exist concerning the concept of a black hole actually containing the lake of fire or any other tenable realm of soulful existence for good or ill. Particularly, inside a black hole the star's collective mass must collapse all the way to a point of zero size at the precise midpoint of the spherical event horizon. This is called a *singularity*, and such must form inside a black hole because any other action would violate the second and third postulates of Einstein's general relativity (*The Physics of Einstein*, 188–89). But what happens at the singularity or in the space between the interior of the event horizon and the singularity itself? This is the frontier of the unknown in physics and even quantum mechanics. Moreover, in that God Himself established all known (and unknown) rules of governing physics, He therefore holds the authority and freedom to violate the same via "miracles." And the field of metaphysics continues to lend greater discoveries into "supernatural" concepts and constructs of our universe at both cosmological and quantum levels. I believe this is by divine design as the heavens declare the glory of God and the firmament/expanse (i.e. spacetime) shows His handiwork (Psalm 19:1).

Astrophysicist Jason Lisle states, "General relativity does not include the effects of quantum mechanics, the latter of which describes how the universe behaves at very small scales. Quantum mechanics disallows a perfectly defined position with known momentum; hence *the singularity may actually have a non-zero (though subatomic) volume*. Unfortunately, quantum mechanics cannot describe what happens in an intense gravitational field [like a black hole], the very kind associated with a singularity. *So there is some mystery here*, and some questions which are not yet answered" (*The Physics of Einstein*, 189; emphasis mine). Dr. Lisle is respected worldwide for his work in astronomy, astrophysics, physics, and mathematics. He is also a devoted follower of Jesus Christ and the founder of Biblical Science Institute. Promoting both good science and good theology, Dr. Lisle refreshingly recognizes the true Architect of creation and thus of every scientific field.

The Avernine star is simply a conceptual idea that the lake of fire would recall the name of Avernus, i.e. hell.

P15a: "fallen principalities, Svarog and Fenrir . . ."

I have borrowed names from Slavic and Norse mythology for these two fallen angels. Svarog is a fire-god of the sky; and Fenrir is Odinsbane, a wolf-god of violence and war with significant affect at world's end—though he is defeated (*Norse Myths*, 121–26, 295–99; *World Mythology*, 190).

P15b: "mystery kept secret . . ."

Romans 16:25–27.

P16a: "at once the High Priest . . ."

Exodus 30:34; Psalm 22; Hebrews 4:14–16. Jesus was "Himself to become the sacrifice burned on the altar, thence to ascend up to heaven on our behalf. He is both altar and incense, both sacrifice and priest" (*The Revelation Record*, 142–43).

P16b: "King of Elysium . . . judge rightly the ends of the earth."

Daniel 2:34–45 reveals the interpretation of king Nebuchadnezzar's dream, wherein a great statue representing a succession of great kingdoms is obliterated by an uncut stone that becomes a mountain—God's kingdom—and fills the whole earth. Notably, the statue's base, its feet, are a fragile mixture of iron and clay. A heavenly figure later appears to Daniel having "arms and feet like burnished bronze" (Daniel 10:6), like unto John's vision of Christ whose "feet were like fine brass as if refined in a furnace" (Revelation 1:15).

Eugene Peterson expounds wonderfully, "The succession of kingdoms of this earth, no matter how impressive and powerful, is set on a base that is flawed. Christ's kingdom is set on a base that is as strong as its superstructure is magnificent. The bronze is firm. Bronze is a combination of iron and copper. Iron is strong but it rusts. Copper won't rust but is pliable. Combine the two in bronze and the best quality of each is preserved, the strength of the iron and the endurance of the copper. The rule of Christ is set on this base: the foundation of His power has been tested by fire" (*Reversed Thunder*, 35–36).

Also see 1 Samuel 2:6–10 concerning God's absolute sovereignty, for "The adversaries of the Lord shall be broken in pieces; from heaven He will thunder against them. The Lord will judge the ends of the earth."

P17a: "Leviathan . . . fleeing serpent . . ."

Psalm 74:13–14; Job 26:13; Isaiah 27:1.

P17b: "take up Your wood-hewn throne . . . mountain of God"

The Cross and the Kingdom (Revelation 21:2–6, 10–27).

Chapter VIII

Paragraph 2a: "new covenant shall satisfy . . ."

Exodus 34:5–10; Jeremiah 31:31–34; 50:4–5; Ezekiel 36:25–28; Luke 22:19–20; Hebrews 12:22–29.

P2b: "new wine, new wineskins."

Matthew 9:17; Mark 2:22; Luke 5:37–39.

P2c: "I have not come to cancel or change the law . . ."

Matthew 5:17; Romans 8:1–4; 13:10; Galatians 5:14–18; 6:2; James 2:8–13.

P3a: "no condemnation . . . conformed to my image."

Romans 8:1–11; 12:1–2; 13:12–14; Galatians 3:27.

P3b: "All are called . . . few will be glorified."

Matthew 7:13–14; 20:16; 22:14; Luke 13:23–24; 1 Corinthians 7:17; 1 Peter 2:9.

P3c: "awaken the Moratani . . ."

A name I have constructed, meaning "children of darkness." In Tolkien's legendarium the *Atani* are the Men/humans of Middle-earth, so named by the Noldor elves of Valinor. The prefix *mor-* means "dark" (*The Silmarillion*, 143, 318, 362).

P4a: "I chastened my city with the beast of Babylon . . ."

2 Kings 24:8—25:26; 2 Chronicles 36:5–21; Jeremiah 21–22; 25; 39:1–10; Lamentations 1—4:18; 1:1–2; 2:14.

P4b: "Her prophets have dreamed delusions . . ."

Jeremiah 23:25–40; 27:9–10; 29:8–9.

P5a: "covering of blood . . . of Abel."

Hebrews 12:24.

P5b: "signs and wonders I do in my name . . ."

John 4:48; Acts 2:16–22; Hebrews 2:2–4.

P6a: "I descended in the cloud . . . I saved Moses . . ."

Exodus 32:30–34; 34:5–17; John 10:14, 27.

P6b: "He asked to see my glory . . ."

Exodus 33:17–23.

P7: "My statutes . . . lived through me."

Romans 6:22; Ephesians 2:1–10; Philippians 1:21–24; 2 Timothy 3:12.

P8: "*contra mundum* . . ."

Latin for "against the world." Jesus here laments the obstinacy of Israel and her failed shepherds, who use God's name to edify themselves above all nations and above God Himself. As Rome/Byzantium underestimated the Germanic, Mongolian, and Muslim hordes, so the world underestimates the severity of God's coming judgment and return to Earth.

P9a: "I am the former and latter rain."

Jeremiah 5:24; Hosea 6:3; Joel 2:23.

P9b: "Israel . . . strive with me as Jacob . . . world will learn righteousness."

Genesis 32:24–32; Isaiah 26:9; Daniel 9:26.

P10a: "Mediator of the everlasting covenant . . ."

Hebrews 8:6–13; 9:15–28; 12:24.

P10b: "blown away by a holy wind."

Isaiah 41:15–16; 57:13.

P10c: "as far as the east is from the west . . ."

Psalm 103:12.

P11: "My Beloved Disciple shall behold . . ."

Prior to his death, John the apostle, one of the Twelve, witnessed the absolute holiness of Jesus Christ and His return to earth via the visionary Revelation Jesus gave to him.

P12a: "Mount of Corruption."

2 Kings 23:13.

P12b: "remnant . . . is accursed . . . Holy One in your midst . . ."

2 Kings 21:10–15; Hosea 11:9.

P13a: "he who increases knowledge increases sorrow."

Ecclesiastes 1:18.

P13b: "Wisdom is a helpmeet for every season . . ."

Proverbs 3:13–18.

P13c: "I will be in you, and you in me."

John 17:22–23.

P14: "I returned to my companions . . ."

Matthew 26:43; Mark 14:40.

P16: "the order of Melchizedek . . ."

Genesis 14:18–20; Psalm 110:4–6; Hebrews 5:6–10; 6:19—7:22.

P17a: "I again prayed for . . . Cup of woe to pass from me."

Matthew 26:44.

P17b: "a redemptive reversal . . ."

God so loves humanity—which He created for relationship—that He is ever at work for His people, "ironically turning their evil into good, their cursing into blessings, their temporal adversity into eternal prosperity." Consider that upon Adam and Eve's fall into sin, God would have been within His divine rights to kill them rather than the innocent animals (Genesis 3); yet by the shedding of blood (though not their own) He covered their shame and their sin was remitted (Matthew 26:28; Hebrews 9:22; 10:14–18). G. K. Beale elucidates: "This principle of restorative irony, of course, applies to the very beginning of the Christian life. One becomes a Christian through God's transforming the sinful heart of unbelief into a heart of repentance and faith so that a person's impending curse of damnation is turned into a blessing of eternal salvation" (*Redemptive Reversals*, 80).

Chapter IX

Paragraph 1: "the widow of Nain."

This brief narrative is found in Luke 7:11–17.

P3: "Chaya . . ."

The name Chaya means "life." It is the female rendering of the Jewish male name Chaim.

P8: "the *pneuma* . . ."

Pneuma is the Greek word for "breath, or breath of life"; in the New Testament the word indicates the Holy Spirit. The Hebrew equivalent is *ruach*; and the Latin is *spiritus*.

P10: "Aviv . . ."

The name Aviv means "new life, freshness, or spring season." Aviva is the Jewish female form, and the male name is often shortened to Avi. A contemporary example of the name in common use is the Israeli city Tel Aviv, which means "Hill of Life" or "Spring Hill."

P11: "Immanuel!"

This name means "God is with us." See Isaiah 7:14; Matthew 1:23.

P13: "Scythopolis near the Jordan."

Also known as Bet Shean, this "city of the Scythians" (Colossians 3:11) became the prime city of the Decapolis ("ten cities") and was the lone city of the ten on the west side of the Jordan River. Located 17 miles south of the Sea of Galilee at the joining of two river valleys (Jordan/Harod), the volume of fresh water and fertility of the region prompted a Jewish saying: "If the Garden of Eden were in Israel, then its gate is Bet Shean."

It was built by the Romans circa BC 63 and thrived until it was leveled by an earthquake in AD 749. Though there is no record of Jesus having ministered there, it is probable that He did; for the city is the same distance southeast of Nazareth as Galilee is northeast from Nazareth, and thus resting within Jesus' well-traveled routes.

P16: "wedding in Cana . . ."

John 2:1–12. From Cana Jesus' public mission truly commences, as here He performs His first miracle—turning water to new wine. After the wedding celebration, Jesus and His mother, His brothers, and disciples make for Capernaum (2:12). I have written that Jesus sends the others ahead as He and His mother travel together first to Magdala per the deliverance of Maryam (Luke 8:2).

P19: "prophecy . . . by Simeon . . . *Behold, this Child* . . ."

Luke 2:25–35.

P20: "Isaiah's woeful Servant . . ."

Isaiah 50:6–11; 52:13–14; and 53. The messianic/prophetic Saga of the Secret Servant is found in Isaiah 42–56.

P25: "seven unclean spirits . . ."

Scripture records that Mary of Magdala had been delivered from seven unclean spirits (Luke 8:2).

P26: "disembodied *shedu* . . ."

Enoch 15:8—16:1. The term *shedu*—plural *shedim*—is Akkadian and means "spirit beings," in this case "demons." Though rarely used (Deuteronomy 32:17; Psalm 106:37), this term was primarily neutral with the utilized context determining whether angel or demon. Likewise with the more common and familiar neutral Hebrew term *elohim*, meaning "gods" or "protective spirit beings," though it is also used to contextually identify Yahweh God via singular *Eloah* (the One God/Lord God/God) and plural *Elohim* (the triune God/the God of gods). See Heiser, *The Unseen Realm*, 30–35.

Psalm 82 extols God's sovereign justice toward the fallen angels/gods. "God [*eloah*] stands in the congregation of the mighty; He judges among the gods [*elohim*] . . . I said, 'You are gods [*elohim*], and all of you are children of the Most High. But you shall die like men, and fall like one of the princes" (82:1–7).

Enoch 15:8—16:1 provides fascinating insight into the origin of the unclean spirits which harass humanity and over whom Jesus exercised authority, continuing to do so through His Holy Spirit in the world via His followers across history. When the Nephilim/Rephaim giants were killed by the great flood and then by war post-flood, their spirits were condemned to wander the earth seeking refuge/habitation (in animal or human bodies; Matthew 8:28–32) until the day of final judgment. Said spirits are "unclean" due to their being conceived by an unholy union, for certain fallen angels procreated with human women and gave rise to supernatural giants of demon-human stock (Genesis 6:1–7). This genetically impure race did not consist of divinely sanctioned souls but rather corrupted spirits that were irredeemable.

The Enoch passage reads: "And now the giants, who are produced from the [fallen angel] spirits and [human] flesh, shall be called evil spirits on the earth, and shall live on the earth. Evil spirits have come out from their bodies [via sexual procreation] because they are born from [wo]men and from the holy Watchers [fallen angels/sons of God] . . . And the spirits of the giants afflict, oppress, destroy, attack, war, and cause trouble on the earth . . . They cause offenses but are not observed [seen] . . . And at the death of the giants, [their] spirits will go out and shall destroy without occurring judgment . . . until the day of consummation, the great judgment in which the age shall be consummated over the Watchers [fallen angels] and the godless."

P33: "Maryam . . ."

The Aramaic/Hebrew name means literally and simultaneously "beloved, bitter, and of the sea" from the root *mara* ("bitter") and *yam* ("sea"). The Greek translates to Mariam or Miriam, with the Latin being Maria. A shortened form is, of course, Mary, which often simply and endearingly means "beloved."

P35: "Nathanael of Bethsaida."

This brief narrative is found in John 1:45–51. Nathanael means "God has given."

P41: "Jacob . . . dreamed of a path . . ."

Genesis 28:10–17.

P45: "Zacchaeus . . ."

This account is recorded in Luke 19:1–10. Zacchaeus means "pure of heart/spirit, innocent."

P49a: "I have left the ninety-nine . . ."

Luke 15:3–7.

P49b: "Come now, let us reason together."

Isaiah 1:18.

P52: "Give me some water . . ."

John 4:7–14.

P55: "Today salvation has come to this house . . ."

Luke 19:9–10.

P57a: "Thales/Pythagoras . . . Plato/Aristotle . . . divine language . . ."

See *Mathematics*, 15–19, 121; *Greek Philosophy*, 1–9.

Before Jesus Christ entered the world via incarnation, the Spirit of Truth and Wisdom had been active on the earth from the beginning (Proverbs 8:22–31). Whether interacting with select individuals (e.g. Adam/Eve/Abram) or people groups (e.g. Hebrews) directly by heavenly encounter or by subtle inspiration (e.g. Greeks/other Gentile prophet-teachers), God steadily prepared humanity for the full revelation of truth that would come in the Person of Jesus Christ and the subsequent arrival of the Holy Spirit from within the Church Body of believers (Isaiah 48:16–17; John 14:16–26; 15:26; Acts 2; 2 Thessalonians 2:13–14).

Upon Jesus' fuller revelation of truth to the world, the times of partial revelation and ignorance are overlooked by God in that He commands everyone everywhere to repent before the final day of judgment arrives (Acts 17:26–31; Romans 3:23–26; Hebrews 1:1–2). For excellent insight into the Spirit-directed aspects of Greek philosophy, mathematics, and worldview, see Bradley/Howell's *Mathematics Through the Eyes of Faith* and Markos' *From Plato to Christ: How Platonic Thought Shaped the Christian Faith*.

Also consider, Johann Kepler wholly believed the reason for the success of mathematics lay in God's creation of both the world and the human mind. Kepler stated, "In that geometry is part of the divine mind from the origins of time, even before the origins of time . . . it has provided God with the patterns for the creation of the world, and has been transferred to humanity with the image of God."

Galileo Galilei likewise acknowledged mathematics to be a divine language when he wrote, "Philosophy is written in this grand book, the universe, which stands continually open to our gaze. But the book cannot be understood unless one first learns to comprehend the language and read the letters in which it is composed. It is written in the language of mathematics." The above quotes by Kepler and Galilei are cited in McGrath, *Glimpsing the Face of God*, 79–80.

P57b: "Euclid . . . *Elements* codex . . ."

Thales (b. BC 640) and Pythagoras (b. BC 570) lived long prior to Euclid, who lived around BC 300. The former duo contributed much to mathematic discipline, but Euclid far surpassed them both in his influence on future mathematics. He is most recognized for his thirteen-volume *Elements*. Bradley and Howell explain:

"This work was so influential that it has been referred to as the 'bible of mathematics.' The volumes contain a total of 465 theorems, but the importance of the work does not lie in the originality of its mathematical results. Most of these, in fact, were not even Euclid's own ideas. Instead, by writing *Elements*, Euclid brought order, rigor, and logic to the realm of mathematics. He was the first to establish a method for systematizing, organizing, and proving mathematical knowledge. Today we call this approach the 'axiomatic method'" (*Mathematics*, 121–122).

P62: "my daughter Afina."

The name Afina means "a female fawn." The account of the woman caught in adultery being brought to Jesus is recorded in John 8:1–11.

P64: "Jeremiah's prophecy . . ."

Jeremiah 17:13.

P69: "Now you are Yeira . . ."

This name—also Yaira—means "to illuminate or to shine brightly."

P74: "my son Nissim."

This name means "miracles or wonders." This account of a blind man healed and the offended priests is recorded in John 9.

P92a: "if you abide in my Word . . ."

John 8:31.

P92b: "chastised you for searching the Scriptures . . ."

John 5:38–40. In this Scripture passage, Jesus calls out the Jews who oppose Him by exposing the fact that they—intentionally or not—worship the Torah, not God; Jesus says, "You search the Scriptures, for *in them you think you have eternal life*." He then reveals that although the Scripture does testify of Him, "you are not willing to come to Me that you may have life." Here we see the danger of neglecting or avoiding a *relationship* with God by hiding behind imagined affiliation with the concept of God.

P92c: "I am the way, the truth, and the life."

John 14:6.

P93a: "rectors have said, 'Cursed is everyone . . ."

Deuteronomy 28:58–62; Galatians 3:10–11.

P93b: "what is the purpose of the Law . . . fulfill the Law . . ."

Galatians 3:19–25; Romans 3:19–28; 7:8–13; Matthew 5:17.

I have written, "the Law only saves by condemnation . . ." G. K. Beale offers excellent exhortation on this: Per Galatians 5:3, "those who attempt to achieve salvation through good works by obeying God's laws are doomed to fail because God *does* expect perfection, and therefore nothing imperfect or unholy can enter into the holy presence of God. The futility of trying to save oneself through obedience to the law is expressed well by James, who explains that you could perfectly obey all your life and yet disobey only once, and that is enough to make you as guilty as if you had broken the whole law (James 2:10) . . . even *one* violation can keep you from the saving presence of God."

Per Galatians 3:19 and Romans 7:7, Paul reveals that the intention of God's law was to expose humanity's sin nature; for without the law, humanity would neither know what is right nor have knowledge of sin. Beale summarizes, "The law has a *condemning purpose* in that it shows people how sinful they really are and how far short they fall from attainting salvation through obedience. . . . showing them that they deserve condemnation for their sin" (*Redemptive Reversals*, 112–113).

Therefore the Law has become our tutor to lead us to Jesus Christ, that we may be justified by faith, for He redeems us from the curse of the Law by becoming the curse for us, that we may gain salvation (Galatians 3:13–24). Psalm 22 is a powerful prophecy of the Messiah's redemptive reversal for those who would be saved.

P94: "the wrath to come . . ."

Isaiah 13:9; Matthew 3:7–10; Luke 3:7–9; 1 Thessalonians 1:10; Revelation 6:17.

P96a: "sober and vigilant in their prayers."

1 Peter 4:7.

P96b: "hated . . . for my name's sake . . ."

Isaiah 66:5; Matthew 10:22; 24:9; Mark 13:13; Luke 21:17.

P98: "Joseph of Arimathea . . . Nicodemus."

References to Joseph are Matthew 27:57; Mark 15:43; John 19:38. References to Nicodemus are John 3:1–21; John 7:50–51; 19:39–42.

P100: "I had cleansed the Temple . . ."

Jesus "cleansed the Temple" on at least two occasions, once at the beginning of His public ministry (John 2:13–22) and again near the end (Matthew 21:12–17; Mark 11:15–19).

P101: "tensity between belief and unbelief."

Matthew 13:58; 17:20; Mark 6:1–6; 9:24; 16:14; Romans 11:19–23; Hebrews 3:12–19.

P102a: "There is one God, yet they are three Persons . . ."

Genesis 1:1–2, 26–27; 1 Corinthians 8:4–6; 12:3–6; 1 Timothy 2:5–6; James 2:19; Revelation 5:1–7.

P102b: "the Father sent the Son . . . God is love . . . God is perfect . . ."

John 1:1–13; 5:17–36; 17:23; 2 Timothy 1:7; 1 John 1:5; 4:7–18.

P102c: "bear witness in heaven . . . by water and blood . . ."

1 John 5:6–13; John 16:33.

P102d: "Word of God made flesh . . . not return void."

John 1:14; Isaiah 40:5; Romans 8:18; 1 Corinthians 9:22; John 14:7–11; Isaiah 55:11.

P103: "Holy Spirit as an inheritance . . . Spirit's direction . . ."

Ephesians 1:13–14; John 14:16–17, 26; 15:26; 16:12; Luke 10:19–20.

P105a: "one's own unique kingdom purpose . . ."

1 Corinthians 12:7–27.

P105b: "discerning wisdom which establishes prophecy itself."

Proverbs 2:1–5; 4:7; John 1:1–5; Revelation 19:10; Wisdom of Solomon 7.1—8.1.

"Wisdom . . . pervades and penetrates all things by reason of her purity. For she is a breath of the power of God, and a clear effluence of the glory of the Almighty . . . For *she is an effulgence from everlasting light* and an unspotted mirror of the working of God, and *an image of His goodness*. And she, *though but one*, has power to do all things . . . she reaches from one end of the world to the other with full strength, and orders all things well" (*New Testament Background*, 301:#254 *Wisdom of Solomon*, lines 56–75; emphasis mine).

In the *Wisdom of Solomon* text, as in the biblical book of Proverbs, we find Wisdom personified with the feminine gender. This was common in Semitic literature per the biblical concept of woman being created to be a helpmeet/companion to man (Genesis 2:20–25). Notably, the Greek Stoic's concept of Logos paralleled the Jewish concept of Wisdom; Logos is everywhere, but primarily believed to be found in those virtuous souls which live in accord to it/Him. As emphasized in the *Wisdom* passage above, Wisdom seems to be a distinct and differentiated being, yet still equal with God (*New Testament Background*, 302). Intriguingly, this theistic conception is more Platonic than Stoic, revealing the activity of the Spirit of Truth/Wisdom in the world as He prepared the Way for the arrival of Jesus Christ and the fuller revelation of the triune nature of the Godhead—Father, Son, and Holy Spirit. For the metaphysical aspect of Platonic ideas, see Kreeft, *The Philosophy of Tolkien*, 39–48; and for a most powerful depiction of Wisdom portrayed as a feminine Teacher, see Boethius' *The Consolation of Philosophy*.

P106: "You have searched me and known me . . ."

Psalm 139:1, 6, 23–24.

P107: "my royal priesthood . . . shepherd many priests into my fold . . ."

1 Peter 2:9; Acts 6:7.

P109: "a new covenant . . . according to the Spirit."

Jeremiah 31:31–33; Romans 8:1–4.

P110a: "I have come to set you free."

Isaiah 42:6–9; John 8:32; Romans 6:22.

P110b: "*orthodoxia* . . ."

A Greek word meaning "correct opinion/belief" and from whence we get *orthodoxy*. Two Greek words form the one: *orthos*, meaning "straight," and *doxa*, meaning "opinion, teaching, doctrine, or glory." Also consider the word *orthopraxis/orthopraxy*, which means "correct practice, or correct worship," from the Greek words *orthos* and *praxis*.

P111: "God's thoughts loftier than man's . . ."

Isaiah 55:9; Job 28. For the concept of a limited canvas *enhancing* creativity, I was inspired by Erwin R. McManus' book *The Artisan Soul: Crafting Your Life Into a Work of Art* (HarperOne, 2014), a treatise on the joy of human creativity meeting its highest purpose when directed by our loving Creator. Also see Jordan Raynor's *Called to Create: A Biblical Invitation to*

Create, Innovate, and Risk (Baker, 2017); and Andrew Peterson's exceptional duology on creativity, *Adorning the Dark: Thoughts on Community, Calling, and the Mystery of Making* and *The God of the Garden: Thoughts on Creation, Culture, and the Kingdom* (B&H, 2019/2021).

P112: "the *neshamah*."

Neshamah is a Hebrew word meaning "breath, spirit, or soul." This word is occasionally used in place of *ruach* or *nephesh*. The Greek equivalent is *pneuma*. Also see note P105b concerning Wisdom being "a breath of the power of God."

P113a: "blood of my new covenant will justify many."

Isaiah 53:11–12.

P113b: "the Law is fulfilled in one word . . ."

Deuteronomy 6:5; 10:12–13; 11:13; 30:6; Joshua 22:5; 23:11; Matthew 22:37–40; Mark 12:29–31; Luke 10:27–28; Jude 1:20–21.

P113c: "What does the Lord your God require . . ."

Deuteronomy 10:12–13; Micah 6:8.

P115: "not come into the world to condemn it . . ."

John 3:16–21; Luke 9:56.

P117: "son of thunder . . ."

Mark 3:17. John and his brother James were sons of Zebedee and of the Twelve. Jesus named these two "sons of thunder" in macabre memorial of the time they desired to call down fire from heaven to consume the Samaritans which refused to receive Him (Luke 9:51–56). Jesus rebuked them sharply for this despite the enduring nickname.

P118: "You are from above and not of this world . . . the Light"

John 8:23–30; 1:6–13.

P119a: "sought my wisdom . . . having no knowledge of me."

For excellent insight into philosophers and religious teachers in pre-Christian history, see Kenneth R. Samples, *God Among Sages: Why Jesus is Not Just Another Religious Leader* (Baker, 2017).

P119b: "chosen an uncommon vessel . . . Unknown God . . ."

Acts 17:22–34. Here Jesus refers prophetically to the apostle Paul in Athens.

P119c: "Epicureans and Stoics . . . Prometheus . . ."

Acts 17:18–21. Stoicism, as a philosophical system, was materialist. More important than this, however, "is the fact that in spirit it was deeply religious and thoroughly moral. The universe, the Stoics held, was not a meaningless place, nor was man's place in it fortuitous. Pervading the whole of the material order was Reason and Purpose [the Logos] . . . itself divine and indeed the only god the Stoics recognized," though some acknowledgment of more popular gods did occur despite apparent philosophical contradictions. The Stoic understanding of the Logos was that of an impersonal god-concept. Over time, "Stoicism became the prevailing philosophy of the ever practical Romans," and revealed itself to be a versatile religion as it produced many prominent adherents from Epictetus, a former Greek slave, to Marcus Aurelius Antoninus, a true philosopher-king and Roman Emperor (*New Testament Background*, 65, 70–71).

Epicureanism, as developed by Epicurus (ca. BC 342–270), resembled Stoicism more closely than either party would admit. Both schools "saw that in a chaotic world the only way to peace was the disciplining of desire." Though labeled an atheist, Epicurus did not deny the existence of gods; yet he taught that while they are benevolent, they remain impersonal (*New Testament Background*, 78). Herein we see that both Epicureans and Stoics sought a generalized Good, but from within the failed context of humanity and humanism, from which salvation could only come from outside, particularly from the Creator God and Savior Jesus Christ.

Prometheus, whose name means "forethought," a son of the Titan Iapetus, was known as the Greek god of fire and friend to mankind. Zeus had vindictively hidden the element of fire from humanity but Prometheus stole it and took it to earth that it might aid in humanity's fated sojourn. This act, however, brought Prometheus into conflict with Zeus (*World Mythology*, 77; *The Myth Made Fact*, 74–79).

Viewed through a Christian lens, Prometheus is a Christ-type. Per Zeus' retribution for treason, Prometheus "hangs, crucified, upon a rock, bearing in his broken body the pain and torment he earned for taking the part of man. The fire that he stole for us brought us protection, but it also brought us wisdom and illumination. Out of love for man, Prometheus gave 'light to every man' (John 1:9), but he did so at a terrible price to himself" (*The Myth Made Fact*, 76). This myth may also prefigure Jesus Christ giving the Holy Spirit to His true followers (John 14:16–17, 26; Acts 2:1–4).

P119d: "the Forms to be a Person . . . the One *and* the Many . . ."

See Plato's Theory of Forms as presented in his *The Republic*; and consider that the Holy Spirit paved the way for the Gospel via the Jewish Law and Prophets and Greek philosophy. The following is taken from my commentary on the book of Revelation, Appendix B #11 (*The Revelation of Jesus Christ*, 302–304):

"Plato described certain ideas such as Beauty, Truth, and Justice as universal Forms—the highest Form being that of God. He believed all Forms to be connected and rooted in the 'invisible world beyond the senses' only to be distorted in the visible world by the division between reality and appearance—the One and the Many.

"For example, information we gather about the world is categorized into 'knowledge and opinion.' Knowledge is sought, but opinion dominates and distorts 'true knowledge.' One who fancies beautiful things will have opinions about them, which may differ from another who fancies beautiful things. Some find beauty in evil. But the one who fancies Beauty itself can indeed possess true knowledge. For though there are many beautiful things in the world, all truly beautiful things are rooted in the universal Form of Beauty (which would appeal to every soul).

"For Plato, seeking meaning beyond the visible world of the senses toward understanding the Forms leads one to ultimately understand the Good, i.e. the meaning of life. This is neatly summed up in his Allegory of the Cave and the Light (*New Testament Background*, 62–65). Notably, the Theory of Forms greatly assisted early Christian philosophers in further developing an understanding of heaven and the soul; however, that is not to say that Christianity is founded on Platonic reason. Far from it.

"In the *Timaeus*, Plato describes the supernatural *Logos* (Gk. 'the Word') through which the world was created and through which the Forms are levied upon the universe. This 'Word' is none other than the Word of God, Jesus Christ (John 1:1–4). Likewise for Aristotle's Changeless Being, the Unmoved Mover. Of course, living in pre-Christian history, Plato and others of like mind would not have *known* Jesus. But the ancient pursuit of the undeniable truths of foundational logic and rational thought are, I believe, evidence of the Spirit of Truth at work in the world preparing the Way that Christ Himself would pave with His perfect Gospel and final revelation.

"In fact, this is the very message Paul disclosed to the Athenians in Acts 17:16–34, even referencing pre-Christian history as 'times of ignorance that God has overlooked, but now commands all men everywhere to repent' (17:30).

"Even the early church father Clement concurs. Marcellino D'Ambrosio states, 'Clement goes so far to say that Greek philosophy is actually of divine origin. Though philosophy is not on a par with the Old Testament, God, in His Providence, sent it to the Greeks as a preparation for the Gospel in a similar way that God sent the Law and prophets to the Jews to prepare them for His Son.

'Granted, Greek philosophy neither comprehends the truth in its entirety nor conveys the strength to fulfill the Lord's command. Yet it at least prepares the way for Christianity by making man self-controlled, by molding his character, and by making him ready to receive the truth' (*When the Church Was Young*, 80).

"For example: Plato, in his *Apology of Socrates*, presents Socrates as a philosophic missionary and martyr who taught men to know themselves, to strive toward improving their souls, to love the God of All Knowing, and to see wisdom as cognizance of one's own ignorance (*New Testament Background*, 60–62).

"Concerning the Torah, Jewish literature may be seen as an inverted pyramid. Barry Holtz explains: 'The Bible is at the base, but the edifice expands outward enormously—midrashic literature, the Talmuds, the commentaries, the legal codes, the mystical tradition, the philosophical books. All this is Torah. . . . The classic Jewish texts are as much "classics" as the works of Greek and Roman culture, and although they are far less known, they are as enduring, as challenging, and no less profound' (*Back to the Sources*, 13–14)."

An outstanding and thorough treatment of this theme is found in Louis Markos' *From Plato to Christ: How Platonic Thought Shaped the Christian Faith* (IVP Academic, 2021). And a vital collection of ancient Greek, Roman, and Jewish writings can be found in C. K. Barrett's *The New Testament Background: Writings From Ancient Greece and the Roman Empire That Illuminate Christian Origins* (HarperOne, 1995). Also enjoy Peter Kreeft's treatment of philosophical theology, epistemology, and ethics in *The Philosophy of Tolkien* (Ignatius, 2005).

P119e: "other Gentile flocks . . ."

John 10:16. This is a prophecy that Jesus is the Messiah for all, not only the Jews.

P120: "turn the Greek world upside down!"

Acts 17:2–6.

P122: "Isaiah's prophecy . . ."

Isaiah 7:14–16; 8:14–17; 9:2–8.

P123: "High Priest of humanity . . . Scapegoat . . . 'outside the camp' . . ."

Leviticus 16:21–30; Matthew 3:13–15; John 1:19–34; 19:28–30; 1 Peter 3:21–22.

P124a: "the baptism of repentance . . ."

Mark 1:4; Luke 3:2–4; Acts 13:23–26; 19:1–6.

P124b: "Jonah learned this hard truth . . ."

Jonah 2–3.

P124c: "John came in the spirit of Elijah . . ."

Matthew 17:10–13; Luke 1:13–17.

Elijah himself shall return at the end of the age amidst the final seven-year time of Jacob's trouble (Jeremiah 30:7), i.e. Seventieth Week of Daniel (Daniel 9:24–27). Elijah will be accompanied by another prophet—most probably Enoch—to prophesy in Jerusalem against Antichrist during this time of God's outpouring wrath on Israel and the world (Malachi 4:5; Zechariah 4:11–14; Revelation 11:3–4). Consider that both Elijah and Enoch are the only two individuals recorded in Scripture to not have suffered physical death, thus being supernaturally taken into heaven alive to be preserved and prepared for their last-days ministry whence they shall be killed by Antichrist; they shall then be resurrected after three days with the whole world as witness (Revelation 11:7–13). For further treatment of this topic and theological reasoning toward Enoch (and not Moses) being Elijah's prophetic compatriot, see Birch, *The Revelation of Jesus Christ*, 132–36.

P127: "bring your mother, Salome, to me."

Matthew 20:20–23.

P136: "we worship You in spirit and truth . . ."

John 4:23–24.

P138a: "prophecies of Your birth."

Micah 5:2–4; Matthew 2:1.

In true prophetic form, Bet Lehem means "house of bread." Bethlehem was also "David's city" (1 Samuel 20:6). Also, Nazareth derives from *netzer*, a Hebrew word for "branch," which may point to messianic prophecies such as Isaiah 11:1.

P138b: "resisting the devil in the desert."

Matthew 4:1–11; Mark 1:12–13.

P138c: "You cursed the full-leafed fig tree . . ."

Mark 11:12–14, 20–24.

P140: "narrow way to the Father . . . wide path to destruction . . ."

Matthew 7:13–14; Luke 13:23–27.

P141a: "the glass sea."

John bar Zebedee eventually receives Jesus' revelation of the end of the age and sees the glass sea before the heavenly throne (Revelation 4:6; 15:2).

P141b: "you shall conclude Daniel's record."

Daniel 12:9, 13. John received the fuller revelation (per the book of Revelation) of that which Daniel received.

P143a: "Though the flesh be in captivity . . ."

John was for a season imprisoned on the Roman penal island, Patmos, in the eastern Aegean Sea. It is here where he received Jesus' prophetic revelation (Revelation 1:9–11).

P143b: "origin of prophecy."

Genesis 1:1–2; Revelation 19:10.

P145a: "seek first the kingdom of God . . ."

Matthew 6:33.

P145b: "Plato's 'cave' . . ."

See P119d above.

Chapter X

Paragraph 1: "Arlisgion—the place of reeds . . ."

In Tolkien's Middle-earth legendarium, *Arlisgion* is an ancient word from the First Age meaning "the place of reeds." It is a region through which the human hero Tuor passed while searching for the hidden city of Gondolin, compelled as he was to deliver a prophetic warning to the king (*The Fall of Gondolin*, 10, 43, 266–67). In that Tolkien framed Middle-earth history as the earliest history of Earth (*Letters of Tolkien*, #131:143), I have had Jesus reference a favored reeded region of seclusion (in Galilee) with this ancient word to reinforce the idea of His eternal nature, particularly His pre-incarnate involvement with our world. Moreover, in my own travels to Israel I had the privilege of spending secluded hours in a strand of reeds on the shore of the Sea of Galilee. Such personal time prayerfully and worshipfully spent with Jesus Christ has much inspired and informed the writing of *Gethsemane Moon*.

P3: "My divine foresight . . . checked and limited . . ."

See Chapter V/P9.

P6a: "You shall adorn Wisdom's robe . . ."

Also known as the Philosopher's Robe, this concept speaks to a mantle of perfect wisdom to be worn, or possessed, by a worthy student who would become the perfect teacher. The search for such perfect all-encompassing wisdom has been with humanity from Creation, yet humanity's fall into sin and the subsequent sin nature we now possess makes perfect wisdom—individually or collectively—impossible to achieve. Therefore, the only way to gain or apply Wisdom's perfection (i.e. foundational logic, rational thought, and divine revelation) is via the discretion of the Holy Spirit. This holds true for those who believe in Jesus Christ *and* for those who do not, for the universe itself is beholden to the Creator God who upholds all things by the Word of His power and grants existence even to those who reject Him (Hebrews 1:1–12).

An early attempt to codify a systematic philosophical worldview is found in Parmenides' (b. BC 515) poem, the *Way of Truth*. It is modeled on the Pythagorean cogency of geometry (ca. BC 540). In the poem, a goddess/Wisdom grants Parmenides his deductive revelation and promises to reveal to him "the unshaken heart of well-rounded Truth," i.e. reality itself. Yet the primary objective of the poem is "to demonstrate that the common-sense belief in the reality of the physical world, a world of plurality and change, is mistaken, and to set in its place a One Being, unchanging, ungenerated, indestructible, shaped as a sphere" (*Greek Philosophy*, 10–11).

Though the revelation is not complete (by design), I believe a Holy Spirit-inspired foundation was beginning to be established concerning a monotheistic worldview which has lingered within human consciousness since Creation, and more specifically the idea of an eternally existing God of supreme intelligence and faculty. Intriguingly, "Parmenides' distinction between appearance and reality and between opinion and knowledge laid the foundation for Platonism" (*Greek Philosophy*, 11), which would much more thoroughly pave the Way of truth as wholly revealed by Jesus Christ and His continuing revelation to the world by His Spirit (see Chapter IX/P57a).

Other than Jesus Himself—the perfect Teacher—King Solomon is the only human to have been granted perfect wisdom, ultimately failing to leverage it for God's glory but rather for his own per his fallen state (see the biblical book of Ecclesiastes).

P6b: "Sophists, and Cynics . . ."

For Sophists, see Chapter VI/P20a.

The Greek Cynics were so named per the word *kynikos*, meaning "doglike or currish," from *kyon* "dog/canine" and *ikos*, denoting "likeness/similarity." The ancient Greeks viewed the Cynical school associates as living like stray dogs, for they proclaimed and followed their own set of rules and mores, dismissing traditional social and political standards—also described as "a cosmopolitan utopia and communal anarchism" (*britannica.com*—'Cynic/Skepticism, Asceticism, Hedonism'). The Cynics did not always deny the existence of God/gods and supernatural aspects, but neither did they revere them.

Notably, in the New Testament era, philosophy as a discipline was not confined to university and eccentric study. It was highly practical and intended to be widely practiced. "The teachers of philosophy saw their own beliefs as the needed cure for men's ills and proceeded to offer them to the public.

The philosopher became the street-corner orator, and the Cynics in particular preached their 'gospel' to all who would listen, and it was often delivered—and received—less as a reasoned system of beliefs about the universe than as a divine revelation" (*New Testament Background*, 81). This assists us in better understanding both the "philosophic missionary" climate within which Jesus operated *and* the multi-leveled impact of the truth He revealed amidst the winds of doctrinal half-truths and untruths (Ephesians 4:14–15).

P6c: "a vessel of wrath, Achilles . . . a seed sown in a lost time."

In the society of Homer's *Iliad* a heroic code existed, particularly among warriors. This code consists of two parts. First, the best warriors possess an honor which can only be won in battle, and the "more honor one has, the more he is entitled to the finer things; conversely, the more one enjoys the perks of his status, the greater is his duty to fight bravely in the front ranks." Such honor could be determined by *meeds*, or prizes, won by great deeds. "These prizes consist of gold, horses, armor, trophies, and women. The more fiercely and bravely one fights, the more meeds of honor he will win; the more meeds he has, the greater will be his honor; the more honor he has, the higher his status will be in society" (*From Achilles to Christ*, 62–63). The second part of the heroic code highlights the glory that honor brings. Unless mortal warriors bring great glory to their name, when they die they will be forgotten.

During the Trojan War (ca. BC 1200), king Agamemnon and his best fighter, Achilles, fall into an epic quarrel wherein Achilles threatens to leave the battlefield. Out of wounded pride and perpetual envy, Agamemnon revokes one of Achilles' meeds, the beautiful woman Briseis (*Iliad*, book I). This is likewise a massive strike to Achilles' honor. In response, Achilles and his elite warriors refuse to fight and they are sorely missed in battle. In time, Agamemnon reluctantly offers Achilles untold meeds of honor. Yet Achilles refuses them. This is inconceivable for the time. Louis Markos explains, "Achilles of all men is the last person we would expect to refuse the gifts, for he is the one most concerned with winning fame and glory as a compensation for his mortality."

When we consider that Achilles' identity was entirely that of a warrior and not a philosopher, we see that his words to an embassy pleading his acceptance of the gifts and return to battle are "radically opposed to the beliefs of society . . . radically different, in fact, from his own beliefs and actions to this point" (*From Achilles to Christ*, 64–65).

Achilles refuses to be persuaded by Agamemnon's three ambassadors, yet it is not simple stubbornness driving him, it is something else. Achilles states,

> Fate is the same for the man who holds back, the same if he fights hard.
>
> We are all held in a single honor, the brave with the weaklings.
>
> A man dies still if he has done nothing, as one who has done much.
>
> (*Iliad*, book IX.318–20)

Markos clarifies that this is not something Achilles believes, or is not something he believed in the past. If taken to the extreme, says Markos, a statement such as this could fracture the very foundation of the meeds of honor system. If honor is the same for both the brave and the weak, then why fight? Achilles later says,

> For not worth the value of my life are all the possessions they fable were won for Ilion, that strong-founded citadel, in the old days when there was peace, before the coming of the sons of the Achaians.
>
> (*Iliad*, IX.400–403)

What exactly is Achilles saying? Is he saying that human life is of infinite worth? Markos recalls, "The Judeo-Christian belief in the intrinsic value of all human beings had yet to be 'invented' when the Trojan War was fought or when Homer composed his epic [ca. BC 700]. We have not even reached the teachings of Socrates and Plato, *who themselves do not fully reach this understanding*" (*From Achilles to Christ*, 66; emphasis mine). Yet in answer to his father-figure, Phoinix, one of the ambassadors, Achilles astoundingly continues,

> Phoinix, my father, aged, illustrious, such honor is a thing I need not.
>
> I think I am honored already in Zeus' ordinance which will hold me here beside my curved ships as long as life's wind stays in my breast, as long as my knees have their spring beneath me.
>
> (*Iliad*, IX.607–10)

Louis Markos illuminates wonderfully by asking if we are listening to a first-century Christian or to a mighty warrior who has killed thousands for honor and glory. Achilles should not be saying or *thinking* these things! "If it is true that we all have honor and worth merely because we are alive, then the whole heroic code and the meeds of honor system on which it rests is an illusion . . . Achilles has no name for the new ethic he is tentatively proposing, but I like to call it the 'fellowship of life.' . . . we are all going to die, so let us live and enjoy the time that is given us. Let us not rush into our deaths more swiftly, but take honor and dignity in the life that is within us."

Understandably, none of the ambassadors, including Odysseus, comprehends what Achilles is relaying. Homer records their reaction: "So he spoke, and all of them stayed stricken to silence/in amazement at his words. He had spoken to them very strongly" (IX.430–31). Upon the embassy's return to Agamemnon and his audience to repeat Achilles' words, they have the same reaction (IX.693–94).

Finally, Markos summarizes, "Ironically, the right ideas have come to the wrong person at the wrong time. Alas, not just ironically but tragically. Achilles' new ethos, a message society needs to hear but will not hear again until Paul speaks at the Areopagus in Athens, prevents him from returning to the war." This plays out in tragic fashion through the rest of the *Iliad*, although Achilles does eventually return to battle when his best friend, Patroclus, is killed by Hector. "As for his new ethic . . . Achilles rejects it completely, blaming it for the death of his beloved friend. And so is lost to the world an idea—that life has intrinsic value apart from one's status or accomplishments—that could have revolutionized the ancient world. Nevertheless, Achilles' shadowy, ill-defined ethic remains one of the greatest 'seeds' of the pagan world, one that will be fully articulated by Christ and go on to provide a foundation stone for the edifice of Western civilization" (*From Achilles to Christ*, 66–68).

P6d: "We taught Solomon the Sage's Psalm . . . Pansophy's shroud . . ."

I have imagined the Sage's Psalm to consist of the biblical books penned by king Solomon: Proverbs, Ecclesiastes, and Song of Solomon. These three collectively form a complete life philosophy by which to live "in the world but not of it" that Jesus perfectly modeled and prayerfully instructed His followers to strive for in the Spirit (John 17:14–19).

"Pansophy's shroud" is simply another name I have given for the "philosopher's robe"; pansophy/pansophia means "all wisdom, or universal wisdom" from Greek *pan* ("all") and *sophia* ("wisdom/knowledge"). I have also envisioned Pansophy to be the feminine personification of Wisdom in the book of Proverbs (see Chapter IX/P105b and X/P6a).

P6e: "Socrates [et al] . . . Epicurus and Zeno . . ."

As detailed previously (Chapter IX/P119d), Socrates, Plato, and many other pre-Christian sages and teachers around the world sought objectively for a divine wisdom and moral law. Others, however, sought self-edification from a humanist worldview; for example, Epicurus and Zeno, a Stoic (Chapter IX/P119c). The Epicureans and Stoics adhered to an untenable conglomerate of materialistic religion wherein the concepts of Reason and Purpose were themselves deified.

P6f: "the congruity of Logos, Ethos, and Pathos . . ."

The Logos (logic) refers to one's reason, word, and rational comprehension. Ethos (ethic) refers to one's moral authority and trustworthiness. Pathos (passion) appeals to one's emotional experience of understanding and feeling. These three are ideally complementary and only properly effected and balanced in the soul by the Holy Spirit (1 John 3:24—5:12).

P8a: "visionary mode of Virgil . . ."

Author Louis Markos posits that the history of Rome, "from its mythical beginnings to the birth of Christ . . . [sets] the stage for the greatest proto-Christian poet, Virgil, who 'read' Rome's history in a way not dissimilar from how many biblical writers 'read' the history of Israel." The battle of Actium that ended with a naval victory for Octavian in BC 31 decisively ended a Roman civil war. Octavian—Caesar Augustus—became the first emperor of the Roman Empire and granted the West the longest era of peace it had known, the Pax Romana (BC 31–AD 14). Markos also explains that in considering the divine events of God calling Abraham out of Ur and Israel out of Egypt at the exodus, for Virgil, Actium marked "an equally divine event toward which all history had been moving since Aeneas left Troy." He adds, "Like the writers of the Bible, the pagan Virgil held an eschatological view of history in which the end not only explained but justified the suffering that preceded it" (*From Achilles to Christ*, 194–201; Chapter VI/P21a).

In like manner, the passionate suffering of Christ was justified by His resurrection (Hebrews 9:11–28).

P8b: "Aeneas left Ilium."

Ilium is another name for Troy.

P9a: "prophecy of Hermes . . . Job and Isaiah . . . true Myth . . ."

When Prometheus is condemned by Zeus to endure perpetual suffering, Prometheus prophesies of his eventual freedom at the hands of Heracles/Hercules (Chapter IX/P119c). Yet after detailing the pain he is to endure, Prometheus receives a prophecy from Hermes that hints at an unexpected hope:

> And do not expect these sufferings to end, until some God agrees to take your place
>
> and volunteers to go down into Hades, the sunless realm, and Tartarus' gloomy depths.
>
> (*The Greek Plays—Prometheus Bound*, 215, lines 1026–29)

Is this passage perchance an occasion of God via the Holy Spirit speaking prophetic glimpses through the pagan poet Aeschylus? Specifically, this passage seems to point to the Scriptures that speak of Christ taking on untold suffering and then descending into the grave and setting the righteous souls free by taking them into heaven (Psalm 22; Isaiah 42; 52:13—53:12; Ephesians 4:8–10; 1 Peter 3:18–22; Hebrews 9:27; *From Achilles to Christ*, 122–23). Even Job prophesied of the Living God coming to earth as a Redeemer to provide salvation and resurrection to eternal life (Job 19:25–27).

The true Myth is the Gospel, the greatest Story ever to exist. Would it not be fitting for the greatest Author to employ foreshadowing "Bread crumbs" within the body of pagan myth and world philosophy/literature, in like fashion to His types and shadows threaded through the Torah and Hebrew writings?

P9b: "death will lose its sting . . . Paradise shall remove . . ."

1 Corinthians 15:55; Isaiah 58:6; Ephesians 4:8–10; 1 Peter 3:18–22.

P9c: "Balder's Gate shall be breached . . ."

Balder was the Norse "corn-god," so named for his death and rebirth which paralleled the seasonal cycle of corn (actually wheat). Every ancient culture practiced rituals of sacrifice and ablution, "but harbored a cherished myth about a god who came to earth, died, and returned to the abode of the gods." C. S. Lewis labeled this multicultural scapegoat (Leviticus 16:10) the Corn-King. "In Greece, the Corn King goes by the name Adonis or Bacchus. In Egypt, he is called Osiris. Amongst the Babylonians and Persians, he bears the name of Tammuz and Mithra. And in the northern regions of Scandinavia, he is called Balder."

Early in C. S. Lewis' faith journey, he and many fellow academics "concluded that Jesus of Nazareth was nothing more than the Hebrew version of the Corn King." However, a conversation with his friend J. R. R. Tolkien "revolutionized Lewis' understanding of myth and the Christian gospel. What if, Tolkien suggested . . . Christ was the myth that became fact? . . . perhaps the reason every ancient culture yearned for a god to come to earth, to die, and to rise again was because the Creator who made all the nations placed in every person a desire for that very thing" (*The Myth Made Fact*, xvi—xvii). For Lewis' profound analysis of the preceding summary, see his essay "Myth Became Fact," in *God in the Dock: Essays on Theology and Ethics* (HarperCollins, 2014).

Balder's Gate is simply a reference to the entrance to the underworld, i.e. the gates of hell (Chapter VII/P13).

P9d: "Conciliation between divinity and humanity . . ."

This heralds the giving of the Holy Spirit and His ministry of reconciliation between God and humanity (John 14:16–17; 2 Corinthians 5:17–21).

P11: "particular prophetic disclosure . . ."

1 Corinthians 2:7–8.

P12a: "problem of evil . . . ruminated by Epicurus . . ."

Epicurus (Chapter IX/P119c) taught that the purpose of life was to achieve peaceful serenity by avoiding pain and suffering. As a thought exercise he challenged the idea of God, proposing that the existence of evil proved there is no God. In sum, cited by Lactantius (4th century AD), Epicurus stated:

> Is God willing to prevent evil, but not able? Then he is not omnipotent. Is he able but not willing? Then he is malevolent. Is he both able and willing? Then from where does evil come? Is he neither able nor willing? Then why call him God?" (Lactantius, *On the Anger of God* 13.20–22)

The fault in Epicurus' shallow musing/challenge is thus: Evil is not defined; therefore valid assessment of his statements is impossible. Epicurus presupposes/imposes a moral absolute that if God can prevent evil, then He should; yet there is no justification for said moral absolute, implying negligence concerning any justification for *not* preventing evil per God's sovereignty. Moreover, the problem of how much active evil—its entirety or in part?—ought to be prevented is not addressed. And the problem of preventing evil thoughts and intentions in conjunction with the issue of denying free human choice is likewise not addressed. Herein, Epicurus' challenge fails.

Whichever god(s) Epicurus had in mind to challenge, he was entirely ignorant of the Creator God of Holy Scripture who has revealed Himself to us in both general and special ways (via creation/nature and His Word).

For additional study concerning the ethics of free will and the war of good and evil, see *The Consolation of Philosophy*; *The Philosophy of Tolkien*, 173–208; and *Tolkien Dogmatics*, 155–211.

P12b: "send fire of division . . . until it is accomplished!"

Luke 12:49–51.

P12c: "By blood and water . . ."

1 John 5:6–8.

P12d: "I lay down my life of my own choice . . ."

John 10:15–18; 15:13; 1 John 3:16.

P12e: "mustard seed sized faith . . ."

Matthew 17:20; Luke 17:6.

P12f: "evil is the soil from which greater good sprouts."

This conceptual phrase was inspired by J. R. R. Tolkien whose elaboration of the idea is concisely captured by Austin M. Freeman: "God is sovereign enough to *use* evil as a soil from which unexpected good can sprout" (*Tolkien Dogmatics*, 71).

A direct sample of Professor Tolkien's thought, however, is surely warranted. He writes in a letter to his son Christopher, dated 30 April, 1944, "I sometimes feel appalled at the thought of the sum total of human misery all over the world at the present moment . . . If anguish were visible, almost the whole of this benighted planet would be enveloped in a dense dark vapour, shrouded from the amazed vision of the heavens! And the product of it all will be mainly evil—historically considered. . . . All we do know, and that to a large extent by direct experience, is that evil labours with vast power and perpetual success—in vain: preparing always only the soil for unexpected good to sprout in" (*Letters of Tolkien*, #64:76).

P12g: "The marvel of the miraculous . . ."

Austin M. Freeman states, "Miracle is . . . distinct from magic and Faerie, though miracle and magic are so similar that they can only be distinguished by Christian theology. The effects may seem identical, but the context and motive are totally different" (*Tolkien Dogmatics*, 78). This truth is starkly evident in Holy Scripture.

P13: "the night I wrestled Jacob . . ."

Genesis 32:22–32; Hosea 12:4–5.

P14: "I reiterated his preceding prayer . . ."

Genesis 32:9–12.

P19: "your name shall be Israel . . ."

The name Israel means "striving with God."

P21: "Fear not, your brother Esau loves you . . ."

Genesis 33:1–4.

P22a: "fallen asleep in Delilah's lap . . ."

Judges 16:15–21.

P22b: "Seventieth Week . . ."

Daniel 9:24–27; Jeremiah 30:7; Romans 11:26–27; Revelation 3:10.

In this prophecy spoken by Jesus, He is referencing the remnant of Israel at the end of the age—after going through seven years of God's judgment, i.e. Jacob's trouble; the Day of Wrath—seeing Him descending from heaven to Earth and finally receiving Him as their Messiah (Joel 2:31–32; Zechariah 12:9–11; Romans 9:27–29).

P23: "my heart grew hot . . . I am as a shadow . . ."

Job 4:14; Psalm 39; 102:11; 119:120; 144:4; Jeremiah 23:9.

P24a: "few will seek to endure their cross . . . I would share the burden."

Matthew 10:38; 11:28–30; 16:24; Mark 8:34; 10:21–27; Luke 9:23; 1 Peter 5:6–7.

P24b: "complete in me, lacking nothing."

James 1:2–4.

P25: "Our more perfect love."

Colossians 3:14; 1 John 2:5; 4:17–19.

P26: "Manoah's altar . . ."

Judges 13:17–23.

Chapter XI

Paragraph 1a: "Shen-lung—Stormbringer . . ."

Shen-lung, which translates as "Stormbringer," is the ancient Chinese storm god, also known as Lei Shen—Thunder-god—due to his roar that shook the landscape. This great blue dragon was said to dwell in Leize, west of Wu, and could at times manifest a human face though its dragon body remained constant. This trait coupled with the idea that dragons are primarily associated with power gives reason for numerous Chinese lineages claiming descent from unions between mortals and dragons (or fallen angels/sky gods) disguised in human form. The five-toed imperial dragon device adorned the robes of emperors as representation of their station [*The Science of Monsters: The Origins of the Creatures We Love to Fear* by Matt Kaplan, (Scribner, 2013), 115–17; *Fantastic Creatures of the Mountains and Seas* by Jiankun Sun, trans. Howard Goldblatt, (Arcade Publishing, 2021), 308.]

P1b: "colossus of Carthage . . . Tiamat of Shinar . . ."

Ancient lore concerning great serpents is reinforced by numerous historical accounts, including the expeditions of Alexander the Great into India (BC 327–325) and the incident in Carthage, North Africa, at the Bagradas River (BC 256).

The Bagradas river incident is most interesting and details a lengthy battle between a Roman army and a "drakon" amidst campaign during the First Punic War. The oldest source for this event is from Aulus Gellius writing in the second century AD (*Attic Nights* 7.3) concerning the now-lost first century BC original record from Quintus Aelius Tubero, who wrote:

"The consul [commander] Atilius Regulus, when encamped at the Bagradas river in Africa, fought a stubborn and fierce battle with a single serpent of extraordinary size, which had its lair in that region; that in a mighty struggle with the entire army the reptile was attacked for a long time with hurling engines and catapults; and that when it was finally killed, its skin, a hundred and twenty feet long, was sent to Rome."

A more detailed record is found in Roman historian Livy's *Periochae* (book 18) from late first century BC, as cited by Valerius Maximus during the reign of Tiberius. Maximus wrote:

"[In] Africa, Atilius Regulus killed an unnaturally enormous serpent with significant loss to his forces . . . The serpent . . . was of such a size that it denied the army of Regulus access to the river. Many soldiers it seized in its enormous mouth and crushed to death not a few of them with its whirling tail. It could not be penetrated by missiles thrown at it . . . they attacked it with many stones launched from ballistae from every side; it was brought down by the weighty blows" (*Facta et Dicta Memorabilia* 1.8.19).

Paulus Orosius, a Christian historian and friend of Augustine (4th–5th century AD), gives a longer report which likely also comes from Livy. The account likewise chronicles the reptile's "astonishing size," its impenetrable and "horrible scaly fins," the loss of many soldiers "with its bites" and being "trampled down by its charge," and the barrage of ballistae that finally killed it. A further more telling trait, however, records the creature lacking feet and having a "sinuous movement . . . upon its scales as if on claws and upon its ribs as if on legs" (*Historiae Adversum Paganos* 4.8). This detail suggests a massive snake or python-like entity, though its identification remains a mystery even today. The Latin records of this engagement use the term *serpens*, meaning both "serpent" and "dragon"; the one Greek source from early third century AD uses *drakon*, also meaning "serpent/dragon" (Cassius Dio frg. 42.43; Zonaras 13.1).

Notaby, hundreds of years after the original event, the intriguing encounter still captured imaginations. A second-century AD epic poem by Silius Italicus about the Second Punic War recounts the battle with the Bagradas Dragon in truly romantic fashion (*Punica* 6.140–293). For *Gethsemane Moon* I have Jesus christen this fantastic beast as the "colossus of Carthage."

Tiamat of Shinar (i.e. Babylonia) was depicted as a great female dragon filled with chaos. According to Mesopotamian mythology, she was the universal primeval mother who embodied the turbulent salt-water ocean at the beginning of time, alongside the masculine dragon Apsu who personified the primordial fresh-water ocean. Their waters mingled and initiated the creation of the gods.

Eventually, a war of the gods erupted and the water-god Ea captured Apsu. Tiamat created an army of monsters and fought against Ea and the other gods until Ea's son, Marduk, was chosen to rise up in victory over her. He destroyed Tiamat's monstrous army then subdued her with a storm, caught her in a net, pierced her with an arrow, and tore out her entrails. Marduk then split her skull and cut her body in two. From one half of Tiamat's body he made the vault of the heavens; from the other half he made the ocean floor. Her eyes became the sources of the Tigris and Euphrates rivers. This is the Babylonian creation myth (*World Mythology*, 326).

P2: "Unlike Eve . . ."

I have written that Lucifer's manifestation as a dragon is an intentional assault on Jesus' physical and spiritual senses. Lucifer's approach to Eve, no matter how he manifested to her, would have been less fearsome and more seductive (Genesis 3).

P3: "Daidalos' labyrinth . . . Ariadne's thread . . . Theseus . . . Pasiphae . . ."

Daidalos/Daedalus was the architect commissioned by Greek king Minos to build the labyrinth within which to imprison the untamed Minotaur—the half-man, half-bull offspring of

Minos' wife Pasiphae and an actual bull (or Zeus disguised as such).

It was to this Minotaur that Minos fed the annual Athenian tribute of seven maidens and seven young men, until Theseus killed the beast. However, Theseus could not have accomplished this feat without the aid of Ariadne, the beautiful daughter of the tyrant Minos. She helped Theseus navigate the labyrinth by giving him a spool of thread with instruction to attach the end of it to the cavern entrance. She also gave him a sword with which he slew the Minotaur (*The Myth Made Fact*, 168–79).

P5: "slow in backing His promises."

Lucifer's mockery here is later dispelled by Holy Scripture: "The Lord is not slack concerning His promise, as some count slackness, but is longsuffering toward us, not willing [wanting] that any should perish but that all should come to repentance" (2 Peter 3:9).

P6: "Erebus' known form . . ."

Medieval author John Milton succinctly captures what the ancient Greeks generally believed about the Beginning: "First there was Chaos, the vast immeasurable abyss, outrageous as a sea, dark, wasteful, wild" (from *Paradise Lost*).

Leaning on their own understanding, although without explanation, the Greeks held that long prior to the appearance of the gods there was only Chaos brooding over unbroken darkness. Then suddenly two children were born to Chaos—Night and Erebus. These two form a kind of yin and yang of darkness whereas the feminine Night (aka Nyx) is benign, being simply the absence of daylight, and masculine Erebus is the malignant "unfathomable depth where death dwells" (*Mythology*, 76–77). Therefore, Erebus is a personification of and/or god of darkness. Although the Greek creation myth presents Erebus as neutral and amoral, from the biblically theological perspective we see that he is indeed evil in that he represents and promotes spiritual darkness, the underworld, and death itself; these characteristics all stand in opposition to the moral Creator and Author of life (Genesis 1–3).

P7a: "Khronos is not on your side."

The ancient pre-Socratic Greeks held three (perhaps more) different conceptions of time, with gods personifying each—Aion/Aeon, Khronos/Chronos, and Kairos. Aion represents eternity and is associated with the afterlife, though in context of earthbound lifecycles he represents the cyclical eternality of seasons. Khronos (not the Titan Cronus) was the embodiment of empirical linear time: past, present, future. And Kairos embodies times of opportunity which concerns actions taken toward fulfilling a task (e.g. cultivation, planting, harvesting; giving birth; tending a wound) as well as recognizing and/or partaking of prophetic convergences (as orchestrated via divine sovereignty).

P7b: "Glaucon's 'wholly just Man' . . ."

In Plato's *Republic*, the devout student of Socrates, Glaucon, appeals to base human (sin) nature and argues (per the tale of the Ring of Gyges) that "man is just, not willingly or because he thinks that justice is any good to him individually, but of necessity, for wherever any one thinks that he can safely be unjust, there he is unjust" (*Republic* 357a–368c).

Glaucon earnestly continues to solidify his argument, playing devil's advocate for an intemperate youth, Thrasymachus, who extols tyranny. He presents to Socrates two contrasting images, one of the perfectly unjust man and one of the perfectly just man, asking which of the two possesses the more enviable life. To quote Louis Markos, Glaucon presents his "hypothetical unjust man as one whose cleverness allows him, 'while doing the most unjust acts, to [acquire] the greatest reputation for justice' (361b). The hypothetical just man, on the other hand, he presents as one who has everything taken away from him but his justice. The former, Glaucon informs us, will go from success to success, but what will happen to the 'just man who is thought unjust'? He 'will be scourged, racked, bound—will have his eyes burnt out; and, at last, after suffering every kind of evil, he will be impaled' (361d, 362a)" (*From Plato to Christ*, 30).

In agreement with Markos, I think the picture of the perfectly just man sounds hauntingly like a prophecy of Jesus Christ.

P7c: "Orpheus . . . Er . . ."

Orpheus, king of Thrace and the world's greatest musician, lost his wife, Eurydice, to the venomous bite of a serpent. Her soul descended to the underworld, but Orpheus followed after by finding the secret entrance into hell. He eventually stood before Hades himself. Then he lifted his lyre and played while he sang a song of love, thus enchanting the underworld entire in an appeal to receive Eurydice and lead her back to the surface. To this, Hades granted Orpheus' request (*The Myth Made Fact*, 24–29).

Boethius, a Christian writer steeped in the pre-Christian philosophers and poets of Greece and Rome, was a one-time Roman consul (ca. AD 510). He was eventually imprisoned for treason, seemingly for his "Christian orthodoxy against the Arian beliefs of Theodoric," king of the Ostrogoths. While in prison, Boethius wrote his most powerful work, *The Consolation of Philosophy*; yet to reach more souls he did not write a distinctly Christian work. Rather, he confined himself "to the kinds and degrees of wisdom available to Plato, Aristotle, Homer, Virgil, Ovid, and Cicero. That is to say, Boethius, though he personally had access to the special revelation of the Bible, only included in his *Consolation* the fruits of general revelation" (*The Myth Made Fact*, 26–27). In books III and IV of his *Consolation* can be found spiritually allegorical exhortations on Orpheus and Eurydice and Odysseus and Circe, purposing to instruct and inspire the reader concerning God, heaven, and hell in a subtly—or perhaps obvious—Christian way (Ephesians 4:8–10).

Toward the end of Plato's *Republic* (book X) he details—in the myth of Er—what we may call a near-death experience. And though Plato did not have the special revelation of Scripture, he "understood that we live in a just cosmos of cause and effect, not a random, capricious universe in which actions have no ultimate consequences." Er was a warrior slain on the battlefield. His body remained undisturbed for ten days and did not decay. On the twelfth day his body was placed on a funeral pyre, and before the fire was set Er awoke and stood, telling a tale unheard by mortals!

Louis Markos summarizes: "During his twelve-day sojourn in the valley of the dead, Er was taken to a strange in-between place from which two paths led to and from the earth below and two others led to and from the heavens above. Souls were coming and going in a ceaseless rush . . . some telling tales, others seeking information. Er wondered what his fate would be, but he was told that he was not destined yet for death but had been appointed as a messenger to bring back to earth news of the journey—and the choices—that await us beyond the grave. The afterlife . . . was a place of justice, of due punishment and reward" (*The Myth Made Fact*, 120–22).

Certainly there is no place for purgatory or reincarnation in Christian theology, yet pre-Christian myths are a seedbed for the prophetic truths that Jesus Christ and the Holy Spirit have now fully fleshed out and illuminated for those who have hearts to perceive. Consider the apostle Paul's experience in 2 Corinthians 12:1–7.

P7d: "saved some like Lazarus . . ."

John 11:1–44.

P8a: "Kairos is an ally . . ."

See above P7a.

P8b: "my Father who intercedes for me."

John 17:18–26.

P11a: "Raphael, Surael, Ananiel."

Although not mentioned in biblical canon, Raphael is cherished in Jewish tradition and is one of the named archangels recorded in the books of Enoch and Tobit (3rd–2nd century BC). His name means "God has healed."

Also not mentioned in biblical canon is Surael/Suriel, another archangel of Jewish and Coptic tradition, whose name means "My rock is God." He is often associated with wisdom, healing, and death. His narrative can be found in the *Synaxarion*, the Coptic/Greek term for a compilation of the lives of martyrs, saints, and religious heroes of the Coptic church. Surael is also found in the book of Enoch and in the Jewish Talmud.

Ananiel, whose name means "Cloud of God," is another archangel not of biblical canon but is prominent in Coptic tradition and is also named in the book of Enoch. Much confusion and uncertainty surrounds this angel's name due to its many variations and their multiple cross-cultural ascriptions to a vast and varied spectrum of characters, holy and unholy. As with Scripture, many different individuals share the same name. I have simply chosen to ascribe a known name to a holy archangel with whom Lucifer once fellowshipped.

P11b: "per the supernal courts . . ."

Job 1:6–12; 2:1–7; Ezekiel 8:3–1; Zechariah 3:1–8.

P12a: "Magi . . . flight to Egypt."

Matthew 2:1–15, 19–23.

P12b: "Ptolemaic and Alexandrian schools . . ."

In the Hellenistic cultural center of Alexandria, Egypt, during the Roman period, the Ptolemaic/Alexandrian schools offered the best blending of Greek, Jewish, and Eastern education, particularly in the arenas of mathematics, medicine, philosophy, history, astronomy, literature, epic poetry, cartography, and geography. Eventually, in the second century AD, the Alexandrian school became a bastion of Christian theological thought and education.

P14: "Emptying yourself of divinity . . . the sacred power you set aside . . ."

See Chapter V/P9.

P15a: "firestones of the Holy Mountain . . ."

Ezekiel 28:13–14.

P15b: "You passed the desert trial."

Matthew 4:1–11; Mark 1:12–13; Luke 4:1–13.

P16: "Melchizedek . . ."

See Chapter VIII/P16.

P17: "covenant I struck with Abraham . . ."

Genesis 15:7–21.

P18: "I lay down my life . . ."

John 10:17–18.

P21a: "the Cleansing . . ."

The great flood of Noah's day (Genesis 7–9).

P21b: "*Anu-naki* . . . Zagros in Babylonia . . . Bab-El . . ."

Anu-naki is a term that literally means "sky-gods," which in a biblical historical context references the fallen angels of the Luciferian insurrection. Their post-flood campaign to deceive humanity concerning the truth of both world history and God's divine plan included establishing themselves as gods, enslaving populations, and disseminating false convoluted creation narratives and epic mythologies (e.g. *Epic of Gilgamesh*, *Enuma Elish*, *Epic of Erra*). The extra-biblical post-flood history of humanity is primarily found in ancient Sumerian and Babylonian records, although recent decades of ongoing discovery have revealed an undeniable connection between *every* ancient culture of the world and *the same* "gods" from the sky—also known as the "shining ones." For example, there is explicit similarity between the *Anu-naki* of Babylonia and the *Tuath De* ("tribe of the gods") of early Gaelic Ireland—e.g. *Tuatha De Danann*, "kin of the goddess Danu."

Certainly, much of the cross-cultural origin-story framework is speculative, mythical, and/or intentional propaganda (as many histories are, whether by human or demonic design). However, such myths (via written records/cuneiform, petroglyphs, hieroglyphs, carvings, temples, tombs, megalithic constructs, etc) provide more actual than fantastical characters and events than many are willing to admit. The challenge is sorting the fantastical details from the core supernatural and actual truths of ancient world history and incomplete (yet swiftly expanding) archaeology, particularly from a proper biblical worldview concerning the identity of "ancient aliens" and giant-gods. A great primer for this level of research is Stephen Mitchell's *Gilgamesh*, which is an engaging history and English translation of the Sumerian epic about a global flood and a historical king of Uruk (Erech/Iraq; BC 2700) who was of both human and divine origin, i.e. Nephilim/Rephaim. I caution, however, that Mitchell's commentary is secular and at times antithetical to Christianity; yet it remains highly informative.

Four excellent resources on ancient civilizations and the surrounding geopolitical developments are: *The History of the Ancient World*, Susan W. Bauer (Norton, 2007); *Babylon: Mesopotamia and the Birth of Civilization*, Paul Kriwaczek (St. Martin's, 2010); *Mesopotamia: The Invention of the City*, Gwendolyn Leick (Penguin, 2001); and *Ancient Worlds: A Global History of Antiquity*, Michael Scott (Basic, 2016).

The Zagros mountains are located in eastern Iraq, a large part of ancient Babylonia (or Shinar; Genesis 11:2) which included modern day Iraq, Syria, and eastern Saudi Arabia.

Bab-El means "gate of God" and refers to God's judgment of the unity construction project in direct opposition to God's post-flood command for humanity to scatter across the earth and subdue it, being fruitful and multiplying (Genesis 11:1–9). Bab-El ultimately became synonymous with the Hebrew verb *balal* which means "to confuse or scatter." For much more detail on this topic, see my commentary *The Revelation of Jesus Christ*, chapter 15 "Babylon 101."

P21c: "Nimroud-bar-Cush . . . the Sanhedrin . . ."

The names and politico-religious body listed are historical tyrants whom had established themselves as gods in direct opposition to the biblical Creator God.

P21d: "The cult of Mother and Child . . ."

This cult began soon after the Bab-El judgment as a demonic corruption of the Genesis 3:15 prophecy. A woman known as Semiramis claimed to give birth to a miraculously conceived son, the god-man Tammuz. She "became known as the 'queen of heaven' (Jeremiah 7:17–18) and the image of her holding a baby boy permeated the world following God's judgment at Babel, leaving only name differences" due to language distortion. In that the mother and child cult was adopted by the seafaring Phoenicians, "namely Ashtoreth and Tammuz, the apostasy spread swiftly far and wide. In Egypt the mother and child were known as Isis and Horus; in Greece they were Aphrodite and Eros; in Italy Venus and Cupid," et al. This "Babylonianism" became a world-dominating religious system from which Abraham was separated by the divine call (Genesis 12:1–4). Later, Israel was often in conflict with yet too often seduced by this satanic influence, eventually suffering captivity in Babylon itself as judgment for rampant idolatry. Early Christianity was tasked with carrying the Gospel into a world saturated by Babylonianism in one form or another. "Unfortunately . . . the mystery of iniquity infiltrated the church when Rome adopted Christianity as its state 'religion' and the draw of power and prestige usurped the desire for truth. Consequently, heresies such as the mother and child cult became 'Christianized'" (*The Revelation of Jesus Christ*, 198–99).

P21e: "Tartarus . . ."

See Chapter IV/P16.

P23: "Through the scions of Ishmael . . ."

Here I have written Lucifer foretelling of long-laid plans to establish a unified global cult to subvert the world and to oppose and crush any followers of the Creator God. True to form, the dragon imitates and perverts divine directives and portents, in this case choosing and weaponizing Ishmael's offspring against that of the half-brother and true child of promise, Isaac (Genesis 17:18–21). The prophetic narrative that foretells of this and directly indicates the rise of Islam and its role of conflict in the latter years is found in Genesis 16 (note verses 10–12). We see this conflict intensifying today.

I have imagined Lucifer being initially on offense and emboldened in his global endeavors. He then believes Jesus to be defeated at His death, thereby solidifying his occupational control of the world. However, following Jesus' resurrection and as Scripture reveals, Lucifer realizes his hubristic downfall and ever after has been on the reactionary defensive, unable to escape God's sovereignty and therefore perpetually striving to steal, destroy, and kill all that God loves.

P24: "warring agency of empire . . . Sumerian pantheon . . ."

Here Jesus foresees the rise of Islam and its growth into one of the seven world empires which stand against God and devour His people—Egypt, Assyria, Babylon, Medo-Persia, Greece, Rome, Ottoman. Notably, the book of Revelation presents a seven-headed dragon that signifies seven specific world empires of satanic purpose—all which have sought to persecute and/or destroy the Jews and possess their land (Revelation 12:3–5; 13:1–4; 17:7–11; Daniel 7).

The kingdom of Antichrist is in fact an *eighth* empire that is *of the seven*, meaning that the seventh (Ottoman/Islamic) empire will be "resurrected" and established as the Antichrist's global kingdom (Revelation 17:7–11). However, this less common interpretation does not insist upon an Islamic Antichrist or a radically Islamic final empire; indeed, no nation would agree to such (Genesis 16:12). Moreover, Ezekiel 38–39 prohibits a radical Islamic context in that Israel's enemies are prophesied to be supernaturally destroyed by God Himself, thus preparing the way for remaining moderate Muslim nations and Israel to formalize an agreement with Antichrist, whose role will begin as a much-desired political messiah amidst an opportune and apocalyptic time near the end of the age. Of course, his offer of world peace will be false and short-lived (Daniel 9:26–27; Revelation 13). I believe the contemporary Abraham Accords (inaugurated in 2020) are a glimpse of this future coalition between Israel and her moderate Arab allies in that today's Arab nations (ally and enemy) were once part of Ottoman territories. For more on this topic, see Birch, *The Revelation of Jesus Christ*, 162–67.

The Sumerian and Babylonian pantheon of gods provided much of the lore and raw idolatry that formed and continues to shape Islam, particularly concerning its corruption of biblical truth and denial of Jesus Christ as true Savior of humanity.

P25a: "God's desire for living sacrifice . . ."

Romans 12:1–2.

P25b: "river which makes glad the city of God . . ."

Psalm 46:4.

P26: "blasting furnace of a parched desert . . ."

Jonah 4:8.

P27a: "God entraps the deceiver in his own wiles."

Proverbs 12:13.

P27b: "house of *shedim . . . ekballo*."

The term *shedim* ("demons") is the plural of *shedu* (see Chapter IX/P26). The term *ekballo* is a Greek term which conveys "a forceful casting out, sending away, or expulsion." This verb is used in the New Testament when Jesus casts out unclean spirits from harassed or possessed human souls.

P28: "trees of Eden . . ."

Ezekiel 31:18.

P30a: "Graeco-Romans . . . Ishmaelite legions/Otori hordes . . ."

The Roman Empire would eventually split in two—Latin Rome in the West; Greek Byzantium in the East; and with separate popes! Both halves of the imperial state were each harried by the rise of violent tribal hordes and their terrorism—Rome initially by the Germanics and Huns; then both Rome and Byzantium by various Islamic and Seljuk territorial iterations. For superb narrative history of this era, see *Sword and Scimitar: Fourteen Centuries of War Between Islam and the West*, Raymond Ibrahim (Da Capo Press, 2018); *Lost to the West: The Forgotten Byzantine Empire That Rescued Western Civilization*, Lars Brownworth (Three Rivers, 2009); *Mohammed & Charlemagne Revisited*, Emmet Scott (New English Review, 2012); and *God's Battalions: The Case for the Crusades*, Rodney Stark (HarperOne, 2009).

My use of the term *Otori* refers to the unknown origin of the Hunnish tribes, veiled as it is in unrecorded history and contradictory speculation. Some scholars believe the Huns originated from Kazakhstan as small tribes that outgrew their region. Other scholars believe their nomadic beginning to be in the fourth century BC terrorizing China during the Qin and Han Dynasties. Failing to conquer, they turned west, and being unrivaled equestrians and archers, they steadily conquered the Eurasian steppe and rode into European civilization late in the fourth century AD. Then they met the bulwark of Rome (and Constantinople) and settled into generational conflict, culminating with the rise and fall of Attila. Linguistically, *Otori* is a Japanese word meaning "large bird" or "swift creature," the latter lending to the Otori-class torpedo boats of the Imperial Japanese Navy. Thus the "Otori hordes" emphasizes the ferociously swift flight of the Huns from eastern steppe to the wall of western civilization.

What may seem anachronistic is not quite that. Within the frame of *Gethsemane Moon* when Jesus addresses the reader He is speaking from a very unique eternal perspective, on occasion utilizing terms and perspective distinctly appropriate and timeless. When Lucifer speaks, his perspective, while not eternal, is closer to such than humanity's. In this instance, Lucifer was already incubating his samurai sect and would thus be familiar with the philology of every language and culture of every tribe since God's judgment of Bab-El.

P30b: "Erra, Ares, Achilles, Iyarri, Sekhmet, and Pallas . . ."

Ares was the Greek god of war; Erra was a Babylonian god of confusion and pestilence; Iyarri was a Hittite and Luwian god of war and plague. These three were likely fallen angels posing as gods. Sekhmet was the Egyptian lioness-headed goddess of war and feminine divinity; Achilles was a mighty warrior, hero of the *Iliad*, and son of the goddess Thetis and mortal Peleus; Pallas was the Greek warrior-god of warcraft and battle strategy. These three were likely post-flood Rephaim, offspring of fallen angels and human women. Also see Chapter IX/P26.

P31a: "save the *world* through self-sacrifice?"

John 3:16–21.

P31b: "lay down one's life for one's friends/enemies . . ."

John 15:13; 1 John 3:16; Matthew 5:44; Luke 6:27–36.

P33a: "You are no Leonidas . . . noble sacrifice . . ."

Here Lucifer mocks Jesus, imagining that Jesus views His self-sacrifice akin to that of Leonidas, ancient king of Sparta, and three hundred of his best warriors as they withstood the Persian war horde at Thermopylae, granting time for the Greek city-states to rally against the invasion. Though vastly significant, this historical event has gained much attention throughout history into the modern era, athough it is indeed much romanticized and embellished by narrative legend. For an exceptionally epic and well researched telling, see Stephen Pressfield's historical fiction, *Gates of Fire* (Doubleday, 1998).

P33b: "Hellen's holocaust . . . Hellas' ideals . . ."

Hellen was the founder of all Greek tribes via his sons; he is also a post-flood Rephaim descendant, son of Deucalion and Pyrrha. Herein we get Greece's ancient/modern national name Hellas/Hellenic Republic. The name Greece derives from the Latin/Roman name Graecia.

Intriguingly, and according to Greek mythology, Deucalion (a pre-flood Nephilim) was the son of Prometheus and was known for his wisdom and good character. Likewise for his human wife, Pyrrha. The gods had become angry at humanity for their divine disregard and violent behavior (hypocrisy much?) and would therefore destroy them by a global flood. Yet the gods deemed Deucalion and Pyrrha to be righteous and chose the pair to survive the judgment and begin anew. Prometheus informed his son of this and thus Deucalion and his wife constructed a boat, survived the deluge, and afterward participated in repopulating the earth. Indeed, this is a mythological version of the truly Divine flood judgment of Noah's day (Genesis 6 10); although Noah and his family were wholly human, not Nephilim/Rephaim.

"Hellen's holocaust" is a reference to Hellen's ultimate destiny in hell, likewise Leonidas and all who worshiped false gods/goddesses. "Hellas' ideals of freedom" refers to the Greek (i.e. western) idealistic and liberating philosophy of freedom both national and individual.

P33c: "The Ephors are my right hand."

In ancient Sparta, the Ephors (meaning "overseers") were a ruling council of up to five individuals. Their authority—both domestic and foreign—spanned the arenas of religion, executive, legislative, judicial, and military.

P33d: "Danite legacy of desertion . . . Lakonia . . ."

The biblical tribe of Dan was a coastal seafaring tribe which was eventually judged for being idolatrous, for remaining preoccupied with their ships (Judges 5:17), and for being unsatisfied with their tribal lot (Joshua 19:47). They were also renowned warriors. The Danites mingled with another seafaring culture, the Phoenicians, along with the Philistines (Judges 14–16). When they lost their tribal allotment, where did they go? Varying tales suggest they assimilated into numerous Gentile cultures and/or mostly migrated to a new homeland—likely both are true. Yet some theories are quite intriguing.

The Greek poet Homer wrote of a seafaring tribe called Danaoi, or Danaan, who fought beside the Greeks at Troy (13th century BC). The Bible directly relates Dan with Greece in Ezekiel 27:19, whereas Javan is the progenitor of the Grecian territory. Moreover, the Spartans—also called Danaans—are *not* native to Greece. Could some of the lost Danites have sailed to the western Aegean sea and settled in the southern Peloponnese peninsula to found the nation of Sparta? For more of this fascinating thread, see *Armstrong Institute of Biblical Archaeology*, armstronginstitute.org/The Spartans: Children of Abraham, Brothers of the Jews.

Likewise notable, Spartan king Areus I (BC 309–265) sent a letter to the Jewish high priest Onias (Nehemiah 12:22) informing of "a certain writing, whereby we [Spartans] have discovered that both the Jews and the Lacedemonians [Spartans] are of one stock, and are derived from the kindred of Abraham." Areus extends a warm offer of brotherly solidarity, offering to share reciprocally in all concerns (Josephus, *Jewish Antiquities* 12.4.10). I suspect a particular angle of political and martial support is implied due to the often volatile climate of politico-religious intrigue that was disadvantageous for the Jews and frequently threatened their national existence. Though no reply from Onias is recorded, over a century later the embattled Jewish high priest Jonathan Maccabaeus sends a follow-up letter to Sparta purposing to assure an alliance (1 Maccabees 12).

Much later, in the first century BC, a Machiavellian Spartan, Eurycles, endeared himself to Jewish king Herod and entrenched himself in the blood politics of the time. We also learn that Herod was much enamored with Sparta (Josephus, *Wars of the Jews* 1.26.1).

Lakonia/Laconia is the southern region of Greece wherein Sparta acted as administrative capital. Spartans were thus also known as Lacedamonians.

P35a: "Zechariah's record . . ."

Zechariah 3:1–9.

P35b: "no offspring or property to judge!"

Isaiah 53:8.

P40: "trial of Choice . . ."

The surrounding and subsequent narrative presents Lucifer in an aching attempt to project the blame of his own prideful Choice onto Jesus, "however innocently" his choice was made (P39). Lucifer wrongly sought more authority and power than his created station allowed.

Austin M. Freeman sums up Professor Tolkien's perspective on both the viability and corruptibility of the divine gift of free will, particularly concerning creativity: "Creative desire seeks shared enrichment and partnership in the delight of making, not delusion or dominion. But this drive is easily corrupted into sin. Nevertheless, God, in order to uphold the great good of free will, even allows the misuse ot sub-creative activity in the production of horrors. When we realize . . . our own absolute power to shape the world of our imagination, we [may] also begin to desire to wield the same power in the primary world" (*Tolkien Dogmatics*, 91; *Letters of Tolkien*, #153:195; *Tolkien On Fairy-stories*, 41, 64). Also see Kreeft's *The Philosophy of Tolkien*, 61–65, for a discussion on fate and free will.

Book V of Boethius' *Consolation of Philosophy* was of great aid in tightening up both my own articulation and the dialogue between Jesus and Lucifer in the proceeding section of narrative.

P41a: "Typhon."

According to the ancient Greeks, Typhon was a terrible serpentine monster with flaming eyes who sought to establish himself as ruler of the world and as the supreme deity. Zeus ultimately destroyed him with a thunderbolt (*World Mythology*, 89). Jesus here identifies Lucifer as Typhon in the mythological, typological, and actual contexts.

P41b: "the one world in the celestial canon . . ."

Just as Adam and Eve were forbidden the one tree of knowledge of good and evil in Eden, so Lucifer and the Host were forbidden to commandeer or interfere with the one world—Earth—in the entirety of the cosmos.

P41c: "Havilah . . ."

Havilah appears in Scripture as both a place name and personal name. Per the meaning of the Hebrew word *havilah*, "stretch of sand," I have imagined it as the expansive and unbroken pre-flood continent within which the vast region of Eden was divinely secured.

P42a: "falsely teaching . . . that darkness preceded Light."

Concerning humanity's first temptation, I have imagined the Luciferian dragon as a philosophical craftsman, seductively awakening new desires in Eve (and through her, in Adam) and offering the gift of "forbidden wisdom." And by his corrupted wisdom, the dragon crafts lies about the Creator God, portraying Him as an enemy seeking their destruction. Lucifer infers that he himself is the master and giver of light, and that God is the Voice of the Dark (Isaiah 5:20–21; *Tolkien Dogmatics*, 163).

That the lie portrays the truth as lie is the ultimate possible rebellion (*Creation and Fall*, 76).

Also see Tolkien's short story, "The Conversation of Finrod and Andreth," wherein a human woman, Andreth, tells an elf—Galadriel's brother, Finrod—the tale of original sin (*The History of Middle-earth, Volume X, Morgoths' Ring*, 301–66). Being set in the fictional Middle-earth yet framed as the earliest history of our primary world, this tale is not a one-to-one parallel to the biblical Genesis record of humanity's Fall; however, the thematic elements of morality, created purpose, and free will are brilliantly presented and expounded.

P42b: "Earth's sister . . . plotting with Yekun."

Earth's sister is the planet Mars, which bears a massive surface scar many times larger than our Grand Canyon. In Jewish tradition, Yekun/Jeqon is a strategist and one of the chief fallen angels who initially conspired with Lucifer concerning an unholy insurrection.

Enoch 68:1–5 is a record of Noah reporting (from his grandfather Enoch) on the divine judgment of the fallen angels which shall befall them. In Enoch 69:1–15 Noah lists names of the leaders of the Watchers who led the vile crime against humanity. "The name of the first, Jeqon, the one who led astray the sons of God and brought them down to the earth, and led them astray through the daughters of men" (69:4).

P42c: "*Imago Dei* . . . disgraced but not dethroned."

Portions of Tolkien's poem "Mythopoeia" are "devoted to the insistence that, while Man is now distant and estranged from his original estate, he retains his inherent dignity, recalling and imaging God through his sub-creative activity" (*Tolkien Dogmatics*, 170).

In like fashion, the author of *Beowulf*—a poetic tale set in pre-Christian history—was "a man learned in old tales who was struggling, as it were, to get a general view of them all, perceiving their common tragedy of inevitable ruin, and yet . . . he was himself removed from the direct pressure of its despair." Throughout history, many souls have wrestled with whether or not there is merit to heathen histories and their doom. J. R. R. Tolkien provides the answer: "The author of *Beowulf* showed forth the permanent value of that *pietas* [loving gratitude] which treasures the memory of man's struggles in the dark past, man fallen and not yet saved, disgraced but not dethroned" (*The Monsters and the Critics*, 23). We embrace future hope by appreciating lessons of the past.

P43: "snare of determinism . . . gift of free will . . ."

Generally, the definition of "determinism" is explained as the doctrine that all events and human actions are wholly determined by causes external to the will. Some take this to imply that individual humans have no free will and therefore cannot be held morally responsible for their actions.

However, Boethius dismantles this hypothesis, limited as it is by the finite human intellect. In Book V, Prose 4, of his *Consolation*, Lady Philosophy states "Let us suppose that foreknowledge exists but imposes no necessity on things. The same independence and absolute freedom of will would remain. [As such, why must the *voluntary* outcome of things be bound to predetermined results?]" To this, Boethius affirms that the results of art would be vain if they were all brought about by compulsion.

Lady Philosophy responds, "Then, since they come into being without necessity, these same things were *not determined by necessity* before they actually happened. Therefore, there are some things destined to [i.e. that shall] happen in the future whose outcome is free of any necessity. . . . But, the point at issue is whether there can be any foreknowledge of things whose outcomes are *not* necessary. . . . If uncertain things are foreseen as certain, that is the weakness of opinion, not the truth of knowledge" (emphasis mine). Herein, God's foreknowledge of future events imposes no necessity or boundary on their future occurrence. Simply put, His all-knowing perspective supersedes our individual and collective limited-knowledge perspective.

Thomas Aquinas reinforced Augustine's ideas about free human choice when he wrote, "A man can direct and govern his own actions also. Therefore the rational creature participates in the divine providence [via free will] not only in being governed but also in governing" (*Summa Contra Gentiles*, III.113; Augustine, *City of God*, book 5, chapter 9).

Rodney Stark states, "the Christian God is a judge who rewards 'virtue' and punishes 'sin.' This conception of God is incompatible with fatalism. To suggest otherwise is to blame one's sins upon God: to hold that God not only punishes sins but causes them to occur." He summarizes with the fact that *free will* did not originate with Christians, and that for them, free will was not a philosophical matter but rather a fundamental principle of their faith (*The Victory of Reason*, 25–26). I would add that free will is in fact a foundational construct of the salvation doctrine itself (John 3:14–21; 10:14–18). Moreover, Jesus' admonition to "Go and sin no more" is ludicrous without an individual free will.

Finally, Dietrich Bonhoeffer distills the sovereignly given gift of free will into a hard discipleship application lived by Jesus and effected only by our unity in Him by the Holy Spirit: Jesus lived and acted "not by the knowledge of good and evil but by the will of God. There is only one will of God. In it the origin is recovered; in it there is established the freedom and the simplicity of all action" (*Ethics*, 33–34). This is only accomplished by and through God's love.

For further examination of the divine gift of free will and human responsibility, see John 10:14–18; Esther 4:13–16; *Consolation of Philosophy*, Book V, Prose 5–6; *Ethics*, 68–69, 244–50; *Tolkien Dogmatics*, 71–75; *Letters of Tolkien*, #54:66; #64:76; #96:110; *The Nature of Middle-earth*, 226–34; *The Philosophy of Tolkien*, 49–70; *The Morning Star & The Melon*, 4–19).

P46: "the Wisdom which treads underfoot . . ."

This phrase (although altered) was taken from *The Imitation of Christ*, 145.

P48: "Fallen man conceives fallen myths."

This phrase (although altered) was inspired by discussions in *Tolkien Dogmatics*, 176 and *Tolkien On Fairy-stories*, 42.

P49: "World Tree . . . gnaw its roots . . ."

The World Tree (of Life)—Latin, *Arbor Vitae*—was a cosmic ash tree known as Yggdrasil in Germanic mythology, but was also common in northern Europe and Asia. It was thought to be the backbone of the universe, its branches spreading above the heavens and the nine worlds, supported by three great roots, one of which descended to the lowest of the worlds—Niflheim, a place of icy mist, darkness, and death. The dragon Nidhogg dwelled in Niflheim, shredding and devouring corpses that ended up there. When temporarily sated with dead flesh, Nidhogg would gnaw at the root of the World Tree in an attempt to inflict damage on the cosmos.

The name Yggdrasil means "dreadful mount" or "death perch," and may refer to Odin's gallows. Odin hung himself on the great ash tree for nine nights that he might learn wisdom, lending to the Viking practice of sacrificial hangings from gallows trees in worship to Odin. The parallel between Odin's voluntary death on the Tree and Christ's death on the Cross is highly notable. "Odin was also pierced with a spear and, like Christ, cried out before he died. Although it is possible that the Crucifixion was known at the time the Odin myth was recorded, there is little doubt his hanging on the cosmic tree had pre-Christian origins" from pagan worship (*World Mythology*, 212, 252). Here again, we see a divine truth prophetically glimpsed, though clouded, until Jesus Himself revealed the universal mystery of His atonement by way of His passion, resurrection, and giving of the Holy Spirit to all who would place their faith in Him and therefore inherit His eternal kingdom of relationship and life.

P50a: "smoking flax . . . serpent's head shall be crushed."

Isaiah 42:3–4; Matthew 12:20–21; Genesis 3:15, Psalm 74:12–14.

P50b: "Avernus . . . Son of Chaos."

For Avernus, see Chapter VI/P22. For Erebus, Son of Chaos, see Chapter XI/P6.

P51a: "Clytemnestra's rage."

Clytemnestra was daughter to Tyndareos, king of Sparta, and was the half-sister of Helen, whose elopement with Paris launched the Trojan War. Married to Agamemnon, Clytemnestra grew to hate him when, in order to gain fair sailing winds to Troy across the Aegean, he sacrificed their daughter, Iphigenia, to the goddess Artemis. Filled with roiling rage, when her husband left for Troy with the warships, she openly flaunted an affair with Agamemnon's cousin, Aegisthus, and with him co-ruled Mycenae. Upon her husband's return ten years later, Clytemnestra feigned joy to see him, despite also having learned of his concubine Cassandra, daughter of Trojan king Priam. As Agamemnon was changing clothes in their home, she entangled him in a literal net whereupon Aegisthus cut him down with a battle axe. She then also killed Cassandra and wrapped both her and Agamemnon's corpses in an expensive robe. Clytemnestra likewise openly flaunted this deed. In retribution, she was eventually killed by her son Orestes (*The Myth Made Fact*, 262–85; *World Mythology*, 34).

P51b: "between a dragon and his wrath!"

In William Shakespeare's *King Lear*, Act 1, Scene 1, the servant Kent interrupts and challenges Lear's decision to disinherit his beloved daughter Cordelia. The king unapologetically informs his servant to stay his criticism or face an ill-tempered draconian demise. "Peace, Kent! Come not between the dragon and his wrath!"

In true Tolkienian fashion, J. R. R. Tolkien borrows and adapts Shakespeare's quote into an epic moment toward the end of *The Lord of the Rings*. In Book V, chapter 6 "The Battle of the Pelennor Fields," the warrior Dernhelm (who is in fact Eowyn, Shieldmaiden of Rohan) is defending her fallen uncle, Theoden, king of Rohan, whom had just been felled and broken by the Lord of the Ringwraiths, himself mounted upon a grotesque winged steed. Dernhelm stood to and cried, "Begone, foul dwimmerlaik, lord of carrion! Leave the dead in peace!" A cold voice answered, "Come not between the Nazgûl and his prey!" (*The Lord of the Rings*, 841)

Chapter XII

Paragraph 1: "dangers of temptation are avoided . . ."

I have written, "many dangers of temptation are avoided through moral deliberation and prayerful constancy." On one level this simply refers to knowing what is morally right and wrong and thus choosing to do right, particularly for the disciple of Jesus Christ. On another level a different and heightened scale of morality arises that is directly allied with Providence and Divine calling.

J. R. R. Tolkien explains that "we do not know our own limits of natural strength (+ grace), and if we do not aim at the highest we shall certainly fall short of the utmost that we could achieve." He continues, "We are finite creatures with absolute limitations upon the powers of our soul-body structure in either action or endurance. Moral failure can only be asserted, I think, when a man's effort or endurance falls short of his limits, and the blame decreases as that limit is closer approached. Nonetheless, I think it can be observed in history and experience that some individuals seem to be placed in 'sacrificial' positions: situations or tasks that for perfection of solution demand powers beyond their utmost limits, even beyond all possible limits for an incarnate creature in a physical world—in which a body may be destroyed, or so maimed that it affects the mind and will." Here Tolkien is discussing the moments and seasons when Divine assistance carries and preserves human limitation beyond itself per love, humility, and resilient perseverance through suffering for a greater and spiritually sanctioned good (Chapter IV/P18–21). Such is ever the perfect blend of the divinely designed relationship, particularly for humanity—the *Imago Dei*.

Tolkien highlights Frodo's quest to destroy the Ring as an example. "Frodo undertook his quest out of love—to save the world he knew from disaster at his own expense, if he could; and also in complete humility, acknowledging that he was wholly inadequate to the task." Truly, he could only do his best to find a way to travel and perform "as far on the road as his strength of mind and body allowed. He did that."

In the end, when Frodo should have tossed the Ring into the fire to be unmade, he failed. His body and mind were broken beneath physical, mental, and demonic torment. But the pure and humble heart with which Frodo began his quest, coupled with all his suffering and perseverance "were justly rewarded by the highest honour; and his exercise of patience and mercy towards Gollum gained him Mercy: his failure was redressed" (*Letters of Tolkien*, #246:326–27).

Recall that Frodo had numerous occasions to kill or incapacitate Gollum, yet pity (and empathy) stayed his hand, believing that Gollum was not beyond redemption. In the end, both catastrophically and eucatastrophically, it was Gollum who saved Frodo. At the moment of Frodo's failure to destroy the Ring, Gollum arrives and wrestles it from the hobbit only to then fall into the fire and end both the Ring and himself. Of course, this was Providence (the Holy Spirit) assisting and completing the quest *with* Frodo when he had reached the end of himself; therefore, Frodo's "failure" could be justifiably forgiven by God and everyone else. In the aftermath of the traumatic confrontation (Book VI, chapter 3 "Mount Doom"), Frodo says to Samwise, "But do you remember Gandalf's words: Even Gollum may have something to do? But for him, Sam, I could not have destroyed the Ring. The Quest would have been in vain, even at the bitter end. So let us forgive him! For the Quest is achieved, and now all is over" (*The Lord of the Rings*, 947).

Despite free will, Tolkien claims that "the power of evil in the world is not finally resistible by incarnate creatures, however 'good.'" No one, he insists, is "good" independently of the grace of God, for such grace comes from outside oneself (Romans 3:23–26). In reading all the passages concerning Frodo and the Ring, Tolkien believes we will realize it was "*quite impossible* for him to surrender the Ring, in act or will, especially at its point of maximum power" per the willing participation of the sacrificial person "being placed in positions beyond one's power" (*Letters of Tolkien*, #191:251–52; emphasis in original). Herein is *why we need God*, to be in true relationship with Him that we may overcome the world by and through Him (John 16:33; 1 John 4:4; 5:4–5).

Another powerful example presents itself in Tolkien's tale from Book V, chapter 6 "The Battle of Pelennor Fields" (*The Lord of the Rings*, 840–42). Merry, hobbit-friend of Frodo and one of the Fellowship, stands with Dernhelm/Eowyn against the terrible Witch-king. But he is so immobilized by fear that he is blind and sick and "his will made no answer," having been overridden by the Enemy. Yet the sudden sight of Eowyn with unbound blonde hair, facing the evil Nazgûl and hearing his declaration that she will be captured and taken to Mordor to be tortured, awakens his imprisoned will from its frozen fright. Thus the woman and the hobbit stand together. Fleming Rutledge observes, "It is an absurd imbalance . . . but their alliance brings forth the best from each," and they defeat the Witch-king. "Thus the two persons who were deemed unfit for battle are the very ones foreordained to be the agents of the transcendent Power [God] in this climactic confrontation" (*The Battle for Middle-earth*, 288–89). And though both Eowyn and Merry survive the battle and the war, they are grievously wounded and scarred for life, despite receiving restorative healing.

Jesus, in His humanity, exemplified for us this type of sacrificial partnership with God. When Jesus cried out to His Father as He took on all our sin, "Not my will, but Yours," this was not a failure of His atoning mission. Rather, His human will allied with the love of His Father and Spirit—even amidst His separation from them—and He was empowered and enabled to fulfill our salvation. I have expressed how this might have been accomplished in Chapter IV, Paragraphs 14–21.

P2a: "What is all flesh . . . shall the clay kick . . ."

Isaiah 29:16; 40:5–8; 45:9; 64:8; Romans 3:20–26; 8:3–4; 9:21; Ephesians 2:11–16; Colossians 1:21–23.

P2b: "carnal contention . . . arrows against my soul . . ."

Job 6:4; Psalm 11:2; 57:1–4; Jeremiah 10:19–21; Micah 7:1–7.

P3a: "Jonah's shade tree . . ."

Jonah 4:6–8.

P3b: "bowels of brokenness and fault . . ."

Jonah 2:1–9; Joel 1:17–18; Lamentations 3:1–32.

P4: "Charybdis . . ."

Charybdis was a monstrous whirlpool "where the sea forever spouted and roared and the furious waves mounting up touched the very sky" (*Mythology*, 170). Opposite this roiling maelstrom stood the sheer cliff-face of Scylla, with treacherous straits passing between. These sea straits were braved by the Argonauts, Aeneas, and Odysseus.

P5a: "Father, glorify Your Son . . ."

John 17:1–5.

P5b: "to become sin . . . reconciled to Us."

2 Corinthians 5:20–21.

P5c: "I have become death."

Jesus' statement here is the fulcrum and final fulfillment upon which all other such statements rest, solely because He not only became sin and death but also conquered it. Particularly, one may think of the infamous Hindu scripture quoted by physicist J. Robert Oppenheimer following the successful testing of the first atom bomb.

"We knew the world would not be the same. A few people laughed, a few people cried, most people were silent. I remembered a line from the Hindu scripture, the Bhagavad-Gita. Vishnu is trying to persuade the Prince that he should do his duty and to impress him takes on his multi-armed form and says, '*Now I am become Death, the destroyer of worlds.*' I suppose we all thought that one way or another."

The Hindu quote is found in Bhagavad-Gita 11.32. Some insist a more direct translation to be "I am become Time . . ."; however, Time and Death are commonly synonymous when personified by various gods in Eastern religions. Another description likely also prompted Oppenheimer's Hindu recollection. Gita 11.12 and 11.17–20 detail a vision of Krishna's universal form as "a thousand suns rising suddenly in the sky . . . an immeasurable blazing fire, brilliant as the sun . . .

marvelous and terrible . . . the space between heaven and earth saturated by you in all directions."

P5d: "Light in the darkness . . ."

Job 12:22; Psalm 112:4; Isaiah 9:2; 42:16; 58:10; Daniel 2:22; Micah 7:8; Matthew 4:16; Luke 1:78–79; John 1:5; 8:12; 12:46; 2 Corinthians 4:6; 1 Peter 2:9; 1 John 1:5.

I have written, "the Light in the darkness when all other lights go out." This is inspired by a line in Tolkien's *The Lord of the Rings: The Fellowship of the Ring*, chapter 8 "Farewell to Lorien." Galadriel gives to Frodo, the Ring-bearer, a priceless gift to accompany him on his perilous journey. She says to him, "In this phial is caught the light of Earendil's star, set amid the waters of my fountain. It will shine still brighter when night is about you. May it be a light to you in dark places when all other lights go out" (*The Lord of the Rings*, 376).

P5e: "bind all of my wounds . . ."

Job 5:18; Psalm 147:3.

P7: "souls standing below me."

Some present at Jesus' crucifixion were His mother Mary, Mary Magdalene, and John. Matthew 27:55–56; Mark 15:40–41; Luke 23:49; John 19:25–27.

P8: "my cherished city . . . negligent nation."

Amos 9:8–15; Matthew 23:37–39.

P10a: "with me in Mother's womb . . . You have been my God."

Psalm 22:10; 139:13; Isaiah 44:2; 49:5–6; Jeremiah 1:5; 20:17.

P10b: "wicked conspire . . . pierce my hands and feet."

Psalm 22:16.

P10c: "Deliver me from . . . sword/lion's mouth . . ."

Exodus 18:4; 1 Samuel 17:37; Psalm 17:8–13; 22:20–21; 144:10; Daniel 6:21–23.

P10d: "My heart is like wax . . . be not far from me . . ."

Psalm 22:14, 19; 38:21; 71:12.

P11a: "netted the notion . . . hard into obedience . . ."

2 Corinthians 10:4–5.

P11b: "by volition made intimately extant . . ."

God sees the end from the beginning all at once (Isaiah 46:10), yet He is not far removed nor unaware of all things (Genesis 1:1; Deuteronomy 10:14). God, specifically by and through Jesus Christ and the Holy Spirit, is both present and intimately involved in affairs both universal, global, and personal—His seeming absence or inattention is a result of His respectful refusal to violate the sovereignly given gift of free human choice.

Although the divine plan of human salvation was conceived and prepared long before Adam and Eve's fateful Fall (Genesis 3), the necessary playing out of history and all of its particular nuances impacts every soul, for better or worse. Herein rests the foundation of God's plan for humanity: loving relationship (John 3:14–17). As such, true love and relationship are only possible and fulfilling when all parties *choose* to recognize and enjoy the overarching purpose for the same. And free choice allows for right or wrong choice, resultant with divinely appropriated justice of eternal reward or eternal condemnation. Love cannot be freely received and given unless one is actually free to choose to receive and give. Even within the Godhead, and in accord with the divine law of logic, the conceived purpose of a plan is not effected until it is acted upon and fulfilled/finished. For example, I may plan to teach a class and discuss the intricacies of all topics that arise, promising clarity and closure for those with whom I share the forthcoming endeavor; however, for such a plan to be effected and fulfilled, I must physically travel to the location of the class (or present myself via media-cast) and actively communicate and relate to all who attend. The intention itself is not substantive. It is the *active employment of and participation in the purposed plan* that catalyzes relational connection, belonging, and completion. This is exactly what Jesus Christ—by His own passionate trial of Choice—has done for whosever would place their faith in Him (John 1:1–17; Ephesians 2:14–22).

P12: "self-evident truth . . ."

John 14:16–21, 26–27; 15:26; 1 John 3–5.

P13: "two luminous individuals appeared . . . Alatar and Pallandros."

Luke 22:43. See Chapter VI/P15b.

P14a: "that Your yoke may be light . . ."

Matthew 11:27–30.

P14b: "Akkadian *shedim* . . ."

See Chapter IX/P26.

P15a: "*Legio Judaica* . . . fallen Watchers."

Latin for Judean Legion, a contingent of holy warrior-angels charged to watch and protect Israel. For the Watchers, see Chapters VI/P22 and XI/P42b.

P15b: "finish the mystery hidden . . ."

1 Corinthians 2:7–8; Ephesians 3:8–12; Colossians 1:26–27.

P15c: "searched diligently all the prophets/approaching salvation."

1 Peter 1:10–12.

P17a: "You stilled the raging waves . . ."

Psalm 89:9; 107:29; Jonah 1:15–16; Matthew 8:26; Mark 4:39.

P17b: "I will hide My face . . ."

Job 13:24; Psalm 27:9; 30:5; 102:2; 143:7; Isaiah 54:7–8; Ezekiel 39:29.

P17c: "like the waters of Noah to Me . . ."

Isaiah 54:9.

P18a: "Phineas with his spear . . ."

The men of Israel committed harlotry with the women of Moab and were seduced into worshiping Baal of Peor, and the anger of God was roused against Israel so that He sent a plague against them (Numbers 25). Moses commanded the judges of Israel to kill every man who had joined to Baal-Peor. Then Phineas, son of Eleazar, the son of Aaron the priest, took a javelin and went after a leading man of Israel [Zimri], walked into his tent as he was whoring himself to a Midianite woman [Cozbi], and thrust both of them through with the spear. God stopped the plague and praised Phineas for his godly zeal, saying to the assembly, "Phineas has turned back My wrath . . . Behold, I give to him My covenant of peace . . . because he was zealous for his God and made atonement for the children of Israel" (25:11–13).

Phineas was a fore-type of Christ, for Jesus likewise turned back God's wrath on all mankind by the perfect and final atoning sacrifice of Himself, gaining the eternal covenant of peace for whosoever would receive Him as personal Savior and God.

P18b: "when You have returned to Us . . ."

John 20:17; Acts 1:9–11; Ephesians 4:10–13.

P19: "all history, prophecy, and eternity converge."

The incarnation, life ministry, passionate suffering, crucifixion, resurrection, and ascension of Jesus Christ is simultaneously the worst and best event in the entirety of history.

P20: "I learn obedience through suffering . . ."

Hebrews 5:5–9.

P21a: "I am the Passover Lamb . . ."

Exodus 12:21–27; Matthew 26:2, 17–19; Mark 14:12–16; Luke 22:7–20; John 19:14–18; 1 Corinthians 5:7–8.

P21b: "As Isaac, I will carry the wood . . . no ram . . . I am the Way."

Genesis 22:1–14; John 14:6.

P22a: "the miry depths . . ."

Psalm 40:2; 130:1–2; Jeremiah 38:6, 13.

P22b: "I will be caught up to heaven . . ."

Acts 1:9–11; Revelation 12:4–5.

P22c: "a new song of my sacrifice . . ."

Psalm 33:3–4; 40:3; 98:1; Isaiah 42:10; Revelation 5:9; 14:3.

P22d: "better than an ox or bull."

Psalm 69:30–31.

P23: "I approached John, James, and Peter . . ."

From this third time Jesus finds the disciples sleeping, and through to His arrest, I have incorporated into the narrative aspects of all four Gospels. Matthew 26:45–57; Mark 14:41–53; Luke 22:46–54; John 18:1–14.

P26: "Yehuda . . ."

This is a form of the name Judas, yet it is also a general name for "Jew," which evokes a theologically heavier aspect to Jesus' rhetorical inquiry.

P28: "I will overcome. This too shall pass."

John 16:33; 1 John 4:4; 5:4; 2 Corinthians 4:17–18; 1 Peter 5:10.

P33: "Peter . . . struck the officer . . ."

Mark 14:47; Luke 22:50–51; John 18:10.

P34: "Sword of the Spirit . . ."

Ephesians 6:17; Hebrews 4:12.

P35: "the scorched hand teaches best . . ."

In Tolkien's *Lord of the Rings: The Two Towers*, chapter 11 "The Palantir", Gandalf instructs the hobbit Pippin about the temptation of evil in the aftermath of Pippin's near fatal mishandling of a *Palantir*, or seeing-stone. The hobbit regrets his ignorance concerning the device and presumes that had he known about it he would not have been tempted to look into it. But Gandalf objects, insisting that had he indeed informed Pippin of the danger "it would not have lessened your desire, or made it easier to resist. On the contrary! No, the burned hand teaches best. After that, advice about fire goes to the heart" (*The Lord of the Rings*, 598–99; *Tolkien Dogmatics*, 193).

P38a: "I prayed and upheld it [the world]. . ."

Hebrews 1:3.

P38b: "Prometheus' fire . . . Secret Fire . . ."

Concerning Prometheus, see Chapter IX/P119c. The "Secret Fire" is Tolkien's reference to both the Holy Spirit and His ministry/activity in the world. Of course, being that Tolkien's legendarium is framed as pre-Christian history, the Spirit's work is more subtle than it is after the incarnation, crucifixion, and resurrection of Jesus Christ via the more personal dynamic of the Holy Spirit in Christ's continuing salvation mission. Therefore, the intricacies and nuances of Christian theology are not expounded within the Middle-earth saga. In this, Tolkien was intentional, for he sought not to proselytize. However, his Ring-cycle was very Christian at its foundation. For great insight into Tolkien's personal view of the Holy Spirit and how he incorporated Him into Middle-earth, see *Tolkien Dogmatics*, 27–36.

In his creation account of Middle-earth, Tolkien writes of the One God informing the Ainur (angels) of His intent: "'I will send forth into the Void the Flame Imperishable, and it shall be at the heart of the World, and the World shall Be' . . . And suddenly the Ainur saw afar off a light, as it were a cloud with a living heart of flame . . . and set it amid the Void, and the Secret Fire was sent to burn at the heart of the World" (*The Silmarillion*, 20, 25; Genesis 1:1–2).

P39a: "no longer will God be closeted away . . ."

1 Peter 2:4–5.

P39b: "syllic spell . . ."

This is an Old English phrase meaning "wondrous tale" or "strange tale" and is found in the epic poem *Beowulf* (line 1769 in Tolkien's translation; *Beowulf*, 74, 358–59). The word "Gospel" stems from this; see Chapter VI/P20c.

P40: "he who blindly prophesied . . ."

John 11:47–53; 18:14.

Epilogue

Paragraph 1: "Simon of Cyrene . . ."

This narrative perspective is inspired by the heart-wrenching events in Matthew 27:32–56; Mark 15:21–41; and Luke 23:26–49.

P2: "young ones, Alexander and Rufus . . ."

Mark 15:21.

P7: "My own breath stole from me . . ."

The devastation of Jesus' body from scourging to crucifixion is carefully drawn from diverse Scripture passages. See Chapter III/P1.

P23: "By My stripes you are healed . . ."

Isaiah 53:5.

P26: "Vengeance is Mine, I will repay . . ."

Deuteronomy 32:35, 41; Isaiah 59:18; 65:6; Ezekiel 7:4; Romans 12:19; Hebrews 10:30.

P29: "I lay down My life . . ."

John 10:15–18.

P33: "To whom has the arm of the Lord . . ."

Isaiah 53:1.

P39: "The chastisement for our peace . . . He shall prolong His days."

Isaiah 53:5–10.

P41: "And by His knowledge . . ."

Isaiah 53:11.

P43: "And who will declare My generations?"

Isaiah 53:8.

Final Postscript

The following list includes the *most* influential and inspirational works that Jesus Christ and the Holy Spirit availed over my lifetime toward preparing me for and inviting me into this Gethsemane project. Solid versions of each work can be found in the Bibliography.

**The Holy Bible* (of the many translations I prefer the New King James Version)

**The Imitation of Christ* by Thomas a Kempis

**The Cost of Discipleship* by Dietrich Bonhoeffer

**Beowulf* (author unknown)

**The Iliad* and *The Odyssey* by Homer

**The Aeneid* by Virgil

**The Divine Comedy* by Dante Alighieri

**Paradise Lost* by John Milton

**The Silmarillion* and *The Lord of the Rings* by J. R. R. Tolkien

**From Achilles to Christ: Why Christians Should Read the Pagan Classics* by Louis Markos

Acknowledgments

HIGH EPIC NARRATIVE GROUNDS me. Whether fact or fiction, this mode of storytelling, for me, is not merely entertainment or an escape from the routine rigors and daily drudgery of our shared earthbound existence. Instead, the immersion into world-building, four-dimensional character development, great life-transforming quests, and the imaginative nuance of profound plotting and outcomes both expected and unexpected, move me to live my present life circumstance with epic intent and a vigilant faith. Certainly, my life is marred with both trivial and epic failures. Yet my life also exhibits both minute and marvelous substance—and solely by God's grace!

As alluded to in the Author's Testament, I was baptized in story long before I was baptized in the name of the Father, Son, and Holy Spirit. But this has been God's plan all along. Whether I am reading Virgil's *Aeneid* or being introduced to Virgil himself through Dante's *Divine Comedy*, I am invited to consider the aspirations of nobility, passion, and the state of my soul. When I immerse myself into the vast richness of Tolkien's Middle-earth, the equally rich history of our present earth, or, most importantly, Holy Scripture, I am challenged to discern my own Quest(s) in life along with the ultimate purpose for which I have been created and uniquely gifted.

Again, I hold deepest gratitude for the triune Godhead—Father, Son, and Holy Spirit. Had I not been raised in a genuinely Christian home and community, I would not have discerned the subtle leading to receive salvation through Jesus Christ and then His eventual call and commissioning into His kingdom mission. Nor would I have been invited to experience *Gethsemane Moon*. God's Story informs my own. I owe them my life.

I also again acknowledge the tremendous role of my parents, Paul and Linda Birch. Prayerfully discerning the Lord God's leading to adopt a son resulted in my blessed upbringing, allowing for my own heavenly adoption into the kingdom of God. This in turn resulted in my divine commissioning to worshipfully consider, contemplate, cautiously write, and finally follow-through and finish *Gethsemane Moon* after a decade of life-changing immersion in the project.

I extend great gratitude and love to Corey Franklin Murphy and his wife Michelle for their life-long friendship and companionship amidst our faith journey. They have both been a constant encouragement for all of my writing projects and indeed for life overall. Corey has been and continues to be a brother, warrior, and best friend whom I will stand beside until death or rapture! Our epic fireside conversations and camaraderie are literally fuel for the literary fire! And I must not neglect to mention the Tuesday night fireside marathons (hosted by Corey) with sister-in-Christ Alaina Murphy and a few other brothers-in-Christ—Jonah Murphy, Noah Theis, Kevin Matthews, Steve Bunda, Bill Cavey, Hunter Adkins—who have likewise "sharpened the iron" and galvanized my motivation to continue writing!

To Mark and Shannon Thomas I likewise gratefully reciprocate the love and trust which has been granted to me. A divine design brought our paths together and I am continuously encouraged by their bold faith and unflagging zealousness to glorify Jesus Christ in all things. Serving with them in ministry and simply laughing together has done much to help revive my spirit amidst a season of the Lord God "restoring the years the locusts have eaten." And thank you, Mark, for being the first to read the entire typescript of *Gethsemane Moon*, reacting and responding in ways which wonderfully affirmed the desired temper of the narrative!

And then there is Lauren Marie Robinson. Following a years-long season of sifting and loss, and amidst a season of restructuring, she literally walked into my life during the last year of *Gethsemane Moon's* drafting. Her unshakable faith, complementary levity, and magnificently artistic spirit have added an unforeseen facet to my personal narrative. Indeed, as the angels encouraged and edified Jesus in Gethsemane, so she has encouraged and edified me. And though I frequently express in countless words how grateful I am for Lauren, there truly are no words to convey the depth of love I have for her. She is a treasure divinely granted.

In no particular order, I express additional affection to those who have offered specific encouragement and assistance as *Gethsemane Moon* developed. Some of you read portions of the typescript if not the entirety; and some of you endured years of my sustained passion for the project as I expressed joys and frustrations, spiritual revelation, unforeseen plot points, and life impact.

Trever and Leanna Pusey, Larry Davis, Steve Adkins, Greg Alexander, Mary Lou Townsend, Carolyn Topper, Billy and Ashley Walters, Booker Jones, the Compass Church discipleship class and spiritual family, the Woodland Community Church discipleship class, Willie (Popz) and Connie Villegas, George and Jan Owens (for reading my first work of fiction—*Love's Legacy*—so long ago, and being enamored by it!), Tracy Hopkins, Trever Wayne Howard, Jodi Beth Birch, James Wade, Bill and Wanda Miller, Brandon Miller, Steve Miller, Mark Warren, Kyle Hubbard, Lindsey English Schilling, Brandon English, David Burkhart, Megan Truitt Temple, Greg French, Aaron Hearn, and the staff at Barnes & Noble (Salisbury, MD)—particularly Doug Collier and Renee Ruark.

And I am exceedingly grateful to Wipf and Stock Publishers, particularly Matt Wimer and George Callihan. The world-class expertise and hard work of the entire publishing team has brought my long-prayed-for Gethsemane project to fruition. You have my deepest gratitude.

Godspeed you all!

Bibliography

A Kempis, Thomas. *The Imitation of Christ*. NY: Barnes & Noble, 2004. Originally published 1418.

Alighieri, Dante. *The Divine Comedy*. Translated by J. G. Nichols. London: Alma Classics, 2012. Originally published 1321.

Allen, Reginald E., ed. *Greek Philosophy: Thales to Aristotle*. 3rd edition. NY: Free, 1991.

Aeschylus, Sophocles, and Euripides. *The Greek Plays*. Translated and edited by Mary Lefkowitz and James Romm. NY: Modern Library, 2017. Originally published 5th century BC.

Barrett, C. K., ed. *The New Testament Background: Writings from Ancient Greece and the Roman Empire that Illuminate Christian Origins*. NY: HarperOne, 1989.

Beale, G. K. *Redemptive Reversals and the Ironic Overturning of Human Wisdom*. Wheaton: Crossway, 2019.

Bennett, Arthur, ed. *The Valley of Vision: A Collection of Puritan Prayers & Devotions*. Carlisle: Banner of Truth, 1975.

Birch, Jon Scott. *The Morning Star & The Melon: Pursuing Truth Through Scripture, Science, Philosophy, and Logic*. Seaford: Signet Ring, 2016.

———. *The Revelation of Jesus Christ: A Disciple's Commentary*. Eugene: Resource Publications, 2022.

Birkett, Tom. *The Norse Myths: Stories of the Norse Gods and Heroes Vividly Retold*. London: Quercus, 2018.

Block, David L. & Kenneth C. Freeman. *God and Galileo: What a 400-Year-Old Letter Teaches Us about Faith and Science*. Wheaton: Crossway, 2019.

Boethius. *The Consolation of Philosophy*. Translated by Richard Green. NY: Macmillan, 1962. Originally published AD 524.

Bonhoeffer, Dietrich. *Creation and Fall/Temptation: Two Biblical Studies*. NY: Touchstone, 1997. Originally published 1959 (Creation and Fall) and 1955 (Temptation).

———. *Ethics*. NY: Touchstone, 1995. Originally published 1949.

Bradley, James & Russell Howell. *Mathematics Through the Eyes of Faith*. NY: HarperOne, 2011.

Bulfinch, Thomas. *Bulfinch's Mythology*. NY: Barnes & Noble, 2013. Originally published 1867.

Bunyan, John. *The Pilgrim's Progress—and Other Works*. Green Forest: Master, 2005. Originally published 1678 (part 1) and 1684 (part 2); as a volume with other works 1876.

Carpenter, Humphrey, ed. *The Letters of J. R. R. Tolkien*. Boston: HMC, 1981.

Charnock, Stephen. *The Existence and Attributes of God*. One-volume edition. Grand Rapids: Baker, 1996. Originally published 1682.

Cotterell, Arthur & Rachel Storm. *World Mythology*. Cambridgeshire: Hermes, 2022.

D'Ambrosio, Marcellino. *When the Church Was Young: Voices of the Early Fathers*. Cincinnati: Franciscan Media, 2014.

Davidson, George. *The Drawings of Gustave Dore: Illustrations to the Great Classics*. NY: Metro, 2008.

Einstein, Albert. *Relativity: The Special and the General Theory*. Translated by Robert Lawson. NY: Three Rivers, 1961. Originally published 1952.

Freeman, Austin M. *Tolkien Dogmatics: Theology through Mythology with the Maker of Middle-earth*. Bellingham: Lexham, 2022.

Hamilton, Edith. *Mythology*. NY: Back Bay, 2013. Originally published 1942.

Heiser, Michael S. *The Unseen Realm: Recovering the Supernatural Worldview of the Bible*. Bellingham: Lexham, 2015.

Holtz, Barry W., ed. *Back to the Sources: Reading the Classic Jewish Texts*. NY: Simon & Schuster, 1984.

Homer. *The Iliad*. Translated by Robert Fagles. Penguin Classics Deluxe Edition. NY: Penguin, 1990. Originally published late 8th or early 7th century BC.

Homer. *The Odyssey*. Translated by Robert Fagles. Penguin Classics Deluxe Edition. NY: Penguin, 1996. Originally published late 8th or early 7th century BC.

Humphreys, D. Russel, PhD. *Starlight and Time*. Green Forest: Master, 1994.

Kreeft, Peter J. *The Philosophy of Tolkien: The Worldview Behind The Lord of the Rings*. San Francisco: Ignatius, 2005.

Lisle, Jason. *The Physics of Einstein: Black Holes, Time Travel, Distant Starlight, E=mc2*. Aledo: BSI, 2018.

Lumpkin, Joseph B. *The Lost Book of Enoch: A Comprehensive Transliteration*. Blountsville: Fifth Estate, 2004.

Markos, Louis, PhD. *From Achilles to Christ: Why Christians Should Read the Pagan Classics*. Downers Grove: IVP Academic, 2007.

———. *The Myth Made Fact: Reading Greek and Roman Mythology through Christian Eyes*. Camp Hill: Classic Academic, 2020.

———. *From Plato to Christ: How Platonic Thought Shaped the Christian Faith*. Downers Grove: IVP Academic, 2021.

McGrath, Alister. *Glimpsing the Face of God: The Search for Meaning in the Universe*. Grand Rapids: Eerdmans, 2002.

Milton, John. *Paradise Lost*. London: Penguin Classics, 2014. Originally published 1667.

Mitchell, Stephen. *Gilgamesh: A New English Version*. NY: Atria, 2004. Earliest surviving texts date from BC 2100.

Morris, Henry M. *The Genesis Record*. Grand Rapids: Baker, 1976.

———. *The Revelation Record*. Wheaton: Tyndale, 1983.

Peterson, Andrew. *Adorning the Dark: Thoughts on Community, Calling, and the Mystery of Making*. Nashville: B&H, 2019.

Peterson, Eugene H. *Reversed Thunder: The Revelation of John & the Praying Imagination.* NY: HarperOne, 1988.

Plato. *The Republic.* Translated by Richard W. Sterling and William C. Scott; with Stephanus reference numbers. NY: Norton, 1985. Originally published BC 375.

Rutledge, Fleming. *The Battle for Middle-earth: Tolkien's Divine Design in The Lord of the Rings.* Grand Rapids: Eerdmans, 2004.

Samples, Kenneth R. *God Among Sages: Why Jesus Is Not Just Another Religious Leader.* Grand Rapids: Baker, 2017.

Stark, Rodney. *The Victory of Reason.* NY: Random House, 2005.

Tenney, Merrill C. *John: The Gospel of Belief—An Analytical Study of the Text.* Grand Rapids: Eerdmans, 1976.

Tolkien, J. R. R. *Beowulf: A Translation and Commentary.* Edited by Christopher Tolkien. NY: HMC, 2014.

———. *The Book of Lost Tales, Part Two.* Edited by Christopher Tolkien. Boston: HMC, 1984.

———. *The Children of Hurin.* Edited by Christopher Tolkien. NY: HMC, 2007.

———. *The Fall of Gondolin.* Edited by Christopher Tolkien. NY: HMC, 2018.

———. *The History of Middle-earth.* Twelve volumes. Edited by Christopher Tolkien. NY: HMC, 2002. Originally published 1983–96.

———. *The Lord of the Rings.* One-volume edition with the Appendices. Edited by Christopher Tolkien. NY: William Morrow, 2004. Originally published 1954–55.

———. *The Monsters and the Critics and Other Essays.* Edited by Christopher Tolkien. London: HarperCollins, 2006. Originally published 1983.

———. *The Nature of Middle-earth.* Edited by Carl F. Hostetter. NY: William Morrow, 2021.

———. *Tolkien On Fairy-stories.* Edited by Verlyn Flieger & Douglas A. Anderson. London: HarperCollins, 2014. Originally published 1947.

———. *The Silmarillion.* 2nd edition. Edited by Christopher Tolkien. NY: William Morrow, 2001. Originally published 1977.

———. *Unfinished Tales of Numenor & Middle-earth.* Edited by Christopher Tolkien. NY: William Morrow, 1980.

Virgil. *The Aeneid.* Translated by Robert Fagles. Penguin Classics Deluxe Edition. NY: Penguin, 2006. Originally published BC 19.

www.ingramcontent.com/pod-product-compliance
Lightning Source LLC
Chambersburg PA
CBHW070631310726
48982CB00001B/251

* 9 7 9 8 3 8 5 2 2 4 8 7 6 *